PRISONER of the DEVIL

Other books by Michael Hardwick include:
    Regency Royal
    Upstairs, Downstairs:
        Mr Hudson's Diaries
        Mr Bellamy's Story
        Endings and Beginnings
        On with the Dance
    The Four Musketeers
    The Man Who would be King
    The Cedar Tree
    The Inheritors
(with Mollie Hardwick):
    The Sherlock Holmes Companion
    The Man Who Was Sherlock Holmes
    Four Sherlock Holmes Plays
    The Game's Afoot (Sherlock Holmes plays)
    Four More Sherlock Holmes Plays
    The Private Life of Sherlock Holmes (novel)
    etc.

MICHAEL HARDWICK

PRISONER of the DEVIL

PROTEUS
London and New York

PROTEUS BOOKS is an imprint of
The Proteus Publishing Group

United Kingdom
PROTEUS (PUBLISHING) LIMITED
Bremar House,
Sale Place,
London, W21PT.

United States
PROTEUS PUBLISHING CO., INC.
distributed by
CHARLES SCRIBNER'S SONS
597 Fifth Avenue
New York, N.Y. 10017

ISBN 0 906071 11 9

First published in U.K. April 1979.
First published in U.S. August 1980.
© *1979 by Michael Hardwick and Proteus Publishing Company*
All rights reserved.

Second Printing, September 1980

Filmset in Monophoto Baskerville by
Asco Trade Typesetting Limited, Hong Kong
Printed and bound in U.S. by
The Book Press.

In all humility
and with the greatest respect
I dedicate this story to the memory of
SIR ARTHUR CONAN DOYLE

to the spirit of whose original conceptions
I have striven to be faithful:

'I feel a second finger lie
Above mine on the pen.'

PROLOGUE

I have often been accused of 'fancifying' the exploits of my eminent associate and friend of so many years, Mr Sherlock Holmes. He himself, on more than one occasion, voiced his gentle rebuke: 'I know, my dear Watson, that you share my love of all that is bizarre and outside the conventions and humdrum routine of everyday life. You have shown your relish for it by the enthusiasm which has prompted you to chronicle, and, if you will excuse my saying so, somewhat to embellish so many of my little adventures.'

I am unrepentant. To Holmes's cynical spirit all popular applause was always abhorrent. Nothing amused him more at the end of a successful case than to hand over the actual exposure to some orthodox official. At my own requests for more detailed accounts of his chains of reasoning he could seldom be troubled to add more to the brisk outline which he had provided at the scene, for the semi-enlightenment, and invariable wonderment, of those of us who had witnessed him going about his enigmatic processes of deduction.

As to the recollection of any feelings or emotions arising from a case he was totally unco-operative, expressing surprise that these should be a subject of any interest to others. Almost from the start of my decision to record our adventures for public eyes, I had recognised that such 'colour' as my narratives contained would need to be noted by me in my journals whilst memory remained fresh. I should be a dishonest man to deny that where this and that other detail was lacking, I never hesitated to provide it, working within the strict limits of truth and my close knowledge of my friend's remarkable and many-faceted nature.

I also recall once—it was during our investigation into the

mystery to which I gave the title 'The Valley of Fear', a murder enquiry in Sussex in 1900 in which I saw my companion's powers at their peak—I recall that he remarked that I appeared to be developing what he termed 'a certain vein of pawky humour', adding that he must learn to guard himself against it. Thenceforward, on the rare occasions when he would bother himself to scan my narratives, I noticed him sometimes frown and raise an eyebrow, as the lips drawn over his pipe-stem pursed. I fancy that such reactions were caused by certain of those passages upon which I had secretly congratulated myself for their pithiness.

Yet, I repeat, I make no excuses. Many of the adventures we shared were so extraordinary, to the point sometimes of absurdity, and the people we encountered often almost laughable in the ingenuousness of their criminal enterprises and in their own persons, that I allowed myself writer's licence. Where amusement was not followed or occasioned by tragedy or genuine suffering, I enjoyed illumining my accounts with a few beams of what I modestly supposed to be wit.

All this having been said, I must now warn my present reader that in the story which I am about to unfold, any wit which might be detected arises purely from recollections of actual speech or situation. In writing what is essentially a grim account of treachery, cupidity, repression and shame, I have restrained my pen from any inclination to 'run away with itself'. The facts shall speak for themselves after their long silence in the notebooks from which I now release them.

By the time this reaches the reader's eye those notebooks and other matter connected with this particular business will have been destroyed by burning. This has been a hard decision to take; harder even than the decision to publish at all. The world has been deprived of invaluable archives of the past due to their destruction by guilty-minded owners or their over-sensitive descendants. The day will assuredly come when every scrap of information concerning my friend Sherlock Holmes will be scrutinised, sifted, analysed, interpreted this way and that, in search of clues to his precise movements and the workings of the greatest investigative mind the field of criminology has ever known. He had a horror of destroying documents, especially those which were connected with his past cases;

though not from any sense of wishing them to pass to posterity as a form of memorial to himself. They were his working materials for future purposes. As he remarked at the culmination of our investigation into the so-called 'Red-headed League': 'As a rule, when I have heard some slight indication of the course of events I am able to guide myself by the thousands of other similar cases which occur to my memory'. Those thousands of documents—letters, depositions, photographs, newspaper cuttings, even visiting cards, train tickets and the programmes of musical concerts, which it was my pleasurable task to paste up for him—were his *aides-mémoire*.

Therefore, the reader might well demand, is it not an offence— nay, crime—on my part to consign any part of that unique archive to destruction? *Mea culpa!* Nevertheless, it is my firm resolve that after this narrative has been set down, the material to which I refer shall be destroyed. Much of it was obtained under vow of eternal secrecy as to its source. A good deal is derogatory to the reputations and names of persons manipulated or traduced by the guilty parties in order to draw suspicion away from themselves. At this remove of time, it is all too possible that new generations of interpreters of it would be led into erroneous inferences, which in turn would start even graver misapprehensions. Mr Sherlock Holmes and I are the only persons knowing—or ever having known—of his full association with this infamous affair, and of the ramifications of his work behind its scenes. Since he has consistently refused to set down any account of it— indeed, declared that it had left so sour a taste in his mouth that he had no wish ever to set eyes on the original material again—I have taken it upon myself to record the details of his part in it, and to nerve myself to that act of destruction which I am convinced is justified, desirable, and even mandatory.

It is with these same considerations in mind that I decree that the following narrative, which I had completed already before appending this preface, shall not be published until fifty years from the date upon which I write these final words. By then, all concerned in the case will have been long dead. Countless scholars will have conducted their researches into the *minutiae* of this episode in history. I remind myself that, by withholding my account for so long, I am depriving them of vital information; yet I have no alternative. Their consolation must be that they will have earned themselves recognition and reputation, not to mention bread and diplomas, as a result of their labours.

The time has come for me to put down my pen and exchange slippers for garden boots. It is a glorious autumn afternoon as I sit here, surrounded by the bulky books of pasted-up documents and the wooden boxes of loose ones. With the addition of the golden brown leaves from the copper beeches at the foot of my lawn they will make a fine blaze on this windless day; and I shall throw upon it other assorted leaves which I have piled ready, in order to provide a pleasing aroma to the smoke, which will overlay the reek of the noxious substance of my fire.

JOHN H. WATSON
London, 1928

ONE

IT was a fine morning in early May in the year 1895. A thin mist, little more than a bloom upon the air, had already evaporated, revealing a clear blue sky and bright sunlight. I felt my spirits lighter than at almost any time in several months as the recollection of winter's mire and fogs retreated before the triumphal march of spring towards summer.

Although the air had smelt quite balmy when I had put my head out of my bedroom window and taken several good breaths before descending for breakfast, I found the fire in our parlour burning as brightly as ever. Our inestimable landlady at No. 221B Baker Street, Mrs Hudson, was a Scotswoman born and bred and accustomed in her native land to a fire in the grate at almost every part of the year. It was only with the utmost difficulty that I had managed to persuade her, at the height of summers past, to leave our fire unlit during the few weeks of greatest heat. Even so, she had insisted upon laying the coals ready for the touch of a match to the paper and sticks upon which they rested, should there occur anything, however brief, in the nature of what she termed 'a cauld spell'.

Impervious as he generally was to his surroundings or to bodily discomfort, my friend Mr Sherlock Holmes never remarked upon the presence or absence of so trivial a thing as a fire. His uncanny sense of observation seemed to be reserved wholly for his professional ventures. In strange surroundings his eyes would be constantly alert, his glance darting everywhere in search of impressions which would inform him of the habits and manner of living of their occupants. On countless occasions I recall his arriving at seemingly miraculous conclusions simply upon the evidence of a single worn chair-arm where a man had been accustomed to lean his weight upon one elbow, a likeness in an ancestral portrait, a patch of carpet laid threadbare by someone's habitual nervous pacing, a sediment in a decanter of port, one volume in a set of Charles Dickens's works more obviously handled than the rest, despite its relative obscurity as literature. I could cite many more examples; but of our own domestic surroundings he appeared to notice nothing, accepting the coming and going of meals and services like the inevitability of day following night.

Despite her stubbornness regarding the fire, Mrs Hudson had long since conceded defeat in the matter of the untidiness of the first-floor sitting-room which served us both as parlour-cum-breakfast and dining room, and, in Holmes's case, consulting room, laboratory, museum and archives. He had absolutely forbidden her to gather together any of the scattered documents which lay upon every surface, to rinse out any chemical equipment, empty his pipes, or even to remove the contents of his overflowing wastepaper basket. She was permitted to dust generally and to tend carpet and fireplace; that was all. Her appeals to me to intercede with him were in vain. To so houseproud a woman he must have seemed at times to be the very worst tenant in London, but she never dared interfere, however much his domestic habits and professional activities upon the premises must have rankled with her. I believe that she was secretly proud of him, and I endeavoured to compensate her for the frustration of her natural instincts by giving her a completely free hand in the tending of my own bedroom, the second floor back. The agreeable consequence was that my dressing set always sparkled, my mirror never showed the least speck of dust, my linen was immaculately pressed and my boots burnished; and my bed was, I would wager, the most comfortable in England, from the almost daily provision of fresh sheets and pillowcases and the constant turning of the mattress.

At the time of which I now write, May, 1895, Sherlock Holmes and I had been back in joint occupation of our apartments for exactly twelve months. The reader who is familiar with my narratives of our two decades of adventuring together will recollect that the three years 1891–94 had been those of his mysterious absence from the country, following his supposed death in hand-to-hand combat with his old enemy Professor James Moriarty at the Reichenbach Falls, near

Meiringen in Switzerland. During that time I had been occupying myself as best I could in medical practice in Kensington, whereto I had removed from my busier one in Paddington, in order to allow myself more time for literary pursuits.

I had lost my poor wife Mary during the Christmas season of 1891–92, through that heart disease which was hereditary in her family. Thus it was that I had been overjoyed when, in April 1894, Holmes so unexpectedly returned from the dead in the dramatic circumstances which I have described in my narrative entitled 'The Empty House'. In the following month I sold my practice, with surprising ease, considering the high price which I had dared to put upon it, to a young doctor named Verner*, and gladly removed myself and my few intimate belongings back to 221B Baker Street.

The twelve months which had followed had been busy ones. Glancing back through the massive volumes which contain records of our work during that period, I find notes of cases galore, some of which are already well known to the public, whilst others, for one reason or another, I have never allowed myself to set down. Amongst the former will readily be recognised those which I, or my Editor of the Strand Magazine, designated 'The Golden Pince-Nez', 'The Three Students' and 'The Solitary Cyclist'. Less known are the story of the red leech (to my mind, too repulsive to be recounted to the family readership), the terrible death of Crosby the banker (dramatic in its way, but dependent upon highly abstruse financial particulars), the shocking affair of the Dutch steamship, *Friesland* (so grotesque that even my best disposed reader would find it impossible to believe); and, I suppose marking the culmination of my friend's reputation on the Continent, the tracking and arrest of Huret, the 'Boulevard Assassin', an exploit whose details I am not at liberty to disclose, but which won for Holmes an autograph letter of thanks from the President of France and the Order of the Legion of Honour.

But to return to this fine May morning of which I write. We were seated at the breakfast table, I at a determined distance from Mrs

---

* It is common knowledge by now that the ready purchaser of my practice proved to be a relative of Sherlock Holmes, who had himself put up the money. Had I been more alert, I might at the time have recognised the proximity of his name to that of Holmes's distinguished ancestors, the Vernet family of French artists. 'I am lost without my Boswell,' Holmes had been gracious enough to remark during my first marriage and separation from him. Clearly, this anonymous gesture, designed to secure my return, was a reiteration of that sentiment.—J.H.W.

Hudson's insistent fire, Holmes with his back to it, oblivious to its heat. As usual, I was shaved and fully dressed for the day, which I intended would take me the short walk up the road to Lord's cricket ground, where I might hope to see the illustrious Stoddart reflect with bat or ball some of the glory which he had gained as England's captain in Australia during our winter, despite his disappointing showing for Middlesex in the summer season past. Holmes lounged customarily in his expensive but carelessly tied dressing gown, over shirt, trousers and slippers. Our breakfast was before us, and, as ever, I felt irritation rise when, occasionally glancing up from my eggs, bacon, kidneys and sausage, I noticed him sitting motionless, egg-spoon poised, his attention distracted from good food by a letter in his other hand.

I cleared my throat, intending to divert his mind back to its proper purpose. He took no notice. I sighed eloquently but without effect and busied myself with toast and butter. At length I heard Holmes stir.

'What do we know of Dreyfus, Watson?' he asked.

I put down the butter knife and answered unhesitatingly.

'A scoundrel. A traitor to his country and a disgrace to his uniform.'

Holmes had lowered the letter and was looking at me curiously.

'You're very warm upon the fellow, Watson.'

'So would any military man be. Such people bring the entire calling into disrepute.'

'I see. Then, will you be so good as to remind me of the details? I recall his name, but not the precise circumstances.'

'I will,' I assented readily, '*whilst* you eat that egg.'

Holmes returned me the winning smile which could so illumine those pale, hawk-like features, and plied his spoon obediently. I poured myself more coffee, and proceeded.

'Alfred Dreyfus is, or rather, was, a captain in the French Artillery. He was arrested last autumn and charged with offering to sell particulars of his country's latest armaments and overseas strategy to a foreign power: Germany, I think. He was court-martialled shortly before Christmas and declared guilty. He has been publicly degraded and transported for life. And good riddance, I am sure.'

'Transported? Surely the charge for such an offence must have been high treason, in which case he would have been shot?'

'I think there was some technical reason why he could not. I forget. We have the cuttings, though. I thought at the time that the case might have some elements you would wish to refer to as talking points during your next French dealings.'

'Stout fellow, Watson! You have a grand instinct as my archivist. Now, when you have quite worked your way through that excessive amount of food which I see before you, perhaps you will retrieve the cuttings and bring me up to date over our post-breakfast pipe?'

'Certainly. May I ask why you are suddenly interested?'

Holmes indicated the letter lying beside his plate. 'We are to have a visitor this morning at eleven. Your traitor's brother, Monsieur Mathieu Dreyfus. It will save a great deal of his time if I am acquainted with all the details beforehand.'

'And a great deal of yours, too!' I snorted. 'I am sure you have more pressing things to do than to concern yourself in any way in this sordid matter.'

'As it so happens, I have not. You see before you, Watson, an idle man. You know how dangerous lack of occupation is to me. Be thankful, then, for any small diversion. Now, eat up like a good fellow. We have not too much time.'

I did as he bade me, although I admit it was with no good grace. It even occurred to me to ring for Mrs Hudson to replenish the toast rack and coffee pot, so that the delay might demonstrate my disapproval to Holmes. But I was restrained from doing so by the knowledge that in his remark about the danger to him of enforced idleness there lay deep truth. Over the years I had gradually weaned him from the use of cocaine. He had never resorted to it, as many of its addicts do, for the purpose of escaping from unpleasant realities of life or from the stress of care or mental over-activity. Quite the reverse: he had only turned to the drug as a protest against the monotony of existence when cases were scanty and the papers uninteresting. All the same, I had often feared that the practice might impair his remarkable faculties in some way. One of the reasons why I had so readily accepted his invitation to return to lodge with him was that I might be on hand to use my influence against any increase in drug-taking to which he might have succumbed during his three years' absence. To my intense relief, I had seen no sign of any use of drugs at all. The syringes lay in their box amongst the clutter of chemical apparatus. By exercising my own modest powers of observation over the year we had now been together again I had observed that the dust upon the neat Morocco case was undisturbed. Clearly, he turned no longer to this artificial stimulant. All the same, I feared that the fiend was not dead, but sleeping, and I should have blamed myself bitterly had I been the one to arouse it.

Consequently I tackled briskly to the rest of my meal, and fifteen minutes later saw us seated in our respective fireside chairs, our pipes well aglow and an open commonplace book of pasted newspaper cuttings upon my knees.

I had not far back to search amongst the familiar typography of The Times to locate the first report to have reached this country of the Dreyfus affair.

'"1st November, 1894, PARIS,"' I read out. '"The following semi-official note has been sent to the press. Presumptive evidence of a serious nature has led to the provisional arrest of a French officer, who is suspected of having communicated to certain foreigners some document of little importance but of a confidential character. An inquiry is being made with the discretion necessary in such cases. The result will be known very shortly."'

And then, '"Midnight: The officer arrested on the charge of high treason is Captain Alfred Dreyfus, of the artillery, belonging to the general staff of the army, and attached to the department for the organisation and mobilization of the army ..."'

'Yes, yes,' my companion interrupted impatiently. 'Pray skip the preliminaries and come to the trial and verdict.'

I soon found the relevant cutting, bearing my own inked record, 'Times, Dec. 24, '94, p. 3 col. 1.'

'This is the most interesting report, I believe,' I said. 'Do you wish it in full?'

Holmes nodded his smoke-wreathed head. 'If you please.'

I proceeded to read out, as follows:

'"PARIS, Dec. 23. At half-past 6 last night, after a speech from his counsel which lasted more than four

> hours, Captain Dreyfus passed from the court-room
> down the staircase, like a man no longer knowing what
> he was about, to the room in which he was to await the
> verdict of the officers who have been trying him. A
> moment later journalists were allowed to enter the
> court-room. Maître Demange was there ..."'

'A moment, Watson,' Holmes interrupted again, withdrawing
the briar pipe from his lips and making a staying gesture with it. 'Do
we take it that the press had been excluded from the hearing
altogether?'

'That is so. The public, too, almost from the outset.'

'How so?'

'There's an earlier piece somewhere which accounts for it. Yes,
here it is: "A morning paper professes to give the statement of an
officer who was present at the opening of the court, and who says that
the reason why secrecy was insisted upon was that the document"—
that is the document Dreyfus passed over ...'

'Is *alleged* to have passed over.'

'As you wish, Holmes—". . . that the document had been stolen
back from the German Embassy, and it could not have been publicly
used without running the risk of a war with Germany."'

'Hm! Very well. Pray continue the narrative.'

I returned to the later report, and read on.

'"Maître Demange was there ..."'

'Demange, eh! Not a defender of clear-cut rascals, from what I
know of his reputation.'

'Holmes,' I expostulated, 'if I am to continue reading ...'

'A thousand pardons, Watson. Do go on.'

> '"Maître Demange was there in a state of exhaustion
> after the effort of his speech. On the large table at
> which the court-martial had sat were five or six
> magnifying glasses, which had, no doubt, been used in
> the examination of the captain's letters. The delibera-
> tions of the court lasted about an hour and a half.
> At 7 o'clock Colonel Maurel and his fellow officers
> appeared, and the orders given to the municipal

guards—'Shoulder arms! Present arms!'—rang
through the room. There was a terrible silence as the
Colonel, with his clear military intonation, read as
follows:—

'In the name of the French people' (the Colonel and
the six other members of the court raised their hands to
their *képis* and gave the military salute) 'is M. Alfred
Dreyfus, captain in the 14th Artillery Regiment,
supernumerary member of the General Staff attached
to the War Office, guilty of having in 1894 procured for
a foreign Power a certain number of secret documents
connected with the national defence, and of having
thus had dealings or relations with that Power or its
agents to induce it to commit hostilities or to undertake
war against France, or to procure it the means
thereof?' The votes having been taken separately,
beginning with the lowest rank, the presiding Colonel
expressing his opinion last, the unanimous reply was
'Yes; the accused is Guilty.' At the far end of the room
a voice cried, '*Vive la patrie!*'"'

'Stirring stuff,' remarked Holmes, at the risk of my further
rebuke. 'Some of our own courts could well do with such a touch of
theatricality.'

'It is no joking matter,' I reminded him. 'Treachery is more
heinous a crime than murder, even, in a military man's eyes.'

'Yes, I dare say it is. But, from what you mentioned earlier, I
gather that the traitor upon this occasion was not called upon to pay
the supreme penalty.'

I scanned the column of print. 'There's a bit about Clause This
and That of the Penal Code. What it seems to boil down to is that a
law of 1848 abolished the death sentence in the case of political offences, while another of 1850—I will read it out—"enacts transpor-
tation as the substitute, and adds that persons thus treated shall enjoy
all the liberty compatible with the necessity of insuring the custody of
their persons." In short,' I could not help adding with disgust, 'they
have patted the fellow on the head and shipped him and his family
and possessions off to New Caledonia, or somewhere comfortable,

where he'll live waited on hand and foot by servants, and ...'

But Holmes's expression was grave, and he was shaking his head slowly from side to side.

'It's not quite as you picture, I fancy.' He flicked his finger in the direction of the letter again. 'But we shall learn fuller details when our visitor arrives.'

'Whatever it is,' I persisted stubbornly, 'it is better than he deserves. When I think of the men—simple, ignorant, but loyal-hearted to the last of them—who fell on their country's service in the Afghan Campaign in which I was proud to play a part, I can almost hear their voices declaring how this man should have been dealt with.' I flourished the cuttings book in the heat of my emotion. 'Even the Times correspondent remarks upon the inequity of this sentence compared with one being demanded for a soldier charged with no more than a serious breach of discipline, but who is expected to be executed for it. He remarks, "There is, it is true, no comparison between the two cases, but breach of discipline may lead up to treason, and the only safeguard for a country is respect for authority from the top to the bottom of society." Amen to that, I say!'

'Incidentally,' I added, 'there is a post scriptum report of a rumour that Dreyfus had committed suicide in prison that same night. Evidently he did not, but many would have seen it as the honourable course.'

'An alternative being that he was confident of his innocence, and determined to live to see it proved.'

'Holmes!' I cried in my exasperation. 'The verdict was unanimous. I always understood that you held the French judiciary in the highest respect. As to the army, it is the rock upon which that unstable country rests.'

'True, Watson, true,' was my companion's mild response. 'But when a man writes to me passionately proclaiming his brother's innocence, and beseeching my assistance where all other means seem to have failed him, it is surely my duty to cast a few doubts? Tell me, is anything adduced in the way of a motive for the crime?'

'Nothing,' I had to admit. 'It states explicitly, "The charge is said to have rested on a document stolen from the German Embassy, but that Embassy has given no sign, and no member of it was summoned as a witness. Nor has any motive been shown for the crime. No extravagance, no love affair or gambling, have been revealed; yet, though these ordinary motives are absent, it is impossible to question the unanimous verdict of seven honourable men." Surely you would admit that as fair comment?'

'I suppose so. And yet, does it not strike you as something of a double mystery that he has been convicted of passing information to the Germans, which in turn has been purloined back by the French; and on the one hand the Germans have made no protest about it, yet the French are said to have called no witness from that side to support the charge for fear of war even? Suppose, for a moment, that no such document ever existed, and that the only ground for prosecution is suspicion based upon hearsay, which the Germans know to be false ...'

'Stop, Holmes!' I cried. 'You are quibbling, and you know it. If you have nothing better to do with your day, I have. I am off to Lord's. The wicket will be lively on such a morning, and Stod is playing.'

I had risen to my feet and was holding the closed volume, with my index finger between the pages to which I had been referring. Holmes sucked and then blew noisily into a now empty pipe, then tapped out the small remains of cold ash against his palm.

'I am given to believe,' he said mildly, 'that in this game of cricket of yours, whose intricacies I do not pretend to understand, certain decisions concerning the batsman are the province of the umpires' judgment, in the light of their observation and experience.'

'That is so. Leg before wicket, for instance. Some catches not clearly from the bat ...'

'Exactly. And I have heard you declare irately after some of your expeditions that So-and-So was incorrectly adjudged by these paragons of fair play.'

'There are ... disputable decisions. However,' I added more firmly, seeing what he was getting at, 'for better or worse, the batsman must accept the umpire's word. To refuse to do so would be totally against the spirit of the game.'

'Even though his whole future should hang upon it?' Holmes asked quietly, only half-addressing himself to me. He stirred suddenly and stood up, examining his watch.

'I must finish dressing. Our visitor will be here soon. Tell me one more thing please, Watson. In those reports, is there anything indicative of Captain Dreyfus's character or background?'

'Nothing at all.'

'Ah, well—we shall just have to learn what we can of them from his brother.'

'*We*, Holmes? Not I, I'm afraid. I told you, I am off to Lord's.'

But my friend had moved slightly to stand facing me directly, and I was surprised to see in his eyes that compound of intense curiosity, serious concern, and the spark of excitement, which had become so familiar to me at the outset of any case which intrigued him.

'My dear Watson,' he said, 'I beg you to do me the favour of remaining. A half-hour of your time at most, perhaps. This gentle-man has come from France especially to see me, I gather at some risk to himself. I must hear him out and make my own judgment. I should prefer your reliable witness to what he has to say, not to mention the benefit of your invaluable opinion afterwards.'

I sighed. That he himself was as sensitive to flattery on the score of his art as any girl could be of her beauty was well known to me. For my part, although I had time and again seen him use flattery of the unsuspecting as a winning technique, a word of commendation to me from Sherlock Holmes remained the acme of tribute.

'Very well, Holmes,' I consented. 'I'll stay and meet the fellow.'

'Good boy!' he cried, with that playfully irritating manner of a man who, at the age of 41 at this time, was more than a year junior to my 42. 'I shall now get ready. Should you hear our client's foot upon the stair, pray entertain him with your delightful conversation until I appear.'

He moved swiftly from the room. As I replaced the common-place book amongst the others, I had to smile. His enthusiasm was the most infectious influence I knew. I could sense that he was willing this affair to bring him the meaningful activity without which he found existence drab and pointless. I very much fancied, however, that he was due for a let-down within the hour.

TWO

I N the event, I was spared the embarrassment of having to receive the visitor alone. Holmes, clad in black morning coat, with soft black bow tie under the turned-down starched collar of the white shirt, and gold albert looped across his waistcoat, was already in position with his back to the fire, hands beneath his coat-tails, when there came a knock at the door and Mrs Hudson announced Monsieur Dreyfus.

He came briskly in, a man of medium height and good build, dressed neatly in a dark serge suit and carrying a black bowler hat in one hand. His carriage was almost that of a military man, although his shoulders were too rounded for a soldier's. I put his age in the late thirties, and was subsequently proved correct. He sported a large, dark moustache, extending well beyond his lips at either side, and had a good broad brow under dark hair.

He introduced himself first to Holmes, whose appearance he evidently recognised at once, and then to me. Throughout my life it has been my habit to base my first impression of a man upon the strength of his handshake and the steadiness with which his gaze returns mine. Despite my readiness to resent him, Mathieu Dreyfus passed my little test notably. His grip was strong, his eyes, in his solemn countenance, unwavering. Those eyes, I was surprised to note, were of the brightest blue, in marked contrast with his general darkness of hair and paleness of skin.

Holmes ushered him into the basket chair in which he generally seated his clients. I resumed my own seat, Holmes remaining standing.

'Mr Holmes,' said our visitor, 'I must commence by thanking you for receiving me. It was remiss of me not to have apprised you in better time of my decision to come, but, to tell the truth, it was an impulse, a sudden inspiration, which stirred me and which was not to be put off for a moment.'

He had spoken in good English, though markedly accented. He was clearly well-educated, a gentleman by breeding, and a person of resolute character. I was impressed again, and from indications familiar to me I could tell that my sentiments were shared by Holmes. He made a gracious little return speech in the fluent French which had passed down in his family from his maternal Vernet ancestors, and which had been nurtured during his childhood and youth by many years of residence in France and wide travels amongst French-speaking communities. To my relief, however, my own command of that language being, in a word, slight, the conversation thenceforward was conducted entirely in English.

'Mr Holmes,' said Mathieu Dreyfus with the most earnest intensity, 'I have come to appeal for your help.'

'I flatter myself that I am the last and highest court of appeal in detection,' Holmes replied. 'To judge from the contents of your letter, you appear to have exhausted all other tribunals.'

'I have indeed. It is as though every avenue were barricaded against me; each a brick wall impassable by any means. Mr Holmes, I am desperate.'

'Then you had better let me have the facts from the beginning. You will not object to the presence of my friend and counsellor?'

The visitor turned towards me and gave a grave little nod of approval.

'Also,' Holmes continued, 'I must warn you at the outset that I cannot bind myself to act on your behalf in any way. I will listen to your account gladly, and judge for myself.'

'Agreed,' said Dreyfus warmly. 'I am in no doubt that when you have heard me, you will entertain your reservations no longer.'

Only now did Holmes take his own chair at the fireside, relinquishing the commanding superiority of his height. I had seen him perform this simple but effective trick so many times: first, to impress his client and add to any feelings of awe which might already be present; and then, to place himself on the client's own physical level, to encourage that confidence and relaxation of mind which would draw forth the freest expression of whatever might emerge.

One characteristic habit of his was strikingly absent on this occasion, though. As readers of my hitherto published narratives will know, Holmes almost always indulged for his new clients' benefit in one of his pyrotechnical displays of observation and deduction. 'Showing off' would be a more everyday term for what was, in effect, a device both for demonstrating that his great reputation was no myth, and as a warning that it would be unwise to try misleading him, since it would not go undetected.

This time he dispensed entirely with this ritual. I sensed that he was in too earnest a mood for it. He began re-lighting his pipe, his chin lowered but the piercing eyes remaining steadily on our visitor.

'It was on the Monday morning of October 15th last year ...' Mathieu Dreyfus commenced, with the confidence of one who has a much-told story to repeat, requiring no search of his memory. But already Holmes was halting him with a gesture.

'From the very beginning, if you please. Your family background, circumstances ...'

'But I was proposing to occupy as little of your valuable time as possible, Mr Holmes, by going directly to the heart of the matter.'

'The heart—the human heart, Mr Dreyfus—is commonly supposed to lie in the left-hand region of the chest. All literature, art and folklore have taken this for granted. As one who has studied anatomy and medicine, I am aware that the belief is false. The heart is central. Similarly, long experience has shown me also that the heart of any matter is by no means necessarily where instinct presumes it to be. So, take no consideration of time, but be as precise as possible as to details.'

This homily provoked a sad little smile of appreciation. Dreyfus sat back more easily in his chair and began again.

'Our family was —is still—a prosperous one, prominent in the textile industry. Until 1872 my father conducted a most advanced mill, as well as other factories, in the province of Alsace, at Mulhouse. Today the town is renamed Mülhausen, for under the Treaty of Frankfurt, after the Franco-Prussian War, the greater part of Alsace, together with much of Lorraine, was annexed by Germany. Under the terms of annexation the inhabitants of our province were given two choices. They could remain there and take German nationality; or they could retain their French nationality by leaving. You can understand that this placed our father in a dilemma. We were a strongly united family—four sons and three daughters, in addition to Father and poor Mama, who was ailing sadly—and totally patriotic to France. Yet, to emigrate would mean giving up the flourishing business upon which our fortune depended.

'This difficulty was solved by our transferring ourselves to Basel, just across the border with Switzerland, but leaving behind the eldest brother, Jacques, to conduct the business on the spot, with the supervision of my father by means largely of the post and through visits by special visa. This was quite a sacrifice for Jacques, who had served throughout the war with the Alsace-Lorraine Legion, and to find himself a German moved him bitterly. However, he acted bravely for the benefit of us all, and the business continues to prosper.

'My younger brother Alfred, who was a mere boy at the time, was considerably unsettled by the move. He was a sensitive, shy fellow, and did not take well to boarding-school in Paris, which is where he was sent. He had to return to live with the family for some time before feeling able to continue there. It had always been taken for granted in our circle that he would eventually assume his place in the business, or, at the most, go into one of the professions. Imagine our surprise, then, when he declared that he desired nothing else than to become an officer in the army. In fact, we did not at first take this seriously at all. It has been remarked that I myself bear more of the natural traits of the military than he. Despite quite a close re-semblance between us, I have to say of my brother that his physique is not prepossessing, his eyesight is imperfect, and he expresses himself without animation and in a voice which lacks both strength and variety of tone. Mr Holmes, I pray you will interrupt me if I am straying into irrelevant details.'

'On the contrary, you are painting a valuable picture,' Holmes replied. 'It is essential to examine happenings in the light of the personalities and character of those whom they concern.'

'Thank you. To continue, then. Although the army seemed a most unlikely choice for Fred, as we call him, his courage was admired and he was allowed, though with some reluctance, to sit the entrance examination for the *École Polytechnique*, which is France's most respected school for military engineers. To tell the truth, we were all relieved to hear that he had achieved very low marks, and Father repeated his offer of most generous terms of employment if Fred would enter the firm. But the marks proved just enough to admit him to the *Ecole*. He entered in 1878, in his nineteenth year, and graduated two years later to enter the army as a second-lieutenant.

'From then onward his career flourished. Promotion to lieutenant. Garrison service with the 31st Artillery Regiment at Le Mans. Five years with the First Cavalry Division in Paris, which was a considerable honour. Excellent annual reports. In 1889 he was promoted again, to captain, and posted to Bourges, to the artillery school, where selected officers are instructed in the use of munitions and learn how they are manufactured. In April, 1890, my brother was accorded the great honour of acceptance to the War College, for preparation for service on the general staff.'

There was a catch in his voice which qualified the pride behind this last statement. Mathieu Dreyfus paused, and I could see that he was struggling with emotion.

'A brilliant career,' I ventured to say, risking Holmes's disapproval of any interruption in the narrative flow. 'Less than ten years from subaltern to captain, and in peace-time! And then, the staff...'

'An astonishing career!' our visitor burst out, no longer attempting to hide his distress. 'A great career! But ruined, shattered to pieces by this bolt from the blue, this disaster of which he is the sole victim and which had its origins in something or other entirely unconnected with my poor brother! Whatever you may have heard or read of his case, gentlemen, I swear to you that the truth has not been in it. He is innocent—completely and utterly innocent!'

Uncomfortable at the sight of a man in tears, I glanced across at Holmes. He was still drawing impassively at his pipe, watching all the time the man who had now buried his face in his hands and whose shoulders were heaving with his sobs.

'I think, Watson,' said he, without shifting his gaze, 'a dose of that medicine which you are in the habit of prescribing for most occasions might prove timely.'

I got up and made rapidly for the brandy decanter, to pour two stiff measures. I knew that Holmes would not indulge at a moment when his concentration was fully engaged, but I had no qualms for my own part in adding some soda from the gasogene and taking an immediate sip, before carrying the other glass across to Dreyfus. It

occurred to me that a Frenchman would prefer his drink un-
adulterated in any way. He evidently sensed that I stood before him,
and looked up. I was moved to pity by his wet cheeks and brimming
eyes, with their wretched, haunted expression. I held out the glass. He
took it without a word and drank readily. Only then did he say, in a
husky tone, 'Thank you, Doctor. I beg your pardon.'

He blew his nose, drank some more of the brandy, and made a
visible effort to compose himself, which he quickly succeeded in
doing. When I made a move to take his empty glass and refill it he
shook his head.

'Forgive me, Dr Watson, Mr Holmes. It was unworthy of me.
But after more than six months of this nightmare I am afraid that my
emotions are no longer under the control which, at the outset, I was
determined they should remain. May I continue?'

'If you are ready, by all means,' replied Holmes.

'When Alfred received word of his acceptance for the War
College, on April 20th, 1890, the world seemed to be at his feet. And
the following day he crowned his triumph by marrying Mademoiselle
Lucie Hadamard, a charming, cultivated, attractive lady of a
wealthy business family, whose father is a *lycée* professor. Thus he had
come to possess, almost at a single stroke, an ideal companion, who
brought him a large dowry, which, in addition to his own income and
the portion he received regularly from our family business, would
insulate him from those financial cares which bedevil most young
officers; and he had set his foot upon the threshold of that
establishment in which he could hope to prosper rapidly and, who
knows, perhaps become one of the youngest men ever to attain the
rank of general.'

Once again, Mathieu Dreyfus paused, although this time not
under the stress of emotion. He simply fell silent, hunched forward,
his forearms upon his knees and hands clasped, as he stared into the
flickering red glow of our fire.

I cleared my throat and remarked, 'Monsieur Dreyfus, all that
you told us of your brother's character earlier suggested that by
temperament and type he was scarcely cut out for a soldier at all. And
yet, his career as one seems to have been little short of meteoric. If you
will forgive me ...'

'Quite, quite,' came the prompt answer. 'Alfred never was the military type. It was resented by some of his comrades, who were. Yet, he possessed great concentration of mind; much application. He was a dedicated student of his calling. To be honest, I would never have termed him imaginative—it is a profession which relies more upon discipline than imagination, so it seems to me. Nor could I call him forceful, or a born leader of others. And yet, he had this quality of applying himself to detail, of working long, hard hours to master any task, which, alas, is not common to all in his position. The hunting horn and the ... the boudoir ... if you will forgive me, are more to many of them than the studies by the midnight oil.'

For the first time since the uncertain commencement of the narrative, Holmes interrupted with a question.

'Are you suggesting, Monsieur Dreyfus, that there was jealousy, perhaps even tinged with contempt, of your brother amongst his fellow officers?'

'Exactly! That a man may advance himself through valour in battle is one thing. To do so through mere study is altogether another.'

'In many other callings, I fancy. But tell me, was he aware of this hostility, if that is not too strong a word? If so, did he not have the tact to ingratiate himself a little to overcome it?'

'You are quite right, Mr Holmes. He was aware of it; but he did nothing to deflect it. My brother is a man of stubborn principle. He would make his mark in his own fashion, despite the ways of others.'

Holmes pressed the tips of his long fingers together before him in a summary gesture.

'So, then, we have a picture of a man who is physically and, to a considerable degree, mentally untypical of the career officer in the French Army, yet who, through ambition and application, outstrips the majority of his comrades in the race towards a most desirable goal; who is, if I am correct, something of an outside runner, in that he is a son of a commercial family, and not a military one; who has money to his name, but not aristocracy ...'

'Precisely!' Dreyfus almost cried. He seemed about to add something else, but stayed silent. Holmes went on, 'How do you view his relations with his fellow officers? Surely, he is not regarded as some sort of pariah?'

Again Mathieu Dreyfus hesitated. Then he said, 'No. But he was not popular, either with his fellows or his superiors. To be honest, he gave the impression of thinking himself above them; in the case of his fellows, in taste; in that of his superiors, in intellect. I have to say of my own brother that he was smug, conceited, rather narrow-minded. A prig, I believe you would say? A good, earnest, dedicated man; yet, I think it is true, in no circles are *such as he* wholly popular.'

A sudden silence had fallen after this, whose cause, I believe, we all knew, but which none of us wished to break. It was typical of Holmes, the relentless searcher for the truth, that it was he who at length did so.

'Monsieur Dreyfus, you speak of your brother in the past tense. Surely, this is at variance with your protestations of his innocence; with your having come to consult me?'

Dreyfus's eyes opened wide. He struck his brow.

'Dear God, I am falling into the habit so soon! No, no, Mr Holmes. All those things which I have said of my brother are valid to this day. Those qualities which I have ascribed to him are true— especially that of courage. As to his regard in the eyes of his fellow officers, I must admit that where formerly were spite and envy are now hatred and rejection. He is not dead. He is not changed. He is what he has been always, except that now, for unknown reasons, he has been branded an outcast and flung into barbarous exile for some alleged offence of which he is wholly innocent.'

As if to punctuate the interview and turn it back to its main course, Holmes leaned into the grate and clapped his pipe bowl into his palm, scattering ash and small shreds of half-burnt tobacco into the pan. He took up the poker and re-invigorated the coals, before reaching down for the Persian slipper in the hearth, in which he stored tobacco, and leaning back with it into his chair, his fingers working at his pipe as he invited Mathieu Dreyfus to come to the crux of his story.

It is at this stage in my own narrative that I believe a temporary change in the style of its presentation is desirable. Up to this point, we have witnessed Sherlock Holmes's sudden access of interest in a case in which he had previously shown none. We have met a foreign stranger, to whose coming I myself had looked forward with distaste, yet whose story, as I have tried to relate it, has sounded sincere, and his protestations plausible. All this has been a relation of fact and openly expressed opinion. Now, however, an episode follows which, though relayed to Holmes and myself in hearsay form, is so subjective in content that my reader might forgive my endeavouring to represent it in a manner more suited to its inherent drama, whatever may or may not be the truth of the emotion depicted in it, which is as described to us by M. Mathieu Dreyfus on that morning in May, 1895.

THREE

THE early morning temperature was low, but the October day fine, as Alfred Dreyfus set forth from his apartment at 6, Avenue du Trocadéro, situated in one of the most desirable of the neighbourhoods of Paris, the 16th *arrondissement*. It required no more than a few minutes' walk to reach the northern end of the Alma Bridge, spanning the River Seine, which he proceeded to cross.

He walked briskly, as became a soldier, proud of his calling; but on this Monday morning the black uniform with gold braid ornamentation on the tunic sleeves and the coveted red stripe of the general staff down each trouser leg had been replaced by a plain, brown civilian suit. The regulation white gloves were absent, too, and Dreyfus swung his arms all the more vigorously, conscious of his cold hands.

It was rare indeed for him to be wearing mufti at any other time than the weekend, when he was off duty; he felt strange in it, and had fussed to his wife, Lucie, about it during their brief breakfast. Lucie was a striking woman, ten years his junior, with chestnut hair and dark eyes, tall and full-figured.

'My dear,' she had said, 'you look as trim as if it were another sort of uniform. No one could doubt that you are anything other than an officer. I am just as proud of you. So is Pierrot, aren't you, my darling?'

Little Pierre, aged three-and-a-half, dutifully piped, 'Yes, Papa.' His infant sister Jeanne gurgled happily in her high chair.

'You are always encouraging, my dear,' replied Alfred Dreyfus in his flat, weak voice. He was an unexcitable man—dull, even— with little interest in anything beside his duty. Much of his spare time

27

was occupied with the study of military history, tactical theory, logistics. He was well aware that some of his brother officers, especially in regimental circles as opposed to the more formal world of the staff, regarded him as 'an old woman', with no taste for escapade, and poor company at any social function. It did not trouble him. He nurtured his ambition upon hard work whilst they idled away their free hours, and consequently outpaced them in advancement, which added to their resentment. His wife could see this, but refrained from attempting to change him. She was content to share his pride in himself, although it did at times take the form of self-satisfaction and even arrogance.

So she had reassured him; yet he had felt strangely vulnerable this morning in the best of the few civilian suits which he possessed. He told her that he felt like an ordinary employee summoned to a special interview with his manager. Lucie appreciated his feeling, but said: 'My dear, don't worry so! I am sure you will bring home wonderful news for us all to digest with our luncheon.'

'Who is to say what it will be? It's all so irregular.'

It was certainly unusual, for several reasons. The summons to the Chief of Staff's office had been delivered by an orderly on the previous Saturday morning, which was in itself strange, since the office was closed on that day. Having completed his two years' probationary attachment to the staff, gaining experience in the four main departments into which it was organised, Dreyfus had recently been posted to duty with the 37th Regiment, stationed in Paris. This was a regulation appointment, as part of his preparation for higher rank. He would have expected the Chief of Staff's message to have reached him through the usual regimental channels, rather than at his apartment. Lucie had persuaded him that there was no significance in this Monday summons at all.

'What can the Chief possibly want with me? he persisted. 'I'm not due to rejoin the staff until the end of the year.'

'It could be anything at all, Fred, but I am sure it is good. You have been singled out for something special, I'm certain. Be thankful.'

'But in mufti! It's unheard of. I've never even *seen* General de Boisdeffre in mufti himself. They say he sleeps in his képi.'

It was rare for Alfred to joke. Lucie was pleased and went to adjust his tie needlessly for him for the last time, as he polished his pince-nez on his crisp linen handkerchief.

'You will see. Good luck go with you, my dear. Hurry back with your news.'

Alfred had kissed his children and, lastly, his wife, had taken up his hat and left briskly, striding down the avenue with the river to his right. The air was keener as he crossed the bridge; and then he was walking away from the river, crossing the Quai d'Orsai, with the round bulk of Les Invalides to his left. It was the route he had taken daily for two years until little more than a fortnight ago. He knew every feature of it, and, almost to the second, how long it would take him to reach his destination in the Rue St-Dominique.

He marched up the steps and through the tall doors, whose attendant recognised him and saluted smartly. Dreyfus nodded stiffly and carried on, along carpeted passages and up more stairs, to the office of the Chief of the General Staff, Lieutenant-General de Boisdeffre. He was aware already of that officer's approval of him, and yet, in spite of his wife's prediction that he had been called there at nine o'clock that morning to hear something to his advantage, he paused to take an extra deep breath, draw in his stomach and square his shoulders, before preparing to knock at the door.

Before he could do so, though, he was hailed by a familiar voice. It was that of Major Georges Picquart, a fellow native of Alsace, some five years older than Dreyfus, whose instructor he had been at the War College. Picquart, like Dreyfus, tended to regard himself as superior to his fellows. His record as a leading graduate of Saint-Cyr and on active service in the 4th Zouaves in Algeria was without doubt more notable than Dreyfus's. He, too, was of a reserved nature, keeping very much to himself and living in bachelor lodgings. Facially, and especially as the cultivator of a large moustache, he bore considerable resemblance to Mathieu Dreyfus.

This morning he greeted Alfred Dreyfus in his usual uneffusive fashion, and invited him to wait in his office for the summons to the Chief of Staff's room. After some small talk between them, Dreyfus enquired whether Major Picquart knew the nature of the business upon which he had been summoned. The answer was in the negative, but Dreyfus had the sharp impression that this was not quite the truth.

At length, Major Picquart left the room, to return shortly

afterward to request Dreyfus to go to the Chief's office. He entered it, to find several men awaiting him, none of whom, however, was General de Boisdeffre. Three were, like himself, in civilian clothing, and he recognised none of them. The fourth, in staff dress, he saw to be Major the Marquis du Paty de Clam, of the Third Bureau, that concerned with Operations. One of his arms was in a sling.

The Marquis du Paty de Clam was an officer of a conscious elegance, who posed, rather than stood, almost in the manner of an operetta character. His head was habitually tilted back, so that his nose pointed ceilingward. A monocle in his right eye, a tightly tailored uniform and carefully brushed receding hair, added to this impression. He was, in fact, an officer of brilliance, though as vain and fanciful as he appeared to be.

He greeted Dreyfus unsmilingly and made no move to introduce the other gentlemen, whom Dreyfus noted were unsmiling, too.

'Kindly be seated, Captain,' Major du Paty said, indicating a chair beside a small table some distance from the Chief's broad desk behind which, in the large fireplace, flames leaped. 'The Chief has sent word that he is delayed, but will arrive shortly.'

Dreyfus took the chair. Sheets of paper, ink and a pen lay in front of him. Du Paty held up his bandaged arm and said, a little less stiffly: 'As you see, I have injured my hand and so cannot write. Perhaps you will be good enough to take down a few lines of dictation from me while we await the General?'

It occurred to Dreyfus to wonder why none of the others present could have performed this task before his arrival. Perhaps they were of too superior rank to be requested to do it, although none of them looked particularly exalted. He obediently picked up the pen and dipped it into the inkwell. Major du Paty began to dictate.

'Being most seriously anxious to have back for the time being those documents which I passed to you before I went on manoeuvres, I beg you urgently to send them to me by the bearer of this note, who is a reliable person ...'

As Dreyfus wrote, Major du Paty leaned forward and his even tone changed abruptly.

'You are trembling, Captain!' he uttered, in accusatory tone. Dreyfus paused in his work and glanced up. He was even more surprised to see the other men supporting themselves by their hands on the table top, craning to see what he had written.

'Not at all, Major,' he answered. 'My hands are a little cold this morning.'

'Be careful!' was the response. 'This is a serious matter.'

The others were glaring, too. Dreyfus could think of nothing more than to dip his pen again and resume. He had written no more than a few words before he felt a hand clapped on his shoulder and du Paty's voice, upraised and tense, declaring, 'Captain Dreyfus, in the name of the law, I arrest you. You are accused of the crime of high treason.'

The nervousness which had been present in Dreyfus all along, and which in the past minutes had been mounting as suspicion grew within him, released itself, causing him to leap to his feet, babbling automatically of his innocence. He felt his face burning, as his usually pale cheeks crimsoned deeply. Du Paty, his head thrown back, was regarding him haughtily from the bottom of cold eyes. The others crowded nearer.

'I have done nothing! This is some absurd trick!'

For once, even Alfred Dreyfus was animated. His head swam. He felt he might swoon. No one said anything, leaving him to rave on.

'Where is the General? What are you doing to me, Major? Who are these gentlemen?'

Major du Paty de Clam spoke at last. 'The evidence is overwhelming. There can be no doubt.'

'Of what? In the name of Heaven, what am I supposed to have done?'

'You know that, better than anyone. These police officers will now search you.'

Two of the three moved swiftly round the desk and laid hands on Dreyfus. He tried to resist, struggling, and felt them dragging at his neat suit, thrusting hands roughly into his pockets, wrenching out what few objects he carried. The fourth man looked on impassively, and du Paty continued to stand in a pose of theatrical hauteur. It was a nightmare to Dreyfus's mind. Reason told him that he should hold his peace, reserving his words for the Chief of Staff, who must surely soon enter to interrupt this nonsensical struggle. But the suddenness of it, on top of the nervousness which he had been feeling throughout the weekend, seemed to have made his tongue uncontrollable.

'I am innocent! What proof have you against me? Show me proof. Take my keys. Search my house. You will find nothing. If you think I am guilty of treason, why not simply kill me?'

The policemen had his keys already, together with his wallet, his pass, some coins, and a few personal items, all of which now lay in a little heap on the desk top. The search completed, they gripped him by the arms at either side, awaiting Major du Paty's further instructions.

He himself moved to the table and slowly, very deliberately, drew aside a sheaf of papers resting on top of a tray. A revolver lay beneath. In a voice of ice he said, 'We are not executioners. If you wish to take the honourable way, however, there is your means.'

Dreyfus stared back at him, aghast. Even in the wildness of his emotion he had felt that this drama must end soon. He was being put to some test of character. At any moment General de Boisdeffre would stride in and he would be released, slapped on the back and told that he had borne up as a soldier should, although he was unhappily aware that he had not. The cold, gleaming reality of the weapon, however, had the effect of bringing him sharply back to his wits. He ceased to tremble, as tongue and mind came under control together. He stiffened, drew up his shoulders, and replied, 'I will do nothing of the sort. Some plan has been set in motion against me, for reasons I do not know. If this accusation is genuinely meant, I will live to prove it false. I am a respected officer. I am an Alsatian who chose to transfer to France and to dedicate my life to her service. The army is my life. Why should I risk throwing it away? For what? Money? I am not a poor man. I do not need a traitor's pieces of silver. I would take up that revolver against any man whom I knew to have acted so. As to myself, I am innocent, innocent! Search every inch of my apartment, only please show consideration to my wife and children.'

Du Paty answered, 'Very well. We shall do so. But, tell us first, have you handled secret documents recently?'

'Only one. It concerned certain dispositions of troops, and preparations concerning Madagascar.'

'Ah! And you say that is all?'

'I swear it.'

'Have you had recent contact with the artillery section?'

'Yes. On two occasions.'

'Answer carefully: have you passed any documents to repre-sentatives of any foreign power?'

'No! I swear it!'

Nevertheless, du Paty rapped the desk top with the knuckles of his unbandaged hand and spoke sharply to the senior policeman. 'Monsieur Cochefert, the prisoner will be taken to the *Cherche-Midi* prison and detained. Kindly take him to the courtyard, where an officer will join you to escort him.'

Protesting still, and struggling helplessly in the strong grasp of Cochefert and his assistant, Dreyfus was led out. Major du Paty de Clam nodded to the remaining man, who was Félix Gribelin, archivist to the War Ministry, who obediently came round to untie the knot in the unnecessary sling. Du Paty unfurled his bandage thankfully and wrung the circulation back into his hand, which Gribelin had secured too tightly in the first place. As they were doing this, one of the floor-length window drapes stirred and from behind it a further man emerged from the place of concealment in which he had been stationed to overhear the confrontation.

This man, dressed in the uniform of a major on the general staff, was a complete contrast in type with the aristocratic du Paty. He was burly and large, with an almost Prussian cranium and features; small eyes beneath a low forehead, and a clipped moustache. Out of uniform, he might have passed for a countryman, a shrewd peasant farmer nearing the age of fifty. His name was Hubert Joseph Henry and he was the second most senior of the so-called Statistical Section. The work of the section was, in fact, Counterintelligence.

Bending and flexing each knee in turn, from the stiffness of standing motionless behind the curtains, Henry came forward to look du Paty in the face. They exchanged nods of confirmation. Du Paty said, 'Kindly go and escort him to the prison, Major. Keep a sharp ear for anything he might confide in you on the way.'

'Of course. He seemed in a fearful fuss.'

'I must admit I was surprised, in one usually so phlegmatic. I had half-expected him to pooh-pooh it all and demand to see the Chief.'

'Significant, eh? I'll see what a few words of sympathy might produce.'

'Send Cochefert back to me, will you? The other fellow can ride outside your cab to the prison.' Du Paty picked up Dreyfus's keys and tossed them in his palm. 'Cochefert and I will accept his invitation to look round his apartment, without delay.'

Henry lumbered away and a few minutes later was seated opposite Dreyfus in the cab taking them the short distance to the *Cherche-Midi* military prison.

'What on earth's all this about?' he enquired, and wrinkled his brow in assumed puzzlement. 'I was just hauled out of my office and told to take you, under arrest, to the *Cherche-Midi*. What's happened?'

Major Henry's shrewd, small eyes were keenly on his charge. Dreyfus's face was deathly pale. His suit, neatly pressed until so recently, was rumpled and his necktie disordered. The military stiffness had quite gone from his frame, as he slumped hopelessly in his seat. No one would now have seen him as unmistakably an officer.

'I am accused of high treason,' he answered through dry lips.

'Eh? The devil you are! But why?'

'I've no idea. None at all. I feel that I might be going mad. I am not guilty, Major.'

The other made a gruff sound compounded of pretended sympathy and wonderment. Dreyfus went on, 'I could have put a bullet into my head. Perhaps I should have done. This accusation is the end of my life, anyway.'

'No, no,' Henry rebuked him in man-to-man way. 'If you are not guilty, you must keep your senses. An innocent man is a strong man. You'll get justice, you'll see.'

Dreyfus nodded limply. 'That is all that supports me, Major, I *must* clear myself quickly.'

'I am sure you will be given every chance. But what, exactly, are you accused of having done?'

'I don't know even that. Major du Paty made some reference to passing documents to a foreign power.'

'What documents?' Henry's question was deceptively innocent.

'He did not specify. He asked if I had handled any secret papers lately. I replied that there had only been one concerning Madagascar.'

'What of Madagascar?'

'I have no idea. It was merely a geographical survey. Now that I recall, I don't think it was even marked confidential, let alone secret.

I was too confused to remember. Major, you must tell them that, please.'

'I can't interfere, I'm afraid. You must make the point when you're interrogated again. What foreign power was mentioned, by the way?'

'None was specified.'

'Italy? Germany?' Major Henry was ruminating aloud, watching the other keenly for any slightest reaction. He saw none. Dreyfus's eyes had dulled with despair. He seemed scarcely to be listening.

The cab clattered towards the heavy door of the *Cherche-Midi*.

'Here we are,' said Major Henry. 'All I can say is, good luck; and remember, you will get justice.'

A short while afterward, Alfred Dreyfus was alone in the gloom of a solitary cell in the heart of the dreary prison. A grated window gave a little light and a depressing view of the prisoners' exercise yard. Beyond the barest necessities, there was no form of furnishing: no writing table or materials, nothing in the way of concession to his rank. He felt benumbed. The delayed shock of the events of the morning caused him to tremble violently. He thought he would faint, and sat down upon the floor. A little rasping sound at the door brought him the realisation that he was under observation through a tiny grating.

A few hours earlier, he had been at the breakfast table with his beloved wife and children, in the warmth and comfort of their apartment. He had been on the point of setting forth, nervous but almost convinced by Lucie's reassurances that something advantageous awaited him. 'Hurry back with your news,' she had bade him. Bitter irony! Even now, she would be waiting impatiently, watching from the window, perhaps; and the aroma of the preparing luncheon would be everywhere in the rooms.

Dreyfus sprang to his feet and began crashing his head against a wall. He heard nothing of the cries in the passage outside, the running feet, the flinging open of the cell door. He was clutched, and dragged, and laid down, and calmed by a uniformed officer, whom he recognised as Major Forzinetti, the prison governor. But even this soft-voiced, worried man, could offer Dreyfus no form of contact with his wife. He had been under orders since Saturday—the morning on which the mystifying summons to the Chief of Staff's presence had reached Dreyfus—to be prepared to receive a prisoner who must be held under the strictest security, who must be allowed to communicate with no one, including his own warders, who in turn should be forbidden to speak to him. That prisoner was now come; and Forzinetti feared that he might not remain alive long enough to face whatever awaited him.

Whilst her husband underwent this solitary torment, Mme Dreyfus suffered an agony of her own.

She had, indeed, peeped many times round the edge of her curtains down into the avenue, hoping to see his briskly-striding form, hurrying eagerly to give her thrilling news of a promotion back to the staff in some appointment which all of military society would recognise as pointing directly towards senior rank. The odour of stewing beef with onions hung redolently upon the air, and a bottle of a superior red wine stood awaiting uncorking, in order to take the air while he told her his news and prepared himself for the meal.

Yet, it was not Lucie Dreyfus's Alfred who stood before her when she at length hurried to the door in response to a ring upon the bell, believing that in his excitement he must have mislaid his keys. She saw three grim-faced men, one of whom she recognised as Major the Marquis du Paty de Clam. He made a sharp bow.

'I regret, Madame, that there has been an unfortunate event, concerning your husband. My companions are Monsieur Gribelin, of the War Ministry, and Monsieur Cochefert, of the Sûreté. May we please enter?'

Lucie stood aside automatically, her hand to her mouth and her heart pounding, as she envisioned some accident. Du Paty turned to her.

'Madame Dreyfus, your husband has been arrested upon the gravest charges. He will remain in custody until further notice. Meanwhile, my colleagues and I are authorised to search these apartments from corner to corner.'

He motioned to the others, who sped away upon their task. Little Pierre, who had run out to greet his father, looked from the haughty stranger to his mother in bewilderment. She gathered him to her skirts, as baby Jeanne, through in the salon, began to cry as a stranger bustled in.

'Major, what is the meaning of this? My husband arrested?'

'As I said, Madame. We are here to impound his papers. Kindly direct me to any drawers which might be locked, and produce the keys.' He held up Alfred's own bunch. 'We have his own to assist us, but it would be a pity to cause damage to any locks which might not yield to these.'

He strode past her into the salon and glanced round. There was much furniture of the Empire period, of richly glowing veined wood with lighter inlay and gilt ornamentation. Almost every piece incorporated sets of drawers, and Cochefert had already dragged some of these out and was tugging impatiently at others. Du Paty tossed him the keys.

'For pity's sake, Major!' cried Lucie Dreyfus. 'What has happened? Arrested for what?'

Du Paty fingered his monocle and regarded her with hauteur.

'You do not know? Well, perhaps not. Perhaps not. It is often the way of such people. At any rate, I am at liberty to tell you nothing.'

'Nothing? Then, please tell me where he is? Where I may see him?'

'Regrettably, Madame, that will not be possible.'

'But ... how can this be? Arrested—for what? Detained— where? There must have been some terrible mistake.'

Du Paty nodded enigmatically towards the piles of papers now accumulating all over the floor, with other objects tossed indiscriminately around.

'Those will give us the truth, perhaps,' was all that he replied.

Lucie appealed to him, 'At least tell me where he is, so that I may telegraph his brother Mathieu to hurry and see him, and bring a lawyer.'

This time the response was sharp and full of dreadful import.

'One word from you, Madame—a single word to anyone—and your husband is certainly ruined.'

Half an hour later, as his two subordinates staggered out with the last of more than twenty piles of documents of every sort which they had managed to accumulate, Major du Paty de Clam turned finally to Lucie and warned her gravely, 'Your only means of saving your husband is by your silence.'

He gave a curt nod and went out, closing the door. Left in the apartment, always so tidy and correct, but now littered and unrecognisably disordered, Lucie Dreyfus and her child stared at one another, unable to comprehend the meaning of what had happened; and the cries of Baby Jeanne beyond conveyed instinctive awareness that the tranquillity of the prosperous Dreyfus household had been horrifyingly, perhaps irreparably, shattered.

FOUR

ONCE more, in our parlour at 221B Baker Street, Mathieu Dreyfus fell silent, save for the muffled betrayal of his emotions. I caught Sherlock Holmes's eye and glanced significantly towards the abandoned brandy glass. Holmes nodded and I got up to pour again for Dreyfus and myself, taking care, however, to dilute both mixtures generously. There was clearly much more narrative yet to come, and it would be imperative that he at least should retain a clear head for the facts.

Lord's cricket ground seemed far away now, as I sat contemplating the sobbing man and the grave, patient Holmes. Vividly, my mind showed me the despairing prisoner in that solitary cell, beating his head against its walls, crying out unavailingly for some explanation, pleading to be allowed to inform his anxious wife at least of his whereabouts. The very air of our cosy room on this mild day now seemed to have become chilled. I moved to make up the fire myself, placing the coals with conscious stealth, so as not to intrude upon Mathieu Dreyfus's communion with his grief.

I resumed my chair and looked again towards Holmes. If I had imagined that he might suddenly leap to his feet in the impulsive way I knew so well, declaring that there could not be a further moment to lose before setting forth to tackle this matter, it was not to be. He had scarcely stirred, so far as I had been aware, throughout our visitor's dramatic and moving recital. Now he did so only to rid his pipe again of its ashes and to refill it. He took a taper from the supply which Mrs Hudson had dutifully replenished before breakfast, lit it, and proceeded to pass the flame to and fro across his pipe bowl, tamping and igniting alternately with meticulous care, until the tobacco was burning evenly and steadily. Then he tossed the remnant of the taper into the flames and sat back again, puffing economically, his eyes fixed upon the piece of burning paper until it had been consumed.

Dreyfus was quiet again by now, leaning back in the basket chair, one hand holding the brandy glass, the other supporting his brow. Holmes seemed content to wait. At length, Dreyfus stirred, glanced at us in turn, and said once more, 'I beg your pardon. If I may continue?'

Holmes withdrew his pipe from his lips and asked, 'Before you do so, there are one or two particulars, if you please.'

'Of course, Mr Holmes. Anything.'

'You have given us a dramatic and disturbing sequence of events, yet at which you were not yourself present. Upon whose account do you base it?'

'Several persons'. My sister-in-law's. My brother's, insofar as he has been able to convey it in his restricted circumstances. His counsel's. The evidence at his court-martial ...'

Holmes nodded. 'Hearsay, to an extent, but generally corroborated. But how came it that you know of this Major Henry's duplicity? That he allowed your brother to believe he knew nothing of the matter, whereas he had been an unseen witness?'

'He testified it at the trial. He gave his version of what had happened in the office.'

'I see. Scarcely open behaviour, but a justifiable tactic, no doubt. Do any questions occur to you, Watson?'

'I had been wondering,' I answered, 'under what circumstances Captain Dreyfus was actually admitted to the military prison. Your account, Mr Dreyfus, gave the impression that he was expected there, unless I am mistaken.'

'You are *not* mistaken, Dr Watson,' our visitor said with emphasis. 'The thought occurred to me some time ago, and I discussed it with Maître Demange, my brother's counsel. He agreed that the rapidity and lack of formality with which Alfred was lodged indicated that the cell had been prepared for him in advance.'

I could not help feeling a little pride in my deduction. 'What do you make of that, Holmes?' I asked.

'A point, certainly. But remember, the interrogation had been planned. The fact that a cell had been prepared against the outcome does not necessarily say that the particular outcome was inevitable.'

I confess that I was disappointed that my first contribution to the matter had not gained more positive results. It was obvious from Mathieu Dreyfus's expression that he was beginning to wonder why Holmes should be so ready to counter each hopeful opening. I had to resist an urge to explain to him that this was in accordance with my friend's method in approaching any new problem: that it was an axiom of his that it was a mistake to begin theorising before all the evidence was to hand. But it was not my place to interfere with his handling of this enquiry, and I remained silent.

Holmes addressed himself to Dreyfus again. 'Pray then, continue your narrative.'

Dreyfus, for whom I was now feeling considerably more sympathy than at the outset, took one more sip from his glass, then placed it on the carpet near his feet. He roused himself, with something like a shake of his shoulders, and recommenced.

'I have recounted how the parting words of Major du Paty de Clam to my sister-in-law had been a warning that one word of the affair *to anyone* would be fatal to her husband. You can imagine the dilemma in which this left her. She had led a sheltered life, under the complete protection first of her family and then of my brother. She had no experience of the harshnesses and menaces of life. The morning's revelation, and the ransacking of her home, had shocked her profoundly. In short, she was left knowing not what to do. Her instinct, as she has since told me, was to fly at once to her parents for comfort and advice; yet she feared to do so, in case she was watched and might by her action give effect to du Paty's dire warning.

'Therefore, she determined to do nothing, comforting herself that it could not be long before some message would reach her from her husband, or that she would be summoned to visit him. Mr Holmes, the poor woman spent a full fortnight in this state of ignorance and suspense.'

'Great heavens!' I could not prevent myself ejaculating. Holmes shot me no glance of reproach, however. His eyes remained steadily on our visitor.

'Yes, Doctor. Two entire weeks without a word, without daring to act; and all that time, her poor little boy asking the whereabouts of his papa. Heaven knows how long this might have lasted, had there not appeared in certain newspapers rumours that an officer, who was at first unnamed, was confined in the *Cherche-Midi* upon a most serious charge. What information or speculation brought a journalist to my sister-in-law's door I do not know. He came to enquire whether the officer in question was, in fact, Alfred.

'Lucie was spared what must have been a painful interview by the firmness of her maid, who told the man that her mistress was out and that Captain Dreyfus was away from Paris. Even so, it was a matter of mere hours before my brother's name began to appear in connection with these reports. Lucie was understandably beside herself with worry. She could bear to keep silent no longer. After several unsuccessful attempts to gain an interview with Major du Paty, she succeeded, and was at last granted permission to get in touch with Alfred's family. This she did by sending a telegram to Mulhouse, where I myself chanced to be at the time. I left at once for Paris and was soon listening to the dreadful tale.

'I immediately set about attempting to see du Paty for myself. It took several days to accomplish, but at last he consented to see me. I found him as she had described: theatrical, pompous, and haughty almost to the point of contemptuousness. He told me at the outset of our interview that he was convinced of Alfred's guilt.'

Mathieu Dreyfus paused once more as Holmes asked, 'Did he appear regretful?' Dreyfus shook his head.

'Scarcely at all. He stated that he had spent much time considering the subject, and had no doubt whatever that the charge was justified.'

'Did he specify upon what precise evidence it was founded?'

'Only that a document had been intercepted, which experts had pronounced to be indubitably in my brother's hand, and which comprised secret information. I replied, "Major, if Alfred wrote it, he will confess as much to me. If I may see him, I will satisfy myself and you of the certainty or not of his guilt. And if he does confess, I undertake personally to place in his hand the weapon with which I shall persuade him to do away with himself." Major du Paty appeared aghast at this notion. He replied, "You do not appreciate what is at stake. One wrong word coming out, and it could be war in Europe." The interview ended, leaving me with no further information, and his absolute refusal to let me visit my brother.'

'But surely,' Holmes observed, 'many words had come out already. The newspapers were busy speculating. Our own newspapers here carried reports, as my colleague was reminding me before your arrival this morning. What, then, do you suppose to be that vital reference of which the major stood in such fear?'

Mathieu Dreyfus shrugged in the eloquent French fashion. 'I do not know. My distinct impression was that du Paty spoke more for effect than from genuine concern. It was his way of warning me not to stir up trouble.'

'Yet I repeat, Monsieur Dreyfus, trouble had already *been* stirred up. It is my experience that there is nothing to surpass the press for causing a ferment by printing rumours without the support of facts. By being so secretive, du Paty and the military authorities must surely have been aware that any disclosures they dreaded—if, indeed, there were any such—must almost certainly be hit upon accidentally by some inventive journalist. Do you not agree, Watson?'

'Most certainly, Holmes. And since you ask my opinion, might I put a question of my own to Monsieur Dreyfus?'

'By all means.'

'It is this. Has the French press not clamoured—as it most certainly would have done in this country—for some frank explanation of the circumstances of Captain Dreyfus's imprisonment, without any sort of hearing, on such vague grounds?'

The look which came into Mathieu Dreyfus's eye, upon my asking this, struck me as a curious one. There was a wariness about it; a shiftiness, almost. He hesitated for some seconds before answering: 'The French press has not been wholly sympathetic to my brother. His treachery seems to be taken for granted. We are of Alsatian origin, therefore our complete loyalty to France is questioned. There have been allegations—totally unfounded—of mistresses, gambling debts ...'

'*Totally* unfounded?'

Holmes's question came like a whip-crack, but Mathieu Dreyfus answered with complete composure: 'On my word, Mr Holmes. There was a time, before his marriage, when I confess I made some deliberate attempts to interest my brother in the pleasures of the flesh and of the tables. I hasten to say that I am not addicted that way myself. It is merely that I sensed he would never achieve popularity amongst his fellow officers if he were to be marked down as the perpetual student, aloof from manly pursuits. My efforts failed utterly. Alfred proved altogether too fastidious. There was for a time a slight attachment, made on his own account, but quite platonic, I believe. Otherwise, nothing. I would swear to it.'

'And the attitude of the press has been mostly unfavourable?'

'Well ... I have to say, yes.'

'Overwhelmingly, in fact?'

Mathieu Dreyfus looked startled by this direct challenge. He remained silent for some moments, then, without speaking, answered with a single nod. Holmes made no comment, however, and, with a wave of his pipe-stem, signified to the other that he expected his story to continue. Again, there came the Gallic shrug, and a slight spread of the hands.

'What more is there for me to say of this nightmare affair? My brother was at length brought to trial, pronounced guilty, and ...'

But Holmes had halted him with a more emphatic gesture.

'You are too concise for us now, Monsieur Dreyfus. So far, your account has been admirably detailed, leaving out, if I am not mistaken, no vital detail. Pray, let us have the rest in similar vein.'

Our visitor nodded, cast his eyes to our ceiling for some minutes whilst evidently mustering his facts into precise order, then proceeded to offer us the final particulars of his story. If the reader will forgive me, I will once more resort to an objective narrative, pieced together by myself from what he was able to recount to us from his own experience, and what subsequently came to my knowledge.

The weeks in his bare prison cell had been as agonising for Alfred Dreyfus as they had for his wife, in the luxurious surroundings of their apartment. Sleep had proved almost impossible, both from the pounding of his mind and heart, and the constant din in the stone passageway outside: clattering boots, shouted commands, jests, laughter, and the repeated scraping of the little grill in his doorway, signifying that he was being scrutinised under the light which he strove to obliterate by dragging the single rough blanket over his face.

He was interrogated repeatedly by Major du Paty de Clam, with Félix Gribelin as note-taker and witness. The more questions du Paty asked, the less information he would offer in exchange, so that the time came when Dreyfus found it hard to remember which part of his answers was given from his own true memory, and which from his stammering efforts to correct assertions and insinuations put to him. He continued to be allowed neither paper, pen nor pencil, with which he might have managed to muster his case into some logically explicable sequence. He could only rely upon his mind, which was a turmoil of impressions, fears, thoughts, doubts, anxieties, interweaving, overlaying and distorting one another, until he began almost to doubt his sanity.

He had only one sympathiser close to him during this time. His guards were strictly forbidden to converse with him. However, the governor of the prison, Major Ferdinand Forzinetti, was one of those whose eyes had been applied frequently to the grill in the doorway, and he had been worried by what he had observed. The incarceration of Dreyfus in his prison had indeed been arranged high-handedly and carried through with suspicious speed. The restrictions upon the prisoner were unusually stringent, including silence, prohibition of all communication, and a diet normally reserved for felons already convicted of serious crimes. Forzinetti had watched the agitated pacing, the weeping, the wringing of hands, Dreyfus's pounding of his head against the wall: his overall mien of despair. He had said to himself, 'This is scarcely the behaviour of a guilty man.' When Major du Paty de Clam asked if his considerable experience of prisoners did not suggest to him that Dreyfus was showing all the signs of guilt, Major Forzinetti replied frankly that this was not the case. He noted du Paty's frown of disappointment on hearing this.

From sheer pity for his prisoner, and fear for his sanity, Major Forzinetti spoke words of encouragement to Dreyfus and conveyed word of him to his family. He would pass no messages in return; but it was enough for Dreyfus's peace of mind to know that Lucie was at least aware of his circumstances, and that he felt certain of speedy release. This was scarcely true, but it helped them both to endure the period of waiting.

Also during this time, the services of Maître Edgar Demange were engaged. This corpulent figure of a lawyer was the very archetype of success in the profession. In his mid-fifties, triple-chinned and complexioned as though he had been nourished from birth on port wine, he was noted for his independence and honour and a success based upon patient application, rather than court-room histrionics. At the very outset, he cautioned Mathieu Dreyfus, as Sherlock Holmes did later, that he would accept the case only if his study of the evidence convinced him that it was a valid one. When he had completed this scrutiny, he had no further hesitation. He agreed to act for Alfred Dreyfus.

Meanwhile, Dreyfus had been undergoing further interrogations, this time at the hands of a Major Bexon d'Ormescheville. He showed Dreyfus a copy of the list of secret information which he was supposed to have offered to pass—the *bordereau*, as it was termed—which had led to his arrest. He almost laughed with relief after the merest perusal.

'But this is not my handwriting, Major!'

'You say not, Captain?'

'Definitely.'

'What if I tell you that experts have made comparisons and pronounced otherwise?'

'Then I say that those experts are grossly mistaken.'

'Come, come, now, Captain. They are the leading members of their profession in the land.'

'I do not care if they are the first in the world. That is *not* my hand.'

'Well, it's your word against theirs, then.'

'I ... admit that there are a few similarities ...'

'Ah! We are getting closer, then?'

'A few similarities only. They are definitely outnumbered by the differences.'

'A man writing a clandestine note which he would not wish to have traced to him would scarcely employ his usual handwriting. He would attempt to distort it. But unless he were expert enough, his lack of skill would show through from time to time.'

'Major, I understood that your task was to take down a plain statement, not to put hypotheses. My statement is that I have no knowledge of this document, and that I was most certainly neither its author, nor its scribe.'

'Very well, then. I shall put that that is what you contend.'

'You might add that no officer of the artillery would have used such inexpert terms in referring to the new 120-millimetre gun, about which the writer of this nonsense proposes to offer information. Whoever composed this was no artilleryman.'

'Unless he were, and wished to conceal it. This, Captain, is merely a summary of items he says he was enclosing: a *bordereau*. I will go so far as to tell you that we have not managed to retrieve those items, merely this one document. It is safe to assume that the items themselves would have been in some detail and accurately expressed. This list is merely a scribbled accompaniment, possibly done at the last moment before handing them over, and under the stress of fear of detection. Absolute exactitude in it would be unnecessary.'

Dreyfus tried again. 'This reference to a copy of the "Firing Manual of the Field Artillery", which the writer says he encloses, but must have back within a matter of days, before it is officially missed: this is nonsense. For one thing, its title is "Firing Manual of Artillery in the Field" ...'

'A mere detail.'

'If you insist. But I can tell you where you may go and buy that manual openly, for a few sous. There's nothing secret about it.'

D'Ormescheville almost sneered at that. 'Captain, I am not wholly an innocent, when it comes to the dirty ways of spies. I know that they are in the habit of passing anything at all which will earn them an extra franc or two, if the recipient believes it to be worth it. They wish to appear to be giving their masters their money's worth.'

'Very well,' Dreyfus sighed. 'One last point, if you will be good enough to note it. The writer concludes, "I am just off on manoeuvres."'

'What of that?'

'Simply that the general staff summer manoeuvres last year were cancelled before the date on which I am supposed by you to have written this. Would I have been likely to append so useless a remark?'

Major d'Ormescheville began to assemble his papers for departure.

'You yourself said it is not my business to deal in hypotheses, Captain Dreyfus. Therefore, do not urge any upon me. They will be the concern of others, at another time.'

When Maître Demange was at last allowed an interview with his client, he snorted at the evidence.

'So much rubbish! No court in the world would convict on this stuff.'

'But if that is obvious to you, Maître, surely the authorities can see it also? Why have they decided to try me at all?'

'Because to release you without putting on some sort of show would be to admit that they had blundered all along. The press would turn round and rend them. No, no, they cannot risk losing face like that. They must have a trial, and the judges will find in your favour. Then, mark my words, the president of the court will state that the authorities were quite justified in acting upon their suspicions, and will congratulate them on their alertness towards any presumed danger to the security of our glorious republic. You'll probably get the Legion of Honour for your pains!'

He clapped Dreyfus on the shoulder and departed, still chuckling. The prisoner sat for some minutes, wondering whether he dared tempt Fate. He decided to do so. He took up the writing materials which had recently been allowed to him and wrote to Lucie:

'At last I have reached the end of my suffering, my martyrdom. Tomorrow I shall appear before my judges, my head held high, my soul at peace.

The experience I have just gone through, terrible though it has been, has purified my soul. I shall return to you better then I was before. I want to dedicate all my remaining life to you, to my children, to our dear relatives.

I have gone through terrible crises. I have had moments of real, wild madness at the thought of being accused of such a monstrous crime.

I am ready to appear before soldiers as a soldier who has nothing with which to reproach himself. They will see my face, they will read my soul, they will become convinced of my innocence, as are all who know me.

Devoted to my country, to which I have consecrated all my strength, all my intellect, I have nothing to fear. Sleep peacefully, then, my darling, and fear not. Think only of the joy which will be ours

when we find ourselves soon in each other's arms.
Awaiting that happy moment, a thousand kisses.
ALFRED'

'The accused is guilty.'
'*Vive la patrie!*'
It was the custom for the accused not to be present in court when the verdict was announced. It was brought to him by an openly-weeping Demange, in the room where he waited, under guard, full of confidence that he would shortly walk from it a free man. At first sight of his distracted counsel, Dreyfus knew the worst. Had he been standing, he would have collapsed.

As Demange had predicted, the court-martial had been a mockery; only not in the sense he had meant. It had seemed to begin badly by being ordered to be held *in camera*, but that disadvantage had soon been nullified by the poor performance of the prosecution's witnesses. Demange told Dreyfus during the first interval that it was bearing out what he had prophesied. The authorities knew they had no case, but had no intention of letting any press or public be present to watch their pitiful retreat.

Dreyfus's confidence grew steadily. He listened to Major du Paty de Clam bumbling helplessly over his evidence about the events immediately preceding the arrest, when he had tricked Dreyfus into giving the specimen of his handwriting. The accused had trembled as he wrote, du Paty claimed. It had been a sure sign to him of Dreyfus's fear of being exposed. The handwriting was examined by the court. At which point had the trembling occurred?, du Paty was asked; there was no sign of it in the writing. Well, he had not *exactly* trembled; but this in itself was suspicious. He *ought* to have trembled, but had not done, because he had suspected what was happening, and had got his emotions under control in readiness.

The handwriting experts were called, and proved not to be unanimous in the opinion that the *bordereau* was in Dreyfus's hand. A blackboard was produced and one of them lectured the court for a bemusing hour of technical terms and complex diagrams, at the end of which he declared that Dreyfus had used a mixture of his own writing, crudely disguised, with clumsy forgeries of his wife's and brother Mathieu's.

Major Henry produced an astonishing display. He deposed that Counterintelligence had been warned that there was a traitor on the staff: 'And there he sits!' he roared, pointing dramatically at Dreyfus. Both Dreyfus and Demange leaped up to protest against this irregular act. Demange demanded the name of Henry's informant, so that he could be called to testify and give his grounds for naming Dreyfus. Henry tapped the side of his nose in a gesture of unmistakable meaning. He replied, 'There are some secrets an officer doesn't even confide to his cap.' The president of the court pressed him to say, on his honour, though without revealing his informant's identity, that Dreyfus had been the officer named as the traitor. Henry raised a hand and declared loudly, 'I swear it!'

Giving his own evidence, Dreyfus relied upon a muted recital of facts, answering every question briefly in his flat, monotonous voice. An impassioned display of outraged honour was what his judges, who were not lawyers but army officers, would have expected from one of their own kind. Even Demange, who addressed the court for three hours, carefully drawing attention to the thinness of the evidence, the conflicting statements of witnesses, and the lack of any suggestion of motive for the crime, was unimpressive. A declamatory tone and gestures of mockery were expected, not painstaking legal stuff.

Alfred Dreyfus was wearing his uniform again on this crisply cold morning of January 5th 1895. But he did not wear it as a reinstated officer of the French army. His appeal against his sentence had been rejected without a hearing, to the almost unanimous approval of the press, in which scarcely a voice had been raised in protest against his having been branded the most odious of traitors. The calls for his execution had been loud. The War Minister, General Mercier, who had had overall responsibility for the arrest and prosecution, had gone so far as to table a bill for the restoration of the death penalty. He had not succeeded, but had taken his revenge by giving secret orders that Dreyfus was not to be sent into the usual form of exile. The leper colony on Devil's Island, off the coast of French Guiana, had recently been evacuated. Arrangements were afoot for the tiny island to become a place of imprisonment for political offenders. General Mercier gave orders for the small amount of building work to be accelerated, and so modified as to accommodate only one prisoner—Alfred Dreyfus.

Dreyfus knew nothing of this as nine o'clock approached on this bitter morning. More than the cold chilled him. A fearful ordeal lay immediately ahead.

His uniform was no longer its trimly-tailored self. Every attachment to it had been loosened by having its threads unpicked: buttons, braid, badges of rank, even the crimson staff stripes down the trouser legs. The sword which he was to handle for the last time had been weakened by an armourer across the middle of its blade.

In the courtyard of the War College, five thousand soldiers and ex-Servicemen were lined up to form a great square, of which diplomats and more than three hundred journalists from several countries made part. Beyond, outside the walls in the Place Fontenoy, a less orderly crowd jostled and chattered in greater numbers. Composed of civilians of all ranks of society, it had been gathering since several hours before, eager to hear, if not to see, the degradation of the traitor.

Precisely at nine there sounded a roll of drums. The crowd outside fell silent. Those within the courtyard saw the prisoner march stiffly out from the room where he had been waiting. He carried his sword erect before his face, in the present-arms position. Four artillerymen escorted him, under the command of a lieutenant of the Republican Guard.

The party marched to the centre of the square, where the commanding officer of the Guard, General Darras, sat astride his horse. The crowd beyond heard the clatter of boots in unison as the party halted, and then thrilled to the general's shouted words: 'Alfred Dreyfus, you are unworthy to bear arms. In the name of the people of France, we degrade you!'

Muffled drums began a terrible, prolonged rolling. There stepped briskly towards Dreyfus a gigantic sergeant of the Guard. Unemotionally, but with fierce strength, he seized hold in turn of buttons, braid, badges, and ripped them off the uniform, so that they scattered about the ground or were left hanging loose. Then he took the sword, raised one leg, and snapped the blade across his great thigh as easily as breaking a twig.

His task completed, the sergeant retreated several smart paces. An order rang out from the escort lieutenant, and the little party commenced its quick march round the entire assembly, so that the traitor should feel every man's contemptuous stare at his degraded form.

Dreyfus had borne his ordeal impassively and in silence so far. But as he marched he began shouting at the top of his reedy voice: 'Soldiers! An innocent man has been degraded! I am innocent! I swear it! *Vive la France! Vive l'armée!*'

The shouts carried clearly to the crowd. A roar of derision arose from men, women and children. People who had never seen Dreyfus and had heard only the most superficial particulars of his case now began howling for his death. The same sentiments were yelled at him by the ex-Servicemen and many of the journalists as he marched past them. There was a moment when it seemed that some might break ranks and attack him. But he shouted all the louder, continuing doing so until at last the awful circuit was completed and he disappeared into the haven of the waiting-room, to be immediately handcuffed and bustled off by prison van to the civilian Santé prison.

The route took him past his home in the Avenue de Trocadéro. He glimpsed his windows through the ventilator grating. At last, the courage which had sustained him that morning deserted him. He wept in anguish for the rest of the way to the prison.

FIVE

ALTHOUGH Mathieu Dreyfus's emotions had not overwhelmed him again during his telling of this grim tale, the effort it was costing him to hold them in check was apparent from the sudden cessation of his narrative flow. For my own part, I felt deeply moved, but wished to make no utterance which might detract from Sherlock Holmes's concentration. He still sat motionless, his long legs thrust out before him, ankles crossed. One hand lay deep in a pocket of his trousers. The fingers of the other supported loosely the bowl of the pipe which, although its stem remained between his lips, gave forth no smoke.

The purposeful bustle of traffic in the street below, and some tradesman's cheerful cry, spoke eloquently of freedom and of the uncomplicated continuance of life's everyday routine. It struck me as a marked contrast with the plight of that man who had been plucked at an instant from all that had been normal and agreeable to him and his family, to be dragged uncomprehendingly into a nightmare.

Our visitor's voice, now strained and subdued, at length broke into my thoughts.

'Of the rest, you are aware from the contents of my note. My brother was conveyed to Devil's Island without notice, without a word of warning to him or to his wife as to his departure or destination. On his way to the port of embarkation, La Rochelle, he was exposed to the stares and insults of all manner of idlers and ruffians; and yet he had not been permitted one single embrace with the wife from whom he was being torn. They had been allowed to meet two or three times briefly, but only in the presence of others and not granted so much as a touch of the fingers. In fact, poor Lucie begged to have her hands bound behind her, if only she might receive one embrace from Alfred; but it was refused.

'He suffered greatly on the voyage, confined like a common felon in a condemned prisoner's cell, without food at first and in the bitterest cold. Now he sweats, day and night, in tropical heat in one small room, watched constantly by armed guards who are forbidden to exchange a word with him. He is given one sheet of paper each day, but allowed to write only to his wife, and in the knowledge that every word will be scrutinised before the letter is allowed to pass. The letters are painfully delayed, as are hers to him, so that there is constant fear on the part of each that silence betokens catastrophe. When his letters do arrive, in batches, sometimes weeks overdue, they are pitiful— quite pitiful. He has shown much courage since this dreadful experience began, but there must surely arrive a time when physical decline and mental torment will overcome even the stoutest resolution.

'I and my family have tried everything open to us in our own country. We have appealed to the War Ministry, to the Premier, to the President of France himself, but always in vain. All respond that the sentence of the court was just, and must stand. The press are adamant, too. Public opinion remains for the most part hostile. Lucie and I have received many anonymous notes of abuse, and she and her children, who, poor mites, know nothing of what has happened, have been humiliated in public.

'Mr Holmes, at the risk of being observed, I have come here to plead with you to interest yourself in the case. It is your reputation that you have often succeeded where all others have failed, and that your concern for the victims of injustice and inhumanity is unreserved. I have said that it was an impulsive decision of mine to hasten here. Please, please assure me that it was the correct one.'

He had leaned forward as he spoke these last words and was looking intently at Holmes, as if willing him to accede. Yet Holmes still did not stir, except to draw the unlit pipe from his mouth and glance into its bowl. Silence resumed and hung for what seemed long minutes, until at last he spoke.

'Monsieur Dreyfus, what is your own solution to this case?'

Our visitor stared. 'I do not quite follow.'

'Surely you have formed some explanation? If your brother is innocent, as you so passionately claim, why is he being persecuted in this way?'

I believed I saw Dreyfus's gaze flicker slightly and that he hesitated momentarily before replying to this. If I had not been mistaken, I knew that Holmes must have noticed it, too.

'Some . . . fearful blunder,' replied Dreyfus. 'An error of identity, perhaps?'

'Then you feel certain that the incriminating document is genuine? That secret information had been passed?'

'I have no proof to the contrary.'

'Yet you insist that the handwriting is not your brother's, despite the testimony of several experts. Do you say they are mistaken, or that they have been misled by someone's deliberate forgery of his hand?'

Dreyfus replied, with a little heat this time, 'I told you, in my account of the trial, that the experts were not unanimous. A majority pronounced against my brother, it is true; but Demange believes that at least one of them did so reluctantly, under Bertillon's persuasion.'

Holmes's eyes flashed as he asked keenly, 'Bertillon?'

'Alphonse Bertillon. He is a well known specialist in the police.'

'Well known, indeed,' Holmes agreed, almost addressing his own thoughts. 'Then, he was prominent amongst this team?'

'Its principal, you might say. It was he who lectured the court at such length about the science of the subject.'

'Hmph! At any rate, he appears to have done so convincingly. Have you brought with you a copy of the document to show me?'

'I regret I was unable to. I do not possess one, and Maître Demange, so far as I know, was lent his only, and had to return it after the trial.'

'That is a pity. I have some small reputation as a judge of handwriting myself and should have liked to form my own opinion. But no matter. Let us return to the consideration of alternatives. Your brother appears to have been convicted solely upon the evidence of this one document and upon the statements of those who examined him in its connection. Was there nothing more?'

Again Dreyfus paused minutely before replying, 'There was a good deal of innuendo as to his supposed immoralities, which Demange refuted.'

'Then, if that is all, we must focus our attention upon the document. The question the judges must have asked amongst themselves was, is this the work of the accused, or is it a forgery, designed to discredit him? If the latter, how did its author manage to insinuate it into some channel in which he could be certain it would be intercepted? And how could he ensure that it would certainly incriminate your brother and no one else? Was it likely that the authorities could not fail to recognise his handwriting? How many of them were even familiar with it? No, no, Mr Dreyfus. I fancy that your forger would have made much more certain—by a signature, or an initial, even—that his work would be attributed without question to your brother.'

Mathieu Dreyfus's pale cheeks had coloured during this. He burst out, 'You are saying that you, too, believe in my brother's guilt!'

'I am endeavouring to put myself in the judges' place. I fancy they must have considered the complications attendant upon a forgery, and decided it too unlikely.'

'But it *was not* my brother's hand!'

'I must remind you that even he admitted to Major du Paty that there were some resemblances. Then there was the evidence of the experts; in addition to which, the judges used magnifying glasses to make their own examination.'

Dreyfus wrung his hands. 'I can see that you do not believe our side of it!' he accused Holmes. He turned suddenly to me, his eyes now wild. 'Dr Watson—for the love of God, do not say that you, too, are in doubt!'

I could only clear my throat and shift uncomfortably under that disturbing stare. From initial hostility my feelings had grown steadily more sympathetic as the wretched tale unfolded; yet there was no refuting Holmes's cold logic.

'If a mistake has been made,' I faltered, 'I am sure that time will see it rectified.'

'Pah! You make your feelings plain, thank you.'

The contempt with which the Frenchman spoke impelled me to answer warmly, 'That is unworthy of you, sir. I have listened with the deepest sympathy. But I am in no position to judge the case upon the facts, and, as a former military man myself, I do not care to question the genuineness of a conclusion arrived at by a panel of officers. That their conclusion may have been wrong is perhaps a possibility. But nothing would convince me that they reached their verdict through conspiracy or from some prejudice common to them all against your brother.'

With an oath, Dreyfus leaped to his feet. His body trembled violently as he threshed his upraised fists in the air, and cried out: 'Can you not? Are you really so ignorant of life outside these cosy surroundings of yours that you do not know what is afoot in the world today? Have you the slightest knowledge of what it is like to be a Jew who dares to trespass upon non-Jewish preserves?'

I confess I was taken aback. The word Jew, the term Jewish, had never been uttered in all that we had heard. I found myself incapable of comprehending its relevance to this matter. Holmes's calm voice relieved me from having to respond to this startling challenge.

'At last we come near to the whole story,' said he, addressing Dreyfus, who swung angrily upon him. 'Pray, sit down and tell us, without passion, that part of your narrative which I believed you were never going to add.'

Dreyfus stood in his aggressive attitude for some moments longer before obeying slowly. He was staring at Holmes. 'You ... knew?' he said. 'Ah, of course! The newspapers.'

Holmes shook his head. 'Our British press, I am happy to say, does not brand the objects of its attention with emotive epithets.'

'Then how ...?'

'Simple deduction. Your family comes from Alsace, where it is prominent in the textile industry. By far the greater proportion of French Jews live in Alsace. That particular industry is especially associated with some of its more prosperous families. Your family possesses markedly Jewish characteristics: a closeness in affection and duty towards one another; a unity in identifying itself with its source of prosperity. Many owners of business interests in Alsace, I fancy, must have sold up completely when determining to retain French citizenship and leave the region. Not so yours, however. An ingenious and tenacious compromise was reached, by which you retained both your French nationality and your mills; that struck me, if I may say so, as being a typically Jewish manoeuvre.'

I glanced at Mathieu Dreyfus, half-expecting him to take further umbrage at this suggestion, but was relieved to see him return

Holmes's little smile and relax from the stiffened posture in which he had resumed his seat.

'I will grant you that, Mr Holmes. But where does your belief in the strength of our unity stand in the light of Alfred's refusal to follow the family trade, insisting instead upon so unlikely a career as the army?'

'That puzzled me, I confess. Yet, when I heard of his dedication to his chosen calling, the intensity of his application and ambition, to the exclusion of more worldly pursuits, I seemed to recognise the Jew again. The fact of his resentment by his brother officers strengthened my conviction. I only wavered seriously when I learned that he had attained the general staff. Now that, of all things, I should have believed impossible to any Jew.'

Dreyfus struck his thigh hard with a blow of his right fist that was almost triumphant.

'He was the only Jew ever to have served on the general staff of the French army.'

Holmes threw up his hands in a rare little gesture, as would say, 'I knew it!' What he did say, however, was, 'To round off my deductions, I will only add that I observed some slight Jewish characteristics in your features, about the lips and nostrils, though only in profile. I recalled that you had said how closely you and your brother resembled one another. Also, you are of a large family. I remembered being told during my last visit to France how strikingly the rate of birth of Jews there had increased in recent decades, in inverse ratio to that of gentile families. The remark, by the way, was made to me with considerable bitterness, and the generally prosperous and confident lot of the Jews compared with the depressed state of the rest of the French.'

'I admire your deduction and memory, Mr Holmes,' said Dreyfus, in a sad tone. 'You must be aware, then, of the wave of anti-Semitism which has been sweeping over our country, and grows ever stronger by the year.'

'Very well aware. It struck me that it might have important bearing upon your brother's case, yet you had chosen not even to mention it. Why?'

'Because I came here fearing that you, too, would close your mind against me if I did.'

Holmes waved a hand languidly in my direction. 'My good friend will assure you that the status of a client is nothing to me. As to religious faith, I think I may claim to be quite unbigoted, eh, Watson?'

'Oh, quite, quite,' I readily agreed. 'But, Monsieur Dreyfus, is the degree of anti-Semitism in your country such that it can inhibit you so?'

'I regret it is, Doctor. It has ancient origins, but there has been a strong resurgence recently.'

'How should that be, when France owes so much to her great Jewish families?'

'Perhaps you do not know the French people as well as your friend does, Doctor? They do not thank the Rothschilds and the Hirschs for what they have done. They resent them for it, and envy their wealth and energy. Their influence is feared, and nowhere is that fear stronger than in the army.'

'Why should that be?'

'Because the army is the very guarantee of my country's stability. Our society is in a state of ferment. Institutions crumble, governments come and go, nothing is constant—except the army. If it should be undermined, people believe, then the very foundations of France will collapse. Our anti-Jewish press, which possesses a shrill voice to which growing numbers listen eagerly, has seized on this. It alleges the existence of a wealthy international organisation—the Jewish Syndicate, it is termed—dedicated to the infiltration of the general staff as a preliminary to gaining control, not merely of the army, but of France itself.'

'Has your brother ever been the specific target of this propaganda?' Holmes interrupted.

'Until this affair began, no,' Dreyfus replied. 'Ever since his identity emerged, though, it has been "the Jew Dreyfus", "the traitor Jew", and so forth. Much of the abuse to which he was subjected at his degradation embodied such terms.'

'Tell me, Monsieur Dreyfus, are your family noteworthy amongst the Jewish community?'

'Quite the opposite. We observe privately the more important festivals. We children have all undergone the rituals associated with the faith. Otherwise, we do not practise the religion. I am afraid we are more French than Jewish, if that is not a *non sequitur*.'

'So there is nothing about your brother which would mark him out as an object of suspicion amongst his fellow officers?'

'Nothing at all. I am positive of it.'

Holmes sighed deeply. 'Then I am afraid there is little I can do.'

Dreyfus stiffened in his chair once more. 'How do you mean?' he demanded, a new edge to his tone.

'Simply that you have talked out your own case,' Holmes answered. 'When I began to suspect that you were withholding an important element from your account, I believed that there might yet prove to be some positive explanation for what seemed to be a somewhat bizarre prosecution upon thin grounds.'

'And I have now given you one!'

'Alas, no. You have stated that your brother, like the rest of your family, is the most un-Jewish sort of Jew. You say for certain that there can be nothing about his religion which could possibly incur against him such fear and loathing that men would plot against him, perjure themselves in giving evidence, and so unanimously misjudge his case as to send him into dire imprisonment.'

Dreyfus was on his feet again, spluttering and gesticulating.

'You have tricked me!' he accused. 'Like an artful prosecutor you have led me into admissions which are contrary to all the facts . . .'

Holmes, who seldom raised his voice in argument, did so now.

'Facts are what you do not offer me, monsieur. Suppositions, suspicions, theories . . . I cannot work without facts, any more than a man can build a house without bricks.'

I felt sorry again for the hapless Dreyfus as he replied, with a renewal of the desperate tone, 'I have given you what facts I can—all that I possess.'

Holmes, too, had risen to his feet. I followed suit. He said, more quietly, and with a more compassionate look to his features, 'Unfortunately, their trend is against your brother, rather than for him. My work is to discover facts, but I cannot change them. I cannot alter the fact, as the judges accepted it to be, that this *bordereau* is a treasonable document, or that the hand which wrote it was your brother's. I can question it, throw doubts upon it, but I possess nothing which will cancel it out. The gravamen of the case against your brother is circumstantial to a considerable degree, but it has more substance than his defence.'

'You ... you believe him guilty, then?'

'I have not said that.'

'Then ...'

'I repeat that it is a mistake to form theories without all the facts. The jury at the court-martial had the opportunity to hear and examine all the evidence. I share your respect for the integrity of the French army. Therefore I must decline to question its conduct on this occasion.'

Dreyfus seemed struck dumb. He turned to me again, but only his eyes spoke. I had no comfort to give him.

Holmes added, 'Should anything new emerge at any stage which you should wish to bring to my attention, I will consider it gladly. Meanwhile, I cannot interfere in a matter concerning a foreign country and its processes of law with so little excuse for doing so.'

With a swift movement, Dreyfus picked up his hat and straightened again.

'I thank you at least for hearing me, Mr Holmes,' he said stiffly. 'It was a hopeless quest from the start, I suppose. It seemed worth any effort, but I was mistaken. I am sorry to have wasted your time, gentlemen.'

With a quick bow in the direction of each of us he strode to the door, grasped the knob, and let himself out without a backward glance, closing the door behind him firmly but without violently emphasising his displeasure.

'Poor fellow!' I declared, sinking again into my chair. 'I mean his brother, of course. I should not care to undergo such an ordeal.'

Holmes regarded me quizzically.

'Not even if you were guilty? Surely, my dear Watson, it is not in your nature to cast the dice and then not to accept the result of the throw?'

'But *was* he guilty, Holmes? It seems a dubious case, to say the least.'

'There are unsatisfactory features, certainly. For example, that fellow Bertillon being permitted to harangue the court for an hour on the science of handwriting.'

'Ah, yes. You pricked up your ears at that. I seem to recall his name ...'

'He is chief of the Indentification Department of the Paris prefectural police. He is also a crank.'

'How so?'

'His special subject is anthropometry, which I need not remind you is the somewhat inexact science of determining characteristics in persons by taking measurements of their heads and features and other portions of their anatomy. There is something in it, but Bertillon goes altogether too far. He claims to be able to pin-point types of criminal tendency by such means. It is as well that he is not at liberty to rush about the streets with his tape-measure and camera, making arrests on the strength of his findings. From what I have observed of so-called "typical criminals", the jails would be overflowing with honest citizens, and the pulpits with burglars and pickpockets.'

'Then how does he hold his office?' I asked, laughing.

'He can talk at such length, and with such abstruse reasoning, that his audiences are virtually mesmerised into accepting what he says. I have heard him. He could make a fortune as a confidence man. It is all such gibberish that it sounds plausible and no one can pin him down on a single point without sending him off on a tangent of thousands of words. I dare say they have ceased trying, and just leave him alone.'

'And this is why you question his part in Dreyfus's trial?'

'No, no. It is the role he took—as chief handwriting expert. Believe me, Watson, he knows less about graphology than you do, which I believe your innate modesty will compel you to admit is not much.'

'Almost nothing, except a few little pointers picked up from you, Holmes. Then, how did he come to be involved, and why did the other experts let him speak for them?'

'Who knows? Perhaps he browbeat his fellows, and the judges merely heard him out, secretly tapping their temples. It may not have contributed much to their thinking, and therefore perhaps can be dismissed as of no importance. Nevertheless, it is a disturbing element. It leads me to wonder whether anything else about the trial was inconsistent with strict justice? If there were, I should certainly begin to entertain doubts.'

'Some of the witnesses seemed to have changed their tune to suit the drift of the questioning.'

'Commonplace enough. Few people have precise memories. A good lawyer, like a good musician, knows how to obtain the effects he desires.'

'Then there was the decision to hold the hearing in closed session. Does the reason for that ring true to you?'

'That there were secret matters to be raised? Possibly. What intrigues me more is the question of how this treacherous document came into the possession of the French at all?'

I reminded him, 'You yourself thought it unlikely that a forger could have engineered that.'

'That is why I seek any other explanation. Could it, for instance, have been a forgery originated inside the foreign embassy with the express purpose of compromising Dreyfus?'

'Why on earth should they wish to do that, Holmes?'

'Perhaps he had been in their service, but had refused to co-operate further, and this was their way of paying him out.'

'But your own argument again—there was nothing in the document specifically identifying him, except the handwriting.'

I felt another idea strike. It seemed so simple, yet persuasive, that I hesitated before giving it utterance. At length I ventured, 'Holmes ...'

'Mm?'

'Suppose ... suppose there were a real traitor ... that the document were part of a genuine act of treachery. Say it was picked up by an agent and brought back to the French authorities, who, in casting about for the identity of their suspect ... hit upon Alfred Dreyfus?'

Holmes did not answer. He sat in deep thought. I could almost hear the mechanism of his mind whirring in full gear.

At length he answered, 'As to the manner in which Dreyfus could have become involved, I am not at all sure. But your theory is an excellent one, nevertheless. It postulates the existence of a traitor, a man, or woman, even, who is at large and perhaps active still, while a scapegoat ekes out his miserable existence instead. In short, if the real traitor is found, Dreyfus must be freed.'

I thrilled in anticipation of what I had precipitated.

'You will take the case, then?' I asked.

To my intense disappointment, Holmes shook his head.

'I cannot. You have heard my reasons. They have not changed. All the same,' he added, gathering up his pipe, I shall certainly give it some thought. I fancy it is going to be a three-pipe problem at least. Off with you to your cricket, my boy, and leave me to ponder.'

'It is almost time for our luncheon,' I reminded him, after consulting my watch. 'Mrs Hudson will be here to lay up the table at any minute.'

'I wish no luncheon, Watson. Pray make my excuses. I will take my pipe into my bedroom, so as to be undisturbed.'

'Really, Holmes . . .!' I began to expostulate, but he waved me to silence and left the room. I wandered to the window to gauge the weather again. The sky was still cloudless, but the smoke haze had discoloured it and given it a cheerless aspect. The temperature seemed to have fallen several degrees. I returned to the hearth, thankful for Mrs Hudson's fire, which I proceeded to mend and prod into new life, while she came in and bustled about me. I decided I had lost my enthusiasm for going to Lord's, Stoddart notwithstanding.

SIX

I should be a proud man, were I able to claim that it was as a result of an inspirational surge in my mind that the notorious Dreyfus Affair was settled. Alas, I can do no such thing. Several more years were to pass—years in which reputations would fall, lives would be sacrificed, dramatic risks would be taken—before anything resembling a solution would be reached. Even then, mystery within mystery would remain, as, to some extent, it does still.

The outcome of Sherlock Holmes's tobacco-induced reverie throughout that May afternoon was disappointing to me. When he at length emerged from his room, his clothing reeking of the fumes, and ash smudged upon his lapels and waistcoat, I looked up from the racing pages of the latest edition of an evening newspaper, hopeful that he would utter some words which would galvanise us both into urgent action. All he said, however, was, 'I fancy I could eat a beef sandwich with my tea'; whereupon he proceeded to punish the bell until Mrs Hudson appeared to receive his order.

When we were alone once more, with our cups and plates before us, he remained distant and abstracted, volunteering nothing. At last, I ventured to question him as to the outcome of his meditations. He stared back at me, as though I had uttered something in gibberish; then, with a look of blank surprise on his face, answered vaguely, 'I thought I had made my position quite plain. There is nothing I can do in the matter.'

'But Holmes . . .,' I strove. It was no use. He rose from the table and went back into his room without a word. I knew better than to feel offended.

The reader of my narratives already in print will be aware that this year of 1895 proved to be one of the busiest and most successful of his career. After its relatively slow beginning, case followed upon case in succession rapid enough to keep his mind at full stretch. I see that at one point I was able to record: 'I have never known my friend to be in better form, both mental and physical.'

Some of those cases of '95 must remain discreetly unrecorded for ever. Certain others I have mentioned, though not described in detail. These included the arrest of Wilson, the notorious canary-trainer, of which I believe I remarked that it removed a plague-spot from the East End of London, as was most certainly the case; the cases of Vigor, the 'Hammersmith Wonder'; of Vittoria, the Circus Belle (certain particulars of this exploit still draw a secret smile to my lips); of the venomous lizard, a truly remarkable business; and, of course, the famous investigation of the sudden death of Cardinal Tosca, undertaken by Holmes at the express desire of his Holiness the Pope, for which he was rewarded with some Papal honour, the exact nature of which escapes my memory.

Adventures belonging to that vintage year with which my reader will be more fully familiar were those which I have described in print under such headings as 'Black Peter', 'The Norwood Builder', and 'The Bruce-Partington Plans'. But here I must admit that, in the past, I have not been wholly frank regarding two of these. The reader will now discover in what way, and why, and I hope will forgive me for not having disclosed the following particulars at the time.

The unusual affair of Black Peter, the retired sealer and whaler who was murdered by harpoon in his wooden cabin in the Forest Row neighbourhood of Sussex, occupied the Wednesday to Friday, 3–5 July. Reference to the closing sentence of my narrative of it will recall to mind Holmes's farewell to Inspector Stanley Hopkins: 'If you want me for the trial, my address and that of Watson will be somewhere in Norway—I'll send particulars later.'

Thus, it has always been assumed that for at least part of the remainder of that month, and possibly the first week or two in August, we were engaged on some Scandinavian enterprise about which my pen has remained still. This was not so: we were in Paris.

'Norway, Holmes?' I asked, when young Hopkins had left our door with his prisoner, whom Holmes had just lured to his arrest. 'What is there for us there?'

'Nothing whatever.'

'Then ...'

'My dear fellow, you will take things so literally. It is that precise mind of yours. If I say Norway when I mean Paris, you must not imagine that I feel obliged to go to Norway instead.'

'Holmes, you are foxing me!'

'It would take a sharp intellect to achieve that, Watson. The position is simply this: we have no investigations pressing for our immediate attention. I wish to pay a visit to Paris, and now would seem to be the opportunity. I trust you will give me the pleasure of your company?'

'By all means.' I regarded him keenly, however. I had never known him go anywhere outside the immediate environs of Baker Street without some good purpose. 'But why did you say Norway? That was no slip of the tongue.'

'If I wish to absent myself from England for a few days' unofficial business, I see no reason why I should advertise my destination, even to the Sussex Constabulary.'

'I see! Then, for what purpose are we to visit Paris?'

'Your questions come at me like bullets, Watson! Your purpose, unless you can think of a better, is to keep me company. It is so commonplace that we go about together that inquiring minds might be alerted if I were to travel alone. As to my reason for going,' he added in less flippant tone, 'it is this.'

From the mantelpiece he took down one of the bunch of letters which had been awaiting our return to Baker Street from our Sussex excursion. I noted that the envelope bore a French stamp.

'It is from Dubuque,' Holmes explained. 'You recall that he is the Sûreté Nationale inspector with whom I had dealings in the Huret case?'

'Ah, yes. Do they require your assistance again?'

'On the contrary, I need theirs. Or rather, Dubuque's alone.'

At that moment Mrs Hudson entered to clear the remains of our interrupted breakfast, and to tut-tut over the disorder which Holmes's struggle on the carpet with the gigantic Patrick Cairns had caused. When she had gone again my friend resumed his explanation.

'You have very patiently forborne in the past three or four weeks to press me upon the Dreyfus affair. I spoke the truth when I told you that there was no action I could take, but my mind has not been idle. Just before this latest little business of ours sprang upon us I had sent off a letter to Dubuque, asking his opinion of the matter.'

'Is it wise to let the French authorities learn of your interest?'

'It would be most unwise. Considerable experience of French public institutions has shown me that a good deal of self-seeking and place-making goes on. There is patronage, jealousy and duplicity. Regrettably, it is difficult for one not familiar with all the personalities involved to know where to place his trust with absolute confidence. Now, Dubuque is a man I would trust in anything.'

'You are sure of that?'

'As I am of you, Watson. He saved my life during the Huret business at risk not only to his own, but to his whole career. By turning a blind eye he could have ensured promotion and the decoration which they were kind enough to give me instead. He himself warned me never to confide in any official whom I did not know most intimately.'

'He sounds a sterling fellow.'

'He is. That is why I wrote to him, at his private address in order to ensure that my letter was not scanned by any other eyes, to ask his opinion of the Dreyfus affair.'

'I see! Then, what has he replied?'

'His letter makes no mention of it. He merely writes, as if to an English cousin, saying that he will be delighted to show him some of the sights of Paris if he is passing that way. So, my dear chap, if you can rise superior to this summer heat, we will allow ourselves a little sightseeing jaunt.'

'In Norway,' I said smilingly.

'That is what we will lead the good Mrs Hudson to believe. I shall conveniently forget to send Hopkins our forwarding address. By the time Cairns comes to trial, we should be back, anyway. So now, let us put our things together and be off, before any further client comes clamouring for my attention.'

Inspector Dubuque proved to be a short, thickset young man, who gave the impression that he would be an asset to any rugby football team. He wore a neat black moustache and had twinkling brown eyes, which, however, he revealed only briefly during the moments of greeting, before concealing them again behind tinted spectacles. He was dressed in an unobtrusive suit, and the place he had stipulated for our meeting was an insignificant café on the Left Bank. The place was full of artistic-looking men and women, seated in groups and leaning towards one another in a babel of argument. No one appeared to give us a second glance.

'I see you are not wearing your ribbon,' Dubuque said to Holmes, referring, of course, to the discreet little crimson lapel insignia of the Legion of Honour. I had never actually seen Holmes sport it at all. Even such modest display would have been abhorrent to him.

'I never draw attention to myself,' he replied. 'I am more than ever grateful to you, Dubuque, for spiriting me away from the Huret scene before any photographers could get there. I wish my features were as unfamiliar in London as they are here.'

The inspector smiled and sipped from his glass of light beer.

'I was able to ensure that your name did not appear in a single newspaper, Mr Holmes, much as it went against my grain to take all the public credit.'

'That is of the least importance. But I gather from your precautions over your letter and the nature of our rendezvous today that the Dreyfus issue is one of some sensitivity.'

Dubuque glanced about him at the mention of the name. No one was paying any heed, but he leaned across and kept his voice low when he replied, in his good English.

'It is still one of the most talked-of matters in France. You may be sure that at least one of the groups about us is debating it. Do not be surprised if fists begin to fly.'

'What are the issues?' I asked. 'His guilt or innocence?'

'In essence, both, Doctor. But it has become so much greater than that. It has provided an excuse for all manner of old rivalries and prejudices to be reawakened. Radicalism, chauvinism, anti-Semitism, anti-Papism ...' He spread his hands. 'Almost any contentious issue over which Frenchmen most enjoy to quarrel has become inflamed on the excuse of Dreyfus.'

Holmes enquired, 'But what of the case itself?'

The inspector shrugged. 'It has become secondary. There has been rumour and counter-rumour. It has been said that he confessed his guilt to an escorting officer. That, in turn, has been denied. The document upon which he was tried is reported to have been filched from a wastepaper basket in the German Embassy. The German government was most indignant at this. Between ourselves, certain threats were made as to what might eventuate if the French press continued to make this allegation.'

'Threats from Germany?'

'Exactly. Their ambassador formally denied, upon the Kaiser's orders, that the embassy is permitted to indulge in any form of espionage. In recent years there have been several embarrassing cases of spying, both proven and unproven, involving foreign legations here.'

'As in most other capitals, I fancy.'

'Of course. Only, you must realise that France today is most sensitive in the matter of international relationships. Our people are by no means of one accord in regard to any major issue. There is widespread suspicion of the motives of this or that movement, any of which it is feared might be aided or influenced by foreign powers. So, naturally, Jewry being the least indigenous of these, it is attributed ambitions which are perhaps based upon nothing more than fears.'

'And Dreyfus has become symbolic of that?'

'A Jewish interloper in general staff circles, convicted of treason? The anti-Semitic press could not have found a better symbol, short of inventing one.'

'Then they are in full cry still?'

'Not now. Our government knows how to muzzle its press. At Germany's demand, it has done so.'

'So while the unfortunate Dreyfus's case continues to be argued hotly in private, it is no longer a matter of public debate.'

'It's true. He is far removed from the centre of it now.'

'Dubuque, I used the word unfortunate of him. Yet you did not object.'

The young inspector's smoked lenses were directed inscrutably between us as he paused, evidently weighing his words. The café seethed and howled about us. At last he said, 'I am glad that the death sentence was not available.'

'You mean,' I asked in lowered tone, 'you believe he might live to see his name cleared?'

The lenses turned to me. I could catch the glint of the eyes behind them.

'I do not say that it *will* be cleared, in his lifetime or after it. But I do believe that, while he lives, justice remains retrievable.'

'You are saying you believe him innocent?'

'No, Doctor. I am saying I do not believe he has been proven guilty. It is a very different thing.'

In that instant I shared Holmes's faith in the integrity of this man. I looked toward Holmes. He had lit one of his occasional cigarettes, no doubt in order to appear less conspicuous than if he had smoked his English-made pipe. He blew out smoke, adding to the already dense haze in the room, and said, 'Dubuque, you have justified my coming here with those words. But are you able to reveal any factual reasons which might lie behind your belief?'

The inspector seemed about to answer, but checked himself, and asked instead, 'Mr Holmes, I am a servant of my country; so you will understand if I enquire what is your interest in the matter?'

Holmes inclined his head, 'I have been appealed to.'

'By Mathieu Dreyfus?'

Holmes nodded.

'Thank you for your directness, Mr Holmes. It is a credit to the man that he has been so enterprising.'

'However, I declined his case.'

The eyebrows rose behind the dark glasses. In a few succinct words, Holmes explained the circumstances. The inspector nodded.

'You were right on every score. You must not be seen to be involved in any way.'

'I am not involved.'

For the first time since the initial moments of our meeting, Inspector Dubuque smiled; a generous, knowing smile.

'Of course you are not, Mr Holmes! Though, tell me, how may I serve you more?'

'Well—purely as a matter of professional interest, of course— has any further evidence of guilt emerged?'

'There have been allegations and suppositions of every sort; but no new evidence at all. Nothing, in fact, since the judges examined a certain dossier whilst they were considering their verdict.'

I recognised at once in Holmes's features those unmistakable

signs of keen interest which I likened in one of my narratives to the
look of a foxhound, as, with gleaming eyes and straining muscles, it
runs upon a breast-high scent. It would be appropriate to the simile to
say that he fairly barked his response.

'What dossier?'

Dubuque glanced round, but the noisy chaos of discussion was
unabated.

'Some papers in an envelope. I cannot say what they were,
because I do not know. I only mention them at all in the confidence
that word will not pass the lips of either of you gentlemen concerning
them.'

Holmes frowned. 'You don't mean, surely, that they are not
common knowledge?'

'That is exactly what I mean. They were submitted directly to
the judges in their anteroom.'

'But not shown to the defence?'

'No.'

'Surely that is most irregular . . . ?' I began to interrupt, but
Holmes waved me sharply to silence.

'Who produced them?' he asked the inspector.

'Major du Paty de Clam.'

Holmes drew the last smoke from the stub of his cigarette and
disposed of the remains. He asked carefully, 'Inspector Dubuque, I
do not ask you to betray any secrets. Will you say, however, whether
your information is that the production of these documents in any
way influenced the judges' verdict?'

'It did. It sealed the case against Dreyfus. I hasten to add that
they may indeed have been of so secret a nature that no public
mention of them has ever been made.'

'Yet they were not shown to the defence, which is against all
principles of justice.'

'There you have it.'

'I hope, my friend, that the mere fact of your knowing that this
occurred is not too great a danger to you?'

The policeman smiled again. 'My informant is also one who
cares for the good name of justice. I have persuaded him of the risk of
confiding in anyone else.' He tapped the tinted spectacles. 'Even so, a
few elementary precautions, such as these, and this insalubrious

meeting place, are in order. Mr Holmes, whether you are even contemplating acting for Mathieu Dreyfus is not my concern. Please be warned, though, that he and his brother's wife are being watched. At all events, keep well away from them, or you may become compromised.'

'Are they still in Paris?'

'No. They have taken a villa a few miles out, at Saint-Cloud, in the married name of one of the Dreyfus sisters. I don't blame them. There has been some very nasty persecution of his wife and children. They are pretty well left alone now, I think, but they are not unobserved.'

'Thank you for your warning. I was not intending a meeting, anyway.'

'Be equally careful if you are approached by any sympathisers for his cause. Many of them are genuine. Some are the sort of fanatics who will seize on anything that will cause a rumpus. Some, though, are infiltrators from the ranks of the anti-Semitic extremists. They are convinced that there is an international plot afoot, and they are alert for indications. So treat any approaches with the deepest suspicion.'

'Thank you again. You will take another glass of beer, Dubuque?'

'If you will excuse me, I must get along. I hope your visit has not been quite fruitless?'

'Far from it. It is my growing impression that there are too many irregularities about this case to be explained by mere coincidence.'

'I agree. But what can one do?'

'In your case, nothing, my friend. You have your duty to your force. As for myself . . .'

'What, Holmes?' I ventured to enquire. He ignored me again, still addressing the inspector.

'I suppose it is beyond all realms of possibility to visit Dreyfus?'

'Eh! Good heavens, not so much as his wife or his lawyer would be permitted!'

'I imagined as much. Then, as you say, there is nothing to be done, is there?'

I fancied that the policeman's eyes flashed, with either interest or amusement, behind their smoked panes. He said nothing; merely shook hands quickly with each of us, then melted unnoticed into the throng.

I stated earlier in this chapter that there was one other adventure of ours in 1895 about which I had not been wholly forthcoming in my printed accounts. It was that regarding the Bruce-Partington plans, an investigation undertaken by my friend at the urgent bidding of his brother Mycroft, the enigmatic *éminence grise* of Whitehall. This matter was to have two sequels, one of which I have already appended cursorily to my account, the other which I did not mention at all. Both had direct bearing upon the Dreyfus affair.

The reader will remember that the case itself concerned a young man, who, without explanation, relinquished his fiancée's arm as they were en route to a West End theatre one foggy evening, and vanished into the murk. His body was found next morning beside the track of the Underground railway, bearing all the signs of his having fallen from a train. In his pockets were found the plans of the highly secret Bruce-Partington submarine, which it was assumed he had purloined from Woolwich Arsenal, where he had worked as a clerk. Several pages of the plans, however, were missing. It was vital to the security of the nation, Mycroft Holmes had averred, that the documents be found, and any link between the dead man and some foreign power revealed.

Acting with his usual despatch and ingenuity, my friend solved the case inside three days. He proved that the young man had been not only innocent, but had been killed by a foreign agent based in London, Hugo Oberstein. Young West had gallantly but fatally tried to intervene between him and the real traitor, Colonel Valentine Walter, brother of the Head of the Submarine Department at Woolwich Arsenal, who had been about to sell the plans in order to meet his debts.

At the outset of the case, Mycroft Holmes had assured his brother, 'In all your career, you have never had so great a chance of serving your country.' Thus it came to pass that I was able to conclude my account of it with a reference to a day spent by Holmes, a few weeks later, at Windsor, whence he returned with a remarkably fine emerald tie-pin, which he would only say had been the present of 'a certain gracious lady' in whose interests he had carried out a small commission.

Although I did not voice in print my speculation as to that august lady's name, I fancy that no reader of mine will have failed to assume that she was no less than her Majesty Queen Victoria; and that her generous gift had been an unofficial token of the nation's gratitude to my friend for saving those invaluable plans from passing into foreign hands.

I can confirm that this was indeed the case, but shall now reveal certain further particulars which I have hitherto withheld.

It was upon a day very late in the year when Holmes paid that visit to Windsor. He had been quiet and withdrawn throughout breakfast, but since this was no novelty I had made no remark. When he had finished his frugal repast he left the table without a word. I was still employed with my coffee and toast when he returned, some twenty or so minutes later, attired, to my astonishment, in faultlessly groomed morning clothes and carrying a top hat whose newness I perceived at once. This immaculacy, and at such an hour, was so uncharacteristic of him that I suspected one of his simple but ingeniously effective disguises.

'I have an assignation with a lady,' was all the reply he would smilingly return to my enquiry.

'You, Holmes!'

The reader will be aware that Holmes's sole relationships with the opposite sex were of a professional nature. He once told me unequivocally that he had never been in love, which I believe to this day; and I have often found it necessary to record utterances of his bearing witness to his cynical and almost contemptuous opinion of womankind's nature and attributes. I am aware that, by not having been rather more explicit about this, I have left room for speculation of an unhealthy and wholly distasteful kind, which the more sensationally-minded commentators have not hesitated to exploit for their salacious purposes.

I shall, therefore, take this present opportunity of placing it upon record that my friend's presumed aversion to women was wholly due to his fear that emotional involvement might in some way detract from, or distort, that true, cold reasoning power which was the very foundation of his genius. Domesticity, with its distracting obligations and limitations of movement, was an impossible notion to him. He preferred the total freedom of 221B, where he could remain a law unto himself, at no one's beck and call save his clients', with the admirable Mrs Hudson to cook and wash and press and clean for him, and myself as undemanding companion and counsellor. It was not selfishness; it was wholehearted dedication to his unique profession. It was certainly *not* from any natural distaste for the female sex. I am well aware that some of his derogatory epithets were delivered with the amused intention of provoking my retort in defence of the ladies concerned and as a pointed allusion to my own confessed interest in the sex. The reader may search my narratives from beginning to end, but he will look in vain for any evidence of harshness on Holmes's part towards women, and will find only one record of an unchivalrous act*. To the contrary, he will discover countless instances of his sympathetic understanding of women and their ways, and almost unfailing gentleness, courtesy and kindness towards them.

But I digress. I had been about to say that, far from declining to reveal the identity of the 'gracious lady' who had rewarded him so handsomely, Holmes gave me a detailed account of his interview with her Majesty. I will pass over the greater part of it, which would be irrelevant here, and move to the concluding portion, when, to his considerable surprise, the Queen commanded her Indian male attendants to quit the room in which he had been received, leaving the two of them tête-à-tête.

'The good old lady evidently perceived my surprise,' he told me. 'She proceeded to add to it by inviting me to be seated.'

'Great heavens! An honour indeed!'

'A most gracious gesture, but not without some indulgence of amusement on her Majesty's part, I fancied. Beneath all that black satin and those severe features, I believe there to lie some vestiges of what she must have been like as a girl, before the worthy Albert taught her to suppress her high spirits. It evidently entertained her to watch my response to this bestowal of privilege.

'The chair she had indicated stood quite close to her own, in the

---

* I refer, of course, to the matter of his deceiving Charles Augustus Milverton's housemaid in the guise of a suitor, a plumber. That he so easily captivated her—and it was purely in the interest of furthering the investigation—is evidence in itself of his latent ability to enrapture the female heart.—J.H.W.

centre of that over-furnished room, thronged with objects and ornaments, its walls crowded with upwards of a hundred pictures. Having seated myself, with a word of gratitude, I waited expectantly. Her Majesty did not speak immediately. I recognised unmistakable signs of nervous hesitancy in the way her fingers played with her great diamond bracelet, in the centre of which I had observed a miniature portrait of her late husband and a lock of hair which I knew must be his. But at length she raised those hooded eyes to look at me. I could see no further twinkle of amusement in them.

'"Mr Holmes," said she—I will not attempt to describe her accent, in which I detected clear influences of German and Scotch—"Mr Holmes, we have upon our mind a matter which is causing us some disturbance, and which we should like to disclose to you, although in the utmost confidence." (And I am placing a similar stricture upon you, Watson.) "It concerns a topic concerning France, which is commonly referred to there as *l'Affaire Dreyfus*. Are you familiar with it, Mr Holmes?"

'I indicated that I had followed its details in the newspapers, but thought it prudent to make no mention of our closer interest in it. Her Majesty was clearly gratified. She went on, "It will be no revelation to you if we say that relations between our country and the German Empire have for some years been somewhat strained. Therefore, it disturbed us greatly last week to receive from our grandson, the Kaiser Wilhelm, a most disagreeable message with regard to the matter. Not to put too fine a point upon it, his Majesty implied that *l'Affaire Dreyfus* is a deliberate machination on the part of our own government, designed to upset the fragile relationship between Germany and France. He accuses Britain of having fabricated some document upon which this officer, Dreyfus, has been convicted of treason, and of having insinuated it into the hands of the French authorities in circumstances which suggested that it had been in the possession of the German Embassy in Paris. His Majesty emphatically denies that any official in the embassy is engaged in clandestine activities, and states that the French government has accepted assurances of this upon more than one occasion. He appears to have no doubt, therefore, that the affair is a subterfuge of our own government. Now, what say you to that, Mr Holmes?"

'I confess I was taken aback by this confidence, and even more so at being required to express an opinion upon it. I answered respectfully that I was in no position to reassure her Majesty, and ventured to suggest that her own Ministers were the persons to whom she should apply for information. At this, she grew quite agitated.

'"That is just the point, Mr Holmes! It has lately become the habit of our Ministers to be less frank with us regarding certain matters. We are positive that certain State papers which should reach our eyes do not do so. Were we to discover that the allegation made by his Majesty the Kaiser is accurate, we should not hesitate to send him our private apology, whilst commanding our Ministers that any repetition of so outrageous a trick would be viewed with the greatest displeasure. Yet, since it has become obvious that a great deal is going on behind our back in regard to other matters, how may we discover the truth of this? As you rightly suggest, we might make enquiries, but with what certainty that they would be unreservedly satisfied?"

'A petulant expression had been gathering upon her Majesty's features while she was speaking. She added, in the crossest of tones, "Of course, it's all over the Munshi. It is too tiresome!"

'I am sure, Watson, that you know, as well as I did, the meaning of this sudden allusion. This Mohammedan gentleman, Abdul Karim, is known in government circles as the Munshi, which your Indian service saves my having to explain to you means a sort of clerk. He has been in her Majesty's service for a number of years, and has risen to occupy a position in her regard almost comparable with that of the late John Brown. I had seen him for myself—indeed, had been received by him before her Majesty appeared for our interview. He is in his early thirties, a civil, well-spoken enough fellow, though with a touch of arrogance which betrays his self-regard. I confess that I could not perceive what connection there could be between him, the Kaiser and the Dreyfus affair, and it did not seem proper for me to ask. Her Majesty, however, proceeded to explain.

'"He has proved himself a treasure to us, assisting in all manner of affairs, especially those concerning India. He has attracted widespread jealousy amongst Ministers and some others close to us. There have been attempts to depreciate his origins and to impute base motives to him. It is even said that he has been supplying State secrets to Afghanistan. Now, is that not the most absurd of things? But it has been made the excuse for withholding documents from ourselves, which it is alleged would have come to the poor man's eyes. We can tell you, Mr Holmes, that he is cut to the heart by such talk."

'It seemed, then, that there was, after all, no connection between the Munshi and Dreyfus, and that it was simply a case of personal resentment against him which was causing Ministers to deny their Queen access to such documents as they saw fit to conceal. In these circumstances, I remained at a loss as to how to advise her Majesty.

'When her brief outburst of indignation had subsided, she said to me, "We beg your pardon, Mr Holmes. We are much irritated by such behaviour; but we have no intention of dispensing with the poor man's valuable services. Yet, it seems that so long as he remains our official secretary, which we recently appointed him, Ministers will continue in their devious activities. For this reason, we determined to put the matter to you, as an independent investigator who has served his country so . . ." (modesty prevents me, Watson, from repeating the adverb used by her Majesty at this point) . . . "We determined to ask you to employ your powers towards discovering the truth of *l'Affaire Dreyfus*. It would enable us not only to return a confident reply to his Majesty the Kaiser, but would inform us as to the mode of behaviour being indulged in by Ministers without our knowledge, so enabling us to adopt such measures as might be necessary to counter it."

'"Your Majesty means . . .", I began, but she stayed me with a hand.

'"Mr Holmes, be so good as to find out whether Dreyfus is guilty of what has been charged against him; and, if so, whether our government is in any way involved in the affair. You have already done the State important service, for which we are grateful indeed. Pray, now, act again, on behalf of your Queen."'

Throughout this remarkable recital, Holmes had stood in a familiar attitude, with his back towards the fireplace, one arm beneath his coat-tails, the other laid across the front of his waistcoat, the fingers of the hand fidgeting with the gold albert attached to his watch. Now, he flung himself abruptly into his chair, his elbows resting upon its arms, the tips of the long fingers spread and pressed together before his eyes.

'What shall you do?' I asked, awed by what I had heard.

For several minutes there came no reply. His eyes were fixed in thought, his whole physical animation temporarily suspended. Then the fingertips were parted, the eyes illuminated, and the body stirring with restless anticipation.

'I must see Dreyfus,' he replied.

'Mathieu?' I returned.

'No. Alfred. You know my methods, Watson. It is impossible for me to investigate a case without ascertaining for myself the character of the protagonist.'

'But he is on Devil's Island, Holmes. Your friend Dubuque assured you that to visit him there would be unthinkable.'

'Officially, yes. But visit him I must. My dear Watson, a gracious lady to whom you and I owe total allegiance has done me the great honour of seeking my help. Her request I consider my command. The issue is as simple as that.'

SEVEN

THE period at which my present narrative has now arrived—the winter of 1895—marks the beginning of almost twelve months which have been termed by certain students of my friend's career as his 'missing year': missing, that is, in the sense that I have previously resisted all efforts to persuade me to reveal what his activites were during that time. I have written elsewhere that some of his cases involved secrets of private families to an extent which would mean consternation in many exalted quarters if it were thought possible that they might find their way into print. Even at this remove of time this remains true; and it so happens that the majority of these cases belong to the year 1896. Therefore, the reader who leans forward now in eager anticipation that I am about at long last to recount the whole story of the politician, the lighthouse and the trained cormorant is destined to disappointment; as also is he who holds his breath to hear the particulars of the journalist and duellist, Isidore Persano, whose correct name I now reveal, but still decline to say more than that he was found stark staring mad with a matchbox in front of him which contained a remarkable worm, unknown to science.

In the absence of information about Sherlock Holmes's doings in this time, certain hacks have foisted upon the public narratives which owe more to imagination than to fact, and lean towards uneasy frivolity. I repeat that it is not my intention now to recount the activities of 1896 in detail; merely one of them. It occupied the months February to May, and the reader will have deduced with certainty that the Dreyfus case was the one at issue.

'I think that will do, wouldn't you say, Watson?' my friend remarked to me over his shoulder, one late January morning. He was leaning towards the mirror above our mantelpiece, fingering the moustache which had been accumulating above his upper lip since Christmas. He turned back to me, twisting both ends of the dark growth downward as he did so, giving him a raffish and somewhat dissolute appearance.

'Very effective, Holmes,' said I; 'if you wish to resemble a confidence trickster, that is.'

'Merely a journalist,' he smilingly replied, and fished from his breast pocket a pair of pince-nez spectacles, which he clipped on above the bridge of the long, sharp nose. I gasped exaggeratedly and cried in mock horror, 'I should never associate with such a bounder!'

I had clearly pleased him. He regarded the effect in the mirror for some moments, disturbing the smooth surface of his receding hair with the palm of a hand, then smoothing it again. He put away the spectacles with a satisfied nod.

'As you know, Watson, it is a maxim of mine that the simpler the disguise, the more effective. An observer looks for what he expects to see—the false hair, the stuck-on-beard, the pencilled lines. It is too crude and dependent upon theatrical artifice. No, by the time I have had my hair re-cut and parted to the right I shall be unrecognisable.'

He rang for Mrs Hudson and instructed her to send out for the little Italian hair-dresser from Chiltern Street. It was Holmes's general custom to frequent barber's shops in varying neighbourhoods, considering them to be useful sources of local gossip. For the past three weeks, though, he had not set foot outside 221B except by night, and well muffled, not wishing his transforming features to be seen. The Italian had attended him before when privacy had been desirable, and could be trusted not to gossip.

'All that is required now is a berth in some humble vessel, at a price within the compass of a second-rate newspaper writer who hopes to attract some attention to his name by gleaning an on-the-spot account of the current boundary dispute between British Guiana and Venezuela,' Holmes continued, when Mrs Hudson had gone. 'It is a felicitous stroke of fortune that the disagreement should have come to a head just now.'

'You propose to take in French Guiana on the strength of that, too?'

'Precisely. What affects the British settlement's boundary might well have consequences for those of the Dutch and French ones. Besides, my journalist is an ambitious chap at heart, if a trifle unsuccessful in his career to date. It has occurred to him that, having travelled so far to this relatively unknown corner of South America, he might as well expand his article into a series. He will visit all three settlements, comparing and contrasting their respective economies, ethnic composition, and anything else which he can show up advantageously to Great British rule. It is the stuff which editors like to have, and therefore his chance at last to become recognised as a responsible commentator.'

'Very good, Holmes,' I chuckled. 'And by what name shall your hopeful freelance be known?'

'Something unremarkable, I fancy. Let me see. Hm! Your own Christian name, Watson John, is it not? Or James? I can never quite recall.'

'It is John,' I answered a trifle stiffly. 'My poor wife sometimes addressed me as James, for reasons which I never discovered. John Henry are my Christian names. I am sorry if they are unremarkable, but there is nothing I can do about it.'

'My dear chap!' he cried, clapping me upon the shoulder. 'I intended no offence. If you will permit it, I will invest myself with a couple of them for this little adventure as a mark in recognition of our long friendship. John James, I think, will serve my purpose inconspicuously enough. I promise to do nothing which shall bring him into disrespect.'

I had to laugh. Holmes had always had this ability to turn aside the least or the greatest displeasure with a gracious remark and a modest quip.

He continued, 'I see that the majority of sailings for Demerara are from Liverpool, but there is one from London on the fourteenth: a merchant steamer with a few berths for passengers prepared to endure without luxury for three weeks or so. It should suit admirably.'

'But Holmes,' I suggested, 'could you not take the same route— the very ship, perhaps—by which Dreyfus went to his exile? The convict vessels no doubt carry paying passengers also. You might learn something from some returning colonist, or a member of the crew.'

He was shaking his head. 'I had considered the possibility, of course. It would be quicker and direct. But it is vital that I equip myself with a plausible identity and reason for going there at all. The English journalist I propose to represent would automatically head straight for his own country's possession to begin his survey.'

'I suppose so. Well, I can only say again that I wish I were accompanying you. If there is to be danger of any sort, I should prefer to be at your side.'

'Stout fellow! Were I travelling openly as Sherlock Holmes, I should not only welcome, but need your company, to allay suspicion. As John James, I cannot justify a companion; besides which, I hope you will play your part here, diverting any enquiries as to my whereabouts with any devious answers which your nimble mind can concoct.'

'Shall I make investigations on your behalf into any new matters which appear relatively straightforward?'

'I, er, think not, my dear Watson. Let the Scotland Yarders justify their offices in the relatively short period of my absence.'

So it came about, a little more than two weeks later, that Sherlock Holmes slipped away from our Baker Street haven, and from his identity, to board the steamship which was to carry him to who could say what danger, merely in furtherance of his principle that, circumstantial evidence being a very tricky thing, it is most necessary to test it by shifting one's point of view a little, with the possible result that all those elements which had seemed to point in one direction might suddenly be found to be indicating quite another. That this was to be undertaken at no small cost to his own time and purse had no influence upon his thinking. His life, as he had put it to me upon many occasions, had been spent in one long effort to escape from the commonplaces of existence. Here, then, lay before him a supreme opportunity to slough off humdrum routine and engage in a hazardous adventure, in exotic surroundings, which might, at the same time, lead to the saving of a soul.

'The sea air, sunshine and patience, Watson—all else will come.' He was not, in fact, to utter these precise words until more than a year later, and then in connection with an adventure much closer to home than that which I am about to write. But they are appropriate; and so, I trust my reader will find, will be my reverting once again to an objective form of narrative of a sequence of events at which, for reasons which I have explained, I was not able to be present.

The voyage to British Guiana, that sole British possession in South America, was uneventful. The steamer, although by no means new, was well found, both as to seaworthiness and internal facilities, which proved better than the company's advertisements had promised. As Holmes discovered, in chat with the Scottish Mate as both leaned upon the lee rail, their pipe smoke streaming down the wind, passengers were not sought, but merely tolerated in exchange for the modest fare which paid for their victuals and left a little profit after. Advertisements of sailings were therefore couched in less than inviting terms, thereby discouraging adventurers and honeymoon couples seeking to score over their friends in the matter of enterprise. Holmes's only fare-paying companions on the voyage were all male, five in number, returning to British Guiana after home leave. Each occupied his separate small but adequate cabin, and they ate communally at a long table headed by the Master or the Mate, whilst the other few officers messed together at a table of their own and paid their passengers little heed beyond the gruff civilities of the morning and night.

Holmes discovered little of value in the course of the alternately rolling and pitching progress across the Bay of Biscay and North Atlantic. All the colonists were British and held a superior view of their Guianan settlement to those of their neighbours. It was the largest of the three—virtually the size of Great Britain itself—the most populated, and the most developed, which was only to be expected. If some unimaginative fools had not abolished slavery (under which system, the five colonists concurred, the natives had been most contented), British Guiana would have become one of the most prosperous possessions of the Empire, with a growing export trade in rice, timber, rum, and the diamonds which in recent years had been exciting the keenest speculation. The consequent shortage of labour had retarded all this, there having proved to be only a limited voluntary population for what was unanimously agreed to be a d——d sticky, swampy, mosquito-ridden territory, of which only the coastal plain was habitable at all.

Dutch Guiana, more properly called Surinam, the British

possession's neighbour to the east, was compared disadvantageously from most points of view by Holmes's informants; while the farthest east, and smallest territory of the three, French Guiana, or Cayenne, was contemptuously referred to as little more than a disposal place for convicts, exiles, and the sort of officials who were too incompetent or corrupt to be found elsewhere the employment to which their grades entitled them. It was added that while French Guiana was bounded to west and east respectively by Surinam and Brazil, its inland boundary was impenetrable jungle, infested with serpents and poisonous insects of every type, whilst its coast was patrolled by legions of sharks of the most malevolent species. Malarial fever, leprosy and early death were avowed to be the almost certain lot of those who dwelt, voluntarily or compulsory, inside these boundaries.

Of the penal settlements themselves, Holmes could learn little from his fellow-passengers. There was a major one at St Laurent, some miles inland from the French Guianan capital of Cayenne. The most fabled, though, were those which lay some ten miles off shore: the three so-called Salvation Islands—Royale, St Joseph, and Devil's. None of the five passengers had ever visited the French territory, let alone the prison camps; but the Mate, McRither, had many times in his life put in at Cayenne.

'Yon's a gae glaikit hole,' he reminisced, and spat over the rail. 'Ye maun tak' tent, gin ye gang yon.'*

Holmes, who had uttered no intention of going there, was quick to shift the conversation to such other limited topics as seemed capable of engaging the grizzled Scot's interest. He was thankful, though, that he had furnished himself with an ample supply of quinine; and that his revolver and a box of rounds lay within his sparse baggage.

He was also to find himself thankful that his trip to the Guianas had coincided with the ending of the winter rainy season. The worst of the weather was over by the time he reached the Demerara River, and the British capital of Georgetown. It would turn for the worse in a matter of weeks, though, McRither had told him, advising my friend that he should not dawdle over whatever task had brought him there.

---

* I trust the reader will forgive any inaccuracy in rendering these words. Their burden would seem to have been: 'That is an insalubrious spot. Should you find yourself visiting it, take due precautions.'—J.H.W.

To Holmes's relief, the European populace appeared to be wholly concerned with itself and its own affairs. His explanations to the few officials with whom he came into contact, and to the half-breed proprietor of his modest hotel, that he was a journalist interested in political economy provoked neither sensation nor even curiosity. Clad in a cheap white linen suit and sun hat, he moved unobtrusively in the unexceptional heat, tempered by the steady trade winds sweeping the long, deep coastal plain on which most of the settlements and developed areas lay. His eyes gauged the varied Eastern and African origins of the majority of those about him, while his ears noted the contorted English which underlaid their language, strange yet comprehensible.

He was anxious to get upon his true mission; yet he compelled himself to expend a week going about, notebook and pencil ready, asking questions of impatient and condescending petty officials about figures for exports and imports of various commodities, plans for building roads and winning back areas of the jungle forests which lay, dense and dark, between the plain and the hills and mountains beyond, and seeking opinions about the border dispute along the ill-defined 'Schomburgk line' which, in consequence of the intervention of the United States of America on behalf of Venezuela, was under examination by an international commission. He found few who knew much about it, or cared. Should the dispute become inflammatory, a gunboat would be sent from Gibraltar, Venezuela would withdraw its claims, and that would be the end of the matter. At the end of the week, Holmes judged that he could move on with confidence. The hotel proprietor shrugged again when he informed him that he would be visiting Dutch Guiana for two or three weeks before returning to conclude his survey, and hoped to manage a few days in the French territory if time and weather permitted. Holmes deposited a few items of his baggage at the hotel, then left by a coastal vessel for the chief port and capital of Dutch Guiana, Paramaribo. During the brief voyage, however, he learned that the small ship would be carrying on from there to Cayenne to load a cargo of rum, the French possession's principal export. He decided to stay aboard and go there directly.

As the vessel neared Cayenne, at the mouth of the Maroni River, Holmes had his first view, on the port bow, of the prison islands.

'Îles du Salut—Islands of Salvation—they call them!' ejaculated the English-speaking French member of the crew who pointed them out to him. 'Isles of Death, more likely!'

'Why are they so called, then?' Holmes asked.

'Because their climate is better than the mainland. The sea breezes keep down the heat a little. Also, the malarial mosquito cannot reach them. But the vampire bats can. They swarm there. They gorge upon one's blood while one sleeps.'

Holmes regarded the speaker carefully. He was of middle age, pallid, hollow-cheeked and bony, a man who had clearly undergone privation which had affected him for life.

'You know the islands well?' he asked.

'Too well. Ten years' knowledge, gained on account of a hell-cat of a woman in Marseilles. Because I spared her the life which I should have taken, she was able to inform upon me and take her revenge with a list of lying accusations.' The man laughed bitterly. 'If I had murdered her, I should probably have remained a free man all these years. By desisting, I sentenced myself to that place.' He gesticulated at the islands. 'It's an irony, isn't it, monsieur?'

Holmes murmured sympathetic agreement. He wished he had made this man's acquaintance at the beginning of the voyage, instead of at its end. Useful information might be forthcoming from him.

'Look here,' he said, after glancing round to ensure that no one was close, 'I'm a journalist from London, out here to write about the territorial dispute with Venezuela. But I reckon it would mean a feather in my cap from my editor if I could work up a piece on life in the prisons here. D'you suppose they'd let me visit them?'

'Easy enough. There are a score or two of fat officials in Cayenne who have been asking for years for a knife under their ribs. You'd be a hero amongst the convicts, and if you didn't get the guillotine you could spend the rest of your life studying the *bagnes*.'

The sailor threw back his scrawny neck and howled with laughter. There was indeed something wolfish about him.

'Seriously, though,' Holmes pursued. The man stopped laughing and looked at him thoughtfully. Then he said soberly, 'Yes, monsieur. Write your article. Get your editor to publish it boldly, so that it will attract attention and everyone will read it and will come to sympathise with the poor devils whose lives are gradually wasted from them by the callous brutes of *surveillants* who starve, and beat, and taunt them into committing misdemeanours which earn them the solitary hole. Do that, and you will have performed a service for which the good God will reward you when your time comes.'

He had spoken with rising passion and a tear gleamed in each of his red-rimmed eyes. Holmes said, 'I will apply to the Governor for permission to visit the islands, then. Do you believe it will be granted?'

'I do not know. It may be that you will be allowed to see the St Laurent camp, which is up the river, but as to the islands . . .' He shrugged, and repeated, 'I do not know. In any case, you may be sure that you would be shown only that which they do not care to conceal. You would see only newly-arrived *bagnards*, with flesh still on their bones and blood not yet sucked from them by the bats, and not yet shaking with the fever while having to work all day in every kind of weather, barefoot and half-naked. No glimpse would be given you into the blockhouses where daytime is as dark as night, and where men lie fettered and kept alive only in order that they should suffer. You would not see the floggings, the guillotinings, the nightly disposal in the garbage carts of the remains of those whom sickness and hopelessness have at last overcome. No, monsieur. I and other *libérés* like me, who have served our sentences and managed to survive to live out our time in what passes for freedom, can tell you the truth of the prisons. For the price of a few glasses of *tafia* and some tobacco you will get all the information you need.'

It seemed to Holmes that his luck could not have been greater. He had known already that ex-convicts and men on probation made up a large part of French Guiana's European population, and that many still serving their sentences were at large to perform menial duties in Cayenne. It had been his intention to try to gain the assistance of some such, but he was well aware of the dangers it would entail: of the chance of his purpose being betrayed for a reward, or of his being tricked out of the money he proposed to offer, and murdered for the rest. But it appeared now that none of this would be necessary. Fortune had favoured him with the confidence of a poor wretch who had somehow retained a spark of idealism through his wasted years.

'Surely, though,' he asked the man, 'you will be going back to Georgetown as soon as the cargo is aboard?'

The man shook his head. 'It is only by chance that I am one of

the crew for this voyage. When the ship was last in Cayenne, a hand
was murdered for the contents of his pockets. I am a trusted *libéré* and
a fisherman. It is known that I have no wish to make an *évasion*. My
days are numbered, and I no longer have the will to remake my life
elsewhere. Therefore, I was ordered to take the man's place back to
Georgetown. Another was signed on there, and I am supernumerary.
When I set foot on the quay here it will no doubt be my final return to
Cayenne.'

Holmes glanced round again, then surreptitiously groped into
his wallet without taking it from his pocket and thereby revealing its
contents. His fingers found some notes which he knew to be in small
denominations. He extracted one and slid it along the ship's rail,
under cover of his palm. The man covered Holmes's hand with his
own, took possession of the note, and stuffed it quickly away into his
trousers pocket.

'You can trust me, monsieur, in case you are wondering. Be
warned, though, to be less generous with others. A few sous at a time
will suffice. You might be killed for more.'

'I understand. But tell me, before we leave those islands behind,
which is which?'

The man pointed to the lumps of land thick with coconut palms.
'To the left, Île Royale. That is where the administrative offices and
the hospital are situated. Also, *La Case Rouge*, which you would call
the Bloody Barracks. Look at that lush greenery, and try to realise
that amidst it lies a hut no longer than this vessel, in which, at this
very moment, several dozen men eke out their lives in despair. Be
certain that last night at least one died, either of disease or by the knife
of another, and tonight will be the same. The bodies will be thrown
into sacks and tipped to the sharks. At least their earthly sufferings
will be at an end.

'To the right there, about the same size as Royale, is St Joseph.
That is where they send the insane and those they would make insane
by solitary confinement for years upon end. No, monsieur, they will
never show you St Joseph, and you will find it hard to believe what I
or anyone can tell you of it.'

'Is it so bad, then?' Holmes worked his imagination hard as he
gazed across the blue sea to the green island, inviting in appearance.

'Worse than anything you can conceive. Can you imagine

dozens of men, each in his individual cell, whose walls run with humid damp, whose only light is the faint glimmer from the ventilator slit; who have no work, no recreation, no bed but a plank and a ragged blanket, no communication with one another? The only sounds they hear are the moans and shrieks of those who are mad, and the tread of the *surveillants'* boots as they pace the iron catwalk above the cells, day and night, up and down, so that even sleep is made impossible. The food is whatever scraps are thrown down, and for drink there is a little water poured into the filthy bucket which each pitifully holds up once a day. It is sometimes the warders' pleasure to forget to toss down any food, and to pour the water in such a way that it misses the bucket. In that state a man must rot in mind and body for perhaps five years. Be warned by me, monsieur, that if it should become known in Cayenne that your purpose is to disclose such things, such a fate could well become your own.'

'But how can these things be?' demanded Holmes, who had listened to this account with mounting amazement and disgust. 'I have always held French justice and liberality in the highest respect.'

The answer was a shrug, and the resigned reply, 'I am no philosopher, monsieur. That man should choose to use his fellow men worse than he would beasts when he has the power to do so is inexplicable to me. I am content nowadays to value each day for itself, and to give thanks for my own little freedom. But if the pen is your trade, and you care to earn some reward, and at the same time perhaps do a good act on behalf of the forgotten inhabitants of this colony and the many who will follow them so long as this system lasts, then you have a rewarding subject before you. But once you have set it all down, I should advise you to ensure that you never fall foul of any French authority, or you might well end up like me, with the blood drained from you by the bats and your mind as empty as a dried out old coconut shell.'

The islands had slipped abeam by now. Between the two larger could just still be seen the third, a little further out and considerably smaller. Holmes pointed with his pipe stem.

'The third, I take it, is Devil's Island?'

'That's it.'

'Its name would imply that it is the most terrible of the three.'

'It is little more than a great rock, about one thousand metres

long and half as wide. Nothing grows there save palm trees. The
lepers who inhabited it until recently found it impossible even to raise
goats. Yes, it is an inhospitable place, but less terrible than the others.'

'I gather that it is where this man—what was his name?—
Dreyfus is imprisoned.'

'Yes, he's there, the scum. I saw him being rowed across. In fact,
I was one of those who worked to prepare his quarters. Now, there's
another irony for you: a man who betrays his country gets an island
and a house to himself, and even some books to pass his time, whilst I,
who did nothing more than give a slut of a girl less than a fraction of
her deserts . . .!'

He went off into a diatribe against justice; but Holmes scarcely
heard. His eyes rested on the receding shapes of the islands and his
thoughts upon the men who suffered out of his sight on them. In
particular, his thoughts were upon the solitary captive upon whom
any real John James, journalist, might well have bestowed the
colourful sobriquet Prisoner of the Devil.

At length he turned to the man beside him. The steamer had
now swung directly towards the mainland and would soon reach
port, but the sailor appeared to have no urgent duties to occupy him.
He had ceased to rave now. He looked gloomily down from the rail, as
if anticipating that within an hour or so his brief experience of
freedom would be finished for ever.

Holmes asked quietly, 'This information you offer to provide—
how may I obtain it?'

The man made no response at first. It was as if he had lost
interest. Then he roused himself and asked, 'Where do you stay in
Cayenne, monsieur?'

'I have no advance arrangements. I had intended to register my
arrival at the Governor's office and ask advice.'

'Huh! I know those clerks. They are all in league with the worst
houses, where you will be welcomed like a milord, and your
belongings rifled the moment you leave your room.'

'Surely there are one or two reputable hotels?'

'Oh, yes. There is the Palmistes . . . But, look here, if you require
a decent lodging, clean and respectable, and where, on my honour,
you will be neither cheated nor robbed, I can direct you to one.'

Holmes hesitated. The sailor had made a not unfavourable

impression upon him, yet how far might he be trusted?

'I have nothing worth stealing,' Holmes said at length. 'As to being cheated, I can take care of myself. A newspaperman gets to know all sorts and learns most of the tricks. I will take my chance, thanks.'

The sailor bared his teeth in a humourless grin.

'Yes, I know I am only an old *bagnard*. You have no reason to think me honest.' He delved into his pocket and brought out the note Holmes had passed him earlier. 'Take back your money, please. Give it me again when I have served you, if you wish, and I will ask nothing more. What would you judge my age to be, monsieur?' he asked, with what seemed sudden irrelevance.

Holmes's observant eyes had already noted the bony pro-truberances of the skeletal frame, the scrawny neck, the face like a thinly tissued skull, with deep-sunk watery eyes and decaying teeth.

'Allowing for the privations you have undergone, and the climate of this place, I place you at fifty,' he replied bluntly.

'I am thirty-six. My name is Albert Gonselin. I carved my initials, one each, on the breasts of a Marseilles harlot, because she had informed the police that I had committed a theft which, in fact, her keeper had done. Ten minutes after I had dealt with her they arrived and found some pieces of the loot amongst my clothing, where he had hidden them. I should have killed them both. But apart from marking her, I never committed a crime of any sort in my life. Now, monsieur, do you, as an Englishman, judge that as deserving of ten years in these prisons—ten years, which have had the effects of almost twenty upon me? If so, here is your money, and may you find yourself in the worst lodging in Cayenne, with a knife in your back into the bargain.'

The crumpled note was held out defiantly, without care that anyone might have been watching. The hand holding it shook with passion. The eyes burned.

'Please keep the money,' Holmes answered.

Slowly, the note was withdrawn and put away again. The fiery gaze remained steadfast, though.

'Listen,' Albert Gonselin instructed. 'Register at the Governor's office by all means. Tell them where you will be lodging. It is a place where many foreign seamen stay. The clerks will not be surprised. On the other hand, if anything happened to you there, the authorities would turn the place upside down. So you may be secure in the knowledge that nothing will befall you in that place, which is kept by a Madame Louveque. She has been good to me in the past year, and I would do nothing that would make trouble for her. You will find it a discreet house from which to come and go, and I and one or two friends can come there and talk with you without arousing suspicion.'

It was good logic. Holmes would need to register his presence in the capital, in any case, before going about asking questions in his journalistic pose. It suited him well to take lodgings in a humble place, where any form of surveillance would certainly be more cursory than at a principal hotel; and Gonselin's assurances had the ring of honesty to them. At the worst, there was always the revolver, and beyond that one or two other forms of self-defence of which Holmes was capable. The balance of risk seemed to be in favour of his accepting.

'Very well,' he replied. 'You will take me there?'

A whistle shrilled twice from the bridge. Land was drawing close ahead, white buildings glimmering against dark green foliage.

'I am needed now,' Gonselin said. 'I shall be helping until late with the unloading. Get someone to direct you to Madame Louveque's. Anyone on the wharf will know it. Tell her that Albert sent you. Make your guide carry your baggage, and do not tip him more than a sou, or you will be marked down as a fool for plucking. I will get in touch with you.'

He went quickly forward, where seamen were gathering around a winch. Holmes remained where he stood, observing details of the shoreline. There stirred within him now the familiar, exciting sensation that once more the game was afoot.

EIGHT

HOLMES had disembarked on to a wharf crowded with a motley throng of natives, Arabs, Chinese, and many pallid Europeans dressed in the red-striped pyjama-type clothes and broad brimmed straw hats, which he knew to be the garb of the convicts. Several of the latter converged upon him, obviously in the hope of being favoured as his porter. None of them was of engaging appearance, and Holmes's faculty for deducing a man's type from little details of his appearance was for once of no use to him.

'Madame Louveque's,' he announced firmly. It settled the matter. All but one of the men turned away murmuring oaths, clearly disappointed that here was no naïve visitor who would be too free with his purse or susceptible to more serious trickery. The remaining convict, a ruffianly-looking young fellow, yet without the glint of cunning in his eyes, picked up the luggage, jerked his head, and shambled off on wooden shoes along the wharf.

The house was situated in a thronged market area, not far from the waterfront. It bore no hotel insignia and there was nothing in the form of a reception desk. The man walked on down a short, gloomy hall, in which the smell of garlic hung heavily, and into a bar room, furnished with many chairs and tables. A worn piano stood in a corner, with a violin lying on its top. There was little decoration, save bead curtains covering what seemed to be alcoves, whose function Holmes could guess.

Behind the bar a fat, swarthy woman was smoking a cheroot, resting her elbows on the counter and conversing with the only other occupant of the room, a man in rumpled civilian clothing. The woman was plainly of mixed blood, from her colouring and crimped black hair. She was dressed in gaudy green. Several large, cheap rings shone on her podgy fingers.

'*Au bateau,*' explained Holmes's porter, dropping the luggage before the bar. '*Anglais.*'

During the short walk together, Holmes had answered the man's questions in the most rudimentary French, preferring not to reveal his fluency in the language. It was his general custom in French-speaking countries. He had picked up many an enlightening remark passing between people who had supposed that rapid speech in their own language would be incomprehensible to him.

'*Bonjour, madame,*' Holmes greeted the woman stiffly. '*Je . . . je . . .* Albert sent me here. Name of James.'

At this the woman's gaze, which had been wary and suspicious, changed immediately. She smiled, showing very white teeth. She was perhaps in her forties, prematurely aged by over-weight and the unhealthy climate, but quite attractive now that she had relaxed her defensive guard.

'You want a room?' she asked. Her English was confident, with an American tinge to her accent.

'*S'il vous plaît, madame.*'

It's O.K. I can talk your lingo better than I reckon you can mine. How long you staying?'

'A few days. A little over a week, perhaps.'

'Here on business?' She answered herself with a laugh. 'You would be. No one comes to Cayenne for anything else.'

Holmes repeated in the briefest terms that he intended to write about the colony's economy. He could see that Madame Louveque was wondering how it had come about that he had been directed to her establishment, and by Albert, but she asked no questions in front of the other men. He gave his porter a sou, which he took without demur and left. The other man tossed off the remains of what he had been drinking, nodded to the proprietress, ignoring Holmes, and left, too.

Madame Louveque took a glass from the shelf behind her and placed it before Holmes.

'Join me in a glass, Monsieur James.'

Holmes had tasted *tafia* in the British colony. This form of rum was the local drink of the Guianas, hot and fiery. He generally preferred to reserve his palate for fine wines and excellent brandy, but had no hesitation in resorting to cruder liquor when it would help ingratiate himself or seem in keeping with a pose. So he accepted readily, and, knowing what to expect, was able to down the drink in a manner which obviously impressed the watching woman as being well suited to a newspaperman.

Then she rang a handbell. A few moments later there appeared a pretty girl, dark-skinned and large-eyed. She wore a crimson dress with decorative embellishments, giving the impression of being anything but a maid. Yet she picked up Holmes's belongings and led the way to the room indicated by her employer. It proved to be plain, but quite clean, and mercifully overlooked a low roof and a deserted street beyond.

The girl placed the baggage at the foot of the bed, then stood beside it, looking at Holmes intently, a hand on one of her hips.

'*Merci, mademoiselle,*' he said, in as execrable pronunciation as he could muster. 'That ... that will be all.'

She gave him a merry grin, tossed her curly head, and went out of the room.

When he had unpacked a few essential items from his valises and secured them again in a way which would betray any attempt to tamper with them, Holmes sauntered out into the town. It was late afternoon, hot and humid. The very heat seemed to smell; but, as he soon discovered, the source of the cloying stench was the rubbish which lay everywhere in the drainage ditches which criss-crossed the streets, waiting for the next rainy season to sluice them clean. Weeds, nourished by the last rains and nurtured by the sun, grew in untidy tufts beside the few unpaved roads and all over the dried mud areas where feet did not tread to crush them. The buildings, mostly single-storeyed, were of wood, thrown together without plan or taste and painted in garish colours which had faded patchily and never been renewed. Apart from a startlingly impressive square, whose sides were each perhaps two hundred yards long and lined with magnificent ranks of palm trees as tall as the mainmasts of sailing ships, there was nothing about the place except dishevellement and that sort of squalor which is bred out of resigned hopelessness.

Holmes knew its history: once a sort of colonial Eldorado, to which misguided seekers after fortune and ease had flocked, to find there only disease and disillusionment. The ending of slavery in the middle of the century had been the final blow to hopes of prosperity. Within a few years, convicts had replaced slaves as forced labourers in the forests and sparse plantations. Then, for a time, this system had been abandoned, to be revived again only in the year of Dreyfus's conviction. By then, Cayenne had declined beyond restoration. France had shrugged her shoulders over it and left it a place of banishment, both for the thousands of men who were deported there from their homeland, and for those who administered them and conducted the few struggling industries.

The sooner, Holmes told himself, he could get his business in this blighted place over, the better.

That evening he took a chair in the bar for a while, making two or three glasses of poor wine last as long as he could, in the hope of seeing Albert Gonselin. The place was busy, thick with tobacco smoke and the fumes of the *tafia* which almost all the customers drank. The piano jangled and the violin shrilled with some style in the hands of a gaunt man who must once have been a professional. Madame Louveque presided at the bar, and the girl who had shown Holmes to his room, and three or four others, were in evidence, from time to time disappearing with men into one or another of the curtained alcoves. Holmes was approached by each in turn during the course of his wait. He ignored them, and, with contemptuous shrugs, they left him alone.

Convicts, and *libérés*, men who had served their sentences but had to spend an equivalent period in the colony afterwards, made up the bulk of the clientele. The ironic thought occurred to Holmes that since prisoners of one degree or another evidently made up the greater part of Cayenne's population, and moved about so freely, it was those who had been sent there to guard them who were the real captives, living in constant fear of retribution, if what Holmes's ears picked out of the conversations about him was anything to go by. But he remembered the camps and the islands, and knew that he had seen nothing of the true nature of this penal settlement which had become known to the outer world as Devil's Island, although, as Albert had told him, that particular island was the least hellish of them all.

Holmes retired at length to his room, thankful that there was a key in the lock. He had only just lain down when there came a tapping and a girl's voice calling in an endearing tone. He made no response. His door was given a single, petulant kick, and then he was left in peace.

He slept as well as he might have expected in the sticky heat, pestered by mosquitoes, and next day started vigorously upon his rounds of the administrative offices. Even more so than in British Guiana he was given to understand that his enquiries were unwelcome and futile. He could find out all he wished to know by applying to the French Embassy in London, he was told. But did the French authorities in Cayenne not wish the world to be told how gamely they were struggling to develop the settlement's economy against all odds? They laughed at the notion. He was wasting his time, they assured him, in their offhanded way. There would be another boat in about a week. He would do well to get aboard it and go home to write about horse racing, or some other useful topic.

No aid was offered him by these officials; no hospitality. They were simply not interested. It was what he wished. When he casually asked if it might be possible to inspect a penal camp, the bored Frenchman, who had been amusing himself by making Holmes repeat each French word three or four times before he would condescend to catch its meaning, dropped his pretence and laughed.

'We'll gladly accommodate you, free of all charge. Sightseers not admitted, however.'

Holmes took the greatest care not to mention Dreyfus or his island. He kept off that same topic also in the evenings, when Albert Gonselin and a pair of cronies took to visiting Madame Louveque's bar and chatting with him in one of the screened alcoves, over glasses of *tafia* for which he paid. They told him dreadful tales, at times sickening, at others heart-rending, of conditions in the jungle camps where diseased men worked naked in the rain and heat, chopping down and hauling great mahogany trees; in the blockhouses, where men would murder over a bad throw of a home-made dice, or for possession of a newly-arrived youth; of the silent agonies of the solitary-confinement pits; of the sound the guillotine made as it sliced through a neck before an obediently-kneeling convict audience.

They pointed out through the beaded screen this man and that in the room. A great murderer, respected by all for the way he had mocked the *surveillants* and done solitary again and again for it: he looked to Holmes as though he would scarcely be able to kill a chicken now, so wasted and hobbling he was. The violinist, who never smiled, had killed his wife in Rouen because she had objected to his hours of practising. The foxy-looking little man with one of the girls on his knee had been a nobleman and a millionaire, until his massive frauds had been exposed.

Holmes took no notes, except mental ones. His quest was a false one, yet no knowledge of criminals and their ways was ever wasted in his view. It added to that impressive catalogue of folly which his mind retained, to be referred to instantly for examples and precedents whenever a fresh problem came his way. But after three evenings he had heard more than enough. The anecdotes were becoming repetitious. Clearly, there were patterns of life and behaviour in the camps, as in any society, and well-defined classes and types and situations had evolved. There remained only one facet unexplored, and this was for Holmes the all-important one.

'What about this Dreyfus?' he asked. 'You say he's in a class of his own?'

Albert and one of his mates, Raoul, made derogatory noises. 'Pampered swine!' Raoul almost spat. 'They should have shot him and had done with it.'

But the third man, Manuel, whose dark eyes and accent betrayed to Holmes his Pyrenean origins, shook his head.

'I've heard talk that he's innocent. They wanted him out of the way.'

'As I say, they should have shot him.'

'Or the guillotine.'

'No,' Manuel insisted. 'They don't want his blood on their hands. Just to keep him where he can't fight to clear himself. They don't mind if he rots, or jumps off a cliff, but they daren't murder him, in case word gets out.'

Holmes leaned forward towards Albert, who was the only one whose English was fairly fluent and who acted as interpreter and spokesman for the group.

'Listen, Albert,' he said, keeping his voice low but speaking eagerly, 'there could be something big in this for me. If I could write up a piece about the way Dreyfus is treated, compared with the rest of the convicts, and what the various feelings about him are, it could be what we call a scoop.'

Albert repeated his ejaculation of disgust, but Holmes went on.

'Don't you see, it would make my series even more of a sensation? Everyone outside here speaks only of Devil's Island. That's the name that's recognised. No one's heard of the other camps. So, I use Devil's Island in the title of my series, to catch attention, and then lead off in the first article about how mistaken everyone is. But, as the last of them all, I come back to the subject of Devil's Island, and tell how it *is* a prison, like the rest, only for one man alone, and how his treatment differs from everyone else's. I tell you, any editor would jump at that. I might even be able to get it syndicated in America and Europe.'

Albert regarded him for a moment, then translated for the others' benefit. Manuel nodded enthusiastically. Raoul continued to look doubtful, until Albert added some words of his own. Holmes knew exactly what he was saying.

'The guy's right. Some of our French rags would pick up a story like that. It'd take some explaining away. Might even cause an enquiry into the whole stinking set-up here.'

Raoul, too, nodded at last, and reminded Albert, 'One-Eye Jules was in the labour gang they took over to do some work on the guards' quarters in the Winter. He could tell him how Dreyfus lives.'

'One-Eye! I wouldn't trust him as far as I could throw him.'

'You couldn't lift him let alone throw him!'

'That's true enough. No, he'd be straight off to the Governor's office to split on what our friend here's going to do, and sell our names for helping him. He'd do anything for a few francs. We'd all find ourselves back inside.'

'And him,' Manuel agreed, nodding towards Holmes, who was leaning back, sipping from his glass and feigning total ignorance of what they were saying. 'They'd accuse him of something and get him put inside, English or no.'

'Or he might just happen to have a nasty accident,' Raoul added.

Holmes judged this to be the moment to break into the discussion.

'I've been thinking, Albert. Is there anyone you know who's seen Dreyfus on his island? Talked with him, maybe?'

Albert indicated the others. 'We've just been talking about that. The only *libéré* we know who has seen him isn't the sort of guy we'd dare put on to you. He'd land us all in trouble. Of course, there are some guards who've done their spell over there, but we're not exactly on speaking terms with their kind, and they wouldn't talk to you. Otherwise, no one visits Dreyfus, except the doctor and inspecting officers.'

'If only I could get there to see him myself.'

'No hope. They don't allow visitors on any of the islands, and that one especially. A newspaperman's the last they'd consider in the whole world.'

Holmes drained his glass and sent Manuel out to fetch the old *libéré* who shuffled about as waiter with another round. He said nothing until after taking the first sip from the fresh glass. Then he suggested carefully, 'If I *could* get to Devil's Island, I could cause a sensation. I can see the headlines now.'

All three understood his words and they chuckled together.

'It is impossible,' Manuel and Raoul said, speaking simultaneously.

'Why?' was Holmes's simple response.

Their smiles faded and they stared at him. Albert said, 'You're not serious?'

'I certainly am. We reporters don't just go around with notebooks, copying down statements from people. We go and see for ourselves. I could tell you stories of guys who've wangled their way into interviews with kings, generals in the middle of battle, a convict in the condemned cell ... There's a way into everywhere.'

'Not Devil's Island.'

'Of course there is. They took Dreyfus there, didn't they? Guards and others come and go, you say.'

Raoul and Manuel were smiling almost pityingly at these naïve protestations, whose gist they had followed. Albert explained to Holmes the simple facts.

'First, the way to Devil's Island is by way of Royale. We've told you already, that's the administrative centre of the islands, so it's crawling with *surveillants* and others. Second, although there's only a couple of hundred metres between Royale and Devil's, there's a really fierce tidal race between them, so if you've any ideas of swimming it, forget them. In any case, the sharks shoal there like mackerel. They get fed well enough every evening, when they dispose of the corpses to them. The landing place at both sides is guarded ...'

'One moment, Albert. Why is it guarded, if it's so difficult to cross? I take it that an official boat goes fairly regularly, but that must be all?'

'Correct. It takes several men, rowing for their lives, to manage it across the current. The boat goes every few days, but not regularly.'

'I repeat, then, why are there guards? Presumably the boat is kept on Royale Island, so that even if Dreyfus were a man of superhuman strength, capable of rowing himself across the strait, he could not possibly steal the boat for the purpose. He wouldn't dare swim for it, you say. So, once more, why are there guards?'

'Well, I did not mean that there are actually sentries. But the landing place at each side is in clear view. Any attempt to cross from either side could not fail to be seen.'

Holmes said musingly, 'Therefore, it is taken for granted that there is no escaping from Devil's Island.'

'With good reason.'

'So there is no point in keeping actual watch.'

'You're splitting hairs, monsieur,' Albert laughed, and gave his companions an amused summary. But Holmes still spoke seriously when he continued.

'We are reasoning from the wrong direction. Dreyfus cannot get off. But supposing someone wished to get on?'

'Who in heaven's name would want to?'

'I do, for one.'

A hint of impatience came into Albert's tone. 'I have explained. Anyone attempting to cross would be observed and he and all his crew—and he would need half a dozen—would be seized, or shot, or simply hurled to the sharks.'

'That is precisely what I am getting at. No one can leave the island. No one could get on to it by the official crossing route. Therefore, there is no need for constant surveillance.'

'As you wish.'

'Therefore, it is in no one's mind that an attempt might be made.'

'There was talk at one time of the Jews getting up an expedition to try to rescue him. Everyone agreed it would be impossible. Their presence in these parts would be known from the moment they set foot in the territory. No one would co-operate with them, in any case. The *transportés* are mostly of one mind about Dreyfus.'

'Perhaps so. But might not a few *transportés* undertake to get a man on to Devil's Island, in order that he might speak with Dreyfus? On the strict understanding, that is, that it would not constitute an attempt to rescue him, but in aid of their own cause.'

Albert translated hastily. The others nodded, but shrugged. Albert answered Holmes, 'It might be arranged ... if it were not impossible to manage.'

'I do not see why. You are a fisherman ...' Holmes narrowly prevented himself from adding the observation that so, too, were Raoul and Manuel: he had not been told, but the callosities on their hands and the deep crevices caused by drying salt water had made it obvious to him. 'I ... dare say you know a few others of your calling who might prove sympathetic to the endeavour. There would, of course, be payment. I'm not a well-off man, but I could manage something on account. If I get my interview, I'll be in the money, believe me. There must be some way I could get a share smuggled over to you.'

Albert licked his lips and translated again. 'There would be no difficulty about the latter,' he said. 'There are safe ways. But the question remains, how could the visit be managed. If you are thinking of using the cover of darkness, forget it. The waters are too hazardous.'

'No. You get me aboard your boat unseen and go out fishing, as usual. Of course you do not go anywhere near the strait between the two islands. You head out to sea beyond Devil's Island, until you are at a point ... (which a simple trigonometric calculation has told me must exist, was what Holmes did not add) ... a point at which we are out of view from both Royale and St Joseph. You then turn completely about and head straight in to Devil's Island. It is the blind side. Dreyfus's quarters and the adjoining guard house are quite close to the landing point which you say is so visible. Unless there are sentries posted all over the island, keeping watch on its seaward sides as well—which I very much doubt, but perhaps may be ascertained, just in case—then you can put me ashore and, in a matter of minutes, be back on your innocent seaward course again.'

There was obvious wonderment in the way Albert conveyed this to the others. Manuel whistled and Raoul shot Holmes a distinctly suspicious look, as if questioning this degree of ingenuity even in a journalist. But he nodded, and said to Albert, 'It could be done. There is a place, at the right tide ... He would have to row himself to the shore, though. There are too many rocks for us to stand right in.'

Manuel added, 'I have never seen a guard watching from that side. Only with Dreyfus.'

Holmes's ears pricked up at this. He asked Albert, 'What does Manuel mean?'

Albert could answer himself. 'Dreyfus is closely watched. There are six guards on the island, on duty two at a time. He lives in his house and they in another nearby. But in a room next to his the guards on duty sit. They can hear his every move, and watch him through a grating. He performs all his own menial tasks, but he is allowed to wander about the island, to gather wood, and so forth. On the side of which you speak he chooses to sit for an hour or two on a white rock like a bench. He remains motionless, gazing out to sea— cursing the discovery of his treachery, no doubt. We have often seen him there. Always late in the afternoon, when the worst of the heat is over.'

'But you mentioned a guard?'

'Beside him. One has to accompany him wherever he roams.'

'Invariably?'

'How can one say?'

'But—think carefully, please— have you ever seen him there alone?'

Albert consulted his friends. After some moments' animated conversation he answered Holmes, 'We think so—almost certainly.'

Holmes was certain of it. Six men, two on duty, four off, guarding one man on an island patrolled by sharks and without means of escape or hope of refuge or assistance could he have managed it ... No doubt each newcomer to the duty performed it faithfully for a while at first, but boredom, monotony and torpor were bound to set in, especially in this humid climate. They would let him wander, positive that he would always return to his 'home'.

He decided to hazard all. 'Then, if I were to get ashore on that far side of the island, and lie hidden for a few days if necessary, sooner or later I might hope to get an hour's chat with him.'

'Put it that way, I suppose you're right. But the whole thing's crazy!'

'Would a thousand francs be crazy?'

The three facing him looked sharply at one another again. Albert shifted his eyes to Holmes's, and his look was steely and penetrating.

'You seem mighty keen on this. You sure you're not up to something?'

'I promise you. All I wish to do is to meet the man face-to-face, get my own impression of him, ask how he lives and what he feels about it. The kind of details you've been giving me so helpfully about your own kind.'

'You sound very ready with your money.'

'I tell you, it isn't my money. I haven't got it. But with a story like that, I can't fail. I put it to you, gentlemen, we've trusted one another these past few days. Trust me that much further, and I won't let you down.'

Albert Gonselin slowly reached across the table with a bony arm protruding from his red-and-white striped shirt. Claw-like fingers encircled Holmes's arm just above the wrist and tightened, with surprising strength. Holmes could have thrown off the hold easily enough, with a quick backward jerk; but he desisted, and gasped loudly as though in pain and fear.

'Let us down,' Albert said in a tone of steel, 'and you'll be chopped up small enough to fit in a bucket! Don't think that once you're clear of this place you're out of reach. We've friends back at home who would enjoy tracking you down.'

He tightened the grasp momentarily, and Holmes allowed himself a grunt of acute pain.

'I promise . . .' he gasped, '. . . you'll get the money . . . Please!'

The pressure remained for a few seconds more, then was slackened. The claw opened and the arm slid back across the table, like a retreating serpent.

'All right,' Albert said, though with no renewal of warmth in his tone. 'I'll see what can be done.'

He threw his drink down his throat and held up the empty glass meaningfully. Holmes nodded to Manuel, who went off to fetch more. While he was gone, Raoul said something to Albert, who suddenly grinned and asked Holmes unnecessarily, 'That's a point—having got on to Devil's Island, how do you reckon on getting off it again?'

Holmes gave him a startled look in return.

'I hadn't thought of that!' he said in the tone of the amateur of all amateurs.

'Then you'd better!' Albert Gonselin said.

NINE

THEY left Cayenne two days later. Once more Sherlock Holmes's appearance had undergone a transformation. This time, however, it was achieved merely by a change of clothing. He wore the red-striped suit, broad straw hat and wooden shoes of a convict.

The change had been made in his room in Madame Louveque's house. Albert Gonselin had confided their plan to her, knowing that she could be fully trusted. She had agreed to keep her girls out of the way when the moment came for Holmes to come out of his room in his disguise and leave the house with Albert, after which she would ensure that the room, in which most of his belongings remained, should be kept securely locked until his return. Anyone chancing to ask the whereabouts of the bothersome English journalist—an unlikely enough event—would be told that he had gone to Surinam for a few days, but could be expected to return briefly before leaving French Guiana for good. Holmes had announced this intention to the fat clerk in the Governor's office, on whom he had been accustomed to call each morning, tiresomely seeking introductions to this person or that who could give him particulars for his study of the territory's economy. The man had shown not the slightest interest.

Not all Holmes's belongings remained behind in the locked room, however. The revolver and ammunition did; it seemed to him that if his adventure went awry, and he was apprehended, things would go far worse for him should he be found to be armed. The convict clothing, too, was a dangerous expedient, to be shed at the first opportunity. He could not have got on to Royale Island under his own identity; yet, to be found at any stage to be masquerading as a convict might obtain him a berth there in his own right. Therefore, he carried his tropical suit and pith helmet in his meagre baggage, and changed back into them as soon as the fishing vessel had put out from Royale on the morning of the venture. In his inside breast pocket lay a waterproof pouch, containing money and one or two other items which might prove useful.

Morning had been selected for a number of reasons. It was the time when most fishing boats sailed, so that this one, to all appearances manned by a crew of four in convict garb, would excite no special attention. By ten o'clock the heat would be intense, and by noon so fierce that it would take the most conscientious lookout to shield his eyes and stare across the dazzling sea. Surveillance on all three islands would be at its minimum. Finally, the afternoon tide would be at its most favourable to enable Holmes to accomplish a safe landing on Devil's Island.

He had, of course, given the matter of leaving the island as much thought as of getting on to it, but preferred to maintain his impersonation of the eager yet artless adventurer. It had been Raoul who had supplied the answer to both landing and escape which Holmes's supple mind had already worked out, but which he had preferred should come from his friends.

Consequently, there lay under the nets piled upon the deck of Gonselin's fishing boat a native dug-out canoe. It was fashioned from a single tree trunk, hollowed throughout its length of nearly twenty feet, and with a stem and stern rising in a curve to assist stability. Such craft thronged the rivers of the Guianas, but were little used in the rougher water of the sea. A dinghy had been considered originally, but without Holmes's having needed to argue against it the idea had been rejected. Any dinghy belonging to Cayenne or the islands would be identifiable if discovered; a *pirogue* would not.

It would not be easy to handle by one man, and a complete novice at that. Normally there would be two paddlers, fore and aft. However, there could be no question of anyone accompanying Holmes on to Devil's Island. He must get there alone and manage to moor the canoe and conceal it well enough to avoid detection during his stay. In its bottom lay a short mast and a small sail, as well as a paddle and a spare. There was a supply of water in a small cask, some food, quinine, matches and cigarettes, a blanket, a bottle of *tafia*, and a few sundry items. Gonselin had impressed upon Holmes most strongly that even if he were to get clear of the island without detection, he could by no means be certain of reaching Royale Island, unseen or seen. The current might carry him along the coast or out to sea; besides which the most serenely calm conditions in those waters could alter suddenly, with winds up to hurricane force and waves gigantic enough to overwhelm far more suitable craft than his.

Practical sailing was not amongst Holmes's many and diverse accomplishments. He was well aware of the dangers he faced. Alone in his room, he had pondered the few alternatives, but found no better solution than this. If the canoe should be lost or damaged even before the time for him to escape in it, he had available to him the last possibility, tried a few times in the history of the penal islands, of making some sort of raft. It would offer him a slender chance indeed. The canoe was his main hope. At least he would have a brief opportunity of learning to propel it in the few dozen yards between the halted fishing boat and the shore of Devil's Island. He dared not chance any more extended practice; the risk of observation was great enough without that.

Yet again, as they sailed from Royale towards the farthest side of Devil's Island, Albert Gonselin stressed, 'You're undertaking this completely alone, remember? If they catch you they'll doubtless beat you about in the hope of finding accomplices. Utter just one name, and you'll be a corpse within a week. Whichever of us stays free will track you down.'

Holmes replied, 'It is said that an Englishman's word is his bond. I have given you mine.'

'Well ... O.K.' Albert seized his arm in a rare gesture of cameraderie. 'Listen, we'd stay around near the island, waiting for some signal from you to help pick you up. But you understand why we can't? They'd be suspicious and watch us.'

'I understand perfectly. All the risk must be mine. I promise you solemnly, though, that if I don't get back to Royale, but manage to survive to land somewhere else, you'll hear from me.'

'We trust you, friend. Remember, though, that as soon as you see you're going to make it back to Royale—if you do—change back into your *bagnard* suit, and loiter on the wharf until you see any of us. An unauthorised stranger on Royale would be in as much trouble as anyone disguised as a convict would on Devil's. Whichever way you regard it, you're taking a colossal risk.'

Holmes grinned wickedly under his flourishing moustache. 'Know what they call me at the Press Club in London? "Daredevil Jack James". Well, boys, I'm going to dare the Devil this time in a way that'll ensure me free drinks for a month when I get back there.'

The sun was at its height when they drifted to a halt in that tiny area north-east of Devil's Island in which they were hidden from view from Royale and St Joseph. Manuel had been scanning Devil's Island for some time through a telescope, his hand cupped above its end to obviate all risk of reflection from the glass catching a watcher's eye.

'Nothing,' he said yet again. 'No one moving.'

'Let's get busy,' Albert ordered. The three Frenchmen, assisted by Holmes, heaved the mass of dark netting aside, revealing the canoe. In its bottom lay a folded basketwork structure. Albert pointed to it.

'When you leave the island, erect that. It will shelter you from the worst of the sun and from the dew at night. If you are in for a long voyage, for heaven's sake keep under cover as much as possible. The sun and the sea will prove equal enemies to you.'

The canoe had mooring ropes secured to its bow and stern. By these, the four men heaved it over the gunwale and lowered it into the sea, on the side of the boat farthest from the island. Holmes shook hands with them in turn, and clambered down.

'Wave when you are safely ashore,' Albert Gonselin instructed. 'We will not wave back, for fear of being seen. But if you do not wave we will linger as long as we dare, in case you have to return. God preserve you, my friend.'

Holmes took up one of the spoon-shaped paddles, which had replaced the long poles generally used to propel such craft in shallower water. In the way Albert had demonstrated to him during the voyage he began to paddle with it, first on the right, then the left, of the canoe. He made headway slowly, until, emerging from behind the fishing boat, he felt the current catch the canoe and start to drive it shoreward. Again heeding Albert's instructions, he dipped the paddle into the water and held it there, and was gratified to feel its resistance against the current cause the nose of his craft to turn as he wanted it to, directly towards Devil's Island.

He had to concentrate fiercely upon holding the canoe in

precisely that same direction. It rocked and bumped, even in this calm sea, giving him some slight indication of the difficulty he would have controlling it in anything rougher. Also, it did not escape his notice that the sinister blue-grey fins of two large sharks, which had been motionless hitherto, turned to converge on him, as the monsters abandoned their basking to satisfy their curiosity. The likelihood of what might happen if one of them should bump hard against his shallow craft was something he did not allow himself to contemplate, but made him thankful that the shore was already only a few yards away.

Close though the shore was, it was less than inviting. Using the telescope during the voyage out, Holmes had surveyed the island as best he could. It was a great rock mass, consisting of two humps with a valley between them, and nearly ringed by a narrow beach or plain. On the smaller hump, at the landward end, stood the stone buildings which constituted Dreyfus's personal prison establishment. The larger hump, the end towards which Holmes was drifting, was well forested with coconut palms and should provide him good cover once ashore, in contrast with the rest of the island which was only sparsely wooded. But at this end the beach had petered out. Only rocks lay ahead, and the sea surged up them menacingly. A misjudged approach, and his craft would be smashed and he likely drowned.

Yet, there was no time for calculation. Another big wave would be enough to throw the canoe on to the rocks. Already, Holmes could hear its rumble behind him. The stern began to rise and the craft was lifted and propelled forward. From his elevated position he just had time to see a channel between the rocks a little to the left ahead. It seemed little broader than the canoe itself, but it was the best hope. He dug deep with the paddle, as the wave raced under and the canoe shot forward, spray drenching down into it as the wave crashed against rocks and recoiled.

The impact he had feared did not come, though. Blinded momentarily by the stinging spray, he recovered to see that his craft had entered the channel as truly as a piston into its socket. There were drenched rocks to right and left of him, from which the sea poured back. Even now, he could feel the contra-movement of the water receding, about to carry him out again by the way he had entered.

Hurling the paddle into the bottom of the craft, he flung out his hands on either side and grasped at rocky fissures. His fingers gripped securely. And then he was having to cling on with all his strength, holding the canoe where it was while the tide surged back under and around it, trying to lift and tug the craft back out to sea.

It was the greatest physical effort he had ever had to make in his life. His arms seemed likely to be jerked out of their joints. His feet, thrust forward, pushed hard to help hold the canoe steady. His teeth were clenched together like a tightened vice. It could only have lasted seconds, but it seemed like minutes before the canoe sank down once more as the last of the ebbing water gushed from under it.

Holmes knew he had only moments to spare before the next wave. Relying upon one handhold alone, he heaved himself bodily out on to the rock. The canoe began gently to drive backward towards the mouth of the channel and the sea. The boom of an approaching wave, a mighty one, sounded. He let the craft drift just far enough for the bow rope to come to hand. He grasped it and swiftly made as many turns of it as he could round the sharp tip of the rock he was holding. Then he clung on, both for the canoe's security and his own, while the great wave rushed in, over the surrounding rocks, over himself, over the canoe, flooding the narrow channel with leaping, bubbling foam.

He managed to hang on until it, too, had receded. Then, knowing that he would have comparative respite only until a seventh such larger wave came, he worked frantically to make his craft more secure, slithering down the rock to fish for the stern rope and tie that as well. Each time a lesser wave came in he had to cling on again and wait for it to pass. But the canoe held firm. There was no room in the narrow channel for the craft to be dashed about to destruction. It lay flooded, but secure. With great difficulty, between inundations, Holmes managed to drag out the few supplies he had brought, feeling thankful that Albert Gonselin had prepared for the worst and had packed them securely in well-tied bundles made out of old oilskin capes. As he got each out, he threw it up beyond him, to where a rim of rock formed a sort of pallisade against the sea. At length he was able to crawl up to this same barrier, and over it, into a basin of hot pebbles, only sprinkled by the spray from each incoming wave, to dry again instantly. Only now did he stand erect, facing seaward, waving his extended arm several times to and fro towards the fishing boat.

This was the calmest sort of day! How his moored canoe would fare under rougher circumstances he did not know. Whether it would have been sucked away entirely by some mighty sea, or dashed to pieces, by the time he would come to need it again, he could not envisage. But there was nothing more he could do to secure it. At least the place where it lay was under an overhang of eroded cliff; it would not be seen from above, and certainly not from out at sea.

He sat down to regain his breath and strength after his fierce battle with the elements. His soaked clothing was drying already, and his skin tightening as the sun baked the salt which coated it. His lips were bitter to his tongue. He knew that he must make for cover without delay. At least, though, he had achieved something, if only the dubious distinction of becoming the first voluntary dweller upon Devil's Island.

The climb up the rock face was a difficult one, but had to be repeated in order to carry up his belongings. After an hour's hard toil Holmes lay in the hiding-place which would have to serve as his home for as long as it took to accomplish his mission. There had been little scope in choosing it. The baked, rocky surface of the island supported nothing in the way of undergrowth. There was a place, however, where a slight declivity formed a basin beneath a circling shade of trees. To his surprise, there were straggling tomato plants within it, bearing a few of their fruit. He recalled that the island had been a leper colony. Perhaps the unfortunates had found out every place where a plant could flourish. It occurred to him that the guards might have discovered these spots, and might come to pick what they could find; but a close examination of the ground revealed none of that scouring which the boots of impatient men would have left. He dared reconnoitre no further. This was the only place where he might conceal himself and also escape exposure to the sun.

His belongings about him, his single blanket spread out to dry, he could do nothing now save settle down and wait. Fortunately, he needed no fire, for warmth or cooking. There was natural warmth enough, and his ascetic eating habits absolved him from the necessity of regular meals. Tobacco was his usual solace, but it was not his master. He had not brought his pipe, for it would have been too demanding of matches, and the smoke of his black shag might have hung and wafted dangerously. His great ability to remain still and patient by the hour would carry him through whatever period of waiting should prove necessary.

It seemed, for a time, that the waiting might be brief indeed. Holmes had scarcely been settled an hour in his lair when he heard a man whistling a tune. His keen memory identified it as '*Voici le sabre!*' from Offenbach's "*La Grande Duchesse de Gérolstein.*" Certainly, if Alfred Dreyfus were in any mood for whistling, it would be a subconscious irony if he were to choose a piece about the proud possession of a sword—he who had watched his own broken across a tormentor's knee. Peeping cautiously over the rim of his hiding place, Holmes saw that, as he had expected, it was a guard, a young man in uniform and pith helmet, with a rifle slung over his shoulder; but Dreyfus was with him.

He walked in front, slowly, his arms behind his back and his gaze cast down. He wore a grubby white linen suit and pith helmet and a short black beard. It was apparent, from a distance of twenty feet or so, that he was emaciated and enfeebled. His carriage was that of a man far older than Holmes knew him to be. Everything soldierly about him was absent.

The guard, Holmes saw, was whistling *at* him. So the irony of the sabre song was meant, after all. Dreyfus's guards, or at least this one, had found subtle methods of extending his degradation. From the way the victim carried himself, he was doing his best to bear it with dignity, if he could not ignore it. He walked gravely on, until at last he came to the tip of the cliff, where Holmes had noted the white, bench-like rock on which he had been told the exile was accustomed to sit.

Dreyfus sat now, lifting his head to stare out across the sea. What were his thoughts, Holmes wondered? Of his wife and children, certainly. Of his homeland beyond the sea ... But what of that homeland? Did he curse the day he had been tempted to betray her? Or was his curse for those who, for whatever reason, had ruined his career, broken his life, and sent him to be consumed by heat and sickness on this stony place, where a loutish boy could have authority to mock him?

After whistling on for a while the guard fell silent and paced about behind his charge. Dreyfus gave no sign of even realising that he was there; his gaze was fixed immoveably out to sea. Holmes began to fear that the bored youth might wander idly in his direction. The circuit he had begun to pace was bringing him closer to where he lay. Holmes had no doubt that, with the advantage of surprise, he could tackle him successfully before the rifle could be unslung, let alone used. But that would gain him nothing. It was imperative that no one should learn that there had been a visitor to the island.

The guard's footfalls were coming nearer. Holmes no longer dared peep over the edge of the hiding-place, and there was no possibility of creeping away unnoticed. For once, he was at a loss what to do. Then, suddenly, the footsteps ceased. After a painful pause there came the scrape of a turning heel, and the derisive whistling began again. It started to recede. Very slowly, Holmes raised an eye above his cover. He saw that Dreyfus had risen and was walking slowly back along the island, the youth sauntering behind.

It had been a merciful escape; but it had not secured him his interview with Dreyfus. That would have been miraculous indeed, so soon after his arrival. Holmes silently admonished himself upon the importance of patience in an impatient world, and began to busy himself quietly and watchfully with his arrangements for spending his first night under an open tropic sky.

His reward came gratifyingly soon, however. After a reasonably comfortable night, despite drenching dew and the whine and prick of various sorts of insects, he crept to the cliff edge and looked down. The canoe was still secure, the sea no heavier than on the previous day. He ate some cold bacon and beans from tins, and settled down to his vigil again. It was soon oppressively hot, but the drooping leaves of the tall palms were between him and the direct sun, so he was as comfortable as could have been possible.

It was late afternoon when Dreyfus came again; and this time he came alone. Holmes watched him pass to his accustomed seat, but made no immediate move to approach him. He continued watching the path along which the prisoner had come, hoping not to see a guard meandering after. There was no one; and now there was no time to lose. Holmes rose to his feet, taking up a position beside a tree trunk which would screen him from the rest of the island, and called softly, 'Captain Dreyfus!'

He saw the hunched shoulders stiffen, and the head lift slightly and turn towards him. And then he was looking straight into the surprised eyes of the Prisoner of the Devil.

Alfred Dreyfus made no verbal response, as Holmes, with a swift glance along the island, came hurriedly from his place of concealment, to squat down almost at Dreyfus's feet, so that the stone on which he sat would hide him from anyone who might approach.

'Listen to me, please,' said Holmes, speaking in French. 'There is very little time, and it is imperative that I speak with you; only, no one must know that I have been here.'

There was indeed a close resemblance between this man and his brother Mathieu; or would have been, had not this one's features been so gaunt and strained. His pale skin was blotched with the angry marks of insect bites. Dark shadows beneath his pince-nez betokened lack of sleep and perhaps the onset of organic disease. The wispy hair showing under the pith helmet was ragged and white.

'Who . . . are . . . you?' he asked slowly, in the halting manner of a person with an impediment of speech.

'My name is John James. An Englishman. I am a journalist from London. I am making a study of your case.'

Dreyfus regarded him long, but again made no reply. Holmes urged, 'Captain, this might be the only opportunity.'

The silence continued. Then, at length, 'What do you want of me?'

It was said with almost no expression: no hope, no interest, no curiosity.

'I wish to know the truth—from your own lips, as opposed, perhaps, to what emerged in court.'

Only now did a little animation show itself.

'I see. Yet another attempt to gain a confession. Save your tricks, monsieur.'

Dreyfus began to get up. Holmes reached out urgently and grasped one of his legs.

'Do not stand up, Captain. Stay seated, I beg you.'

To his relief, Dreyfus slowly obeyed, but said, 'What is this new game? Who sent you—the War Ministry or the Government?'

'Neither. I am here of my own accord.'

'On this place! Nonsense!'

'On my honour, Captain.'

'Honour! Honour and loyalty—those were once my only creed.

I kept to it faithfully, and see where it has brought me!'

'It has brought me here, too, Captain. To seek for truth, in order, if possible, to gain justice and see honour restored.'

Dreyfus hesitated, then said, 'Your French is perfect. Too good for an Englishman.'

'My maternal ancestors were French. I was brought up in the country.'

'Speak to me in English.'

'Very well,' Holmes answered, obeying. 'I know that you speak the language, and will recognise that I am no less fluent than in French. I am no impostor, here to trick you.'

A deeply thoughtful expression had come upon the other's face. He replied in French, 'How do you know that I speak English, if you have not seen my dossiers, which no journalist can have done?'

'Because your brother Mathieu speaks it well. You were brought up together. It is a logical conclusion.'

'You ... have spoken with Mathieu ... in English?'

'At length. He came to London to solicit my aid on your behalf.'

'How can an English journalist help me?'

'By re-kindling public interest in your case.' Holmes spoke in French again. 'I don't know whether you are aware, Captain, that it is no longer discussed in the French newspapers? They have been persuaded to desist.'

'How should I know?' came the response, steeped in bitterness. 'I, to whom no man is permitted to speak a word.'

'You are kept in silence?'

'Like a Trappist. You notice that my speech falters? It is because I have almost lost the faculty. I speak sometimes to my warders, simply in order to practise my tongue. They do not reply. Coarse brutes that some of them are, I should welcome even a few words from them at times.'

'Do you receive letters?'

'A few. My dear wife writes frequently, but they are held up for months at a time. Whenever I see the mail boat from Cayenne approaching Royale Island my heart leaps within me. But, again and again, I suffer only disappointment.'

'When you do receive letters, do they contain details of any moves to re-open your case?'

'None at all. All are censored, as are mine. Expressions of love and encouragement, and heartrending messages from my little ones, who believe I am on foreign duty—these are all I receive. There are times when it is only the thought of those dear ones which prevents me from welcoming the blessing of death.'

'It is so bad, then?'

The captive regarded him with renewed suspicion before replying, 'It is hell on earth. Eternal silence. Fevers. Cramps. Pains of many kinds. Meagre, wretched food, which I must prepare as best I can without proper means. Stifling heat. Days and nights of unceasing rain. Inactivity. Nothing save one or two books to distract my mind from the torments of suspense and hopelessness. I am locked in at half-past six, without any light of my own for reading, yet my mind is so tormented that I cannot sleep. Sometimes, I am so disheartened, so worn out by it all, that I long to stretch myself out, let myself go, and thus passively finish with my life. And yet . . . and yet . . .'

'Yes, Captain?'

As he had been speaking, Dreyfus had been staring unseeingly before him. Now, however, he turned to look Holmes squarely in the face, as he said slowly, 'I do not care who you are, monsieur. If you are here upon the purpose you claim, I thank you. If yours is an attempt to prise words from me which may be twisted into an alleged confession, as was done before, then it matters not, either. I have only the same answer to give: it is, that it is my honour, principally, which keeps me alive. To surrender my life would be the same as surrendering my sword; to hand it over without just cause.'

'"Without just cause"? You are innocent, Captain Dreyfus?'

'Completely. It requires only someone to search hard enough—the government possesses every means for such a search, all the machinery to penetrate the mystery—and I will be shown to be totally guiltless. There must be an end to all this. There must! I am determined to remain alive long enough for my honour and my family's to be restored. Whether your report is for a newspaper, or for the official dossier, I care not. But, pray, put that in it. It is the wretched Dreyfus's remaining creed.'

He had spoken with growing passion, the thin, weak voice rising to a crescendo which was almost a shriek. Fearful that they might

have been too preoccupied to notice the approach of a guard, Holmes
got up on to his knees and peered cautiously down into the valley.
There was no one in sight. He sank down again, reaching a decision.
From his inner pocket he withdrew the waterproof packet and
unwrapped it, saying as he did so, 'You were right, Captain. I am an
impostor. No—hear me, please. I am an impostor, in that I gave you
the assumed name under which I concealed my identity in order to
get to this place at all. You suspect me, my motive in coming to you. I,
in turn, had my doubts of you. I suspected that you might be as guilty
as has been made out. There was nothing more for me to judge by
than the public reports of your case and the testimony of your brother,
which I found too partial and fragile to be convincing. There was
only one way to satisfy my doubts, and that was to come here to see
you face to face.'

'But ... how did you come? They cannot have let you across.
Monsieur, I am confused! You say you are an impostor. You claim to
be here in my interest ... For God's sake, I beg you, explain!'

The oilskin pouch was unwrapped. Holmes drew from it a
document.

'I shall not tell you how I came, Captain. It was by hazardous
means, and the return will be more difficult still. If it fails, it is better
that you should not know anything of it, so that no one will be able to
make you relate it. It would lead to the incrimination of others.
Answer one question, please, and I will then tell you who I am and
show you proof of it.'

Was there the sound of whistling approaching?; or was it some
effect of the wind, which had begun to rise, as the sky darkened at its
rim where an approaching plane of flat cloud loomed?

'My question is, if I can arrange for you to be taken away from
here—rescued—have I your consent to do so?'

The answer was direct. 'You have not. I would resist—report it,
even. To attempt to escape would set the seal upon my alleged guilt.
Only by continuing to endure this torture can I show my unflagging
belief that my innocence will be proved. When that is done, I will quit
this place more gladly than awakening from the worst of nightmares.'

'Captain Dreyfus,' Holmes said, 'you have given me the answer I
sought. Had you agreed even to contemplate an attempted escape I
should not have blamed you, but I should have continued to doubt

you. By insisting upon remaining under these conditions, you convince me. You assure me that you know there is a truth somewhere waiting to be discovered. Please, therefore, read this paper.'

He passed over the letter which the former President of France had written privately to Sherlock Holmes, expressing his and his country's thanks for Holmes's part in the case of the assassin Huret.

Dreyfus read it, then looked up, puzzled.

'I do not understand. What has this to do with me, or you?'

'I am the letter's recipient. My name is Sherlock Holmes.'

'I . . . regret the name means nothing to me. This Huret case . . . I recall it. There was a Sûreté officer at the heart of it. I forget his name.'

'Dubuque. We worked together, in the closest trust and friendship. I am a private consulting detective, Captain, and prefer to remain beyond the limelight. The French Government retained my services in this Huret case when its own forces were at their wits' end. That I achieved some little success, that letter testifies. Before I came here I puzzled as to what message, or token, or sign I might bring which would convince you of my genuineness. A message from your brother or wife would scarcely have convinced you, even in their own hand.'

'You are right enough there. I doubt that I shall ever trust handwriting again after what has befallen me. I admit that I have even stooped to scrutinising my poor wife's letters, in case they are forged.'

'I am sorry to hear it. I could think of nothing other than that . . .' Holmes indicated the letter which Dreyfus still held . . . 'and this.' He opened his palm and disclosed the insignia of the Legion of Honour. 'Your brother argued to me of your honour, Captain, and I confess I believed it to be special pleading. But I have heard you upon the matter, and I am convinced. Now I show you the only proof I can offer of my own honour. Do not think that because it was bestowed by the then President that I remain in your country's employ. It was a mere incident in my career. I ask you to accept that I was approached by your brother to take your case, that I wavered, and then resolved to seek you out and judge you for myself, if that is not too fanciful a way of expressing it.'

Dreyfus reached out a bony hand to take the insignia and gaze at it in his palm. For the first time he smiled, although the bitterness in it was obvious.

'This is what my attorney told me I might receive upon the acquittal of which he was certain. I congratulate you, monsieur. You have fared somewhat better than I.'

With an abrupt movement he handed back both letter and insignia. He glanced out to sea and frowned.

'There is a storm coming. I must go back. They know I always hurry in before a storm, for fear of a soaking which will bring on the fever again.'

The wind was making a soughing sound amongst the rocks. Holmes could feel it beginning to gust about him. He wrapped the oilskin parcel again.

'You accept my word?' he urged. 'You believe that I am whom I say, and that I will act for you to the best of my ability?'

'I . . . believe so. I still do not understand how you came here . . . how you are prepared to accept a risk which might prove fatal to you, when those of my own countrymen who should be most concerned for me appear to be doing nothing.'

'I came,' Holmes answered, 'because my Queen requested it.'

'The Queen of England! But . . .'

'Queen Victoria, Kaiser Wilhelm of Germany . . . There are international implications. Do not think, Captain Dreyfus, in your loneliness and despair that you are a forgotten man. There are people who are more deeply troubled over you than you can imagine.'

Dreyfus's face gleamed even paler in the approaching gloom.

'I regret to be an embarrassment to anyone, Monsieur Holmes. Believe me, it has been none of my causing.'

'Then—whose, Captain?'

'Whoever wrote that document.'

'Forged it, do you mean?'

'*Wrote* it. Whether it was a deliberate forgery, or an accidental one which was imputed to me, somebody's hand held the pen. If it was a forger's, then—why? Why was it done, and why has a government, with all the means available, not found out?'

Dreyfus rose to his feet, the wind catching at the flaps of his jacket.

   'But if it was not a forgery, Monsieur Holmes, then there is a
traitor somewhere. Until that traitor is unmasked, I very much fear
that this will remain my lot. I thank you for coming. I will live with
new heart in the knowledge that someone is acting for me. I only hope
that the day will never come when I discover, at the bottom of the
well of despair and bitterness, that there is, after all, no waiting
draught of redemption for me to drink.'

   He turned to go, Holmes remaining on the ground out of sight.
Over his shoulder Dreyfus said, '*Bon voyage*. Please . . . convey to my
dear wife and brother my fondest love, and say you left me in good
heart.'

   He walked away; and his step was noticeably brisker than
Holmes had seen it before.

TEN

HOLMES crawled back to his hiding place. Now that he was alone he was aware again of the boom of the sea, of the rising wind and glooming sky. He wet a finger in his mouth and held it up. The wind was off-shore. A quick decision was necessary: either he should make his attempt to escape now, or be prepared to wait he knew not how long before the impending storm took to pass and there would come another favourable wind; that was, assuming that whatever the sea did in the meantime left his frail craft, his only means of escape, intact, or that he was not found by the guards.

He made up his mind to go while the odds were still in his favour.

He bundled his belongings together in the blanket, taking care to leave no trace of his having been there. It was easier to take everything down than it had been to bring it up. Inside a quarter of an hour he had everything stowed in the bobbing canoe and was untying the after rope.

The sea was livelier now, but its billows were long and rolling, the sort which, with luck, might be ridden, as opposed to the short, choppy sort of waves which would make the narrow craft impossible to control and soon tip it over. He employed the same technique getting out of the channel as he had entering it. With the bowline untied and sliding through his hand as the canoe floated backward from between the rocks he clambered in and seized the paddle. A wave came from behind, lifted and carried the canoe into the channel again, then surged back, bearing it with it, clear into the sea. In the trough left by the wave, Holmes paddled desperately on one side only, needing to turn the canoe completely round upon its axis in time to face directly the next wave. He just managed it, and moments later found himself riding high as the returning wave lifted the canoe bodily and urged it along.

Holmes put down the paddle and groped for the short mast and sail. He quickly had the mast stepped in its socket and the sail rigged, filling at once with the strong, steady wind and making a noticeable difference to the canoe's progress. It was round the tip of Devil's Island already, and in sight of Royale, but Holmes was less concerned about being observed than about the performance of his craft. The wind which in the lee of Devil's Island had seemed to be blowing from directly behind him, proved to be more abeam, slanting his craft away from the group of islands. He quickly lowered the sail, but it made little difference. Although he dipped his paddle deep and held it firm against the pressure of the sea, the canoe's bow would not turn.

The sea seemed to be rougher, now that he was further from any mass of land. The wind was whistling about his ears and dashing fine spray over him from the wavetops. Holmes cursed his folly. He had taken the wrong decision. He was being borne seaward, and night was not many hours off.

There was nothing he could do. Albert Gonselin had warned him that, in such an event, he must simply strive to keep the craft afloat and let it take him where it would. In those waters many things could happen. The sea and wind could change, or die down, as swiftly as they had risen. He might find it possible to set the sail again and fetch up somewhere on the South American coast, it would not initially matter where. He might even find himself in the British possession of Trinidad, where matters would be easiest of all for him.

The contrary alternatives did not bear thinking about: exhaustion, sunstroke, running out of water and food; or a capsize and the sharks.

He managed to erect the basketwork shelter and doubly ensure that his belongings were as safely stowed as he could make them. Then he settled himself grimly into the steering position, the paddle at the ready to dip at either side to keep the bow directly into the looming waves. Already he could feel the strain upon his muscles. The sea approached with almost hypnotic regularity, each wave a new challenge, and every seventh a dire threat.

Sherlock Holmes's mind was not on Alfred Dreyfus now. The sea and the wind monopolised it. He possessed physical strength considerably greater than the average man's; yet he knew that he was all but powerless in opposition to the mighty forces of Nature. It did not occur to him to pray. His belief in Providence at all times was that what must be, must be. He might survive the storm to reach safety, or perhaps to perish becalmed under pitiless sun. Nothing could avail him but to exert all his strength and determination for as long as he was able.

The sky was darkening ominously. The rising wind howled. The wavetops were jagged with white ridges of turbulence. The canoe bumped and lurched and the paddle no longer made any impression. There flashed into Holmes's mind a recollection of that sickening moment when he and Moriarty, wrestling one another for life or death, had lost their footing and plunged over the rim of the Reichenbach Falls to what had seemed certain doom. And as that recollection came to him, a greater wave than any lifted the bow of the canoe high into the air and hurled it back in a corkscrewing motion, spilling out its contents and its occupant . . .

'Great heavens, Holmes!' cried I, as he paused at this stage of his narrative to reach for a taper and relight his pipe. 'Here am I, trembling from head to toe, yet you sit there as calmly as if you had nothing more dramatic to recount than a row on Regent's Park lake. What miracle enabled you to survive?'

He returned me his whimsical smile, obviously enjoying my incredulity.

'Another day, perhaps?' he suggested, and moved as if to rise.

I shook a forefinger at him. 'Oh no you don't!' I warned. 'None of your Arabian Nights tricks on me, Holmes. I will have the rest of the story now.'

He sighed exaggeratedly and settled into his seat again.

'No miracle, I'm afraid. Simply, the timely arrival upon the scene of Albert Gonselin's fishing boat. Pray don't look so disbelieving, Watson. If you can adduce any alternative means by which I could possibly have been saved, your mind is even more fertile than I have yet acknowledged.'

'You mean to tell me that the course of his boat simply happened to coincide with the point where, at that precise moment, you were capsized?'

'Oh, it was somewhat less remarkable than that. As I discovered when they had got me aboard and restored to my full senses with the aid of blankets and *tafia*, they had been out fishing and were running for port to evade the coming storm. They had spotted the canoe, and knew almost certainly that none other than myself would be at sea in such a craft. At the risk of delaying fatally their own dash for safety they put about and chased after me.'

'And caught up with you just as you went over?'

'Not quite. I was some minutes in the sea. How many, I do not know, except that they felt more like hours. Naturally the canoe did not sink but remained tossing in the waves like the log it had once been. My rude ejection had fortunately not flung me too far from it to prevent my swimming the few strokes which enabled me to grasp it and hang on. It was in this state that the good Albert and his friends found me and were able to haul me aboard and press half the contents of the Caribbean out of my stomach.'

'Phew! All I can say, Holmes, is that if it was not a miracle in the fullest sense, it was as close to one as I shall ever hear related.'

'I must confess that, taking it and the Reichenbach incident together, I have had a generous share of the benignity of Providence. I very much fear that to hope to escape death against all the odds on any future occasion might be asking too much of Fate. That same law of averages which I have so often invoked in trapping an habitual criminal who, sooner or later, will make the error which will bring his downfall, can scarcely be expected to make an exception of me.'

'Well, if I had been inventing a yarn, I should have hesitated to save my hero in such a way. It would be expecting a great deal of the reader's indulgence.'

'My dear fellow, you know my view. Life is infinitely stranger than anything which the mind of man could invent. Besides, who knows, perhaps it was Dreyfus's share of the goodness of Providence which saved me.'

'Ah! Then you are taking his case?'

Instead of answering he clapped a hand to his stomach and cried, 'My word, foreign travel has left me with the deuce of an appetite! Pray summon up Mrs Hudson, and let us find out what is cold in the larder that is deserving of our attention.'

I touched the bell obediently. Mrs Hudson entered and, in

response to Holmes's winning plea, said that she might be able to 'find' a woodcock or something of that sort, although if he had only said at the time that our dinner, which had been of soup, sole, mutton, pudding, savoury, fruit and cheese, had been inadequate to his needs, she would have provided an extra course or two. She departed upon her search.

Holmes got up and went to the sideboard where a row of dusty bottles lay. He selected one and plied the corkscrew.

For the second time in my life I was experiencing the relief of seeing him back in the old surroundings, from which events might well have removed him for ever. His return this time has been less theatrical than that earlier one, after the three years' absence following the Reichenbach Falls incident, when he had come to me in disguise and caused me to faint for the first and only time in my life by revealing his identity in so dramatic a way. This time I had had telegraphed notice that he was returning from British Guiana, with no hint that he had endured any danger, let alone come within a fraction of losing his life.

Our curtains were drawn, for it was mid-evening, and the lamplight half-illumined our cosy, cluttered room, gleamed upon the brass fender-top and items of glassware, and animated the scattered photographs with its twinkling upon the silver decoration of their frames. Holmes's tall figure was distinctly leaner than I had last seen it, his features, when he turned, more hawk-like than ever. Yet his face and the backs of his hands wore a deep tan unusual to him, and he moved with that alertness which I had come to associate in him with enthusiasm and renewed interest in life.

He handed me a glass, and we raised our respective ones to each other. 'A pity not to serve so excellent a wine quite *chambré*,' he remarked, sniffing deeply into his glass, 'but I fancy it will serve our purpose.'

'So,' said I, 'having been so providentially picked up by your friends, what occurred then?'

'Eh? Oh, nothing of interest. They happened to have my convict outfit still aboard ...'

'"*Happened*"?'

'Why, yes. Fortunate, wasn't it? By the time we reached Royale Island, just ahead of the storm—and such a storm, Watson!—I was safe in my former identity as a *liberé* member of the crew. We had to lie there for a couple of days, which gave me ample time to sleep and recover my strength; then, under clear skies and burning sun, back to Cayenne, where I was successfully insinuated ashore in the dress and person of John James, journalist, just arrived back from Surinam to wind up my affairs in French Guiana, before returning to the British possession and thence home, full of respect for the administrative methods of French colonialism. And here you see me. Ah, Mrs Hudson! A Lucullan repast, to be sure!'

To my surprise, however, when the good woman had departed, Holmes made no move to tackle the game pie and cold woodcock with which we had been furnished. Instead, he returned to the sideboard and drew the cork from a second bottle which he had up-ended along with the first. He picked up a napkin and carefully wiped the neck clean, before replacing the bottle to stand there in the shadows from our lamp, surrounded by a gleam of glasses.

'Yes, Watson,' he said, with that way of his of returning suddenly and seemingly irrelevantly to something which had been broached earlier and brushed aside, 'I am taking Dreyfus's case. If the man is not innocent, then my name is Lestrade.'

'In that case, he's innocent for sure,' I chuckled. 'By the way, Inspector Lestrade has been round a couple of times in your absence.'

'Mm? The Yard out of their depth again?'

'He gave no particulars. I told him you were in Scotland and Ireland respectively. He seemed to accept it.'

'Good. No, I have seen Dreyfus for myself. I have looked into his eyes. I have witnessed the conditions in which he lives—exists, would be a better term—and I am convinced that no man who knew himself to be guilty, and who was offered a chance to escape such conditions, would have refused.'

'You offered to help him escape!'

'Merely to test his reaction. He declined, with dignity, without even enquiring the means at my disposal. That I had no means at all, he was not to know. It did not enter into it.'

'Was he able to give you any evidence to work upon?'

'Only that of his character—and his belief, which I accept.'

'Deep waters, then Holmes?'

'Deep and murky, Watson. We shall require all our powers to penetrate them.'

'In that case,' I said, with a meaning glance at the tempting tray upon the table, 'what is that saying of yours about renewing our energies before making a fresh call upon them?'

To my surprise, he shook his head. 'Patience, my dear fellow. The principal member of the feast is not yet here.'

'You are expecting a visitor?'

'Correct, my dear Watson. I am expecting Mathieu Dreyfus.'

Holmes drew the bulky watch from his waistcoat pocket under his dressing gown, flipped open the case and consulted the hands.

'I warned him to come by a most roundabout route, for fear of being followed. He has certainly taken me at my word.'

He explained further that he had telegraphed to Mathieu Dreyfus at the same time as he had notified me of his arrival at Liverpool, which had been his port of return. It occurred to me to wonder whether, in view of the circumstances under which Dreyfus had left us previously, he would accept the summons; but, sure enough, within another half hour he was seated again in the basket chair, sipping a glass of the *chambré* wine, which he courteously pronounced to be excellent, and accepting a plate of food which I had assembled for him at Holmes's request. Holmes himself declined to eat.

Mathieu Dreyfus's face was more deeply drawn, and he appeared to have aged out of proportion to the time elapsed since we had last seen him. His manner was stiff, and he confessed himself surprised to have been summoned by Holmes, but declared that he would do anything which might help his brother, and so had accepted. Holmes asked him whether there had been further developments in France of late.

Mathieu shrugged. 'Nothing positive, alas.'

'Positive or negative—anything at all?'

'Various attempts to persuade our family to accept this or that offer of help—documentary evidence in exchange for money. I have refused all. Anything which could genuinely help my brother would carry no price label upon it.'

'Quite so.'

'Besides which, I am certain that some of the offers have originated with the authorities. There have been suggestions that I should make accusations in the press against certain persons. I believe it is all a trap, in the hope of compromising us.'

'In what way?'

Mathieu Dreyfus answered bitterly, 'To alienate us further from our own people—the Jews. There are many Jews already who hope never to hear our name again. The feeling which has been stirred up against our family has been magnified by certain newspapers and directed against the Jewish people in general. The "crime" of Alfred Dreyfus is seen as symbolic of their aspiration to bring down the French constitution and acquire control themselves. No, Mr Holmes. Alfred is no martyr, in the eyes of many of those Jews who should be employing their money and influence to clear his name. He is an embarrassment, a nuisance.'

I put in, 'I understood that the French newspapers were prohibited entirely from discussing the affair.'

'That is so. But there are hints, innuendos: what I believe is termed "trailing the coat", hoping to provoke us into blind charges which can be skilfully deflected, leaving us stranded and foolish. No, Doctor, however much we are provoked, overtly or covertly, I am convinced that we must avoid playing into their hands by causing trouble until we have concrete evidence as our weapon.'

'You are quite right,' Holmes remarked. 'On no account do anything which will attract attention to you. You must preserve the utmost freedom of movement for when it is needed.'

Our visitor stared openly at Holmes, his fork motionless above his plate.

'You ... are prepared to help us, Mr Holmes?' he asked, on the edge of incredulity.

'I have given the matter much thought. There are elements in it which I cannot reconcile with absolute truth and justice. That there has been misapplication of the law, in so grave and notable a case, is quite astonishing. Even if we accept that this mysterious conclusive evidence against your brother was so secret that it could not be produced in court, that does not satisfy the question as to why it could not even be shown to the defence attorney, Demange. Is the implication that he, too, is not to be trusted? Whatever its dilemma, the clear course for the court should have been to give your brother at least the benefit that, having been disallowed from making a full defence, he should be sentenced much less honorously than has been the case. Either that, or a subsequent appeal might have been quietly allowed, and with the glare of publicity removed from him he could have been permitted to take up his exile in some more bearable place, where his wife and children could have joined him, yet where he would still have been under any restraint deemed necessary. Instead, he is kept in those fearful conditions under the closest watch. What is it they fear of him, Monsieur Dreyfus?'

'That he will get free to find out the truth.'

'Precisely! And what is that truth? That he has been conspired against by means of a forgery and the corrupt manipulation of the law; or that there has been real treachery done, which has been imputed to him either in error or deliberately. An extension of this question leads us inevitably to ask, if this was deliberate, was it in order to ruin him, for whatever motive? or to conceal the real traitor's identity? The addendum to each of those questions must be, why?'

Dreyfus pushed his plate away, his eyes flashing.

'Mr Holmes, I could have put those hypotheses to you before now. It does not require a mind so famed as yours to arrive at them. I can only wonder that you did not do so sooner.'

'Because,' Holmes answered quietly, 'I had not met your brother. Until I had done so, I could not be sure that this was not a perfectly simple case of genuine guilt, proven albeit in a somewhat questionable fashion. My friend here will tell you my principal maxim—that when you have eliminated the impossible, whatever remains, however improbable, must be the truth. Having now met and talked with your brother, I am assured by all my instincts, all my knowledge, all my accumulated experience, that the impossible, in his case, is that he is guilty as charged.'

Our visitor's eyes bulged so much that they seemed likely to pop out of their sockets. The fork he held clattered loudly against his plate, so violently did he tremble. He had to put it down.

'You have . . . met my brother!'

'He sends his most affectionate greetings to yourself and to Madame Dreyfus and their children.'

Holmes went on to describe the meeting, although declining to say how it had been accomplished. Mathieu's mouth tightened when Holmes told him of his brother's weakened appearance and grim mode of life.

'At least,' Holmes concluded, 'I fancy I left him in better heart than I found him. He seemed almost on the verge of abandoning hope.'

'I am deeply grateful, Mr Holmes. If you will be good enough to give me particulars of your fees and the expenses you have incurred ...'

Holmes waved the matter aside.

'I did not go at your request. I went out of service to a gracious lady whom it is my loyal duty to obey.'

Dreyfus stared again. 'You ... you do not mean ...?'

'Her Majesty Queen Victoria.' Holmes quickly sketched his interview with the Queen.

'This is formidable news!' the other cried. 'I myself addressed an appeal to the Kaiser, as well as to many of our own high politicians. He did not respond, and the best any of the others would offer was polite sympathy with my brother's family, though none for him. I sense that all believe him guilty.' Mathieu Dreyfus's brief moment of delight and hope had passed. He set his plate of half-finished viands aside, unable to manage more. 'What can we possibly do?'

'We must turn to that useful institution, the Fourth Estate.'

'The press? But I tell you, they will do nothing to help. Since the degradation there has been a void around our family which none will enter.'

'Exactly,' Holmes agreed. 'That is why it is essential to bring the case back into full public discussion. The longer it is left under a covering of silence, the greater the danger that its details will blur and passions cool. Now, the press is a most valuable institution, if you only know how to use it. If your French press will not respond voluntarily, we must force it.'

'But how?'

'By providing it with an item of news which it cannot ignore. I refer, of course, to the recent rescue of your brother from Devil's Island.'

This time the Frenchman's look of surprise was so extreme as almost to be comical. I should not be surprised if my own had appeared equally grotesque to Holmes, who sat there watching the two of us, an enigmatic smile on his lips and his fingers fanned out, their tips pressed tightly together beneath his chin.

'Holmes . . .!' I began to expostulate, but words completely failed me.

'Yes,' he went on coolly. 'Got clean away in an American schooner with Madame Dreyfus aboard. They had several days' start before news even reached Cayenne. By now, they could be anywhere.'

Dreyfus looked at me, as if to enquire whether Holmes was subject to sudden brainstorms, of which this was one. Then he replied slowly to Holmes, humouring a supposed idiot's fancy: 'I was with Lucie at St-Cloud only the day before yesterday. She has never set foot out of France.'

Holmes nodded. 'For that reason, it would be futile for us to release our news just yet. Those who keep watch on her would know instantly that it was untrue. However, if you can contrive to get Madame Dreyfus into total concealment for a week or two, any report that she is out of the country will appear plausible. Of course, it is not absolutely necessary to involve her in our charade at all, but it will add what will seem a strong corroborative factor. A mere report of the escape would be too bald. It could be immediately denied, while an investigation into it were swiftly conducted.'

I could not prevent myself beginning to chuckle. Holmes flapped a languid hand in my direction.

'You see, Monsieur Dreyfus? My friend here has had more experience of the method behind what you clearly believe to be my madness. Pray explain, Watson.'

'If I read you aright, Holmes, it is this. A report of the escape of this celebrated prisoner from this most notorious of penal settlements is certain to cause a furore. Even the French press would feel justified in breaking the silence imposed upon it by the government. At once, the name of Dreyfus would again be on every tongue. The case would become the cynosure of all attention.'

'Capital, Watson! And, who knows, the belief that Alfred Dreyfus is at large to speak out might well flush from cover the true traitor, if such there be, or cause such panic amongst those who have conspired that each will prepare to save his own skin at the cost of his fellows'. In short, the truth might be precipitated.'

Hope and amazement had returned to Mathieu Dreyfus's eyes. He leaped from his chair and strode to where Holmes lounged, to grasp one of his hands between both of his, wringing it heartily.

'Now I know why your reputation stands so high, Mr Holmes. You can not only deduce situations, but can also manipulate them.'

'It is an adjunct to detective investigation which most of its practitioners neglect. To be at the mercy of events is to lose the initiative and remain forever a step behind them, which is a capital disadvantage. My preference is to lead the way and let circumstances catch up, so that I may ambush them when I am ready.'

'Well, well, well!' Dreyfus laughed, returning to his own chair, though pausing in his delight to shake hands with me, too. 'I have been privileged to witness the great mind in action after all!'

'I must warn you,' Holmes told him gravely, 'that the hoax might bring some reprisals from the authorities. Your family must be prepared for recriminations and even some form of persecution. From all you tell me, the Jewish people might not prove too grateful if it provokes a renewal of the vilification of them.'

'No matter!' Dreyfus exclaimed almost airily. 'The main object will have been achieved.'

'We hope so, at least. It could misfire, in which case I have at present no alternative plan to offer.'

The other frowned as a thought occurred to him. 'My brother . . . What action do you suppose might be taken against him as a consequence?'

'I have to say candidly that it will certainly not ease his situation in the short term.'

'But Holmes,' I objected, 'he will be entirely innocent of any complicity in your scheme.'

'Nevertheless, he is at the centre of it.'

'You don't say that they would do anything dire to him?'

'I fancy not. It would be too obvious to the watching world, and there would be an outcry. No, I envisage, perhaps, closer surveillance, less freedom of movement on the island, for fear of any real attempt resulting. Harsher living conditions, even. But I have met Alfred Dreyfus, and heard him. I believe he is the type of man who will bear it with the fortitude which has sustained him so far. He knows now that independent persons are actively engaged on his behalf. He has that feeling of hope which is vital to the endurance of any ordeal.'

'Well said, Mr Holmes!' cried our visitor. 'When at length he learns that he had been subjected to new harshness as part of your endeavours to clear his name, my brother will assure you that he would have been prepared to suffer far worse in order to regain the honour which he prizes above all things. But now, please, relate in detail what you propose to do, and what precise roles I and Lucie must play.'

Holmes stiffened from his languid attitude and stood up to adopt that pose, back to fire and legs apart, which I associated with him in expository mood.

'The first step must be as follows ...' he commenced.

ELEVEN

HAS DREYFUS ESCAPED?

STORY HOW AUTHORITIES WERE OUTWITTED.

Captain Hunter, of the steamship Nonpareil, recently arrived at Newport (Mon.), tells a remarkable story (says the *South Wales Argus*), amounting to nothing less than that Captain Dreyfus has escaped from the penal settlement to which he was condemned for life. It appears that when the Nonpareil was loading rock phosphate at Connetable Island, about forty miles from Cayenne, Captain Hunter was told that Captain Dreyfus had escaped from Grand Salute, which is a small island some miles away from Cayenne, both of which are used as French penal settlements. At the urgent entreaty of the prisoner the French Government had given permission for his wife to join him, and in due course she arrived in Cayenne.

The only means of communication between Grand Salute and Cayenne is a French Government cutter, which runs at intervals. Soon after the lady's arrival she was invited to go to her husband on board this vessel. She declined, stating that as there was no doctor on the island she would remain in Cayenne until she had become somewhat acclimatised. While in Cayenne she was evidently well supplied with money. Some time after the cutter went out to Grand Salute, arriving about four in the afternoon. After receiving reports and giving instructions it sailed away. The same night at ten o'clock an American schooner, with Madame Dreyfus aboard, sent a boat ashore, and brought off not only Captain Dreyfus, but several of his guards. The schooner sailed away and nothing further was heard of them. The time for the rescue was admirably fixed. The Government cutter only visits Grand Salute at intervals. There are no other means of communication with Cayenne, and as the schooner picked up Captain Dreyfus a few hours after the cutter left, it would be days before the Governor of Cayenne could learn that his prisoner had escaped. The schooner therefore had several days' start. Of course, an attempt has been made to hush up the affair officially, but the news leaked out, and reached Connetable Island, which place Captain Hunter left three weeks ago. Captain Hunter's third officer confirms the story.

THUS, on September 3, 1896, appeared in the London Daily Chronicle the account of Alfred Dreyfus's 'escape'. It had not, as it stated, originated in an earlier report in the South Wales Argus. Holmes would never be quite specific as to the details, even to me; but it was transmitted by him, late on the evening of the 2nd, to a member of the Daily Chronicle's staff who owed him a profound favour for a reason of which Holmes would tell me no more than that the danger of prosecution which hung over the man's head could have become reality had Holmes chosen to pass a message containing only three words to Inspector Lestrade of Scotland Yard. This unnamed journalist—evidently a man in high authority—hurried down to the printing floor and ordered the item to be set up in the edition about to go to press. By the time anyone else in the building could ask any questions about it, it was already on the streets of London. The following day the news was the talk of Paris through the pages of the sensationalist newspaper *La Libre Parole*.

That this scurrilous rag should have been so quickly on to the story was, however, no chance happening. Since the student of Sherlock Holmes's methods is certain to find some points of interest in the chain of events, I will retrace it, first returning to the interrupted conversation with Mathieu Dreyfus in our sitting-room at 221B Baker Street.

Holmes had reiterated his instruction to Dreyfus that he must conceal his brother's wife for at least two weeks before the planned date of the journalistic *coup*, in order to lead watchers of her villa to believe that she might be absent. But there was a preceding duty to be carried out before Mathieu Dreyfus left London.

'I fancy the name Adolphe Meyer will mean nothing to you?' Holmes asked Dreyfus, who wrinkled his brow, shaking his head slowly. 'No, of course. There is no reason why it should. Remember the fellow, Watson?'

'Wasn't that one of the freelance spies whose name you considered in connection with the Bruce-Partington case?'

'The same. Meyer, Monsieur Dreyfus, is one of those unsavoury characters whose presence is unwelcome in any capital, but which must be tolerated against the day when he might prove useful to his hosts. He will spy for whomever pays him best. His loyalties fluctuate accordingly, with the consequence that he comes to know a little of the confidences of all the chief powers and many minor ones, yet never enough to be of acute danger to any of them. His chief nuisance value is that many hours of the authorities' time is wasted in keeping him under observation whenever he makes a move, in case he is up to something which will need to be known.'

'I wonder they don't send him packing. His name has a very German ring to me.'

'He has committed no known act prejudicial to the realm. I expect it is preferred to have him where he can be kept in sight, rather than invisible. Besides, there are slight hopes that, sooner or later, he will lead the way to the headquarters of a suspected Anarchist organisation in the East End. As to his being a German, it is a case of "There but for the grace of God went Mathieu Dreyfus".'

'I do not follow.'

'He is a native of your own province of Alsace-Lorraine. When the partition occurred he was one of those who made the choice of German nationality. Following this, I understand, he became more Germanic than any German, and only conceals his hatred of the French when he is in that country's employ.'

'That is typical of such people. His name also has a Jewish sound to it, though.'

'You are correct. He is of Jewish origins, but his scruples are not such as would prevent him from helping to ferment the anti-Semitic reaction in France, if it were worth his while to do so. It leads me to believe that this is a man who, with the inducement of a tidy sum of money, will seize upon a chance to embarrass the French government and will not hesitate to do it by means of renewing the dispute between those who sympathise with Alfred Dreyfus and those whose hostility to him owes much to religious prejudice. You will almost certainly find him ready to co-operate with you.'

'With me? But I should not wish to do anything which might harm the interest of my fellow Jews.'

'I had not overlooked that certainty. I put it to you, though, that your brother's case is paramount. He is helpless. The Jews as a whole, on the other hand, are capable of defending themselves.'

'Well, that is so. Then, how do you propose to involve this Meyer?'

'As a channel of communication, nothing more. The false item about the attempted escape will certainly be picked up by the French press. It is essential, though, that it be followed up by an amplified version of an even more sensational nature which can be splashed triumphantly and exclusively where its impact will be most influential in stirring up a din. So, before you leave London, I wish you to go to Adolphe Meyer—his address is 13 Great George Street, Westminster—and give him this further despatch which I have prepared.'

Holmes produced several sheets of notepaper from the folder from which he had earlier drawn that bearing the text of the supposed rescue attempt. He passed them to Mathieu Dreyfus, who glanced over them briskly, with my gaze over his shoulder. The article was in the form of an 'interview' with the non-existent Captain Hunter of the mythical steamer 'Nonpareil'.

Dreyfus began to chuckle over it. He raised his eyes to my friend.

'The literary profession has missed a formidable practitioner in you, Mr Holmes.'

'A humble amateur in comparison with my friend,' Holmes laughed, indicating me. 'However, you get my gist?'

'Indeed. Captain Hunter asserts that he was approached by the dreaded Syndicate of international Jewry and paid to take Lucie in his ship, rescue Fred, kidnap his guards so that there would be considerable delay in raising the alarm, and spirit them all away to some undisclosed haven. It is a brilliant conception of yours. But why must we deal through Meyer?'

'Obviously, you yourself cannot simply walk into some newspaper office bearing this in your hand, and I do not wish to be seen to be involved at all. But Meyer—how much money you give him I will leave to your skilled commercial instinct—I fancy he will find the combination of payment and a chance to throw the French authorities into disarray irresistible. He will be accepted as a plausible source of the story—a known opportunist who has had the enterprise to hurry to Newport and obtain this exclusive interview with the captain. He will not only be paid by you, but generously by the editor to whom he sells so choice an item.'

'But surely,' said I, 'it will take a matter of no more than hours for the authorities to give the lie to the whole story? This sequel will be dead before it can be printed.'

'Not if the editor in question acts quickly enough.'

'Even so, he will have to follow it with a repudiation and an apology. He will be in bad odour with the authorities. Where do you hope to find an editor of a prominent newspaper who will not first seek confirmation of the facts before risking going into print?'

'I know precisely where to find him,' Holmes smiled. 'His newspaper is called *La Libre Parole*, and his name is Edouard Drumont.'

'*Ah!*' Mathieu Dreyfus's exclamation startled me by its sharpness. His eyes were shining and he slapped his free palm upon his knee. 'Mr Holmes, you excel yourself!'

'That is most complimentary of you, monsieur.'

'Not at all. Not at all.' Dreyfus turned to me. 'You appear mystified, Doctor. You do not know of Drumont and his rag?'

'I have heard of neither, I'm afraid.'

'Then allow me to inform you. Drumont is the chief spokesman for the anti-Semites in my country. A few years ago he wrote a scurrilous book, "*La France Juive*—Jewish France". By distorting fact and twisting evidence to suit his argument, he set out to demonstrate that the Jews are the greatest threat to French traditions and institutions. He branded them unscrupulous, greedy, devious, untrustworthy—anything at all which might discredit their character, their motives, their patriotism. Unfortunately, the work proved an instant success. It sold in great numbers, not only in France, and had a profound effect upon public feeling. It certainly prepared the way for the formation of the National Anti-Semitic League.

'Then Drumont founded his newspaper, *La Libre Parole*—Free Speech. It, too, has proved highly popular through its flamboyant style and its sensational treatment of controversial issues, especially those which can be fashioned in any way to be detrimental to the Jews. It was this paper which printed the series of articles revealing so-called Jewish plans to infiltrate the General Staff of the Army, as a first step towards gaining controlling influence over finance and industry. It was the first to name my brother after his arrest, naturally with the tag of 'Jew' prominently attached to his name. When his trial was impending, it told its readers that he would not be convicted, because, it hinted, the War Minister and the Foreign Minister were already in the power of the Jews and would quietly ensure his acquittal.'

'Monstrous!' I exclaimed. 'The worst excesses of the gutter press.'

'But an interesting point,' remarked Holmes, who had been listening thoughtfully. 'The suspicion which such a hint would implant in many minds would be that there would be other officers and politicians under the Jewish thumb. A natural reaction to that on the part of those of them who feared that they, too, might be named, however much they knew themselves to be innocent, would be to demonstrate their freedom from any such influence by taking a public stance against any Jew involved in controversy. Alfred Dreyfus is a case in point—perhaps *the* case. By siding themselves with those who were against him, these officers and Ministers could show off their independence and at the same time offer renewed proof of their loyalty to their country's best interests.'

I said, amazed, 'You suggest that the court martial reached its verdict from such motives?'

'It is possible, now that I come to consider it. The verdict went against all the visible evidence, for no other reason which I have been able to deduce. Extraordinary pains have been taken to isolate Dreyfus since and to ensure that his case is not ventilated further.'

'But that professional officers should sacrifice one of their comrades for such reasons . . .!'

'If they had found him not guilty, what do you suppose their treatment would have been at the hands of *La Libre Parole* and others like that? They would have been crucified.'

I had to concede as much, abhorrent though it was to all my instincts, both as a former military man and as one who has always valued integrity amongst the highest qualities desirable in anyone put, however briefly, into a place of influence. I could see now what conflict between justice and expediency might have raged in the minds of the officers of the court and the witnesses who had been called before them. I sought consolation in the belief that such a situation could never occur in the British Army, but restrained myself from saying this aloud, out of respect for our French visitor's feelings.

We had all remained silent for some minutes, each examining these implications in his mind. At length Holmes said, 'So you see, Watson, there is all the more necessity to re-open discussion of the case in as spectacular a manner as possible, and Edouard Drumont is the ideal mouthpiece for us to use. Depend upon it, he will not check the veracity of the Captain Hunter interview. He will most likely suspect it, but it will seem to him like a gift from the gods. It will make him all the more in a hurry to get it on to his most prominent page and into the hands of half of Paris before the authorities can deny it and deprive him of a splendid chance to show the long-feared Jewish Syndicate at its fell work.'

'I agree with you,' Dreyfus declared. 'I will go to this Meyer at once ...'

'But arrange a date not less than, say, three weeks hence. You must have time to make Madame Dreyfus "disappear" first. Inform me as to that date, so that I may arrange the publication in London of the initial despatch accordingly.'

'I understand.'

'And do not pay Meyer more than a fraction in advance. Conceal the precise nature of the matter until the time comes to pass this article through his hands, or he might well betray you for a higher amount.'

'My intention entirely. Fortunately my family is wealthy enough to be able to accommodate him upon a scale which, from the sound of him, he will find it against his nature to decline. Our wealth is one of those factors which have been adduced against us by our own kind. "They are rich," it is said. "They are troublesome. Well, they can afford to buy their way out of difficulty." It comes home to me how it must be to be without money and influence in the face of the forces of prejudice and oppression. Dear me, how one takes the lives of others for granted!'

'Amen to that,' said I.

Thus it came about that the news item which I reproduce at the head of this present chapter came to appear in the Daily Chronicle. That Adolphe Meyer had faithfully and successfully fulfilled his part of the bargain which Mathieu Dreyfus had succeeded in negotiating with him before hurrying back to France was confirmed by a telegram. It arrived from Paris on the same day as the Daily Chronicle's piece appeared, addressed to me, no doubt for security's sake. It read, 'Fishing excellent. Superb catch.' There was no signature.

'Our client has succeeded in his little task,' remarked Holmes, tossing the telegraph form back to me. 'If anyone comes asking for me, I am not at home. Any sort of development could occur, and I wish to be free to meet it.'

The development which did occur, however, was of a sort which neither of us could for one moment have foreseen. It was the arrival of a message, brought by hand of a man of whom Holmes had remarked, chancing to observe his approach along Baker Street as he was staring moodily out of the window, that he was a former navy man, of Petty Officer rank and not less but no more than twenty years' service, following which he had been discharged due to a chronic ailment of an internal organ, most likely the trachea; who possessed a wife and three grown-up daughters in Brixton, but hailed originally from Yorkshire, most likely somewhere along the line of the West and North Ridings of that county. He was clearly in the employ of some government department in Whitehall, though he wore no uniform; and he was in the habit of visiting a public house in St James's Street on Saturday evenings. Other than that, he could tell me nothing of the fellow; and that I omitted to ask him how he had deduced all this was only due to the nature of the contents of the note conveyed upstairs by Mrs Hudson, who reported that she had told its bearer that the recipient was not at home, upon which he had departed, apparently convinced.*

Holmes ripped open the plain white envelope and scanned the single sheet it contained. He passed it to me without a word. It read, in a hand which was disciplined rather than artistic:

'*Diogenes Club at three p.m., if you please.*
Yours,
MYCROFT
P.S. I know you are at home. Do not fail to come.'

There was of course, no mistaking the sender. Sherlock Holmes's

---

*When, in due course, I remembered to ask Holmes how he had summed up so much of the man at a glance, he replied offhandedly that he had been acquainted with him for years!— J.H.W.

elder brother Mycroft was the only person in the world, to my knowledge, possessing that singular Christian name. The Diogenes Club, in Pall Mall, of which he had been a founder member, was his most public place of business. The precise location of his official office in Whitehall was unknown even to Holmes. His brother was never seen anywhere, save at the Diogenes; and that, being renowned as the most unsociable club for unclubbable types of men in London, meant that his acquaintance was strictly limited.

Mycroft Holmes's ostensible position was as a 'government accountant and inter-departmental adviser', at a salary of four hundred and fifty pounds a year; yet I was aware, from his authoritative manner in connection with the cases of 'The Greek Interpreter', in 1888, and more recently that of the Bruce-Partington Plans, that his burly shoulders bore far greater responsibility than those vague titles suggested. His present summons to Holmes, who had never been a man to accept instruction from anybody lower in rank than his Queen, rang with an impressive quality of command. I glanced up from it.

'You will go?'

'I believe I might,' answered Holmes, affecting casualness. 'Perhaps you would care to accompany me?'

'I am not comm ... asked,' I pointed out.

'Never mind. Mycroft knows that your assistance is indispensable to me. Besides, in dealing with my brother, I regret to have to admit that I feel more comfortable with a witness present.'

At precisely two minutes to three we alighted from a hansom-cab outside the looming premises of the Diogenes Club. They were unmarked by any sign, and the uniformed old porter who occupied the hooded, leather-covered chair in the lobby never spoke until addressed, even by persons he knew well. At our entrance, he rose to his feet and regarded us with that baleful stare which had in its time caused men who had fought gallantly for their country at the far ends of the earth to turn and go silently, leaving their appointments upon the club's premises unkept.

Holmes was not to be cowed, however. 'Our appointment is with Mr Mycroft Holmes,' he announced. 'Mr Holmes and Dr Watson.'

'This way, gentlemen,' commanded the servitor. 'The rule is, no speaking whilst passing through the premises.'

He turned his military back and marched off. Holmes winked broadly at me. We were already acquainted with the condition of membership of the Diogenes Club, that no conversation was permitted anywhere except in the Strangers' Room, towards which we were now being conducted. The long passage was partially bordered on one side by glass panelling, which gave on to a spacious, tall room, whose elegant decoration seemed to me wasted upon the men with misanthropic countenances who sat in it, reading newspapers or staring into space, each in his own nook like monks of some silent order in their stalls.

The Strangers' Room was a much smaller chamber. Its only occupant, standing beside the window, gazing down into Pall Mall, was Mycroft Holmes.

I knew him to be seven years older than his brother, which put him at this time on the borderline of the fifties. He was stout to the point of corpulence, with massive features and a heavy jowl, which contrasted completely with my friend's spare frame. But there was that in his face, especially the light in the watery grey eyes, which preserved a family likeness.

He did not smile or come forward to shake hands; in fact, I believed I noticed a brief frown of disapproval at sight of me.

'Well, Mycroft,' greeted my friend cheerfully when the porter had left us in privacy, 'to what do we owe your hospitality in these scintillating surroundings?'

His brother's lips turned down at their corners into a positive scowl. He pointed silently to a newspaper lying open upon the green chenille cloth draping the table.

Holmes and I drew closer. The newspaper was folded in such a way that its title was not visible, but I recognised it instantly, having already scanned a copy keenly only that same morning. Holmes, however, put on one of those impish displays of pretence which he found impossible to resist in the face of unmistakable censure.

'Don't tell me,' said he. 'I am thinking of writing a little monograph upon the detection of typefaces, which is a necessary adjunct to the knowledge of every criminal investigator, and I seize every opportunity to practise my own. That, unless I am grossly mistaken, must be—the Daily Chronicle.'

He reached out a hand, as if to turn over the paper and verify his conclusion. His brother snatched the newspaper petulantly up and shook it noisily in his face.

'Spare me your parlour tricks, Sherlock,' he almost snarled. 'You know perfectly well what paper it is, and what it contains.'

'Really? *Are* we in the habit of taking the Daily Chronicle, Watson?'

I almost expected to witness what would have been the extraordinary sight of Mycroft Holmes dancing with rage. He threw the newspaper down again and pointed to it dramatically.

'You and your confounded meddling!' he shouted at his brother. '"Captain Hunter", indeed! If you had signed your name to the item it would not have been more obvious to me than that it was your work.'

Holmes made no retort. It was plain to me that, despite the pretence of surprise which he maintained, he had been genuinely taken aback by his brother's knowledge of his connection with the newspaper item. He had once told me that behind Mycroft's almost bovine appearance and generally lethargic manner lay an intellect which, in its ability to observe and deduce, was superior even to his own, but that its possessor had neither the ambition nor the energy to become, as he might have done, the greatest criminal agent the world had ever seen. Yet I could not fathom how observation and deduction alone could have shown him that it was my friend who had composed and engineered the printing of the false news item.

Mycroft turned his glare upon me. 'Well, Doctor?' he demanded. 'If my brother is determined to keep up his pose of ignorance, I must turn to his henchman for an explanation, if you please.'

'Hmph!' said I, desperately glancing to Holmes. 'Ha, ha! Er ...'

Mycroft Holmes regarded me with disgust. There came a tap at the door.

'At last,' he said, moving to answer it, 'we can put an end to this pantomime ... Ah, come in.'

The man who had been escorted to the door by the porter was middle-aged and scrawny, with hollow cheeks and eyes and an unhealthy pallor. His outmoded suit hung baggily upon his angular frame, and his shirt collar was a size or two too large. He was unknown to me, but a gasp at my side told me that my friend had recognised him instantly and been taken completely aback.

'*Bonjour, Monsieur James!*' the newcomer cried cheerily, advancing briskly to shake his hand warmly. '*Ça va?*'

I doubt if I had ever seen Holmes more openly nonplussed. His brother was watching him with wicked delight, grinning maliciously as he addressed me: 'Allow me to introduce Monsieur Albert Gonselin, from Cayenne.'

It was my turn to gape. The stranger greeted me civilly and shook my unresisting hand.

Mycroft explained to Holmes, 'Gonselin chanced to be in London on some business, and I asked him to step across. I have no time to waste upon playing your game with you, James. I anticipated that you would have nothing to tell me, so I felt it more direct to let you see proof that I know exactly what you have been doing.'

'Dear me!' my friend said at last. '*Touché* to you, *Mr Holmes*. I must have left my sixth sense behind in London. How are you, Albert?'

'Well, thank you, Monsieur James,' replied Gonselin. He had either not been told our true identity, or was concealing that he had. 'A fish out of water, however.' He indicated his clumsy clothing. 'It is so long since I last dressed for civilisation that I had not realised how much weight I had shed in between. I must accept that my place is in the colony for good.'

'So you are just passing through "on business", eh?'

'That is so,' replied the other, his eyes twinkling.

'Well, I had better not enquire what it is, if it is anything connected with this gentleman here.'

'No, you had not, Mr James, 'Mycroft interrupted quickly. 'I did not invite Gonselin here to supply the deficiencies of the press. It was simply to cut short your evasiveness and enable us to proceed to some plain talking. Thank you, Gonselin, that will be all. The packet will reach you at your hotel by this evening.'

'Thank you, monsieur. And you, Monsieur James, for your bank draft. It was much appreciated. Good-day, gentlemen. Perhaps we shall meet again?'

He shook all three of us by the hand and departed. I noticed the porter hovering near to the door, waiting to escort him. Mycroft

Holmes had planned the interview very carefully, and had gained a well-earned success.

'Now then, Sherlock,' he said, when the door was closed, 'let us have no more shilly-shallying, if you please. I know all. My only regret, and it is a bitter one, is that I did not intervene before your meddling could result in this.' He indicated the crumpled newspaper again. 'I was certain that, sooner or later, you would go into action, but I had no means of knowing what form it would take. I summoned Gonselin from Cayenne to demonstrate to you the extent to which your movements have been observed, after which I intended to warn you off the course. Unfortunately, his arrival came just too late. I need hardly add that the gist of the so-called interview which has appeared in this morning's *Libre Parole* has been telegraphed to me. It is utterly irresponsible of you, Sherlock. Men have gone to the Tower for less.'

My friend laughed and took a chair.

'Oh, come now, my dear chap! There is no need to exaggerate the position. But I am all curiosity. How came you to get upon my track?'

'Through Gonselin, of course. He is a dedicated fellow, but I fear that climate will be the death of him before long.'

'He is not a *libéré*, then, but one of your fellows?'

'He is both. Our former man there marked him down as a person of resource and intelligence, whose crime had been a simple act of passion and not the product of any perversity of mind which might make him devious to deal with. Our man's health could stand no more of the climate—he died a few weeks ago at Woking—and it was vital to establish continuity. Gonselin was resigned to living out the rest of his days there, and he was glad to accept recruitment and the modest stipend which it brought.'

'You mean to tell me that her Majesty's Government finds it necessary to station an agent in Cayenne?'

'It is a very low-grade posting. That is, it was until Dreyfus arrived in the islands. Who knows now when the colony might become the centre of some dramatic development? Why did you go there, Sherlock?'

The direct question was put casually, but Holmes was watchful enough by now to have an answer ready.

'To see him,' he replied simply.

'And to seek his co-operation in an attempt to rescue him?'

'Certainly not.'

'I am inclined to believe you.'

'*Thank* you, Brother.'

'I considered it inevitable that, following your usual method, you would seek a face-to-face interview, in order to assess his character for yourself. I was only surprised that you hesitated so long before going.'

'What made you imagine that I should have the slightest interest in him?'

'His brother's visit to you, of course. Our people in Paris assure me that Mathieu Dreyfus is determined to move heaven and earth to try to establish his brother's innocence. He is a man of acute intelligence and the family has considerable means. Sooner or later, he would certainly approach the Great Detective for help. His was an eleven o'clock appointment, was it not?'

'I give you credit for thoroughness,' Holmes laughed. 'Dear me, though? Are we to take it, Watson, that our humble abode is subject to constant surveillance by agents of Whitehall? We should take that exceedingly amiss, should we not?'

'Indeed,' I supported him, addressing Mycroft. 'There are no more loyal subjects than your brother and myself, Mr Holmes.'

'Oh, indeed, Dr Watson. Your door and yourselves are not the objects of attention, believe me: just occasional persons who come there. From reports of the movements they make subsequently I am able to assess pretty well the nature of the advice Sherlock has given them, and to anticipate their intentions.'

'You appear to have kept a close watch on me after Dreyfus's visit,' objected Holmes. 'It was weeks before I went to the Guianas.'

'It was not until Gonselin reported the arrival of a journalist fellow asking questions about the penal settlements in general, and Dreyfus in particular, that I decided to order one of my periodical routine reports upon you, Sherlock. I learned that you had not been seen for weeks, and that Inspector Lestrade had twice been turned from your door by Dr Watson in person with the story that you were in Scotland, or Ireland, or somewhere. Once away on your own might have been acceptable, however unlikely. Twice was positively suspicious. I made enquiries and discovered that you had been seen nowhere. There was no lengthy official investigation in progress with which you were associated. It was simple deduction that you were engaged in some clandestine affair and using your friend to cover your tracks from enquirers. The visit of Mathieu Dreyfus some time before, coupled with Gonselin's report of the inquisitive newsmonger from London, gave me my answer. Your return, somewhat emaciated and with certain areas of your skin heavily tanned by the sun, brought confirmation.'

'Bravo! I trust that when next the government is pleading lack of funds to spend where they are really needed, someone will query the wasted cost of keeping observation upon one who has never deviated from his service to his country and the Crown.'

'Hear, hear!' I was impelled to cry. Mycroft Holmes cast me a bleak glance, then turned back to his brother.

'You should be grateful for my attention to your welfare. Without it, you would have been a dead man by now.'

'Eh? From what cause?'

'Drowning—or exposure. Your canoe was drifting hopelessly away from land into a storm it could not possibly have survived. Gonselin and his crew fished you out in the nick of time.'

'What had that fortunate encounter to do with you, pray?'

' "Fortunate encounter"! They had been waiting for you to leave the island ever since you set foot on it. It was my express order that, unless absolutely forced by the weather or danger of discovery by the authorities, they were to keep constant watch for you.'

'I never saw them!'

'That is because you did not expect to. I admit that had the storm arrived sooner they might have fled back to Royale Island before you made your escape, in which case you would have perished. But only to that extent was there any coincidence in their being at hand to save you.'

'Well, then, it seems I have to thank you for your solicitude on my behalf, Mycroft.'

'Do not trouble. It was not for you. The reason why I ordered them to keep their vigil was to ensure that when you did leave Devil's Island, you left alone. Had you persuaded Dreyfus to go with you, and got him ashore, the consequences would have been appalling. Gonselin's orders were that if you were seen to be accompanied in the

canoe, he was to close with it and convey Dreyfus immediately back
to his prison, praying that he had not yet been missed.'

Holmes made a gesture of utter resignation.

'So much for my illusions about brotherly love. Then, are you
going to tell me precisely why you are so intent that that poor fellow
should continue to suffer, and for a crime which, in all likelihood, he
did not commit?'

Mycroft shrugged his heavy shoulders.

'Dreyfus himself is not my concern. I agree, the case against him
seems thin almost to the point of transparency. It is what he
represents which affects me.'

'What do you mean by that?'

'The Dreyfus affair is a confounded nuisance,' Mycroft sighed
with the effort of having to explain. 'You must be aware that relations
between France, Germany and Italy are in a delicate state. A sudden
deterioration of feeling between any two of them might lead to a war
which would have all Europe in flames and certainly embroil this
country. Consequently, our agents in Paris, Berlin and Rome are kept
constantly on the alert, watching for anything which might call for
timely intercession by us to save the situation from becoming out of
control. Like agents the world over, they rely for much of their
information upon the tongues of persons in official posts who are
prepared to keep them abreast of affairs—out of concern for their own
countries' well-being, of course.'

'Oh, of course! The health of their own bank accounts would not
enter into it.'

'You were always a cynic, Sherlock. The fact is that the
suggestion that Dreyfus had done treacherous business with the
German Embassy, and the Kaiser's angry statement that no embassy
of his is involved in spying business—which you may believe if you
wish—struck fear into many of those who were formerly ready to talk
freely. They locked up their tongues and took to glancing over their
shoulders, unsure of whom to trust. As a result, the flow of
information to our agents had virtually dried up. It has taken all these
months—more than a year—for the tongues to begin to wag again.
The Dreyfus case and the alarums it had set off had all but been
forgotten when you, with your gratuitous interfering, cause it to
spring back to everyone's notice! Our patient work is undone again

and our agents' activities put in jeopardy for perhaps another year to come. I did not exaggerate when I alluded to the Tower!'

Mycroft's slow manner had given way to rapid speech, flushed cheeks, and agitated gestures. He bobbed in his chair and waved his hands like a foreigner. Holmes continued to sit rock-still, and there came no smile of wry amusement at his brother's antics.

'Do you tell me,' he asked, in his steeliest tone, 'that a man is to be condemned to go on living in a hell on earth so that the underground machinations of governments may flourish undisturbed? You refer to me as a cynic, Mycroft; but I never heard a more cynical proposition than that which you argue.'

'Individuals must sometimes suffer for the good of the many. Can you not conceive the nature of European war?'

'But ... but not one word of concern for Dreyfus's plight! Papa and Mama would have died from shame, had they been alive to hear you in this vein, Mycroft.'

Mycroft was startled by this, and shot me a little glance of embarrassment, returning his brother a muttered answer about its being 'all in the game', or some such. 'Besides,' he went on, seeking to regain the initiative, 'who is to say that Dreyfus is suffering unjustly? He was tried and found guilty. Can you say certainly that he was not? Our information is that someone most definitely offered information to the Germans. Not a finger has been pointed at anyone other than Dreyfus. So, it is a case of the welfare of a man who is probably guilty, against the danger of war in Europe. The life of one in the balance with those of millions.

'Your natural compassion becomes you, Sherlock,' he ended more quietly. And, believe me, it was not merely in order to ensure that you did not rescue Dreyfus that Gonselin and his crew were ordered to keep watch. But I have to repeat that what you have done will have made it harder again for Britain to keep her finger on the hidden pulse of Europe.'

Sherlock Holmes's usually sallow features were pinked over with the flush of anger. His eyes flashed like dagger blades as he got abruptly to his feet and took up his hat and stick.

'Come, Watson,' he ordered, 'before I become incapable of leaving this place without causing such a commotion as will jerk every one of its occupants out of his complacent slumber.'

Without another glance at his brother he swept to the door. I hurried after, not looking back. Before we had gained the passage, however, I heard a snarling growl from Mycroft Holmes, followed by the sound of the newspaper being crumpled into a ball between his hands. It flew past me and fell at Holmes's feet. He gave it an almighty, contemptuous kick, and we strode on past the staring porter and off those oppressive premises.

He spoke no word all the way back to Baker Street, eschewing the use of a cab and walking fast and angrily, looking neither to right nor left. It was all I could do, hampered as I was by my old wound, to keep up with him, but anger lent added strength to me, and I managed it. I was glad, however, when we had ascended the seventeen steps which marked the end of our perambulation and flung ourselves into our respective chairs.

Editions of the evening newspapers had, as always, been laid out on our smoking tables by Mrs Hudson, and we took them up simultaneously. My eye was quickly caught by the name Dreyfus on one of the principal news pages, and I read the French authorities' brief but categorical denial that there was any truth whatsoever in a report that an attempt to remove him from Devil's Island had been made. Then, across the page from this item, another name arrested my attention.

'Holmes!' I ejaculated, heedless of his silent mood.

'I know, Watson,' he answered gravely. 'I have just seen it myself.'

He sprang to his feet. 'Come along. There is not a moment to be lost.'

I followed him down the staircase on weary legs and was glad to see him wave down a hansom. The destination he gave to the cabby, with an injunction to hurry, was Great George Street, Westminster.

The second name which I had noticed in the newspaper had been that of Adolphe Meyer. The report was that he had been found murdered in his apartment.

TWELVE

GREAT George Street today is one of those which flank the island of lofty government offices to the north of Parliament Square. In 1896, however, there remained a few years to go before the many old houses which stood in it were swept away to permit this rebuilding. It was in one of these, No. 13, that Meyer had his apartment. As we drew up at the door I remarked to Holmes upon the impudence of a spy's establishing himself within yards of all of the country's principal centres of government. He nodded abstractedly, paid the cabby hastily, and almost ran into the house.

He had evidently had dealings with Adolphe Meyer at some time, for he bounded without hesitation to the first floor, where a police constable stood guard at an open door. The man enquired our business and raised his eyebrows significantly at the mention of the name Sherlock Holmes, no doubt suspecting some ruse of the press. But my friend's incisive tones had carried to those within, for there appeared at once in the doorway the familiar form of our old competitor and occasional collaborator, Inspector Lestrade of Scotland Yard.

A smile lit up the sallow, ratty features and the darting brown eyes.

'Mr Holmes, Dr Watson!' he cried. 'Step inside, gentlemen. Dobson, close the door on us. What brings you here, Mr Holmes, eh?'

The rooms proved to be those of a wealthy occupant. My tired feet sank luxuriously into carpeting of thick pile. The wallpapers and hangings were of classical dignity and there was the gleam of polished wood and brass at every turn, with almost all surfaces occupied by some exquisite vase or other ornament.

The late Adolphe Meyer, thought I, must have been a most successful practitioner of his dark trade. However, he would enjoy these elegant surroundings no longer, for he lay, face downward with arms and legs sprawled out, in the centre of the study-cum-sitting-room, into which the short vestibule led. The rich carpet was discoloured to one side of him by the blood which had flowed from a wound in his back.

'We have had occasional transactions with the man,' my friend explained to Lestrade. 'The newspaper account of his death carried no details as to the manner of it, and curiosity impelled us here.'

'Well, there's no cause to keep it any secret, Mr Holmes.' Lestrade nodded towards the corpse. 'See for yourself, by all means. Though as to the reason, it'll have you guessing for once, I fancy.'

Holmes and I leaned down from either side of the body. There was no doubt about the nature of the wound. A knife had pierced neatly through the clothing and deep into the body beneath the left rear of the rib-cage.

'Hm!' grunted Holmes, straightening his lanky from again. 'A single wound, inflicted by a half-inch blade—stiletto, almost certainly—wielded by a left-handed man ...'

'Or woman?'

'No, no. A woman would not have made such a wound. The blow was delivered with great power, as well as precision. There is no doubt at all that it was intended to kill him, and that the assailant was an expert at his job. He was also either a friend of Meyer, or at least an acquaintance upon important business.'

'How do you reckon that?'

'See here—the ashtray upon the smoker's companion. Two cigars, both smoked down to their butts before being extinguished. And these indentations in the leather seats of two adjoining chairs. They sat and smoked together, but their cigars were of markedly different varieties. May I, Lestrade?'

'Go ahead, Mr Holmes,' said the other, with a broad wink at me. 'Always good for a smile, you going on about cigars and pipes.'

'I am not in the habit of "going on" about anything,' retorted my friend with an aggrieved look. 'You are well aware that I have devoted a great deal of attention to the study of tobacco ash as an aid to investigation, as I set out in the little monograph I wrote. In fact, I distinctly recollect presenting you with a copy, Lestrade, and commending you to study it with concentration.'

'You did, you did, and very interesting, so far as it goes. But I ask you, how is a man on an Inspector's pay expected to get the chance to compare all those hundreds of types . . .?'

'One hundred and forty, to be precise.'

'Well, all right. Even so, the only chance I ever get to smoke a cigar is Christmas Day, and it's not one of your fancy Havanas, neither.'

'My dear Lestrade, the next occasion you find to call at our humble abode, you shall be enabled to vary your custom. Meanwhile . . .'

Holmes picked up the thicker of the two butts, examined it keenly, then sniffed at it several times.

'Havana,' he pronounced. 'Luis Marx Grandioso, crop of '93. About ten guineas a hundred. The very best. Cut with a proper instrument. I fancy you will find it on Meyer's desk, and somewhere in this room a store of these excellent cigars. As to this other—dear me!'

He fingered the thinner butt with distaste, not troubling to sniff it.

'Regina Regenta. Made in Britain by Morris and Sons. Price threepence. Mm. The corpse is facing the door. Yes. Our picture is quite clear, then.'

'It is?' I asked, being altogether unclear as to any detail of it, except that two men had sat here and had a convivial, or businesslike, conversation.

'Is it not? My dear Watson, you disappoint me.' Holmes made his offensively exaggerated sigh. 'I suppose I must spell it out. A Havana cigar of this size and quality would occupy its smoker for the best part of an hour, unless he were of an exceptionally nervous type, in which case his puffs would have been much more frequent and the butt consequently far more saturated than this one has been. This threepenny thing, on the other hand, may be eked out to perhaps twenty minutes in the lips of a calm-minded man. But see for yourself the ruin caused to what is left of the leaf by the chewing and rapid puffing of its smoker. I give it ten minutes—eleven at the outside. Now, how many used matches do you find in the ashtray?'

'Only one,' said I, after stirring the fine ash with a finger.

'As I expected. A man who lights a Havana cigar of the first quality does not offer the remains of his match to his fellow smoker. His careful lighting of his own will have consumed almost the whole of the lucifer, as I see is the case here; besides which, it is not the custom of smokers of good cigars to share a match. Yet our patron of the Regina Regenta weed has left no matchstalk behind. I see him as the sort who would light up from his own box, puff out the match, then place it back in the box. A tiresome habit, if one has occasion to borrow the box in search of a fresh match, but not uncommon to men whose instinct it is to keep themselves to themselves.'

Lestrade laughed out loud. 'Very useful stuff, Mr Holmes! You'll tell me when to make a note, of course?'

Holmes scowled at him. 'It is more useful than you imagine, Lestrade. It gives us, as I said, the picture of what occurred here.'

'Blowed if I can see it. Can you, Doctor?'

I wagged my head in what I trusted was a gesture of concealed knowingness. The twinkle in my friend's eye informed me that he knew me to be as baffled as was the professional policeman.

He continued: 'Meyer is seated here alone, as he has been for some thirty or forty minutes, calmly smoking his cigar. A visitor calls, and is invited in. He is either already smoking one of his own cheap brand, or lights one up, having either declined—or, more likely, not been offered—a Havana. He is as nervous as Meyer is calm. They finish their cigars simultaneously ...'

'Just a minute—how can you tell that?' Lestrade demanded.

'Quite simply. the Havana has been smoked to its very end. The cheaper cigar has not. Yet you might expect the more economical smoker to be the one who would wish to extract the very last puff. No. As I see it, Meyer finished his cigar and stubbed it out, terminating the interview as he did so. His companion was forced to abandon the rest of his own weed. This suggests to me that they were in one another's company for, say, ten minutes only, before Meyer rose to his feet to show the other out. Stubbing his unfinished cigar hastily—see how its end is roughly crushed and splayed?—his visitor rose, too, and swiftly stabbed his host, who had turned his back to precede him to the door. There was no struggle. It was done deliberately, instantaneously, and, as I said before, expertly. Your wanted man,

Lestrade, may be no connoisseur of tobacco, but he is no amateur at knifemanship. At what time has your surgeon put the death?'

'A bit after noon today.'

'As I had anticipated. See the half-emptied sherry glass to the side of the ashtray where the Havana butt lay? That is obviously where Meyer sat, no doubt enjoying his pre-prandial drink and smoke when his visitor arrived. There is no corresponding glass, however. The interview was not of the sort which runs to the offer of sherry and a good cigar.' Holmes glanced about, then moved swiftly to the sideboard where decanters and a gasogene stood. He peered only momentarily, before beckoning us across.

'Our friend of the cheap tobacco prefers his drink strong and fiery. See this decanter with its stopper removed? What is in it, Watson?'

I sniffed. 'Brandy.'

'Some of which has run down the outside of the bottle and stained the wooden surface. The murderer may not have been offered hospitality by his intended victim, but he helped himself to a good bracer afterward, and is clearly not the sort of person who is averse to raising a bottle, or in this case a decanter, to his lips. Yes, we can positively rule out any degree of gentleman.'

Lestrade had by now dropped his mocking pose and was looking deeply thoughtful.

'I'll have to hand it to you once more, Mr Holmes. Good job for me you happened to step by. But I don't know how I'm going to find out who did it. There's been no theft that we can find out. There's a little safe behind that picture of an old bloke and his missus there . . .'

'The Gainsborough, you mean?'

'If you say so. The safe hasn't been forced, though. We opened it with a key we found on Meyer and it's chock-a-block with French banknotes. A great wad with consecutive numbers. Someone's given him a good pay-off lately. And you can see for yourself how much silver and stuff there is lying about for the taking.'

'Surely, Inspector,' I put in, 'a man of Meyer's trade, for want of a better term for it, would have dealings with all types, the rough and the smooth. This visitor could have come for any of a hundred reasons to do with the spying business?'

'That's right, Doctor, and it's why it promises to be like looking for a needle in a haystack, tracking him down. Don't bother to ask whether the porter saw anyone, Mr Holmes. It was the first thing we checked, and he was off duty from twelve, having his dinner. There's an appointment book there on the desk, but nothing in it for today. And you won't find anything useful in the way of letters, neither.'

Holmes had gone to Meyer's fine walnut desk, on the tooled leather surface of which correspondence and notes lay in neat piles, each with its paperweight. He lifted each weight in turn and carefully riffled through the documents, replacing them exactly. He also quickly examined the contents of the wastepaper basket.

'No. Nothing of interest at all,' he agreed, shooting me a glance whose significance I discerned. I had been wondering whether the draft of the Captain Hunter interview might come to light and spark off some embarrassing train of enquiry; but, professional spy that he was, Meyer had no doubt destroyed all evidence of it when his part had been completed.

This thought, however, raised another question in my mind. I quickly went back to the corpse and squatted on my haunches beside it, peering at the neck. I glanced up at Lestrade, who nodded.

'Move him, if you want to, Doctor. I'm expecting them to come and take him away any minute. I thought it was them when you gentlemen came to the door.'

I needed only to turn the head and shoulders slightly to verify the theory which had come to me.

'At least one part of your reconstruction is wrong, Holmes,' I was able to say with modest pride.

'And what is that, pray?'

'Bruising on the front of the neck—see? Not severe, but quite apparent.'

Lestrade leaned down to look.

'I never saw that,' he said testily. 'The doctor didn't mention it.'

'How long ago was the examination?'

'About an hour after death. Meyer always dined out at night, and the porter's wife made him up a bit of cold luncheon every day. She found him when she brought it in, otherwise he might have laid here till she came up to clean tomorrow.'

'In all probability, then, the bruising had not yet appeared so early. You and the doctor didn't see it because it wasn't there yet.'

'Hmph! What do you reckon to that, then, Mr Holmes?'

'I see precisely what my friend is driving at, and I fully concur with him. Well done, Watson. We shall make a detective of you yet. Pray explain to the inspector.'

'Well,' said I, getting up, 'it occurred to me that a spy so professional as Adolphe Meyer would never turn his back upon anyone with whom he was closeted alone and who had come upon any sort of dubious business. Yet Holmes pictured him leading the way to the door, to show his visitor out. Those marks on the neck, which I looked for and found, indicate that Meyer was not surprised from behind. The murderer had to tackle him and managed to get an arm lock about his throat, twisting him round so as to expose the preferred target for his knife.'

'Quite excellent, my dear Watson!' said Holmes, examining the carpet. 'And if so many feet had not trampled here in the last few hours we should almost certainly have had marks in this deep pile to give your theory further weight. But there is no doubt at all that you are correct, and the overall picture becomes slightly changed. Meyer's interview with his attacker was brief and was ended by Meyer in such terms as caused the other to stamp out his half-finished cigar and grapple with him as they got to their feet.'

'He'd just have chucked the cigar aside,' Lestrade retorted.

'Such a gesture would have given his victim several seconds' notice of his intention; just enough, perhaps, for Meyer to stiffen up to resist. No. The man deliberately, albeit fiercely, crushed out his cigar, then flung himself upon Meyer who stood there waiting for him to leave. He got one arm—his right—round Meyer's neck, and with his left drew out his knife and used it. Your discovery, then, Watson, adds an important element to our image of the man Lestrade must seek. He is not only an expert with the stiletto—a Continental weapon, which perhaps tells us that he is a foreigner—a person of unrefined habits and without scruple when it comes to killing another; but he is also cunning, of quick enough mind to know, and act upon the knowledge, that he is dealing with a man of keen instinct and great wariness who will need to be taken completely off his guard if he is to be attacked successfully.'

There came a knock upon the door and the constable looked in to report that the ambulance had arrived. Its attendants came in, arranged the corpse upon the stretcher and covered it with a blanket.

'Well, I dunno,' Lestrade remarked as they carried Meyer from the apartment. 'A fellow like that might have had scores of folks with reasons for putting him out of the way.'

'Indeed,' Holmes agreed, and I was surprised to note a new grimness in his expression. 'But not all would correspond with the individual whose characteristics we have deduced. At least your field is narrowed somewhat. Don't I take it that Meyer was under some sort of surveillance, most of the time?'

'Sometimes by us, sometimes by others. We weren't on to him lately.'

'So you are aware of no pattern of callers, one of whom might come close to our description?'

'Quite a few regulars, as you say. Men and women. Most of 'em looking as if butter wouldn't melt in their mouths. Definitely none of the rough sort.'

'I fancy he would meet any such types in other sort of surroundings. Well, Lestrade, glad to have been of some little help.'

'Thanking you, Mr Holmes. I reckon there's nothing much more to be done than seal these rooms and keep them under watch for a while, in case anyone interesting comes trying to get in. And thank you, too, Doctor. Care to sign on with the regular Force?'

'No thanks!' I chuckled. 'I have my time cut out assisting the irregular one. And, Holmes, if I don't get back to my slippers directly my feet will refuse to carry me.'

We made our departure, leaving Lestrade a little enriched but clearly lacking expectation that he could anticipate any arrest.

'What do you say, then, Holmes?' I asked, as our hansom cab spun us towards Baker Street and the blissful prospect of slippered feet upon the fender and whisky and soda in the hand. 'Any connection with his part in your Dreyfus scheme?'

'I don't see why. He did no more than to pass a message to a newspaper. That he succeeded, we know certainly, for the article appeared. That he received his satisfactory reward would seem to be proved by that substantial run of French banknotes in his safe. The murderer would scarcely have been the editor of *Libre Parole*, aggrieved that the interview had been proven false, since we have every reason to expect that he had been delighted by it. It could not have been a Dreyfus supporter or antagonist, paying Meyer out for his part in the deception, since that would have been known to the editor alone. We may confidently eliminate Mathieu Dreyfus, who has no cause to feel other than grateful to Meyer for his underhand assistance. And yet ...'

'What, Holmes? The field of possible candidates is wide, and yet I saw you frown at Lestrade's quite reasonable remark that such a man would have had many ill-wishers associated with his activities. What thought crossed your mind just then?'

He shrugged beside me. 'I really don't remember,' was all the answer he gave; but he stopped the cab outside the next telegraph office we reached and left me waiting while he went in without explanation.

'No, Sherlock. Upon the memory of our dear parents, I swear to you that I had absolutely no hand in it, nor even knowledge of it, until I read that same newspaper report which brought it to your attention.'

So spoke Mycroft Holmes, leaning forward with uncharacteristic animation of gesture and expression in the basket chair in our sitting-room that same evening. It was gone ten o'clock. The blinds were drawn, the lamps lit, the fire in good heart, and the air fragrant with the blend of my own Arcadia mixture and the stronger tobacco favoured by my friend. Mycroft Holmes did not smoke. He sipped occasionally at a glass of wine, which he had insisted upon selecting for himself from amongst his brother's choice store.

He had come in answer to the telegram which Holmes had despatched on our way home that afternoon. It had been directed to the Diogenes Club, from which establishment, Holmes had told me, some mysterious contact with his brother's whereabouts at any given moment prevailed. Following the acrimonious exchange between the two brothers earlier that day, I had scarcely expected so exalted a person as Mycroft Holmes to reply, yet alone obey a summons; yet here he was, looking as out of place away from his own surroundings as, in Holmes's words upon another occasion, a tram-car in a country lane.

Holmes had declined to confide in me his exact plan for the

evening. I believe it was part of his method to keep me in ignorance of his intentions in order that, when they came to pass, my surprised reaction would give rise to some remark or gesture which might draw forth some corresponding and revealing one from the third party. I had learnt early in our acquaintance to let fall no information which we did not know for certain that the other person possessed already, and to save my observations until the burthen of the debate was over and what I might term Question Time or Any Other Business had arrived. Yet, occasionally, I fancy that by a lift of an eyebrow or a pursing of the lips, I had given my friend some support which he sought for an impression which he was beginning to form.

The late Adolphe Meyer's part in Holmes's journalistic ruse had not been mentioned during that scene in the afternoon, and I was surprised when he alluded to the man immediately his brother was seated, glass in hand, between us.

'Adolphe Meyer,' was all my friend had said, his eyes steely through the smoke from his freshly-charged pipe.

'A pity,' Mycroft answered without emotion. 'A scoundrel, but useful. It narrows the field, you know. It narrows the field.'

'What field, in particular, becomes contracted by his removal from it?'

'Oh, you know. Chaps like Meyer, La Rothiere, Oberstein, and their sort—the old hands—each has settled into his routine. We know with whom they are in contact, where they meet, what nature of business is likely to be passing between them. Reports from our people abroad, or in the press, generally give us the sort of confirmation which enables us to trace back the chain of events, the method and the motive. Patterns begin to evolve. In course of time we are able to foresee, from the nature of the opening move, what the outcome of the game will be. If it suits us to let it take its course, we do so. If not, a little manipulation may be applied at some stage where it will not be obvious. But every old hand who ceases to be a player is replaced by some newcomer, full of zest and originality and up-to-date methods, conforming to few of the predecessor's habits. It is all too tiresome, having to mount persistent watch until the new pattern of behaviour begins to stabilise.'

'So Meyer's demise is a nuisance to you, then?'

'Decidedly. And so soon after Oberstein's removal. I must

admit, Sherlock, that you did a brilliant job as regards the latter, and at my own instigation; but I can tell you he is sorely missed. There have even been suggestions that his sentence should be commuted, so that he might return to circulation.'

Mycroft Holmes looked so sincere as he spoke that I was for a moment tempted to believe that he spoke the truth. But a smirk which passed between the brothers showed me that they were indulging in a form of private badinage which had no doubt evolved during their youth and had served since as a veil upon truth, through which they could see clearly but most others would not.

'Which of his patterns of behaviour was Meyer following until approximately one o'clock this afternoon?' asked Holmes.

Mycroft shrugged. 'I told you, we don't watch the old hands all the time. For most of it they lie like newts at the bottom of the pond. Every so often they float or swim to the surface and attract our attention.'

'My dear Mycroft, forgive me if I disbelieve you. At the time of the Bruce-Partington affair, you were able to inform me that Hugo Oberstein, whom you had had no cause to connect with it until my intervention, had been in town one day and out of it the next. If that does not speak of a pretty close eye being kept upon him, I don't know what would. This afternoon, Lestrade spoke of Meyer's being watched sometimes by the police, sometimes by "others", whom I take to be your people. In his artless way he admitted that the police were not interested in him currently I can only conclude that it was your turn.'

'As you wish.'

Mycroft sipped his wine. I sensed that Holmes would have to risk a charge across open ground if he hoped to achieve any result. I was quickly proved correct.

'Look here, Mycroft,' he said. 'You were on to Mathieu Dreyfus from the moment he set foot in the country. You traced him to me. I am not so naïve as to suppose that you had him followed no further. You know perfectly well that he went to No. 13 Great George Street.'

His brother gave him a little smile of triumph and held out his glass for me to re-fill, as if I were some form of automatic servant.

'I confess I could not think why at the time,' he answered. 'When that French press report appeared I immediately had my answer.

Typically devious of you, Sherlock. I could admire it, if it were not all so reprehensible.'

'Please do not let us start quarrelling again over that. I have shown you my hand, Mycroft. Now let me see yours.'

'I have no hand to show. I am a spectator, not a player.'

'*Are* you?'

'Pray what do you mean by that?'

'Did you order the killing of Adolphe Meyer?'

For the second time that day I saw Mycroft Holmes's mask of inscrutability fall away, to reveal one of anger.

'I resent that exceedingly!' he railed, looking round for somewhere to place his new glass of wine before getting up. There was no table immediately within reach.

'*Did* you?' Holmes persisted. 'You, or any of your colleagues.'

'I did not. And if it will help satisfy you, no one else carries authority of that nature.'

'Then you do?'

'I did not say so. You know perfectly well that my official duties are a closed book, into which not even my closest relative may peep. Dr Watson, if you will please relieve me of this glass, I shall take my leave.'

I moved to help him, realising that he could not heave his ponderous form out of the basket chair without the use of both arms for leverage, but Holmes stayed me with a gesture.

'Don't take on so, Mycroft,' he said in a boyish tone. 'It was a question which I was compelled to ask. Accept my assurance that I merely did so in order to eliminate the impossible.'

For a few moments his brother remained tense in his seat; then he relaxed again, took another sip of wine, and made the declaration which I recorded at the commencement of this little episode.

'As you have said, my dear Mycroft,' Holmes went on in a sincere tone, 'I hope I am the last man to accuse my own brother of using murder to further his means, though I don't doubt that, in your work, you would do so if it were necessary. Your natural goodness would cause you to hesitate. You would shrink instinctively from it. Yet, if it were in some way vital to the interest of the country which you so dedicatedly serve, you would order it to be done. But should that dreadful dilemma ever face you, almost the unlikeliest means which any of your agents would employ would be a stiletto. Of course, you might wish to give the impression that the attacker had been a foreigner, in which case so characteristically un-English a weapon might have sprung to mind. But I would wager my small fortune that there is no member of your service capable of wielding it to such instinctively accurate effect as was done upon Meyer.

'Besides,' Holmes concluded, with a wink at me and a nod towards his own empty glass and our whisky supply, 'I am certain that the fastidiousness which is innate to us both, Mycroft, would debar you from employing any agent so crudely mannered as to swig brandy from a decanter.'

THIRTEEN

'How often have I said to you, Watson,' asked Sherlock Holmes, 'that every problem has its precedent amongst the thousands which are stored in my memory?'

'Very often,' I answered, thereby earning myself a sharp look over the top of the newspaper cutting which he had been perusing.

We occupied our respective chairs in our sitting-room. It was a sunny morning shortly after the events which I have just recounted. Although it was already warm and promised a return to summer heat by afternoon, our fire burned, Mrs Hudson having forestalled my objection to it by the simple expedient of lighting it before I descended to breakfast.

I returned him what I hoped was a disarming smile and asked, 'So it has happened yet again, eh?'

He shook his head. 'No. It has not.'

'I, er, I don't quite follow you, Holmes. Why do you allude to it, then?'

'What has not happened is what did not happen once before, which is why it springs so interestingly to mind.'

I decided to terminate, by speedy submission, this latest experience of his teasing habit.

'Holmes, I haven't the faintest idea what you are getting at? If you intend telling me something, kindly spare me the conundrums.'

'As I recall, Watson, you earned the plaudits of your readers of the Strand Magazine by the manner in which you dealt with that extremely interesting case of ours concerning the racehorse named Silver Blaze. It was adjudged one of those narratives in which you surpassed yourself.'

I nodded modestly. 'I might return the compliment. Your solving of the mystery was inspired.'

'Inspired, my dear Watson, by something which did not occur, remember?'

'Ah! The dog who did nothing in the night-time.'

'Precisely. It was the curious incident which gave me my clue, showing me that whoever had stolen the horse had been well known to the stable dog, which would otherwise have raised the alarm.' He flourished the newspaper cutting. 'Here we have another instance.'

'I don't recall any recent inquiries where dogs have been involved,' said I, searching my memory.

Holmes smiled. 'I referred merely to the principle of the thing. No dogs this time, but a letter which was not where this newspaper article claims it to have been—namely, on the desk of the late Adolphe Meyer.'

'Really? May I see it?'

'By all means. But since it is in French, permit me to give you the drift of it. It is entitled "*Le Traitre*", which I need scarcely translate for you as "The Traitor". It proceeds to disclose that confidential evidence was shown to Dreyfus's judges and dispelled any doubts as to his guilt. The evidence was in the form of a communication from the German Military Attaché in Paris to his Italian counterpart. It included the word, "this Dreyfus creature is becoming too demanding".'

'Great heavens! Then that settles it.'

'Wait a moment. The reason why this evidence could not be produced openly in court is alleged not simply to be that it would have been embarrassing to the French authorities to have to admit to intercepting messages between other powers; but because the message was in a complex code which, unbeknown to the Germans and Italians, the French had succeeded in cracking, and did not wish them to know it.'

'Understandable enough. If you let someone know you've broken his code, he ceases to use it and substitutes another. If you keep him in ignorance, though, you can go on reading his secrets.'

'That *had* just occurred to me, Watson,' remarked Holmes a little acerbically. 'However, it happens to be the least interesting feature of this report. What strikes me as far more significant is the assertion that this disclosure reached the newspaper, *L'Eclair*, another sensationalist Parisian rag, by means of a letter which had been found lying on Adolphe Meyer's desk after his murder. Now, I myself made a particular point of going through Meyer's papers, as you saw me do. Lestrade assured me he had found nothing of interest, and there is no reason to suppose from his manner that he was concealing anything from us.'

'His murderer must have taken it.'

'It says quite distinctly that it was discovered *after* his death, and forwarded to the newspaper by a person who felt it his duty to remove all doubt as to Dreyfus's guilt from the minds of the French public, and to cause his family to desist from trying to stir up trouble which might harm the country's good name.'

'Then what do you make of it?'

'Quite simply, that our plot has worked. We have flushed our bird from cover, Watson. Someone who read the Captain Hunter interview is concerned lest the renewed interest in Dreyfus should lead to the truth emerging. He has sought to bring finality to the matter by issuing this further report.'

'But why purportedly through Meyer? Who but ourselves knew of his involvement?'

'Quite a few, I dare say. The editor of *Libre Parole* for one. After the story had served his purpose and been given the lie there would have been no especial need for him to keep its source secret. In all likelihood he was challenged by his confrères of the journalistic profession with having made up the Captain Hunter story himself, and allowed it to be traced to Meyer to prove that he did not.'

'Do you suggest that Meyer's murder was some form of reprisal?'

'It is one possibility, but unlikely. What he had done scarcely merited so drastic a revenge. If the assassin's original intention was to make Meyer reveal the real perpetrator of the ruse, he would more likely have overpowered and tortured him to get the secret. Nothing of the sort occurred.'

'So it would seem that your theory is correct. If it had become general knowledge amongst journalists that Meyer was involved, it would make this new report all the more plausible to them if it seemed to come from him.'

'As you say.'

'Yet, Holmes … *could* it be true?'

'That is impossible to answer with certainty. My instincts tell me that it is not.'

'Your impression of Dreyfus and his brother, you mean?'

'That has quite something to do with it. What I ask myself, though, is why it was felt desirable to get this into print? It was not engineered by Dreyfus's sympathisers, for sure. This cutting was sent to me by Mathieu Dreyfus, whose letter is here before me, and he is firm upon that point. But if it was done by his detractors, they have made a misjudgment. Do you not realise that this is the first public admission that Dreyfus's conviction was arrived at without strict regard to legal procedure?'

'But it explains why.'

'That is beside the point. Fair-minded men will be asking questions now. We may be sure that the French Government will wish to deny the whole thing, whilst the Kaiser huffs and the King of Italy blows. But if it denies that the evidence was too secret to be produced in court, it will have to find some other reason for an unfair verdict having been permitted to stand. In our friend Mathieu Dreyfus's view, which I must say I share, Madame Dreyfus now has every ground for petitioning for a review of the case. It is one of the reasons why he wishes to see us—to discuss it urgently.'

'He is coming here again?'

'No, no. He dare not risk it at present. Even his letter is couched in careful ambiguities. He says he has vital matters—the plural, you note—to talk over, and wishes to introduce us to "a new friend". Ring for Mrs Hudson, will you, Watson? We have successfully rekindled the heat and must not let it die again through our own delay.'

In less than an hour we were seated in the train which would carry us to the Continent. Our destination was not, however, Paris. I gathered from Holmes that Mathieu Dreyfus had nominated Geneva instead.

'Less close to the centre of the hot-bed,' remarked Holmes as we sped through the flat, sunlit Kentish countryside. 'Also, his family's business is conducted from Switzerland. I expect he is less rigorously watched there. Why, my dear chap, you are looking positively pensive!'

'I am remembering,' I replied. 'It is little more than five years since we travelled to Geneva last, and within a few days you were, to all intents and purposes, dead.'

'Ah, yes. And much water has cascaded over the Reichenbach Falls since that time. Yet I must say that in all the interesting and dramatic investigations which have engaged our attention, both before that melancholy event and since my resurrection, none has equalled this present one in longevity and mystery. It is a rotten business, with a stink of corruption to it. Corruption, that is, not in the bodily sense, but morally. Whether it emanated at first from one man, or corporately, the decay has become widespread and may yet attack the very foundations of France. Depend upon it, Watson, there is more responsibility upon our hands than the retrieving of one man's reputation.'

He lapsed into silence after this, and I occupied myself with my own thoughts, which were compounded of recollections of that last Swiss visit of ours, and attempts to puzzle out the riddle which was taking us back there. I found it especially disturbing that it was necessary forcibly to remind myself that whilst we were being carried at our ease through idyllic pastoral countryside, on a day whose pleasant heat was touched upon its edges by the outreaching finger of autumn, the wretch on whose behalf we were travelling continued to suffer the deprived existence, in those inhospitable surroundings and debilitating climate, which Holmes had described to me. The contrast was so great that it gave unreality to the fact; as though Dreyfus were no more substantial than a character in some novel which I had half-read and put aside: 'Out of sight, out of mind,' as the old saying has it. Well, I thought with some relief, my friend's ingenuity had succeeded in focussing attention upon Dreyfus once more, and the dramatic events which had resulted had thrown wide open again a door which had come near to closing for ever.

The reality of Dreyfus's suffering was made more vivid still by the disturbing news which his brother had to give us, over glasses of young white wine at a secluded table in one of the many pleasant restaurants on the edge of Lac Leman. The air was crisp and invigorating. The peaks shone clearly in the distance beyond the sparkling lake, upon which white-painted pleasure steamers passed to and fro. A band close to us was playing pot-pourris from the operettas of von Suppé,

Millöcker and Zeller. Straw hatted, white flannelled foreign visitors, with their lightly-clad ladies on their arms and children skipping before, promenaded before our eyes. We watched them, yet did not see them, as Mathieu Dreyfus unfolded his latest description of his brother's state.

'Fettered to his wooden bed from early evening until morning by manacles about his ankles which prevent all movement; prey to the torments of venomous spider-crabs, the size of a man's hand, and every sort of flying insect; in the intensest heat, made more stifling than ever by the new palisade which they have erected to enclose his hut, thus cutting off what little cooling air formerly entered his window, as well as most of the light and any view of the sea. He can no longer roam the island, but must pace to and fro within the confines of this stockade, and for only brief periods of each day. His guards have been increased, with orders to watch him constantly and permit him no comforts whatever. Even the commandant of the penal settlements felt moved to visit my brother and explain to him that these measures were not of his initiating, but as the result of orders from France. The outcome of that was the commandant's removal from his post, to be replaced by a hand-picked brute.'

'This is appalling!' I exclaimed. 'But how did you learn of it?'

'The former commandant told us. He came to unburden his conscience and assure us that he was not responsible. He said that the orders had come after the report of an attempted rescue.'

Holmes's face was grim. 'I am afraid the blame is upon my shoulders,' he said. 'I warned you that the success of our trick might not be without consequences for your brother, but it makes what you have told us no less horrifying.'

Before Mathieu Dreyfus could reply, a white-aproned waiter came into the little cubicle where we sat, out of earshot of others, and ushered in a lady. He withdrew with a bow, as we rose to our feet.

'Lucie, my dear,' Mathieu greeted her. 'Permit me to present Mr Sherlock Holmes and Dr John Watson. Gentlemen, my sister-in-law, Madame Lucie Dreyfus.'

She was a striking figure; tall and well-formed, the shape of her body emphasised by the narrow jointure of her skirt and silk blouse. A broad hat, with veil, was fetchingly trimmed with fabric roses; her gloves were silken, and the slim, yellow sunshade she carried had cream-coloured silken trimmings and tassel. If I had pictured Madame Dreyfus in my mind's eye at all, it had been as broken and bowed by the weight of worry and fear. In fact, she exemplified French *chic*; but when she had seated herself and lifted her veil, I saw telltale shadows under the dark eyes. I should have termed her features well-sculpted by Nature, rather than beautiful, and I seemed to detect Jewish origins in them.

Her brother-in-law informed us that she had wished to meet Holmes in person before deciding to appeal for the case to be re-opened.

'Do you advise it, Mr Holmes?' she asked in good English, spoken in a melodious voice.

'By all means, Madame. Everything that can possibly keep your husband in the forefront of attention is worth undertaking. We have gained the initiative, and must press forward with our attack. Besides ...' He hesitated, and we all divined why.

'Mathieu has told you of Alfred's new plight?' she said. 'You were about to say that time has become more precious than ever. I agree.'

'I have just expressed my regret to Monsieur Dreyfus that it was my action which resulted in this harsh reprisal.'

'You must not blame yourself at all, Mr Holmes,' she answered warmly, Mathieu nodding vigorously in agreement. 'But for you, he would probably have perished a little more slowly, that is all. Besides, your visit undoubtedly gave him that renewal of the will to survive which he has several times come close to losing.'

She opened her small embroidered satin reticule and drew out a letter. Unfolding it, she handed it to Holmes. 'Here is his latest letter. Please read the passage I have marked.'

Holmes proceeded to read aloud:

> '"I have gained control over myself now; I am once more what I was, and I will remain so until my last breath.
>
> We must rise superior to all, but with the firm resolve to prove my innocence before the whole of France.
>
> Our name must issue from this horrible affair as

pure as it was when it was crushed by it; our children must enter upon life with their heads erect and proud.

As to any advice which I can give you, you must, of course, understand that it is merely what is dictated by my heart. You yourself, *all* of you, are in a better position to judge what is best to be done."''

Holmes ceased reading. 'You are right, Madame,' he told the anxiously-watching woman. 'This is not the letter of a man without hope. His meaning is plain, even if his words are guarded.'

He held up the sheet of paper to the light, studying at closely. 'Has your husband access to invisible ink, at all?'

The Dreyfuses exchanged surprised looks. Mathieu answered, 'It is altogether unlikely ... unless he has managed to concoct some from some sort of juice. But ... no, no. It's too much too suppose.'

'Just as well. This letter has certainly been tested for it.'

He passed it to Dreyfus and myself in turn. The stain of some chemical was visible against the light, but there was no trace of secret writing.

'The fiends!' Mathieu exclaimed. 'I would not put it past them to have faked something of the kind, in order to attribute it to him. In fact, the former commandant confided in us that Alfred had received two anonymous letters from supposed well-wishers. He was watched closely when he opened them, but disappointed his guards—who have to note even his changes of expression at such times—by merely looking puzzled and throwing them into his single drawer. Evidently they did contain secret messages, which it was hoped he would be observed to read. No doubt he was suspicious, in any case, since Lucie and myself are his only permitted correspondents.'

'So the attempts to discredit him are unrelenting,' Holmes mused. 'Someone is very much afraid. It would have been interesting to have the handwriting of those secret messages beside us for reference in the future.'

'Aha!' Mathieu responded, and a look almost of triumph came into his face. 'To speak of handwriting ... But now comes the stranger whom I invited you here to meet. We will come to the matter of handwriting directly.'

The newcomer, who nodded to our host and bowed to Madame

Dreyfus, was a tall, handsome man, dressed in neat white linen and a striped blazer, but every inch the soldier, from his erect bearing to his thick moustache, waxed to points at its ends. I placed him at about my age, or a little younger.

'Mr Sherlock Holmes, Dr Watson, allow me to introduce Lieutenant-Colonel Picquart, head of the Intelligence Bureau of the General Staff.'

As I shook hands with this grave-faced newcomer I could not have felt more surprised if he had been the President of France himself. That the holder of so important a post should be fraternising with the family of a condemned traitor to his country seemed unthinkable. I responded to his greeting courteously enough, but set my mind very much upon its guard. I noticed Holmes's own slight frown of displeasure, evidently from concern at his own involvement having been revealed to one who might be expected to turn out a leading adversary.

However, the particulars which the Colonel proceeded to relate, at Mathieu Dreyfus's urging, were as unexpected as his presence. Sipping sparingly from a glass of wine, he spoke as follows, in assured and accurate English, addressing himself directly to Holmes.

'I have known Alfred Dreyfus for a number of years. Following a good deal of service in the colonies, I was appointed an instructor at the War College. Dreyfus was one of my pupils, and I have made no pretence to his relatives here that I was impressed by him. As one who has often been under fire myself, I could never imagine him in action. He struck me more as an intellectual soldier than as a fighting man. I tell you this, Mr Holmes, because I wish to impress upon you my impartiality in the matter of what is to follow.'

My friend nodded, and Picquart continued. 'In '93 I was seconded from the college to the Third Bureau of the War Department—that which deals with Operations and Training. It was in this capacity that I attended Captain Dreyfus's court martial as official observer. I believed the case against him to have been proven, although I admit I was troubled that it had not been done more openly. In the early summer of last year I was suddenly apponted head of Counterintelligence, when my predecessor in that post, Colonel Sandherr, became too ill to continue. It was not a job I relished. I am by nature an active soldier and a fastidious person, and the dark underworld of Intelligence work had little appeal for me. But it was an order, and I obeyed it. One of the first instructions I received upon taking up the post was to keep an eye on the Dreyfus case.'

'A moment, Colonel,' interrupted Holmes. 'From whom, precisely, did this instruction come?'

'The Chief of Staff, General de Boisdeffre, in person.'

'In writing?'

'No. Face to face.'

'Was any reason mentioned.?'

'None. I gained the impression that he was anxious to be shown additional confirmation that the verdict had been a correct one. Yet this struck me as strange, since almost the parting words of my predecessor had been that the less I looked into that particular matter, the greater my peace of mind would be. However, the command of my chief counted for more than this advice, and I admit I was curious on my own account to know the whole truth. Therefore, I issued orders that all future material relating to Dreyfus must be submitted to me as it came to hand.

'As you will have gathered, Mr Holmes, I have met Madame Dreyfus before today, and I have already taken the opportunity of apologising to her for having made myself familiar with the correspondence which has passed between her husband and herself. It was done as a duty, and caused me to feel neither guilt nor intrusive pleasure. Nevertheless, I now apologise once again.'

Colonel Picquart inclined his head seriously in Madame Dreyfus's direction. She made no movement and her dark eyes showed neither appreciation of his gesture, nor resentment for what had occasioned it. He continued, 'I became, of course, extremely familiar with the handwriting of Captain Dreyfus, and even of his style of expressing himself. There was nothing in the correspondence, from either party, to arouse my suspicions. It was necessarily very circumscribed by conditions which had been laid down as to topics which might or might not be discussed, and consisted largely of Dreyfus's accounts of his agonies of mind on his own and his family's behalf, and Madame Dreyfus's responses in much the same vein. What was certainly never to be detected was any hint of remorse on his part for having committed the alleged treason which had brought them to their respective plights.

'Very recently, however, I seemed to detect a new note in Dreyfus's writings. From self-pity and near-despair, even to the contemplation of making away with his life, he had swung to some sudden confidence. This almost exactly coincided with the publication of a false rumour that an attempt had been made to rescue him from Devil's Island. That no such attempt had been made, I quickly ascertained; yet what, I asked myself, had given him fresh hope at just this time?'

Colonel Picquart fell suddenly silent, gazing out across the shimmering water. I did not dare glance at either of my other male companions; yet, from the corner of my eye, I saw Mathieu Dreyfus shake his head ever so slightly for Holmes to see, and felt the profound relief of knowing it conveyed that Picquart had been told nothing of Holmes's visit to the island.

The Colonel's brief reverie ended as he felt inside his jacket and brought out a document.

'Mr Holmes,' he said heavily, 'for what reason, I cannot say; but my new speculations about what might be passing through Dreyfus's mind caused me to send—for the first time—for the papers concerning his trial. You will wonder why I had not done this earlier. I reply that, as head of Counterintelligence, I had many more things to concern me than his case. I had been at his trial, and heard all the evidence. I had had no reason to return to the records of it. Yet now I did. And my eyes fell at once upon a document, a photograph of which I should now like you, please, to examine.'

He swiftly handed across the single piece of stiff paper, long and narrow. So far as I could see it bore no heading; only some thirty or so lines of sloping handwriting.

Holmes scrutinised it intently, then raised his eyes to Picquart, who was watching him. The latter had produced several more documents, this time on their original notepaper. He handed them across, saying merely, 'A few letters written by Captain Alfred Dreyfus at this same period.'

Holmes glaced through them swiftly. Then he fanned them out in one hand, like a hand of playing cards, the photographed document in the other. When he had perused the letters, his eyes began to flick to and from between them and the single document. After serveral minutes he said, 'This is not the same handwriting.'

'As I suspected,' Colonel Picquart replied, and I heard a sigh in unison escape Madame Lucie Dreyfus and her brother-in-law, Mathieu.

I quietly reached my hand out towards my friend, and he placed in it the documents he had been comparing. As the others sat silently considering the implications of Holmes's confident pronouncement, I looked from the one set of papers to the photograph of a document which had been torn up and later reconstituted. At first sight, the handwriting of them all was identical: forward sloping and spiky, with little difference in the thickness or weight of the upward and downward strokes of the pen. It occurred to me that the writing of tens of thousands of educated Frenchmen might resemble this, being no doubt a style generally taught in schools.

'Look closer,' Holmes prompted me. 'Notice how the lines of writing in Alfred Dreyfus's letters are meticulously parallel, though they tend to slope slightly upward from left to right. But observe the sloping tendency in the photographed document. It is downward, is it not? The spacings are more irregular, the writing more slapdash.'

'Written hastily, perhaps?' I suggested.

'No doubt of that. Yet there is a decided impression of two different hands. The one is neat, thoughtful, inhibited: quite fitted to what we have been told of the personality of Alfred Dreyfus. The other is dashing, impulsive, the product of quite another nature.'

'But I can't understand . . .' I began.

Holmes stretched a long arm to retrieve the papers.

'You are right not to, my dear Watson.' He turned sharply to Madame Dreyfus, whose cheeks, I had noted, were coloured from the excitement of having heard Colonel Picquart's suspicion so definitely confirmed. 'I do not claim to be the first in the field of graphology,' Holmes explained. 'Yet half an eye shows me that your husband's writing and this are not the same. An hour with a magnifying-glass, and I would wager to come up with a score more dissimilarities.'

'But . . . but then, how could the court have found Alfred guilty?'

'Because it had to, or wished to. Which of these, I am not yet in a position to say. It accepted the ravings of Bertillon, the so-called expert, because it could not afford to reject them.'

'*Why?*'

For answer, Holmes turned silently to Colonel Picquart, and

raised his eyebrows in enquiry. Picquart shrugged.

'Believe me, I wish I knew. But I intend to find out.'

'Do you, Colonel?' It was Lucie Dreyfus who rapped out the question, which caused him to colour up instantly and grip the arms of his chair.

'Upon my honour, Madame, and that is something which I hold as sacred as your husband does his own. Yes, I can appreciate your suspicions. You have come to believe that no one is to be trusted any longer, and no wonder.'

He turned to appeal to Holmes and me with a gesture of his arms flung wide.

'When I made this discovery, I was appalled. I knew, as everyone does that there are many questionable things done in the name of security. Having taken command of my department, I soon became aware that my subordinates were in the habit of conducting matters each in his own way, without seeking consultation or permission. I asked Colonel Sandherr about it and he told me it was the usual practice. Intelligence officers, like policemen, are jealous of their own informants and other such people, and so long as they achieve results it is better not to ask too many questions of them. It is perhaps why my department's records are so incompletely and haphazardly kept, although that is a matter to which I am presently giving attention. It is certainly a reason for my instinctive distaste of this business, which involves encouraging and even inciting people to betray their countries and to double-deal for money, a far cry from my notion of operating.

'Yet, instead of keeping my discovery to myself, and pursuing an investigation by stealth, without hesitation I approached Monsieur Mathieu Dreyfus and showed him what I had found. In doing so, I have as much as placed myself before the firing squad, should I be found out. I have nothing to gain, and everything to lose, Mr Holmes, by swallowing my professional pride and seeking the counsel of the greatest practitioner in the field.'

Holmes leaned forward, with his eyes fixed intently on Colonel Picquart's.

'A Frenchman once told me,' he said slowly, 'that the greatest danger I should face in conducting any investigations involving your country's higher circles would have its origins in corruption and betrayal. He warned me to trust no one of whom I could not be absolutely certain. Yet, the Chief of Intelligence apparently risks his life inviting me to trust him. Colonel, if you were in my place, what would your reaction be?'

A slow, engaging smile lightened the military man's taut features.

'I knew you had been given that advice,' he answered. 'Inspector Dubuque is my friend, too.'

FOURTEEN

I T was heartwarming to watch the two of them shake hands all over again, only this time without formality or reserve. Mathieu Dreyfus took his sister-in-law's hand in his and smiled reassuringly. I was delighted by the relief in her eyes and the happy smile she was able to return him.

Colonel Picquart now went on to reaffirm that Holmes's friend Inspector Dubuque was, in his case also, one of very few in whom he would dare to confide his deepest secrets. None of the others was connected with politics or the army general staff, so it was to Dubuque that he had turned when, shaken by his certainty that the *bordereau* was not in Dreyfus's handwriting, he had felt in need of confirmation and counsel. Dubuque had urged upon him the highly unorthodox step of consulting Sherlock Holmes.

'Fortunately, I was well aware of your great reputation,' he told my friend, 'otherwise the notion of approaching an English detective would have seemed a ludicrous one. I confess, though, I had no idea at all of your involvement in the Huret case. Dubuque gave me the details. Your achievement is beyond praise, my dear sir.'

'Dubuque is too generous,' Holmes murmured. 'But to return to our business in hand ...'

'Mr Holmes ...' Madame Dreyfus said suddenly, her face serious again; but I saw her brother-in-law tighten his grip on her hand and give her a slight shake of his head. Holmes turned to her enquiringly, but it was Mathieu who said, 'Madame Dreyfus has a suggestion to make. With her consent, though, I believe it should wait until Colonel Picquart has finished all he has to tell you.'

She nodded, and all our eyes turned again to Picquart, who resumed addressing Holmes.

'I mentioned that I had found the records of my department to be in unsatisfactory order. Much of my time since I assumed command has been spent in examining files dealing with matters of current importance.

'I have made some disturbing discoveries; notably, that various documents of considerable interest do not bear the initials of my predecessor, Colonel Sandherr. It is a practice in which he was meticulous to the end, so the inference is plain: the documents had never been brought to his attention. Regrettably, Sandherr is mortally ill with an incurable affliction of the mind, so I have been unable to discuss this with him. I debated with myself whether to tax my deputies with having omitted to show their former chief documents which he certainly should have seen, for it naturally occurred to me that this practice might well be still continuing, and that I myself was being deprived of important information. However, instinct caused me to say nothing for the time being. Instead, I examined all the uninitialled papers which I had so far found, curious to discover some element common to them all which might uncover a motive for their suppression. Nothing revealed itself, though, and I put it all down to that secrecy with which my assistants preferred to pursue their individual enquiries. I resolved at last to issue strict instructions that in future everything must come before my eyes, at the same time calling for a tightening up of other procedures which were not being followed meticulously enough for my liking.

'I was on the point of doing this when, in the course of going through a file for a point of information, I made a discovery as startling in its way as that of the *bordereau*. It was a report from a woman agent of ours, one Claudine, who for a time had a position as a translator in the *Nachrichtenbüro*—the German Intelligence department—in Berlin. She disclosed in it that a Frenchman was supplying items of military information to Colonel Schwartzkoppen, the German Military Attaché in Paris. That document, Mr Holmes, was yet another which did not bear Sandherr's initials and so had not been shown to him; and the file in which I found it was one dealing with a relatively obscure matter which had been concluded long ago. It was by the merest chance that I happened to turn to it, and so found this most disturbing report, which had no business to be there at all.'

'Was the report dated?' asked Holmes, his eyes alight now with eager anticipation.

Picquart did not disappoint him. 'It was. April 1895—by which time Alfred Dreyfus was on Devil's Island, or at least en route there.'

Holmes brought the palm of one hand down resoundingly on to his thigh.

'Now we are coming close to it!' he exclaimed. 'But tell me, did the agent not name this traitor?'

'Unfortunately, no. Her report is extremely brief. She does not even say whether he is a civilian or a soldier. Only that he is in his mid-forties and wears in his lapel the ribbon of the Legion of Honour.'

'Surely, though, whoever in your department received the report must instantly have demanded more particulars of so serious a matter?'

'If he did, there is no trace of them. It might be that they, too, lie in some other innocuous file. It is a troublesome thought, if so. It would prove conclusively that the report had been kept from Sandherr's notice and filed where it would not be expected to come to light. It might also suggest that, for some reason, a blind eye was turned upon this treachery, which, for all I know, is perhaps still continuing.'

'Great heavens!' I could not help crying at the enormity of this idea.

He turned to me. 'Indeed, Dr Watson. And I will tell you a final detail which will appal you even more. Upon turning to the personal file of the agent Claudine, I discovered that in the same month in which she sent that report, she was withdrawn from her posting in Berlin and her services dispensed with.'

The significance of this was so obvious and so stunning that we all remained silent for some minutes. The band still played and the cheerful sounds of laughter and conversation and the rattle of cutlery and crockery reached our ears. A steamer's whistle blew as it approached one of the busy landing places. There could have been no more incongruous setting for this dramatic narrative to have been related.

Holmes broke the silence at last. 'Colonel, are you able to identify the officer in your department who would have handled this report when it arrived?'

'It was not in code, which eliminates the cypher officers. In view of its importance it would certainly have been passed immediately to one of the chief's immediate deputies.'

'Who, at the time, would be ...?'

Almost with reluctance, Colonel Picquart replied, 'Major Henry and Captain Lauth. They are my own deputies today.'

'I see! Presumably, you have never had cause to doubt the loyalty of either?'

'He would certainly not be serving me if I had.'

'Is either, to your knowledge, strongly anti-Semitic?'

The answer which came astounded me.

'The only officer in my department holding anti-Semitic feelings, Mr Holmes, is myself.'

There was no stunned silence following this remarkable admission, for Colonel Picquart went on immediately to explain.

'This is no revelation to Monsieur and Madame Dreyfus. Also, I hasten to assure you that my prejudice against the Jewish race is neither virulent nor active. It is instinctive. It has been within me throughout my life. I am a Roman Catholic. Like the Dreyfus family, I am a native of Alsace, and a great many of those Alsatians who are not Jews inherit prejudice against them almost with their mothers' milk. Logic tells me that it is unjustified. The Jews gain wealth and influence by the simple means of working devotedly and ambitiously for these things. We others envy them their achievement, and put it down to some non-existent privilege of Nature, which has been denied to the rest of us. Yet, although I am aware of this, if I am to be honest I must confess that my attitude towards the Jews is one of natural antipathy. I am glad, at any rate, not to have to put it in any stronger term.'

'You are honest, indeed, Colonel,' responded Holmes warmly. 'Had I known at the outset of this meeting that, holding the view which you have just expressed so candidly, you were risking everything on behalf of a Jew, I should have felt none of that suspicion which only left me when you mentioned that there is mutual trust between yourself and the admirable Dubuque.'

I murmured my own recognition of the Colonel's honesty and courage. Holmes went on to question him further.

'And you can say with certainty that your views on this subject are not shared by your deputies?'

'Absolutely. Lauth is an Alsatian, too, but we have chatted about the Jews and I know that he has no fanatical prejudices. Henry comes from the Marne—an ex-ranker of peasant stock. The Jews do not trouble the minds of such people.'

'And yet it was almost certainly one of them who handled and suppressed the agent's despatch. You have not spoken to them about this aspect, either?'

'Not a word. I realised that the moment had arrived when whatever step I chose to take might be the wrong one. I knew not which way to turn, hence my approach to Dubuque and then yourself.'

'It is as well,' Holmes agreed. 'Now, as to this Claudine, do you possess any note as to her present whereabouts?'

'Here, in Geneva. It is one of the reasons why I suggested we meet here. I had half made up my mind to interview her, though on reflection I decided it better to hold myself personally aloof for as long as possible.'

'A shrewd decision. Has the lady no other name?'

'None appears on our files.'

'A woman of mystery, then!' Holmes intoned jocularly, yet clearly beguiled.

'From what I can gather she is one of those agents who will work for anyone who will pay her, regardless of any form of loyalty. Yet, no, perhaps I wrong her there. She is Anglo-French, and her record, so far as our knowledge goes, contains nothing that has been to the detriment of either of our countries. She will work for the Germans against the Italians or the Turks, or for either of those against Germany. Or for France or England against anyone else. She is not ostentatiously wealthy, yet she is seldom out of employment. I fancy she might be a little like yourself, Mr Holmes—one who chooses to work ... What is your own saying?'

'Only upon those matters which present some interest or difficulty,' I put in for my friend, who rewarded me with his little nod of acknowledgment.

'Thank you, Doctor,' the Colonel smiled. 'As to her personality, her file shows her to be resourceful, brave, and—a useful asset, no doubt—alluring. Unmarried I think, and perhaps thirty-four.'

'An enticing combination, indeed. And I take it she has not yet been approached?'

'That is correct. I had thought of Dubuque, but I should not wish it to be discovered by anyone that he was carrying out enquiries on my behalf. He is too useful where he is, in the Sûreté, to risk compromising him.'

'Then you wish me to see her?'

'I had hoped . . .'

'I have a better idea, but it wants a little thinking out. In the meantime, Colonel, have you anything further to tell me?'

'That is all. Heaven knows, it is more than enough, is it not?'

I cleared my throat and asked, 'Is there necessarily a connection between the treachery which this agent reported and Captain Dreyfus's case? Couldn't they be altogether separate?'

Colonel Picquart nodded sadly. 'That is my fear. It would mean that not only is there another complex business awaiting investigation, but also that the light which I had fancied might be beginning to fall at last upon the Dreyfus Affair is extinguished, and that we are in complete darkness again.'

'Colonel . . .' It was Lucie Dreyfus again. This time her brother-in-law made no move to restrain her.

'Madame?' Picquart responded.

'Now may I put my own idea to Mr Holmes?'

The Colonel glanced at Holmes before answering, 'By all means.'

'Mr Holmes,' Lucie addressed him, 'your imagination will have told you what pain has been my lot, ever since that terrible morning when our happy life disintegrated at a blow. My private despair has been greater than I have allowed to be seen. My darling children depend entirely upon my example, and I have therefore maintained as brave a bearing as I have been able to do. In a curious way, this has helped me, since to pretend confidence seems to create it within oneself, even when there is little enough foundation for it.'

'I fully agree, Madame. I have a theory that the individual may to a considerable degree shape his or her own destiny through the habit of thinking positively or negatively.'

'Yes! It is an attitude which I have found it bitterly hard to sustain at times. And yet, there always recurs the knowledge that my husband is guiltless, and the belief that God, in his goodness, will restore him sooner or later. But there is ... there is another, more specific, reason for my believing this ...'

She hesitated again and glanced uncertainly at Mathieu Dreyfus. He took her hand once more, and nodded to her to continue.

'Shortly after Alfred had been taken away into his exile, and my plea to be allowed to join him had been dismissed—at a time, in fact, when all our expectations were at their lowest—I was approached by a clairvoyante from Le Havre. She expressed her sympathy with me and said she had had some remarkably clear visions of Alfred in prison and aboard the ship. She believed strongly that there was some message waiting to be conveyed, but that she felt that it would only manifest itself under the strengthening presence of myself or a member of Alfred's own family.

'Our first instinct was to suspect her motives. Ever since the case began there have been approaches by strangers professing sympathy. Some have undoubtedly been sincere; but there have been others who have wanted to discuss aspects of it in detail, and ask many questions. Two even offered to arrange to rescue Alfred if we would pay them sufficient money. We were certain that these were *provocateurs*, sent by the authorities to tempt us to discredit ourselves.

'All the same, you can appreciate that I was eager to know whether the medium's claim was genuine, and to hear what message she might be able to obtain. I discussed it with Mathieu, whom she had not met, and he offered to go to her, without identifying himself, as an ordinary client seeking communication with passed ones. He will tell you himself what transpired.'

'You must understand,' explained her brother-in-law, 'that I have always been highly sceptical of clairvoyance, and increasingly so in recent years, since it has become almost a fashionable game, with some of its obvious frauds accepted as amusing tricks. However, I went to see this woman at Le Havre. She quickly went into a trance and almost immediately called me by my name and recited certain accurate particulars about me. I was only slightly surprised at this. If she were a fake, I thought, she could easily have observed me and found out these things without my knowledge.

'But then she began addressing someone else. It was Alfred. He was aboard the ship which carried him to Guiana. He seemed to be replying to her. Although I did not hear any reproduction of his own voice, she repeated what he was saying. He described his embarkation, the lone cell he occupied in the ship, without food and in bitter cold. The cell was covered by a grating open to the weather. The sea, for the first few days, was rough, and he suffered extremely. Only upon the fifth day was he allowed on deck for exercise, accompanied by two warders, and on the eighth day the weather began to turn warmer, so that he was soon being tormented as much by heat as he had been by cold.

'All these particulars, I kept reminding myself, this woman could have obtained, if she were acting for the authorities. And yet, I was impressed by some element of sincerity in what would have had to be a fairly impressive performance, if such it were. She said that Fred was telling her that he was sustained by the confidence that he would some day be reunited with his family in freedom. This could have been an invention of the sort of thing she would expect me to wish to hear. But then occurred something which struck me as a blunder on her part. She was describing Alfred pacing the deck between his guards and referred to his taking off his spectacles to wipe some spray from their lenses. I had been able to speak to her and ask questions, even though she was supposedly in a trance, and I now asked, as casually as I could, if she could describe the spectacles. She appeared to concentrate very hard for quite some minutes, before replying that they had nickel plated frames and sides, with a plain, low bridge for the nose, and were of a type specially designed not to corrode in humid tropical heat.

'This was enough to convince me at last that the woman was a fraud. I knew perfectly well that Fred always wore gold-rimmed pince-nez, of the folding type, and that they would be all he had with him when he was arrested and imprisoned. I told her this, rather curtly, in fact, and stated that I wished to hear no more. She came out of her trance quickly and I prepared to take my leave. At the door, though, she said, "I know what I said, monsieur, and I was correct. They were spectacles he was wearing."

'I reported all this to Lucie, to her disappointment, and we thought no more of it until letters at last began to arrive from Fred on Devil's Island. One of the first of all contained a reference to his glasses. His pince-nez had become broken during the voyage, and the ship's captain had given him a pair of spectacles in their place.'

Mathieu Dreyfus paused, to see what effect this remarkable information would have on Holmes, but the latter pursed his lips.

'If this medium were some sort of agent for the authorities, that is just the sort of information they would have given her,' he pointed out. 'Such seemingly trifling details, casually thrown in, are precisely the touches which impress disbelievers most. My experience of good clairvoyants of both sexes is that they have a highly developed knowledge of human psychology, and can apply it with skill.'

'You do not believe in them, then?' Lucie Dreyfus asked, in a depressed tone.

'I am not so categorical as that, Madame Dreyfus. I have a saying, "The world is big enough for us. No ghosts need apply." It fairly reflects my view. On the other hand, I am the first to recognise that life, and the forces which govern it, of many of which we are unaware, are infinitely stranger than anything which the mind of man could invent. Allowing generously for what it is possible to disprove or explain away, there is still that residue which baffles understanding. While it remains, the capacity for belief stays, too.'

'My view entirely!' cried Colonel Picquart, to my surprise. He saw my expression and explained, 'Because I am a professional soldier does not mean that I am entirely without imagination or any tendency to ponder the mysteries of life and death, Doctor. As a matter of fact, Spiritualism interests me. I recall first plucking up the nerve to attend a séance to see for myself. The medium caused a hat to rotate on a table top. Such was my suspicion that some mechanical device was being used that I offered my own hat and placed it on the table myself. It began to spin round almost at once. Not only that, but it acquired such an impetus of rotation that it continued to spin upon my head as I walked home.'

We all laughed at the spectacle conjured up by this, but Lucie Dreyfus was eager to return to her subject.

'What I wish to say is this, Mr Holmes. From what I have read of clairvoyants, they often achieve striking results by handling some object connected with the subject with whom one desires to make contact. I have Alfred's letters now, which I did not have at the time of this earlier sitting. Might it not be worth our while to try again now? Who knows what we might learn, what small clue you might receive, which could help us solve this mystery?'

Holmes remained thoughtfully silent for the moment, so I pointed out to her, 'But if it is still uncertain whether the woman is influenced by the authorities, how could anything she might add be trusted?'

'You mistake me, Doctor. Of course I would not propose returning to her. But I see that this extraordinary woman Eusapia Palladino, who is travelling Europe giving test sittings to any professors who wish to investigate her, is in Geneva at this moment, for the benefit of the University. Surely, we could accept anything which she might be able to communicate to us as sincere?'

'An excellent idea, Madame,' declared Holmes before I could reply. 'A remarkable woman, by all accounts. She has come through countless investigations without discredit. No medium in history has been more thoroughly tested. My friend Professor Lombroso, the eminent psychiatrist and criminal anthropologist, had two sittings with her a few years ago. He entered into them in the most detached, even sceptical, frame of mind. He told me subsequently—I recall his very words: "I am filled with confusion and regret that I combated with so much persistence the possibility of the facts called Spiritualistic."'

'You agree?' cried Lucie Dreyfus. 'You see, Mathieu, I was right! We shall get our answers now!'

Mathieu Dreyfus glanced at Holmes and Colonel Picquart, and I could see clearly his uneasiness. Holmes answered for him: 'Do not build your hopes too high, dear lady. Regard this, at most, as a byway off the main road of our journey. Should it lead us to some metaphysical destination, there will have to be physical investigation to establish its validity. But I agree; by all means, let us try any ways at our disposal, and the proximity of Signorina Eusapia Palladino would seem to be a happy coincidence at this juncture.'

The interview was quickly arranged by Holmes, acting in a manner he did not explain to me, through some friend in the University. Within forty-eight hours our party was on its way in two cabs up the steep ascent to the Old Town of Geneva, whose University occupied ancient and scattered premises at the very crown of the hill overlooking the lake.

My friend had given me a brief description of the woman we were on our way to see. Eusapia Palladino had been born in Naples in 1854, of peasant origins. Although she was regarded as almost a simpleton, some of the strange manifestations of psychical phenomena of which she had become the centre had attracted the interest of a Professor Chiaia, who in turn had brought her to the attention of the celebrated Lombroso, then Professor of Psychiatry at Pavia and already noted for his theories about the origins and appearance of criminal types. As Holmes had told us, Lombroso had been deeply impressed by her, following which she had submitted herself to tests by psychic investigators and others in many countries, including my own, where Sir Oliver Lodge and F.W.H. Myers had been amongst those to conduct sittings with her.

It would be less than honest of me not to admit that I travelled to our encounter with a sinking feeling of trepidation in my stomach. Unlike Holmes, I had had no experience of clairvoyance. I had never been a man to wonder much about the so-called 'life-after-death', or the separation of the soul from the body. When I had been under fire in the Afghan campaign I had expected merely to survive or be wiped off the earth by whatever Jezail bullet happened to strike me. It might be fired at me intentionally, or find me accidentally, according to some unknown tribesman's aim. It never occurred to me to wonder what hand Fate might have in the matter. As a doctor, subsequently, I had come to equate death with the breaking down, or wearing out, of the body's machinery, as a mechanic would diagnose a seizure in the working of an engine. I had been present at countless deaths, and had been pleased to note that most had seemed to be accompanied by sensations of relief from pain and worldly suffering of other kinds; but that pleasure I had felt more on behalf of those relatives who stood beside me in their grief than out of any wish to be assured myself that there was some process of 'passing-over' from our own plane to another more blissful and enduring.

The anticipation of the medium's antics and their possible effect upon Madame Dreyfus was disturbing to me, and I confess that I did not relish them for my own part. I did not know whether I should feel revulsion or amazement; whether I should be impelled to shudder or to laugh aloud. At any rate, I repeated inwardly as we drove, the subject of our enquiry was a live one, separated by distance, not death; and the presence of four other witnesses, including my closest friend and the impressively military Colonel Picquart, was reassuring.

Eusapia Palladino, into whose presence we were ushered in a small, stone-walled room, was anything but the flamboyant sorceress type which I had half-envisaged. She was squat, dark, and clumsily shapen. Had I not been told by Holmes that she was in her early forties at this time, I should have adjudged her older. She spoke English, though with a thick accent, grotesque in its rendering of some words. I saw a resemblance in type to the wife of one of the Neapolitan ice cream vendors who were permitted to frequent Lord's cricket ground, who had served me with a wafer early in the summer.

Signorina Palladino answered modestly enough our polite enquiries about her career. Her mother had died in giving birth to her, and her father when she was a child. Her mediumistic powers had first appeared when she was fourteen years old. A table at which she and some friends were sitting rose into the air, while chairs, glasses, bottles and other objects in the room danced and the curtains swished to and fro. Psychic investigators who heard of it proceeded to carry out tests on all those who had been present, in order to discover which of them had been responsible. Eusapia was found to have been that one.

Subsequent manifestations attributable to her had brought her to the attention of the entire world of psychic investigation. Countless individuals and committees of the most reputable sort had tested her. She told us of her ability to write on cards without touching them, to play on musical instruments which she neither saw nor touched, to speak in languages of which she had no knowledge, to levitate her body no matter how securely it was bound to a couch or chair.

The identity of none of our party had been revealed to her, and I was on my watch for her to ask questions which would enable her to make deductions about us. None came, however. She was content to answer ours, in a simple, straightforward manner.

'Of course!' she declared with a little smile when Picquart asked her if her had ever been accused of cheating. 'Many time. The Society for Psychical Research in London calls me complete fraud. They test me no more. They will change mind, however.'

'*Have* you ever cheated?' Holmes asked her bluntly.

She smiled again. 'Yes. I have cheat often. I explain. I am in trance. Some people in room is expecting tricks, but nothing is happening. They are getting impatient. Their minds are on tricks. They wish to see. Their wishes pass into my mind, and I automatical respond. Afterwards comes real manifestation, but by then they don't believe.'

Having spent a quarter of an hour or so establishing rapport with the medium, whose open manner had impressed me, we prepared for the sitting. I was immediately upon my guard again, looking for every possibility of trickery. But Eusapia Palladino, no doubt from long experience, had anticipated scepticism and invited us to take any measures we wished to ensure that the small room contained no apparatus. One corner of it was curtained off to form a cabinet, which she explained served the purpose of an enclosure in which power would gather. In turn we went inside and looked about, examining the curtains and their means of attachment. I tugged heartily at them, and found them totally secure. We drew and opened the window curtains several times before closing them finally, satisfied that nothing was concealed. An oil lamp and two candles, lit by Colonel Picquart after examination by us all, provided the only illumination now, but it was more than adequate to dispel any deep shadows. The door key was in its place, and Madame Palladino invited whichever of us who wished to turn it in the lock, test the door for security, and place the key about our own person. I performed this task and put the key into a trouser pocket, where I kept it in the grip of my hand throughout the proceedings.

The only other contents of the room were enough chairs for us all and a plain wooden table, on which stood tumblers and a decanter of water, and the oil lamp. The two candles stood in tall iron holders placed upon the floor. Our party seated ourselves like a little theatre audience, facing the proscenium formed by the curtained cabinet. I fully expected the medium to take her own chair into the cabinet and draw the curtain upon herself, and confess that although I had examined the space minutely I still believed she had some means of trickery which she could only work in concealment. To my surprise, then, she placed her chair outside the cabinet and a foot or two away from it, so that her back was to it when she sat down. I had already noted that her light clothing, which I should have thought was of a chilly nature for that stone room, had no suspicious voluminosities in which objects might be hidden; but before we sat down, we four gentlemen turned our backs briefly whilst Madame Dreyfus accepted the medium's invitation to examine her clothing and pat her body wherever she wished.

With every suspicion thus satisfied we sat in the secured room and awaited what might transpire.

FIFTEEN

MADAME Palladino folded her hands upon her lap, closed her eyes, and composed her body in an attitude of calm relaxation. She commenced breathing deeply and her head slowly tilted itself a little backward. Within what I adjudged to be less than a minute she gave a little wriggle, as if to shift her position into one of even more comfort, and spoke.

I recollect my surprise that the voice which emerged was no unearthly intonation, but her own. The singular exception was that she now spoke in perfectly cultivated English, of agreeable melodiousness. Indeed, her very features seemed to have become transformed from their dark homeliness to something more finely chiselled, made almost attractive by the serenity which they now wore.

If this surprised me, however, I was quickly to be downright astonished.

'John?' she asked, 'John? Are you there?'

Here was dilemma! The name was mine, but quick memory warned me that it had been borrowed by Sherlock Holmes for his Devil's Island expedition. I shot him a quick glance. He gave me a little nod, clearly signalling me to respond.

'I am here,' said I, and my lips were dry.

'So you are, my dear old fellow! How comforting it is to see you in such good health again after your wounds.'

The first thought which flashed across my mind at this was that the observant medium might well have detected my slight limp and the small stiffness of my upper arm, my twin legacies from the battle of Maiwand. What was less explicable, though, and caused a sharp thrill to pass through me, was that the form of address she had used had been precisely that favoured by my dear father, dead these long years, and that the words had been delivered in his exact manner.

She continued. 'Old fellow, your dear mama and I have watched your career with love and pride. You worked most diligently at your studies. You served your country gallantly. And now you serve posterity in another field.'

Suddenly too overwhelmed emotionally to feel embarrassment or to pause for logical enquiry, I blurted out, 'Papa! Is that you?'

'Of course, old fellow! And still you wear my trusty old watch! Goodness me, how well it has served, in spite of poor Henry's neglect.'

Now, this was truly remarkable. The reader familiar with the long narrative which I entitled "The Sign of the Four" * will call to mind at once Sherlock Holmes's deductive demonstration centred upon this self-same watch. I will not repeat its details here; suffice it to say that, by simple examination of it, he had been able to state that it had been engraved for my father, had passed, upon his death, into the possession of my elder brother Henry, and, subsequent to his own death, which Holmes had accurately ascribed to disillusionment and drink, had come to me. None of these details had been known to Holmes.

The old watch lies open before me as I write these lines, ticking away as reliably as ever, a potent reminder to me of several remarkable experiences in my life, of which the sitting with Eusapia Palladino must remain without doubt the most dramatic. (But I digress once more.)

'Is ... Henry ... with you?' I faltered.

'Of course, of course! He is restored to health and vigour. He only regrets that he could not enjoy these throughout his life upon earth. And Mary sends you her most devoted love.'

'Mary!' I cried, the tears starting to my eyes. 'She is there, too?'

'Naturally. Some day, John, your family and your wife will greet you here. Meanwhile, though, may you be happy where you are, and may the enterprises in which you and your gifted friend engage yourselves prove fruitful. You are both acting upon the side of the angels, my dear old fellow. God bless you and keep you both.'

---

* It has come to be more commonly known abbreviatedly as "The Sign of Four", a less effective form, to my way of thinking. —J.H.W.

I was near to weeping by now. Only a nudge from Holmes, who sat beside me, and a quick whisper in my ear, prevented me from succumbing altogether, and reminded me of our business. Thickly, I managed to ask, 'Papa ... Our present business ... Can you help us?'

There was a silence. When the voice resumed it was fainter, beginning to trail away. I strove to catch each word.

'No ... no more ... strength ... need more str........'

I looked towards Holmes again. He was frowning perplexedly. When I glanced back to the medium I saw that her head was lolling forward. Overwhelmed though I had been personally by my experience, I felt urgently the need to re-establish that contact which would assist us all toward the object of our coming there; but although I asked beseechingly for assistance from the dear father whom I was now convinced had spoken to me from across the abyss between Death and Life, the tongue of our intermediary remained still and her breast heaved in what seemed to be unheeding slumber.

It was Colonel Picquart who brought her back to animation. He stirred in his chair and I saw him draw out of his inner pocket a folded sheet of paper. He stood up quietly, took a silent pace forward, and, with outstretched arm, slid it between the medium's clasped hands and her lap.

She did not move. Picquart resumed his seat and, turning towards Holmes and myself, mouthed silently, 'The *bordereau*.'

We all waited. I had just experienced something totally unexpected, which, more than thirty years later, I cannot explain or dismiss, and therefore must believe—as, indeed, I wish increasingly to do as I grow older and my own passing comes closer. The fact that I, without doubt the most stolidly materialistic member of that assembly, should have been singled out for attention from Beyond both puzzled and impressed me. It had been startlingly convincing; yet I confess it renewed my suspicion that here was consummate trickery in play. The nature of the piece of paper which Picquart had passed across showed me that it was merely that same photographed copy of the *bordereau* which he had shown us earlier. If an Italian peasant with certain extra-sensory powers could make anything cogent out of that, I thought, I should find myself required to revise entirely such notions as I already possessed of the established tenets of religion and science.

For long minutes Eusapia Palladino sat totally still. Even the signs of breathing had virtually left her now. She appeared to be in the deepest slumber. The only sounds in that room were the slight stirrings of my companions and myself, as we fidgeted on our chairs.

My own principal discomfort was from the coldness of the place. It had not seemed excessive at first, although, as I have said, I had thought the medium's garb scanty for the stony surroundings. Perhaps it was as a result of sitting still for what, by now, must have been half an hour, that I began to shiver slightly. I remember consciously wriggling my toes to keep the circulation going. From the corners of my vision I noticed Madame Dreyfus draw her fur tippet closer about her neck, and even the usually impervious Holmes button his jacket and thrust his hands into his trouser pockets. It confirmed my belief that there was something exceptional about this onset of chilliness.

A sudden sound re-engaged my attention. Madame Palladino had begun to breathe deeply once more. Her breast commenced rising and falling in ever more rapid movements and a corresponding rasping sound issued from her partly-opened mouth.

She spoke again, and this time it was in the manner I had often heard patients murmur under anaesthetic, at that stage when the operation is ended and drowsy consciousness gradually begins to return.

'Officer ... Officer ... Black ... black hair, eyebrows ... Black eyes. Moustache. All black ... black. Tall. Thin. Bird ... Yes, bird. Vulture. Black vulture ...'

The voice ceased again. Picquart leaned forward and asked softly but urgently, 'His name, please. The officer's name.'

No answer was returned. Instead, there occurred something which was both wonderful and frightening in its abnormality.

In the air, between us and the medium, and at a little above the level of our eyes, there began to materialise a shape. It was perhaps some three feet in length and stick-like. It hung vertically, and as its detail became clearer I made out the gleam of silver upon black and saw quite distinctly that it was a musical instrument—a clarinet or oboe.

As it solidified, there began to emerge from Eusapia Palladino's body, from her left shoulder, a white extrusion which, with an involuntary gasp, I recognised to be a perfectly formed hand and arm. The gasps of my companions told me that it was not of my sole imagining, or that the charged atmosphere had caused some hallucination in my mind alone. There sat the medium, utterly motionless, her hands still clasped upon her lap, the sheet of paper under them, whilst this third arm stretched itself forward until it could grasp the floating instrument. The fingers divided to set themselves upon separate keys; and then they began to move, and, although the mouthpiece was far from the medium's reach, the silvery tone of solo woodwind began to be heard.

It did not play for long. The brief, attractive phrase was infinitely tender, with a dying fall. It ended. The fingers lifted from the keys and our astonished eyes saw the simultaneous dematerialising of the instrument and the withdrawal of the arm back into Madame Palladino's shoulder, to vanish completely.

I saw Madame Dreyfus sway on her chair, and her brother-in-law quickly place an arm round her, anticipating a faint. She sagged forward and would have crumpled to the ground, but for his grasp.

'Water!' he requested. 'Please, water.'

I was the first to move. Heedless of the medium's trance I stepped swiftly across to the table where the decanter stood, and poured out. I was turning to carry the glass to the swooning woman when something arrested my movement momentarily. Under the decanter lay a square piece of white pasteboard. To my certain knowledge it had not been there before, as I had made a point, whilst searching the room, of lifting up every piece of glassware and replacing it some inches from its original position.

For the moment, though, I paid no further heed to this discovery, concerned only to restore Madame Dreyfus, which was quickly done. I noticed that the medium herself was beginning to stir. The two ladies regained full consciousness at about the same moment.

'Madame,' Colonel Picquart repeated anxiously to Eusapia Palladino; 'Is there a name?'

'Name? Name? What name?' Her Neapolitan accent was as thick as ever. Every last trace of feminine attraction had left her features, and as she roused herself in her chair she scratched the armpit beneath the shoulder from which what I can only term that ectoplasmic third arm had issued forth.

'The officer. The black one. Like a black vulture, you described him.'

She stared back at Picquart, then shrugged.

'I can no say. No remember. Eusapia in trance is no Eusapia awake.'

Holmes spoke at last. 'Madame Palladino, are you aware of your ability to project an extra arm from your body?'

Her eyes, which had been dull as though from interrupted sleep, glowed suddenly.

'Eey! Has done? Sir Lodge has said has seen, but Eusapia no feel.'

'Sir Oliver Lodge described it to me in detail,' Holmes answered. 'Now we have seen it for ourselves. An arm issued from your shoulder—the left one—and its hand grasped a floating musical instrument of the woodwind family. Some bars of music were played ...'

'But I knowing no music—except to sing, like all in Napoli.'

'You do not know what was played, then? It had no meaning?'

The medium's expression was blank. 'I no play. I no feel. I no speak. Eusapia in trance. Is always same.'

I was still upstanding at this moment. I returned to the table where the decanter and glasses were and picked up the square of white card. I turned it over. The reverse side bore a single letter, inscribed in ink so fresh that it had smeared slightly. It was a capital E. I brought it over to Holmes.

'I found this under the decanter. It was definitely not there before. And see, the ink is still wet.'

He examined the card briefly, turning it over, holding it up to the oil lamp's light. Picquart craned across to look at it, too. Holmes held it up for Madame Palladino to see, the lettered side toward her.

She shrugged again. 'Am writing in trance. Often.'

'The letter E, madame? Pray think. What can it mean?'

A pause for thought, then another shrug. She yawned suddenly, and got up.

'Eusepia tired. Sleep now. Eusapia sleep.'

Yawning copiously, she gave a little bob in the general direction of us all and went to the door. She turned the knob, but the door would not open. She turned back to us, smiling tiredly.

'Someone has key?'

I recollected that it was I, and hurriedly produced it. Sure enough, the door proved to be as firmly locked as when I had turned that key in it before the seance. I turned it again now and the remarkable woman left our presence.' *

'It was astounding!' Colonel Picquart declared. 'In all my admittedly limited experience of mediumship I have seen nothing to compare.'

'Did you see the instrument?' Lucie Dreyfus almost babbled. 'That music ...!'

I noticed that Holmes was beating his brow with the palm of one hand.

'That music,' he repeated. 'What on earth was it? I know, and yet ...' He hummed the notes, precisely recalled. 'Ah, how memory lets one down at times. Does anyone know?'

We all shook our heads. I had the dimmest recollection of the tune, heard, perhaps, at one of my visits with Holmes to the Queen's Hall; but I have never been one to be capable of putting a name to a tune, or vice versa, and this occasion was no exception.

Colonel Picquart was scribbling busily in a pocket book, murmuring aloud: 'Tall. Thin. Black hair, eyebrows, moustache, eyes. Overall impression of blackness. Bird-like—vulturine. A beaky nose, perhaps.'

'Not Alfred, at any rate,' remarked Mathieu Dreyfus, stooping to pick up from the floor the photograph of the *bordereau,* which Madame Palladino had let fall unconcernedly. 'Does it call anyone else to mind, Colonel?'

'Not at once. Nor to you?'

'Likewise. I will think hard—but ...'

'Early Mozart?' Holmes was muttering. He hummed the phrase again. 'No, no. Haydn ...? Haydn! Ah, I have it. The "Farewell" symphony. The finale of the last movement.' Once more the tune was hummed. 'Recognise it?'

None of us did, however. Holmes frowned. '"Farewell." *Abschied* in German. Key of E? No, no. F sharp minor, for a certainty; a most unusual key. A black bird. Blackbird? *Schwarzervogel?* No, no—

---

* I met her but this once. She died in 1918. Her incredible gifts were studied in much detail in a book, "Eusapia Palladino and her Phenomena" by Dr Hereward Carrington.—J.H.W.

Amsel, of course. No *E*, however. No *E* anywhere.'

He turned to us all. 'A tall, black-haired, black-moustached officer. The letter E. The finale to Haydn's 45th symphony. These and the *bordereau*. Does any connection occur?'

It did not. 'Ah, well,' he sighed, 'it was worth the trying. At any rate, Watson, she sounded convincing enough in your case.'

'Remarkably so,' I admitted readily, and outlined briefly to the others the accuracy of the medium's observations. I was able to show them the watch itself, with its scratch marks around the keyhole caused by my poor brother's shaky fumblings. They were clearly impressed.

'Then, are there no conclusions to be drawn?' Madame Dreyfus asked, her voice heavy again with disappointment.

Colonel Picquart glanced at Holmes, who was still frowning to himself.

'I fear not,' Picquart replied. 'But perhaps we are a little further forward, even so. It only remains for me to go through the descriptions of the entire officer corps of the French Army, making out a list of those with black hair and moustaches ... I beg your pardon, Madame Dreyfus, but I am not jesting. It is the one and only possibility that has occurred to me as a result of today's experience, and it would be a failure on my part not to pursue it. Who knows, but what it might lead somewhere?'

'Who indeed?'

The response came from Holmes. The frown had left his brow and his eyes wore that expression of thoughtfulness which told me that his mind had fastened upon something which it would not release until it had examined it as thoroughly as we had examined the room in which we stood in a chilly cluster, wondering what to do next.

'Madame Dreyfus,' said Holmes, as though suddenly arrived at a conclusion. 'Monsieur Dreyfus. If you will be so good as to leave the three of us alone now, I have a further little scheme to put to my professional associates.'

'What is it, Mr Holmes?' asked Lucie Dreyfus pleadingly. 'Please tell us if you have hope.'

'It is not a matter of hope, Madame, but of leaving no stone unturned, as we say. Remember that you are often watched and might be questioned at any time. What you do not know about, you cannot be persuaded to tell. Comfort yourself with the knowledge that where there is possibility, there is hope. My friend here will vouch that my favourite axiom is that when the impossible is eliminated, whatever remains, however improbable, must be the truth. That is the task immediately facing us. Take my advice, then, and return home and resume normal life. You may depend upon us to communicate with you the instant occasion arises.'

The brother and sister-in-law made their formal farewells.

'By the way,' Holmes added, as they were about to leave; 'under no circumstances make mention in your letters to Captain Dreyfus of a black-browed brother officer, Haydn in F sharp minor, or the letter E.'

They looked at him expectantly, hoping for some elaboration; but he offered none, and they went.

Holmes closed the door of the little room again. I could have wished for some warmer quarters in which to continue the discussion, preferably somewhere with a waiter within call; but Holmes proceeded to stride to and fro, speaking rapidly.

'We have completed our little excursion into the World Beyond, and it has not been without its points of interest. Let us now, however, return to this more materialistic plane upon which it is our present lot to move and see what we can learn by more mundane methods of enquiry. I refer, of course, to the woman agent Claudine. Your notion, Colonel, was that I should visit her, to save you from exposing yourself to the view of the curious. I answered that I had a better idea, to which I would return. Well, it is simply this. I propose that since neither of us wishes to be seen to be showing an interest in her, my friend and associate here should carry out the duty instead.'

'*I*, Holmes!'

'My dear Watson, never let it be said that I underestimate your powers of subtle interrogation.' He turned to Colonel Picquart, who, I noted, appeared amused by my reaction to this unexpected suggestion. 'You must appreciate, Colonel, that Watson has some remarkable characteristics of his own, to which, in his modesty, he has given small attention amidst his exaggerated estimates of my own performances. Added to which, he boasts an experience of women which extends over many nations and three separate continents. You inform us that Mademoiselle Claudine is a woman of charm and attraction, as well as intelligence; therefore, what more qualified emissary could we appoint?'

The colonel laughed aloud, and I fancied that he eyed me with a new form of respect.

'Excellent, Mr Holmes. Be careful, though, Doctor. The form of witchery practised by female spies is somewhat different from the sort we have seen here today.'

'My mind will be wholly concentrated upon the work in hand,' I assured him, and he laughed again, this time with a wink.

Holmes resumed his serious tone. 'This is my plan. Watson will visit the bewitching lady, and, with the inducement of money, not to mention his winning charm, will find out all she can tell him about the Frenchman whom she reported was in the habit of carrying secret information to the Germans.'

'Hold on,' I protested. 'What makes you believe she will tell me anything? She would never mistake me for French Intelligence in a thousand years.'

'*Ten* thousand,' Holmes affirmed gently. 'She will see you for the honest, true-hearted Englishman that you are. We have learnt that our own country shares her loyalty. Say you are from London, but add nothing more. She is a professional at her game. She knows the devious ways in which it is played, and will not question how you came to know of her or her forgotten report. Only let her believe that you are acting in your country's interest, and I fancy she will help you.'

'Very well, then. What exactly do you wish me to do?'

'I have told you: get her to repeat what she has reported already about this traitor, but press her to search her memory for anything additional which might help us. Above all, try to learn his name.'

'You believe she knows it?'

'I do not know. It may be that she has done all along, but withheld it from her original report in the hope that more payment would be forthcoming to persuade her to give it.'

'But why has she never revealed it since?'

'How can we know she has not? Perhaps some other document, lying forgotten in one of Colonel Picquart's files, could clear everything up for us at a glance. Or perhaps there was one which has been destroyed.'

'Or,' Picquart put in, 'since she had no cause to thank my department for her summary dismissal, she has kept it to herself, in case it should prove useful in the future.'

'A dangerous piece of knowledge to carry about with her, if there are people intent upon suppressing it. That is an argument which you might find convincing, Watson, if you get the impression that she knows, but is refusing to tell.'

'Very well,' said I, feeling eagerness beginning to glow. 'But, loyal though she may be, suppose she is the sort who places self-interest first. She might merely fob me off with what we know already, deny any further knowledge, and pocket the money.'

'You see, Colonel,' said Holmes, 'I did not exaggerate my friend's knowledge of women and their ways. He calls me ungallant for declaring that they are never to be entirely trusted—not even the best of them; yet here he is implying the self-same thing!'

He turned again to me. 'You are more familiar than anyone with my views upon the essential secretiveness of women, so you will not be so naïve as to imagine that I had not foreseen the possibility you outline. No, I am not unprepared for it, and therefore I have devised a little refinement to my plan which, I hope, will enable you to extract the whole truth from this lady. Not only that, but unless I am much mistaken it will throw much-needed light upon the characters and actions of one or two other people, and might even cause them to lead us to our quarry.

'But, my dear Watson, I read in your expression the signal that you are in that form of distress which requires a glass or two of something short and sharp to alleviate it. Come, Colonel. Let us continue our debate in some place where there are better drinks to be had than water, and where a cigar may be smoked in greater comfort than this cell can afford.'

SIXTEEN

MADEMOISELLE Claudine's apartment proved to be situated in an old building overlooking a corner of the Rue Maurice, not three or four hundred yards from the place in which our séance had been conducted. Colonel Picquart provided me with the address and I sent her a brief note stating that I was in Geneva on business from London and that I should welcome the opportunity to call upon her with a view to proposing a commission in her capacity as a translator. I signed myself John Phelps, borrowing the surname of my old school chum 'Tadpole' Phelps, whose reputation Holmes had saved in the case of "The Naval Treaty".

Her note of acceptance was brought back by the messenger boy to the bureau in the lower town through which I had engaged him. Holmes had advised me not to put it beyond her to make enquiries about Mr John Phelps before agreeing to meet him, and therefore not to use our hotel notepaper or request her to address a reply to me there.

It was mid-afternoon of the following day when I made my call. I must confess that I had passed the greater part of the morning in a restless state of excitement and a little trepidation. An encounter with a female spy had not been a part of that experience of women to which my friend had alluded, and upon which I was sometimes wont to look back with modest pride. Colonel Picquart had referred to her alluring qualities. I had no doubt that she had put them to positive use on occasion, and would not scruple to do so again. I knew my susceptibility, and resolved to gain control of the interview and not find myself the one being wheedled, by whatever means, into giving answers. Nevertheless, I took extra pains over my dressing and drew from Holmes a jesting comment which came close to the improper.

The concierge directed me to the apartment upon the third floor, high above street level. My ring was answered by a pretty, dark-eyed maid, whom I took to be one of the many Spanish immigrants working in Switzerland. I was conducted through a tiny lobby into a spacious, sunny room, and invited to take a seat; Mademoiselle would be with me in a moment.

I retained my hat and stick in my hands, as was the custom in those days before being greeted by one's hostess, and looked about me from the comfortable chair. The furnishing and decoration of the room I found entirely agreeable. The walls were yellow, a bold innovation in defiance of the custom of dark greens and browns, but one which proved itself entirely justified by the result, for the light from the broad window was reflected back from every side, giving an impression of exuberance and feminine influence. There were many tasteful ornaments and at least half a dozen vases of blooms of various hues. The furniture was light and in the modern style. I recalled the expensiveness of the late Adolphe Meyer's possessions, and thought that spying might be a dangerous game, but that success in it seemed to ensure enviable rewards, not least some interesting works of modern art.

'I painted them myself. You like them?'

Her voice was soft, but it made me jump, for she had entered the room entirely silently. I struggled to my feet, feeling already at a disadvantage, for my chair was of that soft sort which it is not easy to quit hastily, and she was smiling down at me as I strove.

The enigmatic Claudine was no exotic beauty of the type I had half-imagined. She bore less resemblance to one of those tropical flowers which attract and devour live creatures than to a lily or daffodil or tulip. There was something very compact and orderly about her: her features were symmetrical, the mouth and eyes not luxuriantly large, but exactly proportioned to the shape of her face, which was oval, and the curve of her high forehead; her hair, the colour of new copper, was drawn back above her neck, in a plaited bun, and shone sleekly, with not a strand trailing; her figure was orderly, too, with nothing dramatically noticeable about its contours, and she was dressed unostentatiously, with no more jewellery than a cameo brooch on the raised border of white lace at her throat. Her eyes were a greenish grey, of the sort in which either colour tends to predominate according to the light they reflect. She wore a plain rose-coloured dress and a cream-coloured velvet jacket with a red and white gauze flower in the lapel.

When I had quite got upon my feet I was slightly relieved to find that she was less tall than had seemed; an inch or two less than my own height, and I was not a tall man, even in early middle-age. She held out a hand in the frank English manner and shook mine with a warm grasp. I noticed how white the skin was, and that she wore no rings.

'You painted all these, Mademoiselle?' said I, waving at the many framed pictures upon the fireplace wall.

'Oh, no. That, and that, and that. The little pastel of ballet girls is a Dégas—he gave it me only last year. And the impression of the Thames, of course, is Sisley.'

'Oh, er, ah!' I answered, trying to sound more knowledgeable than I knew myself to be. Once more I felt uncomfortable, aware that whilst I had been surveying her pictures, she had been subtly testing me out, assessing me in turn.

'You know he is Anglo-French, like myself,' she said. Her accent was almost pure English. 'But please sit down again, Mr Phelps. You are just over from London, you tell me. Where are you staying?'

I placed my hat and stick upon a small table and resumed my chair. The act of doing so helped me to cover any sign I might have shown that I was lying when I replied, as I had already planned to do, by giving the name of an hotel which was not the one in which my friend and I were lodged.

She sat opposite me, her hands rested demurely in her lap. She was as neat and light as the decor of the room. Anyone less like my conception of a woman spy I could scarcely have conceived.

She was smiling all the while, conveying the impression of complete openness and an absence of suspicion as to my motive for coming to see her. I knew that she must be aware that I wanted more from her than assistance in some translating project, which would scarcely have brought me from London in person without pre-liminary written enquiry and some explanation of how I had come to hear of her.

'A pleasant enough place, I believe,' she responded to my

naming the hotel. 'I am not terribly familiar with the hotels here. I prefer my own surroundings and I have an excellent cook. But, tell me, Mr Phelps, how do you wish me to help you? Is the work you have come so far to consult me about English, or French, or German, or Italian? I am very conversant with all those, and several others beside.'

It sounded like a deliberate cue to me to unburden myself, and I took it boldly, telling her exactly what Holmes had instructed, and no more. The little smile did not leave her lips, and I saw no reaction in the eyes fixed upon me, but her light tone seemed a trifle forced when she replied.

'You appear to know a good deal about me, and it would be a waste of both our time to deny any of it. However, I cannot help you.'

I must say that this impressed me a good deal, having fully expected the financial bargaining to precede any results. As I understood it, even negative conclusions cost money in the catalogues of the spying trade.

'Cannot? Or will not?' I responded, as crisply as I was able.

She shook her head, her expression serious for the first time.

'There is no question of the latter. My assistance to France was terminated almost immediately after I had reported a Frenchman peddling secrets. For no good reason that I could see I was removed from my post before I was able to see him again. I assumed that the Germans had found out something about me, and that my masters had withdrawn me hurriedly for safety's sake. Yet I have heard nothing from them since, which is strange.'

'Nothing at all? Not even an enquiry about the Frenchman?'

'There was one visitor—also a Frenchman, obviously using an assumed name. He asked whether I had reported all there was to tell, and I assured him I had. He seemed satisfied.'

'And since then?'

'As I told you, nothing.'

'Mademoiselle Claudine,' I tried resolutely, 'if you were to rack your memory, could you not produce a name?'

'No. I never knew it.'

'I . . . am empowered to offer you a sum of money.'

She suddenly threw back her head and laughed.

'Dear me, Mr Phelps, I suddenly feel in need of a chaperone. Oh, poor man, you're blushing! Look here, would it embarrass you totally if I were to ring for some tea? I see that the fifteen minutes which propriety allows for a business tête-à-tête is up, and that to offer you tea would, in some circles, be tantamount to making you a proposition of a certain kind. But my maid is broad-minded, so if you can bear the implication, I dare say I can manage it, too.'

I accepted with pleasure. I was aware that I was being charmed, and my defences were at the ready; but I had liked her instinctively, and I sensed that, professional spy though she might be, she was of a very different sort from a Meyer or an Oberstein. The alternative to accepting her invitation would be to take my leave, and I felt it my duty to persevere a little harder. To be honest, also, I was enjoying her company.

'Mademoiselle,' I continued carefully, after the pretty maid had been summoned and sent for the tea things, 'I am unable to divulge the reason behind my enquiries. I hope it will be enough to say that they are in the interest of the security of France and that her Majesty's Government is concerned for it. You will not deny that these considerations are of overriding importance to you?'

'No, I won't deny it.' She paused, as though hesitating to make a decision, then went on. 'I have not asked who sent you, Mr Phelps—if that is even your real name, which I should doubt. I do not know how much is known about me to you personally, but you know what I am, and I can't apologise for it. The trade of an agent is not the most honourable one. It involves deceits, deceptions, pretences—all right, lying and downright fraud, to be blunt. I will not bore you with the story of how I came to deal in such things, the very thought of which would at one time have made me shudder with revulsion. But here I am. This is Claudine as she is now and will probably remain until she becomes beyond use—or is put down like some dog who is poisoned for inconveniencing someone. All this you probably know. What I wish to assure you, though, with my hand on my heart, is that I am truly loyal to the two countries of my parentage, France and England.'

I murmured a protestation, but she ignored me.

'You speak of money. Of course I will accept her Majesty's money, or France's. If I am to be saddled with this sort of life, then I prefer to live it in some style, as you can see. Other women of my independence and tastes have keepers, whose money they thankfully accept in return for whatever they can give in return. To my mind, the chief element of that return should be loyalty. If loyalty is not regarded as the linchpin of the bargain, then the woman is little better than a ... Dear me, you do blush easily, Mr Phelps! You are not so toughened to this trade as you would like me to believe. I will spare you the word I nearly used, then. But I will substitute another— traitor. Well, my keepers during these years have been the governments of England and France, and I have kept true faith with them both. They have not always been faithful to me in return. Like men with women in keeping, governments can be less than scrupulous about their own behaviour. The French government's dismissal of me from the Berlin post, where I was doing my duty dedicatedly and living a private life the sudden uprooting from which caused me inconvenience of more than one kind, is a case in point. There has been no frank explanation, and although I know better than to expect one, the lack even of some attempted pretence makes me suspect that I have been used in some way.

'At times, I have taken the money of other powers, and have cuckolded them, so to speak. I have had to be a traitor to them, but never, I repeat, to my own two countries. I have served them, debased myself for them. It has never ceased to distress me that my report about the French traitor was not followed by the most active enquiries. I console myself that perhaps it was, but that no one saw fit to inform me. But then I ask, why? Why was I removed and paid off, never to be employed by the French government since, when I was in a perfect position to get conclusive proof about the wretch?'

During this increasingly impassioned recital, Claudine had leaped to her feet and begun to pace to and fro before her empty fireplace, only looking at me to wave me down when I began to get up out of respect. As she ceased speaking she snatched up an enamelled box from a small table and without apology took out a cigarette, lit it with a silver pocket lighter which had lain beside the box, and puffed rapidly, in a manner which ill suited her ladylike mien and those carefully ordered surroundings.

'You are agitated,' I remarked.

She turned to face me at last, and seemed about to return some reply which, to judge from the new expression on her face, and the flashing of her eyes, would have been of a withering nature. Only, at that moment the door opened and the maid came in with a large, galleried silver tea tray. She gave no sign of concern at her mistress's angry smoking, but simply laid out the things and departed.

'"*Agitated!*"' Claudine almost roared as soon as the door was closed. 'I am furious! Something very nasty is afoot. I feel it. In some way unknown to me, I have been made a part of it, and I am being punished in order that others may be able to cover up their own misdeeds. And if you are here as some sort of representative of them, *Mr Phelps*, I suggest you leave as fast as your legs will carry you.'

She made a fierce gesture, and for a moment I thought she was going to seize the teapot and hurl it at me. I could not possibly have escaped a severe scalding.

'I assure you,' I cried, 'I am from England and acting for England. My name is not Phelps. I am not staying at the hotel I named. Please, Mademoiselle, accept that I am here in complete good faith, and that the solution to my problem might well lead to the ending of yours.'

She stood poised for attack for some moments longer, and I thought how she had changed suddenly from the playful doe to the raging tigress, and how little I should care to find her my genuine antagonist. Then, without taking a last puff, she ground out the cigarette in a porcelain ashtray, wafted disdainfully at the smoky air with a white hand, and came to sit near me and pour tea, as though her outburst had never occurred. She made no apology, however. As she poured, I plucked up courage to pursue my quest.

'Your report, as I understand it, referred to this man merely as French, in his mid-forties, and that he wore the riband of the Legion of Honour.'

'That is correct. Whether in his civilian lapel or his uniform, he always wore it.'

'He was a soldier!'

'But yes. An officer.'

'Your report did not say so.'

'I gave the barest details initially. I expected them to be investigated later if necessary. For all I knew, he might have been one of our agents, changing his disguise from day to day.'

'Then you think all this might have been engineered by French

Intelligence, from the start? That it is some red herring, to which you unwittingly drew attention? It would account for your sudden withdrawal from the post.'

'But hardly for my complete lack of employment since, wouldn't you say?' She passed me a delicate cup and saucer and silently indicated a plate of sugared biscuits, which I ignored. 'Mr Phelps— for want of another name—I no longer know what to think. I can't begin to imagine what your interest in him can be.'

'Believe me, it is serious enough. And you have helped me already.'

'How?'

'By telling me this extra detail. You do not know his name ...'

'No.'

'But you saw him.'

'Several times.'

'Then please describe him.'

'Oh, not the most impressive of figures. That was one of the things which made me wonder whether he was really soldier or civilian. I couldn't imagine him in the Brigade of Guards, for instance.'

'Please, Mademoiselle.'

'Well, as I've said, in his mid-forties. Tall. Lanky. Hollow-chested. Very black hair. A great big black moustache. Bushy black eyebrows. Why, what is it? Do you know him?'

My hand had begun to shake so much that the tea slopped from side to side of the broad-brimmed cup. I put cup and saucer carefully down and asked, 'Is ... is there anything more?'

'Well ... his eyes were very dark, too. There was a sort of general blackness to him—like some sort of ruffled up crow. Yes—even his nose was like a beak.'

My head whirled. Eusapia Palladino's words echoed back to me from that stony room, and once more I seemed to hear my father's reassuring tone. Any doubts which had remained within me about the power of genuine mediumship evaporated now. I stared at Claudine, and saw that she was making no attempt to conceal surprise and even concern.

'Are you all right?' she asked. 'You've gone quite pale.'

I required effort to shake my head and say, 'Quite all right, thank you. Perhaps ... perhaps a little fresh tea, if you please?'

She poured the remaining contents of my cup into the slop basin and gave me a fresh fill-up. I took several sips, and felt better for it.

'You know him,' she said. It was not a question, but a statement.

I shook my head. 'You have brought me nearer to him, but the field is still a wide one. If only we had his name! Tell me, though, is there anything more you can add? Any detail at all?'

She thought for some moments, before answering in the negative, and I believed she was telling the truth.

A task now lay before me which I knew I must go about carefully. I put down my cup and saucer again and summoned up my most authoritarian manner.

'We wish you to give us your assistance. You will be paid generously. I shall hand over the first instalment before I leave you. The rest will be transmitted to you by some safe means after you have done what we ask, to our full satisfaction. I am compelled to add that should you be tempted to play a devious game with us, it will go hard for you.'

I made a point of giving her a little glare as I spoke these last words. They seemed to strike no particular alarm in her; on the other hand, she did not do as I had feared she might, and give me that winning smile and expose me for the novice I was at this kind of thing. She merely sat listening, obediently awaiting my command. It was plain to me that she was capable of sustaining as many roles as a consummate actress. I wondered which of them was the real she? But duty forced the speculation from my thoughts, and I continued, in a less harsh, though still brisk and businesslike, manner.

'You will receive a visit within the next few days. Four men will come, and will ask you questions similar to those which you have just answered me. You will treat just as frankly with them, omitting nothing of what you know of this mysterious traitor.'

'And what will follow?'

'Nothing. The money will reach you, and that will be an end to it, so far as you are concerned.'

I saw that I had surprised her this time. She asked slowly, 'It is not for agents to reason why. But since I have told you all I know, what is the point of others questioning me all over again? I hope you don't think there is something still to be bullied out of me which you yourself are too much the gentleman to try to get?'

'Nothing of the sort,' I hastened to reassure her. 'I am afraid I may explain no further, except to emphasise that you are to give no sign that you know what is going on, and are to suppress any temptation to manipulate the conversation.'

'Am I to know whom I am expected to receive?'

'Two will be senior officers of French Intelligence. The others will be inspectors of the Sûreté Nationale.'

'All Frenchmen? Are you going to tell me their names?'

'Those of the policemen are immaterial. The officers will be a Major Henry and a Captain Lauth.'

'Henry and Lauth! But I know them both. It was they who instructed me in the field.'

'And to whom you sent your despatches?'

'Always. Henry's work is principally assigning agents. Lauth is his deputy.'

'Are you personally acquainted with them?'

'We have never met. They make a point of that, I believe. In fact, why do they propose to show themselves to me now?'

'That I cannot answer. By the way, who, precisely, ordered your recall from your Berlin posting?'

'It was an unsigned telegram.'

This startled me. I wondered whether I had stumbled upon something which had been quite overlooked. I asked quickly, 'How do you know it was genuine? I mean to say, the Germans themselves could have had it sent, as the simplest means of getting rid of you from their midst.'

She smiled. 'It was in a code which my work in the *Nachrichtenbüro* enabled me to know had not been cracked by the Germans. Otherwise, I should certainly have been suspicious and signalled back for confirmation.'

'I see.' A further thought had occurred to me, but I kept it to myself. 'Well, Mademoiselle, that is all I have to say to you.'

'Except to ask whether I agree to do this.'

'I, er, took that as understood.'

She got to her feet, still smiling, but saying in a voice whose quality caused a little cold shiver in my lumbar region: 'Mr Phelps, should we chance to have any further dealings, please bear in mind that no one—*no one*—takes Claudine for granted.'

Then the smile became radiant and the room seemed to be flooded with new light.

'But I will do it,' she said. 'Your instructions shall be obeyed to the letter.'

I got to my feet and retrieved my hat and cane. 'Do you prefer to meet them here, or at some other rendezvous?' I asked.

She shrugged. 'This is my base. It is in their records. There is no reason to pretend otherwise—at least, I hope there is not.'

'No, no. Mademoiselle, thank you. I fear there is not much likelihood of our meeting again. It is my loss, I assure you.'

'That is extremely kind of you, *Mr Phelps*. I wish all my "clients" were as courteous.'

We were moving towards the door.

'However,' she added, 'there is one little detail I must trouble you with before you go. Sordid, but necessary.'

'Eh? I don't ... Oh, of course!'

Chuckling, I drew from my inner pocket the bundle of francs, secured with an elastic band, and put them into her hand. She riffled them briefly and raised an eyebrow.

'So much?'

'And as much again afterwards. *Adieu*, Mademoiselle. Good-day.'

I hesitated fractionally. She smiled again, and raised a white hand for me to kiss. I left the building, full of elation and twirled my cane jauntily as I stepped out the short distance to where Holmes and Picquart were awaiting me, in a quiet café at the other end of the Rue Maurice.

'Well done indeed, my dear Watson!' cried Holmes, when I had given them my full description of the proceedings. 'You obviously put your heart into it; wouldn't you agree, Picquart?'

The colonel smiled. 'I take it you were not disappointed in the lady, Doctor Watson?'

'Even Holmes would have to admire her,' I answered. 'A second Irene Adler.'

'Indeed?'

'Every bit as attractive and self-possessed. A pity you won't be there to watch her being interviewed, or you'd see what I mean.'

Holmes and the colonel exchanged a glance at this, and smiled at one another. I hurried on to unburden myself of the thought I had restrained myself from expressing aloud to Claudine.

'This telegram ordering her to leave Berlin. There seems to be no doubt that it was genuine, because of the code. But who sent it? Colonel Picquart, might I suggest that when you return to Paris you search your files for any record of its origin? For all we know, it might have been sent without your predecessor's authorisation or even knowledge; in which case, whoever despatched it would surely have some answering to do?'

'A very good point, Doctor,' replied the colonel gravely. 'It is worth following up, and I will do so at once; though I fancy that if what you suggest is true, the person concerned will have been careful to leave no trace.'

I turned to Holmes. 'Well, Holmes? What next? I say, though, what a remarkable thing that her description of the man should tally exactly with Madame Palladino's!'

He nodded. 'It is a good job for us that you proved to be so receptive a subject. As I have said before, I never get your limits, Watson. It must also be gratifying to you that your late father was able to give us his help.'

I stared at him. Colonel Picquart explained. 'No doubt of it. Your father was the one speaking through the medium all the time. It is only fortunate that, just as his powers were fading, I managed to give her the *bordereau*. Even though it was only a copy, it proved sufficient to renew his energy, which in turn enabled the medium to pick up influences associated with the document.'

'I had no idea it worked in that manner,' I confessed. 'But what have we gained in total? A corroborated description, the fact that the man is a middle-aged officer, and has the Legion of Honour. A letter E mysteriously appearing on a card ...'

'And Haydn in F sharp minor,' put in Holmes.

'Well, I don't see what that has to do with anything.'

'No? Does it not occur to you that since so much significant detail supplied through the medium has now been shown to have been correct, this also might be expected to be capable of having meaning?'

'Then, I suppose you are going to tell us you already know what it is?'

'I fancy I could, but I prefer not to, just yet. There has been enough injustice perpetrated on the strength of flimsy evidence, and I do not wish to be the cause of more.'

'Come along, Holmes!' I rallied him. 'Between the three of us, let us have your theory. It will go no further, and you might have the satisfaction in due course of saying, "I told you so".'

'I am prepared to forgo that pleasure, rather than name a name on the basis of the admittedly *outré* notion which is in my mind. I'll tell you what I will do, though. If Colonel Picquart can lay hands on a copy of the French Army list, here in Geneva, and give me just five minutes with it, I will, if I am then able, write down a name and seal it in an envelope. Either of you shall keep it secure and we will have it opened in due time. A bottle of Pommery '89 shall be my prize if I am proved correct.'

'Done!' I declared with a happy laugh and the colonel laughed, too, but Holmes's expression had turned suddenly grave, and when he spoke again it was in a sombre tone.

'Let us not forget, that while we sit here, playing our games, a traitor is at large, wreaking we know not what harm. In all likelihood there is at least one accomplice, possibly similarly engaged. Above all, let our thoughts not be deflected from the poor creature who suffers upon his rock, and the wife and children who share that suffering through their thoughts. No, this is no game we are playing. We are in the thick of a grave enquiry which might yet set off a cataclysm which could affect all Europe.'

Colonel Picquart nodded, equally seriously. For my part, the exuberance which my afternoon's adventure had lit in me was dramatically quenched. The colour of Mademoiselle Claudine's apartment, and the stimulus of her personality, which I had carried away like a bright light in my mind, gave way to the picture of a solitary figure, in rumpled clothing, weeping under the mocking stares of his jailors, in the stifling confines of his living tomb.

SEVENTEEN

I T will no doubt sound ignoble of me, in view of Holmes's reminder of the gravity of our quest, but it had been my hope that as soon as our business in Geneva was at an end we might return to London. The cricket season of that year, 1896, was proving to be one of outstanding interest. The Australians were our visitors. They had not won a Test Match in England for eight years, and Harry Trott, their captain, had announced that he proposed to rectify this with a team in which such seasoned players as Ernie Jones, Darling, Trumble and Gregory were joined by several young newcomers, amongst whom was Clem Hill, then aged 19. Our stalwarts, who included Hearne, Lilley, Tom Richardson, Bobby Abel, Lohmann and Stoddart, under our immortal captain, W.G., were equally determined, and some battles royal had been anticipated.

The First Test, at Lord's, ended in cheers as Stoddart made the winning hit, a superb cut to the boundary.* At Old Trafford the Australians exacted their revenge, and all depended upon the third and final encounter at the Oval, which was drawing near. I was a little piqued, therefore, to be told by Holmes that we were to linger in Switzerland until everything had been quite completed. It would have been churlish to have protested, and I well knew that he always had his reasons for whatever he did; so I acquiesced, and rather hoped that I might even be compensated with another meeting with the intriguing Claudine.

Upon the day following my interview with that lady , Colonel Picquart left for Paris. He intended to arrange his deputies' visit

*I have never since known England to win a Lord's Test against Australia.—J.H.W.

without delay. The plan was that he should 'find' the misfiled report, fly into a fury about its apparently never having been acted upon, and, unless his deputies could provide a sound explanation for this, order them to Geneva to interrogate Claudine. His reason for sending Sûreté officers as well was that it was to be a safeguard upon his department's reputation. Should it emerge publicly that his predecessor had lapsed in his duty by not having the report investigated, at least Picquart and his deputies would have official witnesses to the prompt action which they had taken upon finding out about it.

It sounded plausible enough to allay any suspicions Henry and Lauth might have that they were the ones being investigated. The Sûreté men were to travel independently of them and were to be present at the interview as silent witnesses, taking no part in it whatsoever. Holmes was as vague as ever to me about the precise effect he hoped these tactics would achieve. It seemed that the general notion was to test the agent's answers against those which she had given me, and to gauge the officers' reactions to them.

'You will need two paragons of honesty from the Sûreté,' I had remarked. 'No doubt Inspector Dubuque will be one?'

'The very first choice.'

'Is there another you can trust as much? Why not Dubuque alone?'

'Because one man's word is always assailable against that of two, if it comes to a difference between versions. I dare say Dubuque knows at least one man whom he can rely upon as trustworthy as himself.'

Yet, when Inspector Dubuque presented himself at our hotel a few days later, he was alone. The receptionist was under instruction to despatch any visitor for us directly to our simple suite, preceded only by a discreet message by the porter. As Holmes explained, the less we were observed publicly with anyone closely associated with our business, the better. So much, I thought wistfully, for a growing inclination to invite Claudine to dine with me in one of those beckoning lakeside restaurants.

'Well, then!' exclaimed the boyish-looking policeman, rubbing chubby hands together with enthusiasm. 'We're getting somewhere at last!'

'I would not be too confident, my dear Dubuque,' Holmes

replied. 'We have uncovered something for certain, and it merits looking into. Where it might lead is another matter.'

'To a swift solution to the Dreyfus Affair, is my hope.'

'Ours also. There is no certainty of that, however. The possibilities are many and varied. We have been afforded an excellent chance of proximity with two men very close to the case. It may be that they acted irregularly at some stage; but that itself may have been caused by carelessness or laxity, rather than intent. Their chief at the time is beyond questioning. We have nothing whatever to go upon other than the incomplete description of this woman Claudine's alleged traitor—yes, Watson, I say alleged because even her word is not necessarily sacrosanct—and whatever reaction either of them might show during the interview. For all we know, the case we are pursuing may run parallel to Dreyfus's, but not intersect with it.'

'You mean, there could be another traitor?'

'Why not? Too much time has been allowed to elapse before this report has been followed up. The original man may have ceased operations long since—died, even. If there ever was any connection between him and the Dreyfus case, it might now be impossible to discover, let alone prove.'

'Well, that's the pessimistic way of looking at it. I'm looking for a scoundrel, and if I find him I'll dog him until he leads me to the solution.'

'Bravo, Inspector!' I echoed, and ignored Holmes's muttering about the trickiness of circumstantial evidence. 'When is the interview to be, then?'

'Tomorrow. Major Henry and Captain Lauth arrive by a morning train. Our assignation with the woman is at three.'

'What about your colleague?' I asked. 'When does he come?'

'Oh, he's here already. Didn't Mr Holmes tell you?'

'Mr Holmes tells me very little indeed, Inspector.'

'Dear me, Watson!' Holmes exclaimed. 'How utterly remiss. There has been something on the tip of my tongue, and I have kept forgetting it.'

'Perhaps you would care to tell me now, before you forget again?'

'It is not so earth-shaking as all that. Merely the name of Dubuque's Sûreté colleague: an Inspector Vernet.'

'Vernet?' I echoed, puzzled. Dubuque was the only Sûreté officer whom I knew by name; and yet . . . '*Vernet!*' I cried. 'Holmes, you don't mean to say . . .!'

'My ancestral name should serve as well as any. With all due respect to our friend here—not to say to your good self—I have trained myself to see things which others overlook. This is my one chance to come face to face with these two officers without having to reveal my identity. Although my French is fluent, I am required, like Dubuque, to be a silent witness. I can watch; I can listen. I can draw my own conclusions. It is an ideal opportunity.'

'But . . . but . . . supposing it occurs to them to make a check upon the identity of this so-called Inspector Vernet. As Intelligence officers, they must surely have some access to current police records. They will be put upon their guard the moment they discover he does not exist.'

'Ah, but he does, Doctor,' Dubuque grinned. 'That is to say, his name is in the official list, with the usual brief particulars. I inserted it myself only the day before yesterday. One would need to be very suspicious indeed to wish to know more than that about the fellow.'

'There are moments such as this, Holmes,' said I, 'when I wonder why you trouble to retain my company.'

He came across and put an arm around my shoulders.

'A confederate to whom each development comes as a perpetual surprise, and to whom the future is always a closed book, is an ideal helpmate. By Jove, there is something else I had quite forgotten!'

'What now?' I enquired grudgingly, as he delved into his inner pocket.

He produced an envelope. 'Colonel Picquart had gone before I could look up the Army List he had sent round to me. Now that I have glanced at it, I have written down a name and sealed it in this envelope. You know that I trust you implicitly, my dear Watson, but, so that everything shall be seen to be above board, please be so good, Dubuque, as to sign your name across the flap, so that this cannot be opened without detection.'

The inspector's grin changed to a look of puzzlement as he complied, using the fountain pen which Holmes offered him.

'Keep it safely, Watson,' Holmes commanded. 'Unless I am very much mistaken, the name I have written on the slip of paper which lies in this envelope is that of the man we are seeking.'

The interview was over. Holmes and Dubuque were back at our hotel and a bottle of cognac was dying under our combined exertions.

I had waited patiently for them to conclude their own discussion of what had taken place before giving me any account of it. At length they had deigned to do so, and I gathered that it had proved illuminating.

'Not a doubt of it,' Inspector Dubuque told me. 'They were doing their best to persuade her that the fellow she'd seen had been Dreyfus. Every point in her description was argued. She said he was tallish. They asked what such a term meant? Either he was tall, or he wasn't. Dreyfus wasn't small, but he wasn't tall. Therefore, the man she'd seen was somewhere between; *therefore*, he could perfectly well have been Dreyfus.'

'It was certainly my impression,' Holmes concurred, 'that they were much annoyed by their errand, and had gone about it predetermined to use it to strengthen the evidence against Dreyfus.'

'That's it. When she said the man's moustache was long, they asked how long was a piece of string? She described his nose as beaky, and Henry said, did she mean a Jew's nose?'

'Then you say they really browbeat her?'

'Tried to , more like. If the two of us hadn't been there with our eyes on them they'd have gone much further, I reckoned.'

'Poor woman!' I exclaimed.

'Poor them, you mean,' Holmes retorted, and the two of them laughed. 'She gave far better than she got.'

'I'll tell you, Doctor,' said Dubuque, 'I've met some women handy with their tongues in my service, but never one to touch her. Sitting there one minute as still and quiet as a nun, and the next tearing into them like a Seine bargee—and some of the same language.'

'Good for her, then! So they retreated in disarray, eh?'

'Dudgeon, at any rate,' Holmes answered. 'Despite its entertainment value, though, the encounter was instructive in several ways. It showed up the prejudice of both against Dreyfus. It verified in every detail the account you gave me of what she was able to tell you, and convinced us both that she had withheld nothing. That she does not know the identity of the traitor is beyond doubt. Her description of him, however, had a marked effect on them both. Although they tried to argue it down in every particular, it was obvious to us both that it was too accurate for their comfort, and that they knew the man concerned.'

'That's right,' Inspector Dubuque agreed. 'It's not my place to slander a couple of officers, but, between these walls, I wouldn't give too much for her safety, if it wasn't obvious that she doesn't know his name.'

'Great heavens!' I cried with genuine alarm. 'You aren't suggesting that she is in danger?'

'I do not think so,' Holmes answered. 'The knowledge she possesses is certainly embarrassing to them, and it is perhaps just as well that she so obviously knows nothing further. But the fact of official witnesses having been present ensures that nothing will happen. It would be accounted to those two, whatever it might be and whoever perpetrated it.'

'Thank goodness for that, at any rate.'

'Your concern for the lady does you much credit, Watson. But, I repeat, she is eminently able to look after herself. She went so far as to mock them by offering to track the fellow down, if they would pay her for it.'

'That got them really worried,' said the inspector. 'Major Henry warned her that if she made any such move he'd get her arrested on charges of spying against the French Army. I won't repeat what she answered to that.'

'All the same,' Holmes told me, 'when you despatch the balance of her remuneration, a little note from Mr Phelps might not be amiss. Thank her for all she has done, and advise her to do nothing more, lest it should confuse your own activities on her country's behalf. That will ensure that she does not intrude into danger.'

'I will do that at once.'

'By the way, she sent you a little message herself.'

'Me?'

'It is very brief. "My kindest regards to Mr Phelps, if you should run into him at the Café Maurice again". She whispered it to me as I was the last to leave her apartment.'

'But...how does she know about that?'

'My dear fellow, you yourself termed her another Irene Adler.

To judge from the way you carried your head amongst the clouds when you joined Colonel Picquart and myself in the café after interviewing her, it did not occur to you that she might have followed you. Obviously she did. It was an elementary enough precaution, but it demonstrates that she is a true professional.'

'You don't suppose she has discovered our identities!'

'Unlikely. It would not much matter if she has; she would be unlikely to use the information against us. In any case, I fancy our dealings with the lady are now at an end. I can see that that is a matter of some regret to you, Watson. I console myself on your behalf with the fact that she addressed you through me as Mr Phelps. At least you had clearly not got on to "Tadpole" terms with her.'

When our mutual laughter at this observation had ceased, and another round of cognac been poured, I asked them both, 'What was your impression of the two officers, then?'

'Real army types, at different ends of the scale,' Inspector Dubuque replied. 'Henry's the ex-ranker peasant. About fifty. Big as a bull, piggy eyes, strutting as a cock—all farmyard, in fact. I know a fair bit about him, as it happens. Got his commission after ten or twelve years in the ranks. Served with the Zouaves at Oran. He was wounded and decorated. Fought well against the guerillas in Indo-China, then was made Town Major of Peronne, until he wangled his way into Intelligence. He's not my idea of Intelligence by any means. Peasant cunning, of course, but not much imagination. The infantry was his real home.'

'How did he get into Intelligence, then?'

'Influence. Any officer in our army who really wants to get on needs someone high up, or in politics, who will pull strings for him. That was one of Dreyfus's drawbacks. He didn't give a fig about patronage, or he might not be in the mess he's in now, poor devil.'

Holmes asked the inspector, 'Could Major Henry have had any ulterior motive in wishing to enter the Intelligence service, do you suppose?'

'He isn't that sort. The army is his life. I think he found himself in a backwater at Peronne and wanted to start moving up again. He married a village girl just a few years ago. I expect he's working towards a decent pension that will see them through their old age.'

'If someone had offered him the means of supplementing his

savings by rendering a few quiet services, might he have accepted?'

Dubuque shook his head vigorously. 'I'd put money on his loyalty, even though I don't care for him as a man.'

'And he would be scarcely the sort to care for a Dreyfus.'

'He'd loathe him. He was all the things that Henry couldn't be— well brought up, comfortably off, climbing smoothly towards the top of the tree. You heard the resentment in some of the things Henry said to Claudine, surely?'

Holmes nodded. 'What about Captain Lauth, then?'

'Again, you've seen and heard him, Monsieur Holmes. Far above Henry in class. The monocle and all that. Cavalry type. There must be times when he resents being junior to a peasant, but I believe they get on well enough. Henry relies on Lauth good deal, because he can speak German, while Henry only knows French.'

'A fine thing for an Intelligence officer!' I declared.

'I don't like to say it of my own country, Doctor, but there's a good deal about the army that oughtn't to be. Colonel Picquart's found that in his department, with a vengeance.'

'Thank goodness he has, or our enquiry would not have leaped forward in the way it has.'

'As you say, Watson,' said Holmes. 'And we must hope that he will uncover something else before our satisfactory progress begins to lose its momentum.'

'Then what is our own next move?'

'To return to our humble abode in Baker Street. For the time being, the matter is in Picquart's hands. We have advised him to search his files quickly and thoroughly in the hope of finding more evidence. Dubuque will report to him the proceedings of today's interview, and he will draw his own conclusions from it. No doubt he will keep a closer eye on those deputies of his, and perhaps delve discreetly into their connections with the Dreyfus affair. In any case, it is time I was getting back to London. You know how restive the criminal element is apt to become whenever I am absent for long.'

An agreeable image of the pavilion at Lord's at start of play floated before my eyes; but something else obtruded upon it.

'Holmes,' I said, 'what about the name? The sealed envelope? Don't you think Colonel Picquart should have it, even if it is to some degree speculative? It would give him a new line to work upon.'

He thought for a few moments, then nodded.

'Quite right, Watson. I will confide it in Dubuque here, who can whisper it to him.'

'Then, shall we open the envelope now?'

'No, no. Don't deprive me of my little moment of drama, Watson. Keep it intact. As soon as I know I am right, or wrong, I will tell you, and you may grovel or gloat, as the case may be.'

Relatively little time was to pass before I was to unseal that envelope, and other matters kept each of us busy meanwhile. Holmes was occupied with the proofs of one of his monographs upon some hitherto overlooked aspect of criminal investigation. I myself sought with difficulty to catch up with my neglected medical work. At the Oval I saw our team take the series two-one, but the match was marred for me, as for many others, by the absence of Stod, in an atmosphere of rancour over the differing remuneration accorded to gentlemen "amateurs" such as he, and the £10 a match received by professionals of the standing of Tom Hayward and Tom Richardson.

When L'Affaire Dreyfus came back to our immediate attention it was in the form of a letter, delivered by what Mrs Hudson described as a rough-looking foreigner, who did not linger for an answer or reward. We were nearing the end of luncheon at the time, and Holmes carefully wiped his knife clean before using it to slit open the long envelope.

It contained several sheets of paper, one of which I saw to be another photograph of a document which had evidently been pieced together after being torn into fragments. As usual, he read everything in silence before vouchsafing me any particulars.

'From Colonel Picquart,' he disclosed at last. 'Things evidently have reached such a pass that he dare not trust the posts, so he has had it brought by a seaman's hand.'

I reached out my own hand, expecting Holmes to put the papers into it, but he retained them, giving me only that secret smile which told me he was exulting in something and would, in all probability, tease me before revealing it.

'He has been busy at his files. Nothing more has come to light about Mademoiselle Claudine's despatch. Either it was ignored at the time, or any subsequent references have been destroyed.'

'What about the sender of her telegram of dismissal?' I reminded him. 'Was there anything about that?'

'Evidently not. He says he questioned Major Henry and Captain Lauth about it, and both maintained that it was a direct order despatched to her by their then chief, Colonel Sandherr, who, incidentally, is now dead, which places him beyond consultation for ever. No one was appointed to replace her, or he might have been able to find out who arranged that. So I'm afraid, Watson, your promising avenue terminates in what (not in any indelicate sense) proves to be a dead end.'

'Ah, well, it was a shot in the dark, I suppose. Have there been any other developments, then?'

'Have there not! He has been looking very thoroughly into the particulars of the gentleman whose name I passed him via Dubuque. They prove to be very interesting indeed.'

'Oho! You are going to tell me you were right, then?'

'Judge for yourself. This is what Picquart has to say about him. He is almost fifty years of age and of French birth, though not entirely French lineage. His father was a general. Both he and his widow died before our man was more than a youth, and he was left with estates and considerable means, which he gradually disposed of in the time-dishonoured pursuits of gambling, betting, drinking and a variety of costly forms of debauchery. He wasted his time at school and failed the entrance exam to the military academy of Saint-Cyr. However, he managed to become an officer by the back door, so to speak, by joining the Papal Legion. An uncle of his, also a general, got him transferred to the French Foreign Legion, but he was soon recalled to play a brief part in the Franco-Prussian War.

'In the years following, his career followed the more-or-less standard pattern of a young regular officer's in peacetime. He cuts a considerable social dash and has a winning manner, both with the ladies and with people in high places, whom he seems to have persuaded successfully to obtain him various appointments and postings which he fancied for himself. In short, he seems to have got on pretty well, for the slapdash sort of soldier he appears to be.'

'I have known them like that,' I assured Holmes. 'The conscientious fellows slog away at their careers and, as often as not, fall to the first bullet that comes their way, while these sort of fellows enjoy charmed lives, in every sense.'

'A fair summing-up of our man, from what I read here,' said Holmes. 'But Picquart credits him with enterprise and a good deal of energy, so long as he is expending it on his own behalf. He also seems to possess a natural literary talent which has stood him in good stead. He is a prolific contributor to the military journals and to the public newspapers, when it comes to dealing with matters military. He is close to *La Libre Parole*, for example. Evidently he has needed to be, for his social excesses cost him his complete fortune, and he has been a chronic debtor ever since. He made a most unsatisfactory marriage in order to get his wife's dowry, and proceeded to spend much of it, trying to live up to the title of Count, which he affects without justification. Have I given you a clue there, Watson?'

'Eh? A clue? I don't think so.'

'You shall see. To bring the fellow's career up to date, he is now judicially separated from his wife, who discovered in time that he was ruining her. He is a major of infantry, stationed at Rouen, which is near enough to Paris to enable him to enjoy himself in his favourite haunts and with his mistress, who is a general's widow, but far enough for him to be able to hide from pressing creditors. The influence of political friends obtained for him the Legion of Honour. In short, he boasts of noble birth, position, heroism under fire, and goodness knows what else, but in fact is a desperately hard-up sham.'

'A classic recipe for a traitor.'

'Yes. And there is another detail which will interest you, Watson. To save description, Picquart has sent a photograph of him. See what you make of it.'

Holmes flipped a small card across the table. I picked it up, and found myself regarding features which were without any doubt those delineated by Madame Palladino and corroborated by Mademoiselle Claudine.

'This is incredible!' I exclaimed. 'Picquart has him, then. Dreyfus will be a free man in no time.'

'I wish I could share your optimism as to that. There is a lot of work to be done yet, and this is a slippery customer, with powerful influences working for him.'

'But why should they? Once he is exposed they will surely not dare to.'

'You don't suppose they will fall over themselves to admit that they have been dupes or rogues all along, do you? They are more likely to do all they can to cover up for themselves, and him as well, perhaps.'

'That would be monstrous!'

'It would also be human nature, of a certain sort.'

'Well, Holmes, you have made your point.' My hand went to my breast pocket where my wallet lay. I drew it out and took from it the sealed envelope. I wiped a knife of my own on a napkin and held it poised.

'Now?' I suggested.

'One moment more. Take a look at this other photograph first. Wait, though—I will just turn down the top half, so as to conceal the name upon it. There. You will see that it is of a reconstructed document which has just come into Picquart's possession. Now, don't cheat, there's a good chap.'

I took the folded paper and examined the photograph. It appeared to be of some sort of form, with perforations at the edge, which had been crumpled and torn into many fragments, later to be reconstituted. The few lines of the message on it were in French. I puzzled over them, a task made more difficult by the disfigurement of the original.

'Don't trouble yourself,' said Holmes. 'It is a somewhat impatient-sounding note from one person to another, chiding him for delay in supplying some expected information, and casting doubt on whether they can continue to do business together.'

'I see. And the addressee, I take it, is our traitor?'

'Correct.'

'The sender?'

'It was never sent. The writer had second thoughts after drafting it and tore it up.'

'Then. . .'

'He threw the fragments into his wastepaper basket. It appears that the waste paper of the German Military Attaché in Paris is still a subject of interest to the French authorities.'

I began to chuckle and slyly made as if to turn the document over. Holmes reached across and snatched it from me.

'Oh, come now, Holmes!' I protested. 'You're not going to keep me in the dark any longer.'

'I assure you, my dear fellow, the name will mean nothing to you when you read it. So why bother?'

'Because you have tantalised me with it ever since it came into your head. Besides, how do I know that you have even got it right? No, I'm sorry, Holmes. No name, no champagne.'

He sighed exaggeratedly. 'Oh, have it your own way, then. But before you pick up that knife again, pray make one last attempt at deducing it for yourself.'

'How on earth can I, when you say it will mean nothing to me anyway?'

'It would if you spent less time concentrating upon cricket and more upon music.'

'Not that Haydn gibberish again!'

'Gibberish! Ye Gods! For that, I shall play it on my violin.'

Stuffing the folded photograph into his pocket so that I could not sneak a glance at it, he got up from the table and went to where his Stradivarius lay in its well-worn case on a side table. He lifted the lid, picked up the instrument and bow, and played a few trial notes in order to test the tuning.

'You said it was a symphony,' I said. 'You're not going to play all that at me!'

'Merely the very end. The passage which Madame Palladino enabled us to hear on a woodwind instrument with no visible player. Listen carefully. It is your last chance to distinguish yourself.'

He tucked the fiddle under his chin and played the phrase. I recognised it, but he played it over two or three times more, before returning the violin to its case. I thought hard, but inspiration would not come.

'Haydn's Symphony No 45 in F sharp minor. As I observed before, a most uncommon key,' he said. 'It is a most uncommon symphony, too. Towards the end, one by one, the players snuff out the candles over their desks and creep away into the shadows, until two violins alone remain; hence its nickname, the "Farewell". It is a musical joke; a respectful hint by Haydn on behalf of his musicians to their employer and his that they were not being released early enough in the evenings to get back to their homes in Vienna before the small hours. Don't you regard that as a delightful gesture?'

'Yes, I suppose it was. Did the employer take the hint?'

'He did indeed. And we should take our hint from it, too. Open your envelope now, my dear Watson, and you will read the name of that patron of Haydn, which is the same as that of the man with whom the German Military Attaché has been transacting treachery.'

I slit the envelope with a single movement of the knife and took out the scrap of paper from within. In Holmes's bold hand it bore the one word: ESTERHAZY.

EIGHTEEN

M Y friend's reminder of the story of this symphony's origin produced
in me an unanticipated upsurge of emotion, from the recollection of
my dear father.

He had been a man of many cultural attainments, in all of which
he remained an amateur, thereby safeguarding his enthusiasm from
becoming jaded. Music had been foremost amongst them. He had
naturally longed to be able to fire his sons with his interest in it,
repeatedly urging upon us the lifelong satisfaction and solace which it
could offer. My poor brother responded better than I, possibly
because of that somewhat maudlin quality of his which was to
contribute much to his downfall. Father persevered with me, but with
little success, alas. Although we were of comfortable means, good
concerts were few and far between in those days. He took me along
whenever anything worthwhile offered and accompanied the performances with whispered observations about which section of the
orchestra was predominating, which about to introduce the subsidiary theme which in its turn would become predominant, and so
forth, thus demonstrating the pattern of the composer's intention
which he had outlined to me beforehand. I have to confess that my
inclination remained less towards the salons of Europe than to the
green turf of England, and that the solo of willow upon leather and
the concerted thrum of massed hooves upon hard going have
continued more musical to my ears than anything which the concert
hall can provide.

Perhaps in desperation, Father had tried to engage my interest
in the symphonies and sonatas by way of such little stories as attached
to some. Thus it was that I had learned of Chopin watching George

Sand's dog chasing its tail and writing a valse about it, and of Beethoven's "Moonlight" sonata, about which Holmes subsequently disillusioned me by asserting that the imagery and title owed nothing to the composer, but to the imagination of an untypically soulful critic. Of the "Farewell" symphony I could not remember Father having made any mention, although the story was just such as would have appealed to his romantic nature. Had I been a better son, I should certainly have taken it in; thus, it saddened me profoundly that it had been a phrase from this work, above all of them, by means of which he had endeavoured to send me a message.

The name Esterhazy stirred some chord of memory within me, though.

'Wasn't that a Polish line?' I asked Holmes. 'Not French, surely?'

'Hungarian, to be precise. Picquart's outline states that this man is a member of an illegitimate branch. His true name is Walsin-Esterhazy. In all other respects, he is a Frenchman, born and bred.'

'Holmes, I must admit I have been very impressed, not to say moved, by recent events. . .'

'So I observe, my dear chap. It does you credit.'

'Everything that is known about this Esterhazy chap certainly marks him as a candidate for villainy. All the same, is it not still possible that, although he is manifestly a traitor, he is unconnected with Dreyfus?'

'I am glad to say it is not, otherwise we should have to begin looking further. Look at Picquart's two final documents, if you will, and tell me if this is not our fellow.'

Two more sheets of paper were passed across our tablecloth. The first I recognised at once as another photographed copy of the *bordereau*. The other was a letter, bearing the signature *Esterhazy*. Even to my inexpert eye the handwriting was identical.

'But this is incredible!' I said. 'How could the experts have been so wrong?'

'Not every one of them was,' he reminded me. 'It was Bertillon whose opinion carried most weight.'

'But, as you yourself pointed out, he is an anthropometrist— nothing to do with handwriting.'

'As full of high-sounding jargon, though, as an inferior sausage is of spice and breadcrumbs. Such a sausage tastes convincing enough to anyone unacquainted with the genuine article, and Bertillon's nonsense would be just as acceptable to any hearers who perhaps wished to be convinced. Besides, as in the medical profession, there is great rivalry between the exponents of varying systems and techniques, and, no doubt, between those who champion the exponents of one or another. Bertillon was the only one of the experts who appears to have come out strongly with an opinion, which he fired home with such a verbal bombardment as must have impressed most of its audience by its assuredness, and bewildered the rest.'

'Even so, the trend of the other evidence was in Dreyfus's favour. It would take more than talk of anti-Semitism and army pride to persuade me that decent men would not have given him the benefit of the doubt.'

'Then you will accept the assertion that secret evidence was produced which undoubtedly showed him to be a traitor?'

'You are putting words into my mouth, Holmes!'

'Not at all. You are aware that the police, when certain of a felon's guilt for a crime which they cannot prove against him, are not above taking him for something else with which circumstances, if not facts, connect him, in the certainty that they will obtain a conviction, thereby getting him put away.'

'I am. And it is not to their credit.'

'I wholeheartedly concur. Nevertheless, it happens, if only occasionally. Perhaps Dreyfus's is such a case.'

'I don't believe it, and neither do you, Holmes. Hang it all, this business is tangled enough without your adding to it.'

'At the heart of a crime there is usually something far simpler than the surrounding detail might suggest. At the same time, we must consider every possible aspect.'

'Such as the eminently simple one that this Esterhazy is a traitor, and by some mischance Dreyfus became suspected instead. You yourself admitted that there were similarities between his handwriting and the *bordereau*. It is only now that we have seen Esterhazy's that the mistake becomes obvious.'

'My dear Watson, you cannot have it both ways. Just now you argued that the handwriting evidence was subsidiary to the other, which itself was not strong enough to produce a conviction. You will not accept that there was secret evidence . . .'

'There you go again!' I cried, in my exasperation. 'I maintain merely that any secret evidence could not have been genuinely detrimental to Dreyfus, because from all that we have learned of his character and career it is obvious that he is guilty of nothing.' I broke off as he slapped a fist into a palm with an exclamation. 'What now, Holmes?'

'See how valuable you are to me, Watson?' was his reply, eyes gleaming. 'The precision of your vocabulary has helped me time and again.'

'What have I said now?'

' "That any secret evidence could not have been detrimental to his character," was what any other person might have said. But with that command of the English tongue which is the envy of your readers you inserted the word "genuinely". Between "detrimental" and "genuinely detrimental" lies all the difference in the world.'

'I merely expressed what I mean—that if there was evidence against him, it was mistaken.'

'Or concocted?'

'Concocted? By whom? Don't say that Esterhazy had enough influence in Intelligence circles to persuade them to get Dreyfus convicted so that he himself could continue spying. That would make them all traitors.'

'It is far-fetched, I agree. Stranger things have been known, though, especially in this murky world of espionage.'

'Then, the sooner Picquart has Esterhazy arrested, and there is a public confrontation between him and the others, the better.'

'I don't believe our friend will be quite so precipitate as that. There may well be even further people involved, too. My belief is that he will watch those he suspects very carefully indeed, and see where they lead him. It must be a calculated risk that there will be further treason in the meantime. But I fancy they will be too much on their guard to risk anything. Picquart's curiosity about Mademoiselle Claudine will have set them wondering how deeply he is looking into the background of the matter. If they do lie low, it means he will have no active lines to follow, but at least it will give him more time to delve into the past.'

'Then, what does he ask you to do in the meantime?'

'Nothing. There is nothing we can do from here, and in any case the balance is too delicately poised now for us to risk interfering. He states that he is not even mentioning the names concerned to Mathieu Dreyfus, for fear he might take some precipitate action of his own. I sense that Picquart has sent us this material out of some instinct for self-preservation. If the people he is investigating are capable of ruthlessness, they will scarcely hesitate to turn upon him, either in physical form or simply by ensuring that he is discredited. He is very reticent in his covering letter, which he begs me not to answer. I think he will feel a little more at ease to know that there are copies of his proofs where they cannot be tampered with by those who would wish to suppress them.'

'Remember Adolphe Meyer,' I reminded him. 'Somebody's hand reached out as far as London when he became involved in the Dreyfus affair. His murder has never been explained, has it?'

'True. We must be on our guard, too, and hope that the wretched business will move quickly enough now to ensure that no one can stop Picquart before the whole truth is brought to the public gaze.'

The year passed over the threshold which stands between summer and autumn. We were briefly engaged in that most tragic case of Eugenia Ronder, the "Veiled Lodger". Other than this, little that is remarkable appears in my journal for some time. There came no news from France, and nothing untoward happened to ourselves which might have indicated that we were known to possess the copies of Picquart's evidence, which Holmes had promptly lodged in the safe-keeping of his bank.

It was upon an evening in mid-November, when a keen wind was rumbling in our chimney and whining through the window-sashes as it dashed flurries of heavy rain against the panes, that we heard our doorbell peal. The clock upon our mantelpiece showed half-past nine. We had been passing our time contentedly, I chuckling over the recently-published collected volume of stories, "Many Cargoes", by my fellow contributor to the Strand Magazine, W.W. Jacobs, whilst Holmes, surrounded by tomes and strewn papers, scribbled notes for his definitive "Study of the Chaldean Roots in the Ancient Cornish Language". Our fire burned well, the wind causing an occasional puff of smoke to issue into the room. Our slippers were upon our feet; I was comfortable in my old smoking jacket and Holmes in his dressing gown. We were completely at our ease.

At the sound of the bell Holmes raised his head sharply to listen, with that aural equivalent of his of a hound sniffing the air. He frowned and remarked, 'We appear to have a visitor. On such a night it should scarcely prove a trivial errand.'

His keen ears had evidently detected Mrs Hudson's opening and shutting the front door and the tread of feet upon the lower stairs. I myself heard nothing until they sounded upon the landing and halted. Mrs Hudson entered, shutting the door behind her back.

'I didna wish to disturb ye, Mr Holmes,' said she, in lowered tone, 'but there's an artist sort of man saying he maun see ye. He couldnae give me a card, but he says ye'll be knowing him, and his name's Dubook.'

'Dubuque!' Holmes exclaimed. 'Show him in at once, if you please, Mrs Hudson.'

She opened the door again and beckoned, somewhat peremptorily, to the visitor to enter. When he was inside, and the door closed, I could perceive the reason for her curious description of him. Had I passed him in the street I should not for a moment have recognised the young policeman. He was muffled deeply into a threadbare coat, with a long scarf coiled about his throat and a broad-brimmed soft hat flopping down upon his head. He wore cheap, wire-framed spectacles, and carried a large, oilskin-covered portfolio, of the type artists use to convey their wares. He was excessively damp, the rainwater dripping from every part of him.

'Good evening, gentlemen,' he greeted us, though noticeably without his usual ebullience of manner. 'I regret to disturb your comfort, but thank heaven I find you here.'

'My dear Dubuque!' cried Holmes, who had jumped up. 'Is it really you? Come, off with those things, man, and in front of our fire. Watson, be unstinting with the brandy, if you please.'

I needed no urging. It was not our custom to sip drinks as we sat at our evening occupations, preferring to restrain ourselves until the time was reached for a nightcap. Only when we engaged ourselves in animated discussion did we have recourse to the decanters. But on this evening, so cosy within and so wild without, I had been warding off special temptation with difficulty, so that Dubuque's arrival proved providential.

By the time I had poured for us all he had divested himself of the wet things and was seated in the basket chair, thankfully chafing his hands before our blaze; but he rubbed them together in a way which suggested to me that something more was chilling him than the wind and rain. He sipped at once at the brandy which I gave him. Then, cupping the glass between his palms, he said, 'Picquart is in a devil of a spot. They're on to him, with a vengeance.'

'Has he been attacked?' I asked.

'Not physically. In the other sense, though. He's been sent out of Paris, on some supposed inspection mission. It seemed to be a matter of a few days at first, but it was extended, and now it's been extended again. He's wanted out of the way.'

'Do you know why?' asked Holmes.

Inspector Dubuque nodded. 'Have you a cigarette, if you please?' he asked. The edge upon his voice was a sharp one.

I hastened to comply with Holmes's nod towards me. In all our acquaintance, I never resented these little acts of servitude to which he put me, knowing that they left him free to give his full attention to the subject before him. There was no doubting the inspector's agitation as he lit up, with trembling fingers.

'Thanks,' he repeated, and jerked a thumb towards his discarded street clothes. 'I took every precaution to avoid being detected and followed; but it's almost certainly the last time I dare be in touch with you tête-à-tête, Mr Holmes.'

'Calm yourself, Dubuque, and tell us every particular.'

The inspector took another hasty sip of brandy. 'Things have started to move fast in France. You've had the Lazare pamphlet?'

'No. Who is Lazare?'

'Bernard Lazare: a young Jew, very strong for the Zionist cause. He's been after Mathieu Dreyfus for long enough to let him publish an attack on the case against Dreyfus. Mathieu asked him to hold on for a while, until things seemed to be quietening down, when it would be a good idea to stir them up again. Well, Lazare held off until a few days ago; then he published. Not only that; he sent a copy of his pamphlet—"The Truth of the Dreyfus Affair", it's called—to just about every politician, every judge, every high-ranking soldier, every journalist, in France. I would have sworn you'd have been sent one—unless it's been intercepted, that is,' Dubuque added, with a renewed frown.

Holmes got up and began to pace about, growling, 'Picquart required a period of peace and quiet in which to conduct his enquiries.'

'But why should this pamphlet have affected him anyway?' I asked the inspector. 'You don't mean to say it names Esterhazy?'

'I was relieved to find it didn't. Lazare's main theme is that Dreyfus was prosecuted because he was a Jew, and that the court was prejudiced against him for that same reason. There's nothing new in that, and I hoped it would all fall flat as just another volley from Dreyfus's sympathisers. It might have done, if *Le Matin* hadn't followed it up by publishing the *bordereau*.'

Holmes halted abruptly. He appeared thunderstruck.

'A few days after the pamphlet came out,' Dubuque went on, with a nod which reaffirmed his words. 'How they got it they didn't say, of course. I have my theory. I happen to know that Teysonnières, the handwriting expert who flatly refused to identify the hand as Dreyfus's at the trial, has been smarting ever since because the court was swayed by Bertillon instead of by him. Either he had managed to hold on to the photograph he had been given to study, or had it copied before he gave it back, thinking it might be useful some day. Pure sour grapes, is my belief.'

Holmes asked quickly, 'Did the newspaper print the text, or a facsimile?'

'A photograph. Of course, it's the first time the public has seen the *bordereau*, and all Paris started clamouring for a sample of Dreyfus's hand to compare with it.'

'Has the newspaper obliged?'

'No; but Mathieu Dreyfus has. He's had posters printed, with the *bordereau* and a letter of his brother's side by side.'

'The devil he has!'

'Look at it his way—it must have seemed a chance not to be missed. Now everyone's arguing again. There have been blows exchanged in some of the most exclusive clubs. And imagine the feelings of Schwartzkoppen and the rest of the German Embassy at seeing it all revealed. Imagine what the Kaiser must be saying. Worst of all, though, is how it has affected Picquart.'

'How should it?' I asked.

'Because, Doctor, his superiors think he sent *Le Matin* the photograph.'

'Picquart! I ... I'm afraid I don't follow at all.'

'I'm sorry. I should have explained from the beginning. You see, when Picquart received orders to leave Paris and make what seemed to him to be an unnecessary tour of all the frontier commands, he knew why this was being done. He managed to get an urgent message to me, and we met, with the most elaborate precautions on both our parts. I'd never seen him so grave before. He said to me, "Listen, Dubuque, I look like being away for a long time, and it is possible that something might happen to prevent my ever coming back. Well, there are some secrets I do not intend to take to the grave with me. I want you to know them, but to repeat them to no one, unless you can manage to see Sherlock Holmes." So that's why I'm here tonight, Mr Holmes, and why I must get back to Paris before I'm missed. If they begin to suspect me, I might go the way Picquart fears; but at least you'll have all the facts.'

Holmes resumed his seat. 'I trust your vow of secrecy enables you to regard my friend here as an extension of myself? It is my invariable custom to share professional confidences with him.'

'Of course I include you, Doctor,' Dubuque answered warmly, giving me a brief smile. Then he turned again to address Holmes, though occasionally sending a few words in my direction as acknowledgment of my *locus standi*.

'It seems,' he resumed, 'that Colonel Picquart's reopening of the case of the spy Claudine's neglected report of a traitor worried certain people more than appeared at the time. We saw that it annoyed Major Henry and Captain Lauth to be dragged into it, but we thought they had satisfied themselves that there was nothing to fear from her, and that they had scared her enough to keep her from trying to identify the culprit by her own efforts. Evidently, this wasn't so. They must have brooded over it, and discussed it together, and decided they'd better take steps to throw Picquart even further off Esterhazy's scent. In short, some more documents have turned up which give the impression that Dreyfus had been trading with the Germans.'

Holmes put a hand to his brow. 'What sort of documents?'

'Communications between the German and Italian attachés, who are known to be close friends, referring to relationships with a Jew. The initial D appears here and there, it seems. Picquart was summoned by the present Minister for War, General Billot, who read out the notes to him. One of them was particularly damning. Picquart asked to be shown it, but he was refused. He asked where it had come from. Billot replied, "Through the usual channels." Now, Picquart knew that this must either be an untruth, since he had given orders that everything intercepted between the foreign embassies must reach his own eyes first; or that Major Henry, the officer responsible for handling this traffic, had kept it from him. He also knew that there had been no recent delivery of wastepaper basket gleanings by his department's agency inside the German Embassy. He suspects that the documents are new fakes.

'Rashly, as he admitted to me, he decided there and then to chance all. He told General Billot that he suspected Major Esterhazy of being a traitor, and asked for permission to have him put under surveillance. The request was refused, and Picquart said he could have bitten out his own tongue for having spoken Esterhazy's name. He was right about that, for three days later he was carpeted by the Chief of Staff, Boisdeffre, his deputy, Gonse, and Billot. They accused him of working to secure Dreyfus's release and of neglecting his official duties in doing so. It wasn't said in so many words that he was suspected of giving *Le Matin* the *bordereau*, but it was hinted plainly enough. On the principle of in for a penny, in for a pound, Picquart told them all about his belief that Dreyfus was innocent. Gonse actually replied, "Dreyfus's innocence or guilt has nothing to do with it."'

'Disgraceful!'

'You're right, Doctor Watson. Picquart was determined to try his best, though. He put it to them that there was no secret that the Dreyfus family were doing all in their power to prove the captain's innocence, and he, Picquart, was sure they would eventually succeed. He pointed out how low the public's opinion of the army would sink when that happened. General Gonse replied, "If you say nothing, no one will be any the wiser." Well, you can imagine what effect that had on a man like Picquart! He said, "That is an abominable thing to say,

General," and marched out of the room.'

'Good for him!' said I, but Holmes, looking his most serious, asked, 'Was my connection with the affair mentioned?'

'Not at all. Picquart particularly wanted me to tell you that. He said, "Through my own fault it has become impossible for me to take the matter any further. I'm being sent as far from Paris as possible, and you can be sure they'll keep me away. You and Sherlock Holmes are Dreyfus's only hope now. Even so, I expect that impatient brother of Dreyfus's has damaged the cause irreparably. He's put them on their guard, and now I've been fool enough to name our suspect."'

'But what about Esterhazy? Didn't the mention of his name seem to interest them at all?'

'They said they would have him investigated. That was all. In my view, it will prove a waste of time. If it was Esterhazy who sold the secrets and wrote the *bordereau*, seeing it published will have been enough to make him drop his relations with the Germans for good. He'll have burnt any other incriminating documents and provided himself with enough cover-up evidence to ward off all suspicions.'

'There is the reconstructed message bearing his name,' I reminded Dubuque.

He shook his head. 'Picquart drew their attention to that. They told him that because it had been torn up instead of being posted, it couldn't stand as evidence.'

'Technically not,' Holmes agreed. 'But it should have convinced them that Esterhazy required serious investigation.'

'I know. Picquart got the distinct impression that they didn't wish to investigate him, for fear of what they might find. As we've feared already, they feel it better to let one obscure Jewish captain rot away on an island than admit that there's been an unholy blunder, and that all of them contributed to it.'

'If that is correct, this is the most loathsome business with which I have been associated in my whole career. But tell me, Dubuque, did Picquart form the impression that Esterhazy's guilt was known to these generals?'

'I asked him that myself. He answered that when he blurted out Esterhazy's name to Billot when they were alone the general looked mighty startled and surprised, and repeated the name before he could recover himself. No, Picquart saw that he'd shocked Billot, but he genuinely believes the general had never connected Esterhazy with the business before.'

'Mm. And yet they are proving lukewarm about following up what must have been a sensational discovery. I fear you are right, Dubuque. They dare not find out the truth.'

'But that places Dreyfus beyond all hope!' I protested. 'The longer they decline to relent, the harder it will be for them ever to do so.'

'Quite right. For that reason, anything we can do for him will have to be done soon. Picquart is clearly in danger for knowing too much. The good Dubuque here can do nothing further. You and I alone are free, Watson.'

'There is your brother and the British Government,' said I. 'Surely, an appeal to his better nature, backed with the evidence we now possess, will persuade him to get the government to approach the French.'

'It is worth trying, certainly. I am bound to say, though, that from what I have learnt of Intelligence agencies over the years, and from Mycroft's cynical response to our earlier protests, the chances of his helping must be slender. But, as you say, we will try him before resorting to any more drastic plans.'

'Such as?'

'I am not sure at present. If I were, I fancy it would be better not to discuss them in the presence of our friend here, who is a patriotic Frenchman. Nor is it truly our place to presume to sit in judgment upon the morality of men in the high places of his country.'

'As to that,' the inspector responded, 'you may say what you like. No Frenchman feels more strongly than I do about my country's state. Corruption is in every place—in politics, the law, the press, the church: all those institutions upon which the people ought to be able to rely for integrity and impartially. Ordinary folk are bewildered and don't know where to turn for justice and truth. The extremists of every sort know this and are out to use it for their own ends. The pity is, our younger generation listens to them. Who can blame it? It gets few enough good examples from its elders; so the young ones throw it their lot with the hotheads, whom they regard as the only idealists remaining. Believe me, gentlemen, you in England are more to be envied than you may know.'

'And yet,' said I, 'our impression is that the French hold us in contempt. "A nation of shopkeepers", "Perfidious Albion"—all that sort of thing.'

Inspector Dubuque returned me a little smile. 'We have never forgiven you for Trafalgar and Waterloo, Doctor. Seriously, though, there is a greater gulf between us than the small breadth of the Channel. Our approach to life's problems is totally different. We French are governed by reason. When it tells us that such-and-such is the course to take, we follow that way with blind assurance. Our Revolution began for the right reasons; yet when it degenerated into a bloodbath provoked by envy, spite, and mob-madness, our instincts did not make us stop and think again. We continued on our mad progress. Now, you English follow the instincts of your hearts. You are not averse to changing and improvising as circumstances alter. The French regard this as unreliability in you; but so far as I am concerned, it is that very quality which produces the more effective and honest results.'

I saw Holmes nodding approval of these sentiments, which the policeman had uttered eloquently and with every sign of sincerity. Dubuque saw him, too, and added, 'So you see, gentlemen, whatever you think might save Dreyfus will come from your instincts, and although it's better that I don't know what it is to be, I am certain it will be what is right. He won't be saved by anyone in France, of that I'm sure. Those who have put him where he is will be convinced by now that it has been for the best, even if something in their hearts whispers to them now and then that they've acted wrongly, they will have reasoned themselves out of that. Those of us in France who believe he's being wrongfully treated see him, first and foremost, as a martyr to prejudice and corruption. These are the considerations which inflame us, more than the plight of the man himself, which is what moves your good English hearts.'

The young man got up and began to resume the disguise in which he had arrived.

'This talk of danger to Europe,' I reminded them both dubiously. 'How much does that weigh in the scales?'

Without hesitation, Dubuque answered, 'Nothing, against that man's life. Do you know, Doctor, I sometimes feel that a war is the only thing that is going to draw the French people together again in a single cause? Who knows, it might bring us a little closer to England, into the bargain.'

His disguise was complete, save for the hat and wire spectacles. Before putting these on he gravely shook hands with us both.

'Tell Picquart, if you are able,' Holmes said, 'that whatever can be done will be towards vindicating him, as well as Dreyfus. The less he is seen to be involved himself, the better. And you, my dear Dubuque—look to your own safety. Unless something of the gravest urgency occurs, I think we shall not meet again until all this is over.'

The inspector hooked the spectacles over his ears, pulled the hat on to his head, so that the brim curled concealingly down about his face, took up the artist's portfolio, and left.

We resumed our chairs. The winter storm, which had escaped my consciousness whilst we had been conversing, sounded all the wilder against the silence which now fell upon us as Holmes rekindled his pipe and each of us thought his own thoughts.

'Well, Holmes?' I asked at length. 'A visit to your brother in the morning, no doubt?'

Surprisingly, he shook his head. 'Upon further consideration, I think not. I prefer Mycroft to believe that I am no longer active in this affair. In fact, I profoundly hope that none of his agents recognised Dubuque and followed him here. Depending upon how well informed Mycroft is about the situation in general, which I fancy will be very well indeed, any apparent renewal of interest on my part might result in his taking measures to head me off. If I am rendered powerless to act, then I fear Dreyfus is done for.'

'What action do you propose, then?'

'In the first place, I shall call upon the only other person whom I believe capable of interceding. If nothing comes of that, I am very much of the opinion that the only means of restoring Alfred Dreyfus to his family and saving him from further physical and mental decline, and even death, will be to remove him from that place—bodily.'

NINETEEN

WHEN I saw the mode of dress adopted by my friend for his visit to his hoped-for intercessor, I had no doubt as to whom that person was to be. Several days had elapsed since Inspector Dubuque's visit, since when Holmes had prowled impatiently, awaiting a summons. His unconcealed restlessness transmitted itself to me, and I was relieved when he at length departed in the rare immaculacy of frock coat, spats and gleaming top hat.

He returned long-faced, however, and threw off the coat thankfully, dragging on his dressing-gown over shirt-sleeves.

'Hopeless,' he said, in answer to my unasked question. 'A complete dead end.'

'I take it your visit was to Windsor?' I said. As usual, he had not favoured me with any information, but I had been able to make my own deduction.

'I might as well have remained here,' was his reply. 'In fact, I could have saved several precious days by not having had to wait for an audience.'

'Her Majesty could not help, then?'

'Wouldn't. She rides to orders, like so many others.'

'The Queen!'

'The poor old soul, it was quite pathetic. My excuse for approaching her, of course, was to report upon the sequence of events since our earlier interview. I had been feeling remiss at not having returned to her sooner, but I wished the matter to resolve itself to some point where she might be able to intervene upon positive grounds. In the event, she heard me out, then told me there is nothing she can do.'

253

'Forgive me, Holmes, but I have been trying to envisage what you could have hoped from her Majesty at all. This is an internal matter for France.'

'For anyone having susceptibilities, you mean,' he returned. 'The best I suppose I had hoped for was some hint to the Kaiser; the French are more likely to be influenced by his displeasure than by our good Queen's. I gathered, though, that all is not quite well between grandmama and grandson, since she declined to invite him over for her Diamond Jubilee.'

'The people would not have welcomed him, you know.'

'Be that as it may, her inability to help us was not due to it. Someone has been instructing her, Watson. I could see as much in her eyes and hear it in her voice. There was an infinite sadness in both, as she told me that she wished to hear no more of the matter, and requested—I would not quite say commanded—that I take no further action. "We understand that it would be better for our country's good if you were not to do so." Those were her words, Watson, and I could sense how personally abhorrent to her it was to have to utter them. Without question she had been put up to it by someone: most likely the Prime Minister, encouraged, I don't doubt, by that brother of mine.'

'You will see him after all, then?'

'Certainly not. He may know what he knows, but I no longer care.' He got rapidly to his feet again and crossed to the cluttered desk from which he conducted correspondence. He seized a scrap of paper, took up one of many pens, and proceeded to scribble violently, saying as he did so, 'You will be going out shortly?'

'I was not intending to do so . . .'

'Good. Call at the news agency on your way and instruct them to insert this in the Globe, Star, St James's, Evening News, Standard, Echo, and any others that occur to you.'

Without looking at me he passed the paper over his shoulder, and I took it without demur. The message upon it read: 'Good berths for up to twenty able-bodied hands ready to sail for Trinidad within the week. Strong young men only need apply to Captain Basil, care of . . .' I needed to read no further. The address was that of the shipping agency through which, using that same pseudonym, he had pretended to recruit hands for a whaling expedition, thereby drawing the murderous Patrick Cairns into his fatal trap.

'Trinidad?' I asked.

He turned to me with a sigh. 'Really, Watson, would you have me put "French Guiana, en route for Devil's Island", and give the whole of the game away?'

He jumped up and bustled off to shed the rest of the formal outfit, leaving me to go about my errand, obediently and automatically, dazed by the implications which jostled for places in my mind.

Within twenty-four hours the familiar response began. This time, however, Holmes had given no instruction to the agency to send the applicants for interview at our Baker Street abode. He dragged me prematurely away from the following morning's breakfast table and into a cab which bore us to Sumner's Shipping Agency, in the Ratcliff Highway. There, a grubby little room was placed at our disposal, and shortly after ten o'clock the men began to file in.

Holmes was dressed for the occasion in the sort of uncompromisingly heavy garb of a master of his own vessel. He lounged back upon the plain chair behind the small table, jacket flung open, hard-peaked cap set upon one side of his head, his lips clamped upon the stem of his foulest pipe, causing his jaw to jut aggressively. I occupied a small hard chair in a corner, ill at ease in a cheap bowler and a shoddy coat which he had thrust upon me. He had delineated no precise duty for me, but I knew that I was enjoying the privilege of being present at the outset of a dramatic undertaking, and I was content to sit unobtrusively and observe his method of dealing with the stream of applicants who came through the door.

'Name?'

'Murphy, Cap'n. Seamus Murphy. Twenty-six and niver a black mark agin me name, so help me.'

'Only one against your left temple. How did the other fellow fare?'

'Ah, well, sorr, put it this way—he won't be among them able to apploy to yer honour, unless yer honour's willin' to wait a day or two afore he can crape along.'

'Fancy yourself with your fists, then, Murphy?'

To my alarm, Holmes flung back his chair with a jerk which sent it crashing and came round the table towards the fellow, who matched him in height but outweighed him by easily thirty pounds.

Murphy was clearly taken off his guard, but he quickly recovered and squared up to Holmes, who, however, merely grinned at him and held up a palm for the man to drive a big fist against with a resounding smack.

'You'll do, Murphy,' "Captain Basil" told him, and pushed across a paper to be signed, whilst he recovered his fallen chair, with a broad wink at me. As the man was writing laboriously he was told, 'Put the word about the others that unless they fancy they might last half a round or more with you, they needn't waste my time.'

'Oi'll do that, yet honour, though ye'll not be foindin' many could.'

'Poor looking bunch, eh?'

'Lot of 'em Jew boys. Handy enough, but nothin' to compare with a good mob of Irish. Now, if yer honour'll give me a day or two, I can . . .'

'No, no. I'll see everyone who's waiting. Good-day to you, Murphy.'

The man lumbered out and Holmes murmured to me, 'The more Jews, the better for our purpose. Our East End Jew is a tough enough customer at any time, and resourceful, too. When we're safely at sea and he can be told what we're about, I fancy he'll find some special enthusiasm for our quest. Come in! By the Lord Harry, call yourself able-bodied?'

So it was with each of them: an early taunt to discover the mettle of the fellow. On one occasion it actually led to a brief exchange of blows, which ended with the applicant staunching blood from his nose with a grubby handkerchief in one great paw, while shaking Holmes's hand with the other. Within an hour he had signed on the number he required, and it occurred to me that I should not have cared to encounter them en masse in hostile mood. Some two-thirds of them I judged to be Jewish, although some of them were at pains to conceal the fact.

'A pity, Watson,' Holmes said, as he shuffled the documents together. 'A race of extraordinary talents and capacity for endurance, driven upon the defensive by the envious malice of those who surpass them merely numerically. If Dreyfus himself were not Jewish he might not be surviving still for us to rescue.'

'You really believe we can manage it?' I asked, instinctively keeping my voice low.

'It will not be for want of trying, if we don't.'

'But what of the consequences. Surely, there will be all sorts of repercussions between the nations?'

'I hope not. One of my reasons for recruiting a high proportion of Jews is to give the thing a semblance of a coup by this mythical Jewish Syndicate. There will be some backlash against the Jews in France, undoubtedly; but once Dreyfus has been enabled to publish his case, to which we shall append all the evidence we have obtained, I fancy that both fury and sympathy will take their respective turns-about. World opinion will be aroused against that kind of unreasoning prejudice which has contributed so much to his sufferings. I said before that he is not a mere symbol, but that does not mean that he isn't one at all.'

'What is your plan of action, then?'

'To land our raiding force and bring him back to the ship.'

'As simple as that!'

'The simplest plans are frequently the most effective.'

'No doubt. But you seem to have discounted the presence of his guards ...'

'If necessary, they will have to be overpowered, though with as little violence to them as possible. I doubt that we shall find them in much state of readiness, and the sight of our plug-uglies will scarcely enthuse them for a fight.'

'... And Dreyfus's own determination not to be rescued. He told you that to accept that way out would be tantamount to admitting his guilt.'

'That convinced me of his sincerity. But the time for passive acceptance based upon mere conjecture is past. He stands no chance while he remains a prisoner. Whether he wishes it or not, he must be got away to some place where he can recuperate and, with our assistance, assemble his case for publication. Then, when the whole world is up in arms about it, and the French authorities are being pressed from all sides to grant him a public hearing, he must offer to surrender himself for that purpose. Such a gesture will show him in the most honourable light. They will have no alternative but to accept.'

'I see your point. Are you going to inform Madame Dreyfus and his brother?'

'Not until our task is accomplished. For all his qualities, Mathieu

Dreyfus is too impulsive to be let into our secret. He might do something rash which could ruin everything. As for Madame, I'm afraid she must endure in ignorance for a few weeks longer. It is for the best.'

'Well.' I said, 'I don't know what the niceties of international law are. Is it kidnapping? Piracy? Violation of foreign territory?'

'I do not care,' he almost snapped; then smiled. 'Besides, you know how unorthodoxy attracts me?'

'It certainly seems unorthodox to recruit a crew without asking a single one of them whether he can hand, reef or steer.'

'Oh, that is by the by. My old friend Captain Muros is providing both vessel and crew. These fellows will sail as supernumeraries.'

'Captain Muros?'

'Not an acquaintance of yours, Watson. The circles in which you are accustomed to move are infinitely more refined. Muros is one of those mongrels of the species *homo sapiens*. His name is distinctly Mediterranean, but his complexion bears the shadows of the slave plantations. The product of some exotic liaison in squalid surroundings, no doubt, It is immaterial. So long as he has money and liquor, he will go anywhere and serve us as faithfully as his mendacious instincts will permit him. His crew are rogues to a man. The vessel itself is sound, if less than luxurious. I would suggest your most expendable wardrobe.'

'You ... I ... *We* are going?'

'But of course, my dear boy. It would be a poor admiral who would not sail with his own expedition and deny his trusty aide his share of the excitement.'

I rubbed my hands joyfully.

'I shall oil my service revolver this evening.'

'I desire you will do no such thing, Watson. No arms of any sort will be permitted on this venture. What plain fists cannot achieve will have to remain beyond us, for any wounding by a weapon would undoubtedly produce those repercussions which we most hope to avoid. Besides, the worst danger you will face will probably be from Muros's crew. I will threaten him suitably before we sail, but we will keep our cabin door bolted, just the same.'

We sailed from London five days later. The passage to the

Guiana coast was accomplished without any major hitch. The weather was cold for the first fortnight and rough enough to keep everyone preoccupied with his own difficulties. Then it began to warm up, the seas calmed, the skies cleared, and our force began to skirmish within itself as unoccupied seamen are wont to do the world over.

It was only in the latter stage of the voyage that Holmes satisfied the curiosity which had been mounting perceptibly in them as to its purpose. He spoke to them in hushed conclave, outlining the details of the Dreyfus affair in simple, lucid terms, working up to an impressive peroration which subtly appealed to the sense of unity of the Jews amongst them, the sentimental sympathy of the Irish, and that dislike of the French which seemed common to them all, and sprang, so far as I could judge, from a mistrust of a people who could so far turn against their betters as to seize their lands and cut off their heads. More practically, he promised them a bonus upon their agreed wages if the mission should succeed, and warned them severely against using any more violence than might prove absolutely necessary. The warning he added about the risk of their finishing up in the penal settlements evoked only a general growl and some uncouth utterances. Thereafter, they ceased to fight amongst themselves, and took to squatting about in groups talking in low tones, glancing up with eagerly flashing eyes whenever either of us chanced to pass by.

The days became hot and humid, and I was glad to change into some of the remnants of my Indian kit which I had thought to bring along. Holmes wore his linen suit again. He had allowed his moustache to grow throughout the voyage, telling me of his hope to continue anonymous in case our venture should fail and he should have to try something else subsequently. I asked whether, by that same token, I should grow my beard, and felt a little piqued when he replied that it was scarcely necessary, as if implying that my appearance was so nondescript anyway that no one would be likely to remark it.

Our plan was to land at Georgetown, British Guiana, where the arrival of a score of British seamen would raise fewer eyebrows than would be the case in the French territory. Supplies of fuel, food and water were necessary for the escape run, and Holmes judged it desirable to let his men get the feeling of land under their legs after a month at sea and with a further voyage of uncertain duration in prospect. So it was that our vessel entered the port one hot, sticky evening and we filed thankfully ashore, watched enviously by Muros's ruffians who had their duties to perform before they, too, could enjoy such pleasures as were to be found on the land.

With unerring instinct, the entire force made for a plain doorway in a rough-cast building near the quay, and went in. There was no sign of any kind above or beside the door, and I glanced enquiringly at Holmes, who nodded to me to follow. I went in, with him behind me, and had to admire the instinct, common also to the British soldier, which had enabled our men to single out a commodious although anonymous bar-room. Tables and chairs were set about without any attempt at uniformity, a few of them occupied by nautical-looking types of European and African origin, drinking and smoking. Heads were raised and turned at the entry of so many men together, but the display of curiosity was short-lived, although I noticed one man rise quickly and slip away through a curtained doorway with some air of purposefulness.

There was a long bar, tended by a fat, grizzle-headed man in a grubby vest, with a cigarette drooping from a corner of his mouth. A middle-aged woman beside him I took to be his wife, and there were two young half-caste girls, of a sallow prettiness, whom I hoped were not their daughters; for, if they were, parental laxity was abundantly apparent in the absence of any rebuke from the elders for the way the girls positively dashed forth to serve the newcomers, making no attempt to withdraw from the crude embraces with which they were welcomed.

A little man began to clamour upon an old upright piano in a corner. Glasses and bottles were hurried to the tables by the girls, cheroots were lit, the volume of gruff chatter rose, with a descant of giggles from the girls, and the disregarded accompaniment of the piano beneath. An air of festivity prevailed. Holmes and I took a table to ourselves. The girls ignored us at first, until Holmes snapped his fingers sharply and Seamus Murphy jerked a thumb in our direction, enabling us to obtain two bottles of beer whose contents tasted of warm soapsuds.

I felt myself excited. It was like India again, and the first night of landing at Bombay, to the unaccustomed sights and smells of a strange land after several weeks insulated from the world in a ship at sea. My years of adventuring in my friend's company had carried me into many stimulating situations, and some dangers; but no adventure of ours had been upon such a scale, and with so momentous a stake to play for, and the eager throbbing of my heart and pulse attested as much.

We sent one of the girls for some of the local cheroots and were soon adding our smoke to the clouds which filled the room, and our coughing to the general din. There was nothing else to do with our time, so we ventured upon two more bottles of the beer, preferring not to risk the effects of the local spirit. As we sat there, sipping, and puffing, and watching with some amusement the men's pawings at the waitresses and at a group of more gaudily clad girls who had been ushered in from the back premises by the middle-aged woman, and were almost *certainly* not her daughters, we were joined by a thick-set man who came through the smoke like a traveller emerging from fog. It was the hybrid Captain Muros.

He had brought with him a large glass of some spirit which I imagined to be *tafia*, of which Holmes had told me. He took a chair at our table and smacked his lips over a long pull at the glass.

'All fixed, Mr Holmess,' he announced in his heavy accent, which seemed to me to owe a good deal to Greek. 'Six canoes.'

'When can you get them aboard?'

'Tonight. The man, he gonna drift 'em on down the tide, an' we hooking 'em up as they come alongsides. Easy.'

He took another great swig, and looked into his glass as if surprised that its contents had disappeared.

'What time?' Holmes asked.

''Bout midnight. No one around then. Easy.'

'You're quite sure there will be enough sober men to manage it?'

'Ah, ass to that, Mr Holmess, men is saying if they can't come ashore, they wanting extra dough. You pay?'

'Within reason,' Holmes nodded. 'It will be worth ensuring there are no blunders.'

'No blunders. Easy.'

Muros got up and hurried away in urgent quest of replenishment for his glass. He had scarcely left us when another man sidled unsteadily up to our table and sat down heavily on the chair just vacated. My first impression was that he was one of the roisterers, in need of support which failing legs could no longer give him, and who had thankfully espied the empty seat. He was certainly drunk, carrying in one hand a half-emptied bottle of the spirit, which he raised to his lips and drank from messily. But he was not one of our fellows. His physique was more that of a scarecrow, and his loose clothing hung upon him in marked contrast to the way our men's brawny frames filled their garments. He was older, too, with sparse, straggling grey hair; and when he raised his face towards us I saw death behind his deep-hollowed cheeks and staring eyes. I also recognised, with a start, that I had met him in London.

'Ça va, Monsieur James,' he addressed Holmes, but his tone was not that chirpy one which I remembered. He asked the question flatly, in a slurred, wet voice, and had to wipe his mouth with the back of a skeletal hand.

'Albert!' Holmes exclaimed. 'What the devil are you doing here?'

Gonselin made no immediate reply, but raised the bottle again and drank. His eyes were half-shut now, and he was obviously having difficulty focussing his gaze. He roused himself sufficiently to answer at length.

'Been waiting you. Got message. Waiting with message.'

He would have raised the bottle again, but Holmes reached across and restrained him, seizing the other's wrist in a strong grip which made his eyes come open again. The bleariness of them was replaced momentarily by a flash of anger at being handled. He began to mouth a protest in French, but suddenly broke off. The yellowed, watery eyes widened in what seemed to be surprise and even horror; the parchment cheeks stiffened as the chin fell, dragging open the mouth, which exuded a dribble of saliva from one of its corners. Then a great shudder shook him. He sagged and crumpled on the chair, like a marionette whose strings had been released, leaving it totally devoid of support. The bottle fell to the floor without breaking and rolled away.

I got up swiftly and hurried round to help him into a posture which would save him from following it; but something about the feel of the skinny frame caused me to feel for his pulse and his heart. I looked up at Holmes.

'He is dead.'

'Quickly, Watson,' was his response. 'Lay him forward on the table, as though he's drunk. The last thing we require at this moment is the police to be called.'

I did as he ordered, and retrieved the bottle to stand it near the dead man's outflung hand. Then, at Holmes's gesture, I delved into the pockets of his jacket and trousers, seeking the message which he had mentioned. Apart from some small items, there was nothing resembling one; not even a scrap of paper.

I resumed my seat, completing a grim tableau in the midst of that movement and hubbub.

'What do you make of it, Holmes?'

'Whatever it was, he was carrying it verbally. If he had lived another minute, even . . . !'

'But why did he not approach us sooner? I would swear he was not in the room when we arrived, and we have been more than an hour already. Why delay?' A recollection struck me then. 'Wait a moment: I noticed a fellow slip out as we entered. There was something furtive about the way he went.'

'Then that is it. Albert had his lookout stationed here, and no doubt others in equally likely bars, with orders to carry him word of any unusual comings and goings. From the state of him, he has been too ill to leave his lodging. His delay in reaching us reflects the effort it must have cost him to do so. It proved just too much for him.'

'He has deteriorated terribly since we saw him in London. The drink was perhaps all that was keeping him going.'

Holmes nodded. 'Poor Albert. He knew he would never leave the colonies alive. His death poses several questions for us, however. What was his message? And from whom? Was it intended specifically for us—in which case, how could he know we were coming here?—or was it meant for anyone at all who might arrive with what might be construed to be suspicious intentions? Watson, I am afraid that whilst we endeavour to puzzle out these matters, it will be necessary to order some more of this disgusting beer. It is not exactly etiquette to sit at table with a corpse, but I fancy it would have pleased Albert's sense of irony. At all events, we must keep up our pose and not attract anyone's curiosity, or it might be all up with us.'

I picked up an empty beer bottle and waved it towards a girl with a tray and glasses. She nodded and soon brought three more bottles to our table, placing one before each of us, without even a glance at the slumped, dead customer for whom she had automatically catered.

Signs of full-scale debauch were beginning to manifest themselves. Men—ours and various locals—clung to one another in maudlin conversation, sharing bottles. Some were slumped on their chairs, the girls on their laps supporting themselves there with arms locked around necks. The piano jangled hopelessly while a group of men across the room from it wailed a sentimental chorus quite at variance with what was being played.

And as I watched, over the shoulders of the dead man who was our table companion, I saw a new flurry of movement. The smoke clouds swirled from the violent throwing open of the street door and the mob and the noise swelled together, as a body of men surged in. I feared for a second that they were police; but they were obviously sailors and roughnecks similar to ours, except that there was an alien uniformity to them which marked them as un-English. They were all large and short-haired and wore pea jackets. I had the impression that they were Americans.

'Correct, Watson,' Holmes said, divining my thoughts. 'Hear the twangy drawl and the rolled r's? I must make time one of these days to set down some thoughts upon the differentiations in the American and Australian dialects as derived from English roots.'

'Never mind that,' I answered. 'There's going to be a pitched battle.'

I recalled having seen before, in India, no doubt, a ship's company of one sort plough into its counterpart of another without any apparent provocation having been offered. I had seen English soldiers fight Irishmen, and Naval men wade into Marines, and Scotsmen fall upon one another as if on murder bent. It seemed to be some sort of instinctive reflex, like strange dogs snarling and snapping at one another before settling down to familiarity; a primitive ritual which had to be observed.

Yet, there seemed to be something beyond the requirements of ritual about the affray which immediately commenced. The newcomers, who had entered talking and swearing amongst themselves, let out a chorussed howl at sight of our fellows and flung themselves at them with the utmost viciousness, scattering squealing girls to the floor, where they lay ignored and in dire danger of being trampled upon. Chairs went flying; the contents of tables were swept off, and the tables themselves overturned. Our men, who had been drinking steadily and copiously, and were mostly seated or supporting one another, were at a disadvantage. Nevertheless, the shock attack seemed to galvanise them back to their senses and they were soon giving as good as they received.

The locals slipped away as quickly as they could, whilst the girls crawled to safety, whimpering and cursing. As to ourselves, no one did more than glance briefly in our direction. I supposed that we were taken for a couple of locals, enjoying a quiet conversation at our corner table, whose slumped companion had not been able to hold his drink. I looked at Holmes, but he motioned me to sit still; so there we sat, watching the mêlée like two comfortable spectators at some violent sporting event. It was certainly interesting to witness the amount of punishment which men could take from the fists and boots of others, and yet come back to return it.

We were not to be left alone for long, though. Through the flailing throng came Captain Muros again, proceeding this time with a curious, stiff-legged gait, arms held out at his sides like a penguin's flippers, eyes bulging, and his swarthy face swollen and almost crimson. The reason for this proved to be that he was being propelled by a huge man who had him so tightly by the collar that he was near to being throttled. With a great effort, Muros succeeded in pointing towards us. For his reward, he was flung aside to vanish amongst the legs of the fighters, while the big man come on towards us.

'You James, eh?' he demanded of me, posturing himself as though daring me to rise.

'Certainly not!' I returned.

'So you're him, eh!' he addressed my friend, who sat back, arms stretched before him on the table top, regarding the man coolly.

'My name is James,' he said. 'John James. But you have the advantage of me, Mr er . . .?'

'Cut the malarkey!' The accent was strongly American-Irish, and the way the words were delivered denoted an excess of fury. I was ready to spring to Holmes's aid if the attack which seemed imminent materialised, but he continued to sit motionless.

'If there were a spare glass handy, I would invite you to relieve us of the necessity of finishing this beer,' he told the glowering man. 'Excuse our friend there, by the way. It would be difficult to awake him, in his state.'

How often had I seen this pose of Holmes's, combining nonchalance with aloof disdain, take the wind out of the sails of a blustering bully accustomed to cringing deference. This man hesitated and glanced again at me. I raised my nose a few inches and returned him my hardest stare.

Holmes asked him, in the same mild tone, 'Won't you sit down and tell me your name? It is always difficult doing business with an unintroduced stranger.'

The look of fury returned to the other's expression, but he complied with the request.

'Name of O'Brien. Johnny. "Dynamite Johnny", they call me.'

'How do you do, Mr O'Brien? Allow me to introduce my friend, Mr John Henry.'

'How do you do?' I repeated. The man mouthed something indistinguishable and roughly dragged up a chair for himself.

'You know what I'm doing here?' he demanded of Holmes, who shook his head blandly.

'Well, I'll tell yez. It's the same as you. Out to snatch that god-damned Dryfoos—and you ain't gettin' in my way, see!'

This startled me considerably. I wondered what reaction it would produce in Holmes. He replied carefully, 'There seems to be some misunderstanding, Mr O'Brien. I am a journalist from London, here to write ...'

'Baloney! I know why you're here, and that bunch of Limeys with yez.'

He glanced briefly towards the centre of the room. The battle raged unabated, neither side seeming to be gaining ascendancy.

'You've come to take Dryfoos, and so have I—and I'm the guy who's gonna do it.'

The former flippancy was absent from Holmes's tone as he responded, 'You still seem to have some advantage over me, in the matter of information.'

'Yeah? Well, I've been here twenty-four hours, and you only just got in. When I see you mob comin' ashore, I knew there was something fishy. No ship your size carries a crew that big—'sides, the crew was still aboard workin'. So I kinda makes it my business to git alongside for a chinwag with your skipper. He wasn't doin' his share of the talking, so I called the boys around and he changed his mind. Git it?'

'I see. May I ask who is sponsoring your expedition, then?'

'Who's behind yours?'

'Mine? Oh, *I* am.'

'Don't you try to kid Dynamite Johnny, mister!'

'Not at all. It's perfectly straightforward. Captain Dreyfus is one of the world's potentially biggest newspaper stories. Before long, his case is going to blow up in the faces of everyone involved in it. I want him secure in my keeping to write his own account of it, before any other newsman can get to him. The whole world will buy the book and my stories accompanying it, and my cut of the takings will pay for my expedition ten times over at least. Now, Mr O'Brien, I've told you my interest. Pray let me hear yours.'

The big man stared at him long and hard, mustering his thoughts to the point of deciding whether to reply. Then, looking a little less ferocious, he leaned forward and admitted, 'There's this guy in New York, see. Jew, I guess. Said he and a bunch of others had gotten together to raise a fund to get Dryfoos out.'

'For what purpose?'

'Search me. Buddies of his, I guess. None o' my business.'

'What *is* your business, Mr O'Brien? Your usual one, that is?'

'You ain't bin around much, mister. Dynamite Johnny O'Brien'll go anywhere, do anythin', provided only the money's right. Soldier of fortune, fixer, provider—you name the handle, and it fits. So, somebody wants this Dryfoos, and Dynamite Johnny obliges, no questions asked.'

'You've weighed all the possibilities, I suppose? The effect upon the balance of power in Europe, etcetera?'

'You're kiddin'! Like I said, no question asked.'

'I see. Might one ask where you had proposed taking him?'

'Cuba, mebbe. Mebbe not.'

'And then?'

'The spondulicks change hands and he's my client's. Leastways . . .'

O'Brien paused, and I saw a craftly gleam in the fierce eyes.

'... Leastways, unless someone else wants to raise the ante.' He made that universally understood gesture of rubbing together the thumb and first finger of one hand.

'Ah! I take it that there is a possibility of a commercial transaction between us?'

'D'yez have to use them English words? You mean a deal, say so.'

'A deal, then.'

O'Brien reached out and took my bottle of beer. He raised it to his lips and drained it. I was not sorry to see its contents disappear. He went on cautiously to Holmes. 'You want this Dryfoos. So does those guys in New York. The hell, what's it matter to me who gets him, or who's payin'?'

'You seem to be taking it for granted, Mr O'Brien, that you are the one who is going to get to him first.'

'Sure I am. You ain't figurin' on tryin' to stop me, mister?'

'No, no. I dare say you are right. You have been here twenty-four hours, as you say. First come, first served. You have done your coaling and provisioning. You're ready to leave. You know perfectly well that we cannot hope to get away in time to overtake you.'

'Ye're durned right ye can't.' O'Brien stretched across again and took possession of Holmes's beer this time. I wondered whether there would be any profit in keeping him drinking, and looked round in the hope of a waitress's eye. In view of what was going on in the room, however, the notion was impractical.

'Then listen,' said Holmes, drawing forward to the table and fixing the other with his steel-grey eyes. 'Why don't we join forces?'

'The hell with that! I'm not splittin' my take with anybody else!'

'I am not suggesting it. I was merely going to propose a means by which you might increase your fee.'

'You what?'

'It's quite simple. Let us take Dreyfus together. Incidentally, I know my way about Devil's Island already, which I fancy might give me some slight advantage in the proceedings. When we have him safely aboard one or other of our ships, we carry him to some mutually agreed destination where he will be safe and where I can have the advantage of his company in peace, in order to question him at length and assemble the material for my book. Meanwhile, you play a delaying game with your New York employer—stall him, isn't that the term?—promising to hand him over when your original fee has been increased to your satisfaction. I somehow doubt that such a tactic will surprise your client.'

O'Brien shot Holmes a baleful look, but I could tell that the proposition was receiving his intense consideration. Holmes added quickly, 'Thus, you will finish up better off than you had hoped. Not only that, but I shall expect to make my own contribution for your assistance. What it amounts to is, that you will make perhaps twice the profit for half the effort—that is, if your force and mine do not succeed in decimating each other before we can even get started.'

The bottle was motionless at O'Brien's mouth. His eyebrows high, he regarded Holmes with the suspicion a wild beast might show upon being tempted with a domestic morsel. Suddenly, the bottle was crashed down upon the table top. He leaped to his feet and swung round to face the milling mob. In a voice which I should have compared unfavourably with that of a bull elephant's he roared, 'QUIT IT!'

The effect was magical. Like one of those pantomime dances, where the whole stage freezes into motionless tableau for the curtain to fall, the fighting ceased. Men stood face to face, leg to leg, fist to fist. I could almost see them shake themselves back into consciousness. Rigid shoulders relaxed, arms fell, and, as one, the entire assembly moved, hobbling and even crawling in some cases, towards the bar, where the proprietor and his womenfolk arose from cover and in their turn sprang back to animation. Americans who had been trying to pulverise their English opponents now shoved them forward to be served first, crying over their shoulders that the drinks were on them. Londoners and Irishmen who, moments earlier, had almost reached that stage where bottles would be smashed for use as many-pointed glass daggers, turned back to help up fallen adversaries and dust them down.

O'Brien gave vent to another bellow: 'Beer—over here!' My heart sank as I saw a girl hastily assemble half a dozen bottles of the stuff on a tray and hurry towards us.

Salvation, though, was not far behind. We had scarcely got through the first rounds, to a background accompaniment of cheerful and unified singing of Irish ballads and Anglo-American ditties, when the bar room door opened yet again and another party of men filed eagerly in. They paused at the threshold, surveying the scene. A terrible silence had fallen upon the drinkers at the bar. The notes of the piano faltered and died away. Suddenly, there sounded a whoop such as I imagine a band of attacking Red Indians would have uttered as they fell upon some Yankee waggon train, and the occupants of the bar surged en masse towards the hesitating newcomers, dragging them inside and setting about them. Their cries of alarm brought their comrades pouring in, and once again chaos and racket reigned.

The three of us stayed watching wonderingly and with rising foreboding; for the new arrivals all wore the dark blue uniforms and distinctive caps of *matelots* of the French Navy.

Released beyond recall from whatever may have been his involvement in this transpiration, Albert Gonselin slumbered on.

TWENTY

Less than two hours later we were at sea, heading eastward in the direction of the Salvation Isles.

We were aboard Captain O'Brien's vessel, which had the advantage of having taken in her coal, water and provisions and was already in the process of raising steam. Our complement was a mixture of his and ours, made up of those who had emerged least scathed from the affray. Those able to do little more than crawl had been left behind to fend for themselves and tend those who were not even capable of that. They were to drag one another aboard Captain Muros's ship, which would wait at Georgetown for a message reporting that our mission had been accomplished. Then Muros was to sail from the area immediately and back to England. Every man would receive his compensation as soon as Holmes could get back to attend to it.

After the shock of the initial onslaught the Frenchmen had fought valiantly, and with the advantage of not having their strength and faculties reduced, as had ours, by drink. A quick conference between Holmes and O'Brien, with some small contribution from myself, had concluded that whatever the significance of the sudden appearance of part of the French Navy implied for us, we had better act without a moment's delay if we were to have any hope at all of success. O'Brien shouldered his way into the fight and extricated his First and Second Mates, who were both relatively intact and sober, and ordered them to get the more capable hands out of the bar unobtrusively and down to the wharf. Holmes and I went ahead with O'Brien; the rest followed soon after, in dribs and drabs, to set about the urgent work of preparing to sail.

Across the pool from us stood a French cruiser, grey and menacing. Her deck was a-bustle with activity. It was clear that she was making ready to sail again quite soon. The party who had been set free to visit the bar would presumably have been the engine-room and other hands who would not be needed for a few hours and could be granted brief respite from the arduous conditions under which they laboured between the decks of an iron ship in tropical heat.

As soon as he saw the warship O'Brien turned to the Second Mate.

'Get the hell back to that bar and keep 'em brawlin'. Try and find at least one guy able to man the door alongside yez. If any Frenchie tries to get out, belt him back in. We're gonna need every spare minute to get up full steam without that there man-o'-war rumbling us. Got it?'

'Yeah, Cap'n.'

'I'll give three toots on the whistle when we're near ready to sail. If yez can make it back in time, ya get to come with us. If not, tough luck.'

The officer saluted by spitting and hurried off. In the event, he scrambled aboard, bloodied and panting, just as the lines were being cast off.

'It's O.K.,' he mumbled through a broken mouth. 'None of the Frenchies got away, and half of 'em's out for the count.'

So we had slipped away. Watching the cruiser from our stern, I saw nothing which suggested that our departure was causing consternation aboard her.

As the land fell behind, I ruminated upon why she should be at Georgetown at all, when the French possession towards which we were heading was no great distance away. I comforted myself with the notion that she was not proceeding thither at all, but was about some business entirely unconnected with us and had simply put into the British base for some urgently needed supplies because it happened to be convenient. All the same, I puzzled over the coincidence of her arrival and the message which Gonselin's fatal seizure had prevented his conveying. I could make out no connection, though, and gave up the attempt, following instead Holmes's example of getting some hours of sleep in order to be fresh for what lay ahead.

I awoke at length and went gladly up on deck from the stuffy little cabin which I had had to share with the Second Mate, whose snores and unconscious babblings had made dozing off no easy matter. It was very dark and evidently overcast, for no stars were visible. I could discern a faint string of lights at some distance on the starboard bow.

'Quite perfect conditions, don't you agree?' came my friend's voice at my side. He was leaning on the rail, the smoke and occasional spark from his pipe streaming away down the warm breeze caused by the ship's steady movement.

'Holmes,' I replied, recollecting one of my drowsing thoughts; 'the canoes. We never picked them up.'

'There was no time. It would have been impossible to remake the arrangement at such short notice, and we could not linger until the agreed hour.'

'What is the plan, then?'

'The only one open to us. We must get ashore in the ship's boats. The sea is calm enough for anything at present, although O'Brien declares he doesn't like the look of this overcast and the state of the glass. At the worst, we shall have to stage an all-out assault: take the place by storm, and run for it. Remember, we have the great advantage of surprise. We are not expected, and it will be the early hours, when man in the tropics gets the deepest sleep he is able to between the cooling and re-heating of Nature's furnace.'

'There must be some system of alarm, though.'

'Indeed; but picture it in action. One relatively alert sentry hears a noise. He peers and listens, wondering whether his imagination has deceived him, or if it had been caused by something quite innocent. He hears something else, yet still he hesitates, seeking to satisfy his own mind before risking the ire of his guard commander and comrades upon being roused. Even when he does that, there will follow minutes of questioning, the struggle into equipment, the manning of lights and deployment of the guard. If we move swiftly and resolutely we can overwhelm them before they know enough of what is going on to raise a general alarm and alert the other islands. Even so, from what I observed during my previous sojourn, there is nothing in the way of a swift patrol boat kept constantly manned and ready to deal with any such enterprise as ours. The sharks in the strait are the only seagoing sentries around Devil's Island.'

'Then we are bound to succeed!' said I, feeling real optimism surge at last. 'From the way these fellows fought one another and the French last night, I have no doubt they will prove more than enough for a handful of guards.'

'I agree. By the way, O'Brien had not intended to be so scrupulous about not using weapons as we were. I have talked him round to our way of thinking, though. We are risking enough as it is, invading another nation's territory and abducting one of its nationals. Events will justify us; but not so easily if we leave a corpse or two behind.'

'You trust O'Brien? I mean, we are in his ship, manned by his crew. Granted that our raid succeeds, we are very much in his hands afterwards.'

I saw my friend's eyes gleam as he turned to me.

'I had not overlooked that. Although he has given me every assurance, I intend that when we sail from the island there will be one of our men doubling the duty of every one of his. Fortunately, our stout fellows acquitted themselves so well in the fight that I reckon we are in an overall majority of three, which gives us sufficient margin for a roving patrol. And that is not counting you and me, my dear Watson. I fancy we are match enough for "Dynamite" O'Brien, are we not?'

His hand found mine and we exchanged a firm grip.

'The game's afoot, Holmes,' I murmured, echoing his immortal phrase.

We fell silent, our eyes searching the horizon where the shore lights gleamed nearer now. Peering down, I was able to discern from the way the phosphorescent bow-wave was widening that our vessel was turning gently landward. Men were beginning to flit about the deck, making ready the falls of the boats for swift lowering when the command should come.

'Well, Mr James?' came the gruff voice of Captain O'Brien, as he loomed large behind us. 'What d'yez reckon to it now?'

'How long, do you fancy?' was Holmes's question in reply.

'Not more'n an hour. Still won't be full light.'

'The weather?'

O'Brien sniffed the air. 'Wouldn't trust if for long. I guess it'll hold up long enough for us, though. Depends how we're gonna play it. Sail right up to the landing place and go in hell for leather, and it could be over in minutes. Only, we'll be a sitting duck there in the strait. Any kinda barrier they can set in our way—a string of canoes, mebbe—and we're cooped like a hog in a pen for to be picked off from Royale. If we go round the seaward side, though, why, then, supposin' the boats can get in like you did before in that canoe, and get away sameways, it's gonna take at least an hour. And you know how quick the sea can get up in these parts.'

I saw Holmes nod and fancied his mind flitting back to the experience of that scuppered canoe. He answered, 'I have all along considered the direct assult from the strait to be the most fraught with danger. If the sea had been really adverse, it would have been our only remaining hope. While conditions give us at least a chance, I favour the seaward approach. Surprise is everything; beside which, there would be infinitely less danger of any French getting killed in the shooting match which an invasion alert would certainly spark off between Royale and Devil's Island. They would report that we had been responsible for any deaths, and the moral motives behind our action would be diluted.'

I sensed, from the way 'Dynamite' O'Brien sucked in his breath, that my friend had put his argument a trifle abstrusely for his taste. But he appeared to have got the gist of it, and agreed that we would make our approach to Devil's Island from seaward, relying upon stealth, and would only pursue the dramatic alternative if a landing on the blind side proved out of the question.

To all our relief, the weather was no worse by the time we found ourselves creeping the last few miles towards the hump of rock, already changing from black to grey as the faint light of first dawn fell upon it. The tide was running directly, and lightly, towards it. The Mate hurried away to order the engines to be shut off, rather than risk the ring of the telegraph in the quietness.

My heart thudded almost audibly with the excitement of seeing Devil's Island with my own eyes. The time was about four o'clock, and I pictured the wretched prisoner oblivious for a last hour or so to his suffering, before awakening to face yet another hopeless day. It seemed incredible that instead, within an hour or so, he would be aboard with us. That he would prove a reluctant passenger I had no doubt. We could only hope that the inevitable protests and indignation would be overcome when he listened to Holmes's reasoning for what we had done and had in mind for him. I prayed that he would quickly come round to our point of view, and that soon after our sailing away towards safety and eventual reunion with his wife and family in some Cuban hideout he would be asleep again, this time with almost forgotten bliss, between clean sheets in the deck cabin which had already been prepared for him.

Barely had I thought this than the sky was light, so swiftly came the tropical dawn. Had it not been thickly overcast, the sun would have been well up already. There was no wind. The humidity was great, and the sky seemed to bear down upon my shoulders. There was an atmosphere of tension and menace.

The boat falls had been well greased, so that the operation of lowering them, when we were at last hove-to a hundred yards from the island, was carried out almost silently. A party of O'Brien's men entered one of the four boats, and some of our lads filled another. Holmes, O'Brien and I occupied a third, with the Second Mate and two oarsmen. Two other men, under the Bosun, were to follow with the fourth boat, as a reserve in case of mishap. The First Mate stayed in command of the ship; and the look upon his face and those of the few men remaining with him was eloquent with disappointment at having been excluded from the raid.

We were rowed quickly and quietly to the shore. The sea was completely calm, with none of that wash upon the rocks which Holmes had so graphically described to me. When the men in the first boat had scrambled on to the tiny beach they were able to assist the rest of us and secure the first three boats by their painters. The fourth lay off at a short distance, scarcely bobbing on the calm water.

We assumed the formation which had been agreed before disembarking. Holmes, the only one of us with any knowledge of the terrain, led the way up the cliff. I followed at his heels, with Captain O'Brien immediately behind me. Then came the men—some two dozen of them—with the Second Mate bringing up the rear.

As each of us reached the cliff top he scurried forward a few yards, bent double as though under fire, before flinging himself down flat, to lie still until all had assembled. The narrow land sloped down away from us, and I could clearly make out the little white buildings housing Dreyfus and his guards. No one was stirring about them.

Holmes surveyed the island minutely through a small glass. He gave a murmur of satisfaction, and addressed us all in a low incisive tone; he had assumed unquestioned command of the operation.

'Spread out well and keep bending low. Move quickly and as quietly as you can. If anyone appears, drop down at once or stand perfectly still, and the odds are that he will not notice you. But if he gives the slightest sign of having done so, rush in as hard as you can go. No shouting, though, and the minimum of force to be used, even if we are fired upon. The guards are to be secured in such a way that they cannot fire after us or raise any sort of alarm until we are well clear. I repeat, though, they are *not* to be harmed. As for Captain Dreyfus, leave him to me and Captain O'Brien. Now, my lads, come along!'

In a manner which would have done him credit in action with a regiment of the line he rose to his feet and set off at a loping gait. The rest of us followed suit, spreading ourselves obediently. In the excitement of it the slight incapacities caused by my old wounds were forgotten. It was like the Battle of Maiwand all over again.

The rocky ground was rough and did not make for easy going, and the clatter of our boots sounded loud enough to alert any sentry. Yet, to my surprise, not a man appeared. My suspicion grew that we had been spotted already and that they were cunningly remaining inside their guardhouse, weapons at the ready, waiting to run out and open point-blank fire. I think we all sensed this, for our pace instinctively quickened. I, and a few others who had perhaps known army service, began to zig-zag so as to offer a more difficult target.

We were within yards of the buildings, yet no shot rang out. No guard emerged. It would have felt uncanny, had we not been so breathless and busy. We simply dashed on, and within another few moments had surrounded the tall stockade. Its gate stood slightly ajar. Every man of us must have been wondering the one thought: what awaited the first to dare enter?

I never admired my friend more than in that moment. Having paused only to get a few breaths after the run, he strode forward, pushed the gate wide, and passed in.

There came no sound. I hurried after him, Captain O'Brien beside me and the men pressing close behind. The place seemed to be deserted. The door of the small, whitewashed house which I took to be

Dreyfus's lodging also stood half open. As we had been told from his own description, it was gloomy within, the pallisade excluding both light and air.

Holmes called out: 'Captain Dreyfus?'

I peered over his shoulder, and saw a movement. A man had risen slowly from a low bed or bench. We could not see him for the door, but we heard him clearly when he spoke.

'It is a lovely morning, my dear Sherlock. I am glad you have been so prompt.'

It was the voice of Mycroft Holmes.

TWENTY ONE

'MY dear Sherlock,' sighed Mycroft Holmes, 'I assure you yet again that I had no alternative. You had to be prevented. To have employed the Royal Navy would have been to attract questions which could not have been answered to anyone's satisfaction. Accordingly, we passed word to the French that rumours of a rescue attempt had come to our ears. They were most grateful and despatched their cruiser at once, inviting me to accompany it,'

'And witness them blow us out of the water, had the need arisen.'

'I did my best to warn you off. Gonselin waited for you in Georgetown with my message, which he unfortunately failed to deliver. I myself put up with the discomfort of that hut, in case you came there without even touching Georgetown on your way. I can tell you, it took some persuading the French to transfer Dreyfus to Royale for those few days. They were all for reinforcing Devil's Island and having you walk into an ambush. Had it not been for the international implications, I'd have been sorely tempted to allow them their way!'

Holmes gave vent to his disgust.

We were seated in our Baker Street parlour. Less than twenty-four hours had elapsed since my friend's and my return to England. The weeks occupied by the voyage home had been a torment to him. He must have paced scores of miles round and round the limited deck of the steamer, unable to settle down to read or laze, so intense was his agitation to reach London and have matters out with his brother.

He had been in no mood for it, that morning on Devil's Island. His anger had been so great, upon learning how we had been tricked, that he would hear no explanation. Naturally, Captain O'Brien's curiosity had proved intense, to put it mildly. His costly prize had been whisked away from him, and a ferocious glint was in his eye as he pushed towards this bland stranger and demanded to know what it was all about.

Fortunately, perhaps, for Mycroft Holmes's physical wellbeing —for I cannot say certainly that his brother would have made wholehearted effort to protect him—there had sounded at that moment a low moan, so sharp and sudden that it startled us all. The Mate had pushed his way in and addressed O'Brien.

'Cap'n, we gotta go. The wind's gettin' up fast. We wait much longer, we're never gonna make it.'

The wind moaned again through the stockade, in witness to his words. O'Brien had hesitated, glaring still at Mycroft, an oddly unkempt figure in a rumpled tropical outfit. It was my friend who had made the decision to evacuate the place.

'There is nothing for us here,' he had announced curtly. 'Back to the boats, as fast as we can.'

'We'll take him, then,' snarled 'Dynamite' Johnny. 'He's got some talkin' to do.'

'No!' Holmes overrode him. 'He and the French have achieved their *fait accompli*. Explanations are not going to bring Dreyfus into our hands now. We have lost him for good.'

He turned to his brother and gestured around the squalid little room, pitifully bare of furnishing and lacking anything in the nature of comfort. I noted with a surge of revulsion the fetters at the foot of the miserable bed.

'Stay on here,' Holmes told Mycroft, 'until your French friends can get over to rescue you. The experience might just do something for your soul. We will meet in London, by which time I might be in a fit state to listen to you.'

Mycroft looked pleadingly towards him, then to me. But Holmes turned sharply and almost pushed me and O'Brien out of that place. It needed only a glance at the sky to urge us to take to our heels after our men.

We reached the boats in the nick of time, and even then had a hard job to get aboard the pitching ship. It carried us back to Georgetown through such seas as I am thankful never to have encountered since. And so, when several days' storm had abated,

Captain Muros carried us back to London.

This time there came no Summons to the Presence from Mycroft. Holmes demanded he visit us instead. Blandly as ever, Mycroft proceeded to explain that, in any case, he could not have entertained us at the Diogenes Club.

'Your behaviour at the Club last time was quite outrageous, Sherlock. Postlethwaite was deeply shocked at your kicking a ball of paper about in the passage.'

'Who the devil is Postlethwaite?'

'The porter. He threatened to make it a resignation matter, and I almost felt it my duty to resign myself in order that he should stay on.'

'I wonder you should. He's a surly old donkey.'

'Precisely. It is why he has enjoyed twenty-seven years of the members' highest esteem. Haven't you noticed the general run of club waiters today? Ingratiating fellows, eager to go errands and carry messages and call cabs, and expecting tipping for everything. Postlethwaite isn't that sort at all. He hasn't done a service for a member in his life, and never gets tipped from one year's end to another. We could never replace him.'

So the mountain had come to Mohammed, as it were, and now voluminously occupied the basket chair before our grate, with Holmes and myself in our usual places at either side. It was mid-morning and too early for refreshments other than coffee to be served. Holmes had made no move to call even for that. His resentment at his brother's having spoiled his plan was unconcealed and he was in no mood for sociability.

'I see,' he resumed. 'So you would sit back and allow your own brother to perish at the hands of the French Navy, rather than allow him to complete a mission of common humanity?'

'Come, come, Sherlock, that is too strong! I was quite confident that you would accept the warning-off.'

'And what about O'Brien's expedition? Were you so confident about it?'

'Ah! That was what I might term a bonus. We knew nothing of it. The information we have been able to secure since is that it was financed by this Jewish Syndicate, which had for so long been rumoured but has only recently taken formal shape. They put up half a million dollars for the attempt, and presumably singled out O'Brien, whose base is Florida, because of his gun-running and other illicit experiences in the Caribbean, which he knows intimately. He mustered his force in no time and set sail. Very fortunately for all concerned, his arrival at Georgetown virtually coincided with yours. The deterrent intended for you was enabled to be applied to him, and he had to return to Florida lighter in pocket but doubtless enriched in his soul.'

'I pray he never crosses your path again, Mycroft—although I am not at all sure that I do, now I come to think of it. "Fortunately for all concerned" you say? But what about Dreyfus?'

'Ah. Ah. What about Dreyfus, indeed?'

'That is no sort of an answer at all.'

'No, I confess it is not.'

For several minutes thereafter silence reigned over us. The clip-clop of horses' hooves and other general murmurings of a busy street were the only sounds in our room, as Mycroft Holmes, podgy hands clasped together upon his knees, leaned slightly forward, regarding our fire with thoughtful gaze. Eventually, he roused himself and said, 'If I were to tell you the truth about Dreyfus, would I have your most solemn assurance that it would go no further?'

I myself was ready enough to assent, and was all eagerness to hear it; but I checked my reply so that Holmes might give me his lead. He in turn stayed briefly silent, before answering, 'Is it so discreditable to you as all that?'

Mycroft looked surprised. 'Discreditable? Why do you jump to that conclusion?'

'Because, my dear Brother, an innocent man is being made to suffer for some expedient or other, and I cannot frankly envisage any which might be great enough to justify the sacrifice.'

'Not even the peace of Europe?'

'Balderdash! That is your typical Whitehall excuse for everything which you do not choose to explain honestly. You are like the Jesuit, who can block any argument by telling his opponent that if he does not possess utter Faith, then he cannot be expected to understand.'

'I assure you, Sherlock, I am speaking the truth. I . . . hope you do not believe that your own brother has lost every scrap of decency?'

'No, Mycroft. What I do think is that your occupation, which I am sure you pursue with the greatest dedication and from the loyalest of motives, is of that sort which demands the suppression of too many of the best instincts of those who are engaged in it, and that you yourself can be no exception. It would be less than honest of me to pretend to trust you wholly.'

His brother's look turned exceedingly grave. He answered, 'Upon all that Mama and Papa taught us to hold sacred, I assure you that what I am prepared to tell you is the absolute truth. You ... might not regard me in any better light, once you have heard it—and you, Doctor Watson, whatever your opinion of me may be, will perhaps have some cause to modify it—but that I must accept. In return, though, I must have a completely binding oath from each of you that you will not act in any way upon the information I shall give you; that you will not pass it, or even hint it, to anyone whomsoever; and that you will terminate all your dealings with the Dreyfus family and their sympathisers.'

Holmes shook his head angrily and got up to stand with his back to the fire. His pipe had gone out and he prodded sharply at its contents.

'That is too much to ask. There must be some sort of compromise.'

'There can be none. You compel me to warn you, Sherlock, that since you have already gone further than is acceptable to her Majesty's Government, steps will be taken to ensure that you do not get the opportunity to do so again. We know who your visitors are— yes, even Inspector Dubuque, with his floppy hat and spectacles. If any of them approaches you again they will be warned off, and who knows but that word might chance to reach the French authorities' ears? As for yourself and your friend here, any further trips abroad will be monitored from beginning to end.'

'Allow me to say, Mr Holmes,' I told him warmly, 'that I should regard any such restriction as an intolerable intrusion upon the liberty of one of her Majesty's subjects!'

'So it would be, Doctor Watson, were it not that the command emanates from her Majesty in person. Yes, I appreciate your astonishment, and I am prepared to provide each of you with a facsimile copy of the order bearing her gracious signature.'

'It has come to this, then!' snarled his brother. 'Whitehall tells even the Queen what she must do nowadays.'

'Oh, it has always been so, except that we tell the Government, and it in turn instructs her Majesty. I must say, life would be a good deal easier if she would always obey. She is positively wilful at times, and there is a good deal which we dare not let reach her eyes, or she would complicate it inextricably. If you only knew what pains it has taken us to cool off her relations with the Kaiser. They were too cordial for anyone's comfort.'

'He happens to be her grandson!'

'That is quite irrelevant. All that concerns us is that they are heads of State, and must behave as such to one another. How can their respective Ministers be expected to maintain the delicate balance of amicability and hostility if they will meet one another on yachts and in drawing-rooms and agree upon matters for themselves?'

'Mycroft, what you are saying is either ludicrously comic or utterly horrifying.'

'It is neither. I am merely telling you how orderly international relations need to be conducted. We live in a modern age. These are not the times of George the Third, who told Lord North what he wanted the Government to do, and was obeyed without question. The Queen—and may God bless her!—is the figurehead of our Ship of State. The Members of Parliament are its crew, signed on for only as long as each of them is needed. But the Captain and Chief Officers—the professionals in charge—you must look towards Whitehall to discover them.'

If anyone else had made this statement I should have called him the most pompous jackass I had ever met, and gone out for a walk in the fresh air. But he was my friend's brother, and I felt that if any such sentiment were to be expressed it should come from Holmes. Besides, I reminded myself that the conversation had only diverged from its true course, and not left it altogether. I saw from the tightening of Holmes's jaw and lips that he, too, was having difficulty restraining himself. But he succeeded, and without making further allusion to Mycroft's high-handed assertion said quietly: 'Tell me this, Mycroft. If I relinquish the Dreyfus case entirely, what will become of him?'

His brother looked him straight in the eyes, and I could hear the sincerity in his reply.

'Let me put it this way, Sherlock. If you do *not* relinquish it, there may be war in Europe and no one will give another thought to him. There is always the added possibility that someone—some individual—might feel more at ease if Dreyfus were placed beyond all possibility of being rehabilitated.'

'He might be murdered, in short?'

'Or suffer an accident.'

'The sort of "accident" which befell Adolphe Meyer, no doubt. *Did* you have him killed, Mycroft?'

I was disturbed to note unease in Mycroft Holmes's countenance at this challenge. He stammered slightly as he answered, 'The . . . the death of Meyer had no connection with the Dreyfus affair.'

'If you know that, you know how he came to be killed, and who did it. I understood that the case was unsolved.'

'I . . . Please, Sherlock, let us return to the main point. I know that you have Dreyfus's best interests at heart, and your country's also. Will you not accept that by ceasing to interfere on his behalf you would be serving both?'

'Is that the whole truth, Mycroft? Or is it that I have come too dangerously close to the heart of the matter for your comfort, and you are warning me off before the final strand of the pattern comes into my possession?'

'Yes and no. You *are* very near to the truth—exceedingly warm, as we would have said when we were boys. But should you come into possession of that final strand of which you speak, and triumphantly produce your finished design, you will thereby perpetrate the immaculate blunder which I have been fearing—because although you will have proved your case, you will have done so from a false premise, and will be totally wrong. You are very close to the truth, but you are running parallel with it, and parallel lines never converge. Believe me, you will never get on to the main line unless you listen to what I am willing to tell you; and I shall not do that without your oath that it will be the end of the affair for you.'

He had leaned far forward as he said this, and had spoken in tones of great deliberation and emphasis, addressing his brother but including me by implication. Now he leaned back; the thick fingers entwined on his lap again; and he waited.

Holmes turned in my direction. 'What do you say, Watson?'

I cleared my throat. 'It seems to me that we have to consider two things. The first is that if you refuse to give the undertaking, you will find it next to impossible to progress any further in the case. Your brother has spelt out the restrictions which will be placed upon you—restrictions, remember, which might have the effect of severely limiting your ordinary work.'

'True, true,' I heard Mycroft murmur.

'. . . And the allies upon whom you have had to depend for all the information and evidence which has come your way have been made virtually incommunicado. Picquart has been sent away where he can do no harm. Dubuque told us he himself would not be able to visit you again. The same, I am sure, applies to Mathieu Dreyfus.'

'True. True again.'

'The second point, if you will forgive me , is whether you can so doubt your brother's word and her Majesty's own complicity in this matter as to feel yourself impelled, like some journalist on a popular rag, to ferret out the last bit of truth, regardless of the damage which we have been assured its discovery could cause.'

Holmes looked surprised and a little displeased at this. I added quickly, 'What I mean to say is, your brother has assured you that you will not get the truth by your own efforts. You will almost certainly arrive at something which appears to be it, but which will not be, and whose effect would be worse than no solution at all.'

'Admirably summarised, Doctor,' Mycroft congratulated me. 'In a nutshell.'

'Very well,' Holmes said. 'Since you put those considerations to me, Watson, I can only conclude that you have mentally confronted yourself with them. Pray, what is your answer?'

'That the balance goes down in favour of accepting your brother's terms.'

He frowned and proceeded to go through the business of re-lighting his pipe, giving himself a few extra moments of thought. Then he tossed the smoking taper into the fire and turned again to face us both.

'I agree . . .'

'Excellent, Sherlock!'

'. . . Only, upon one condition.'

'There can be no conditions at all.'

'There must. It is quite simple, and it is this. If, in my judgment, what you see fit to tell me is a product manufactured out of the devious materials of your trade in order to further whatever process of deception you are engaged upon, then I shall feel myself free to pursue my own enquiries to their end.'

'You have agreed to compromise with me, Sherlock, and I must make the same gesture to you. I accept your reservation, on the strict condition that your line of investigation shall continue to be as at present, and shall take no advantage from what I am going to tell you.'

'Agreed.'

'Doctor Watson? You occupy the dual role of collaborator with my brother and witness to the bargain between us. How do you say?'

'As the former, I agree to the stipulation. In the latter capacity, I promise to serve as reminder and conscience to your brother, should any further developments in the case come to our attention. Further than that, I will insist that he take no action upon them without first consulting you.'

I felt, rather than saw, Holmes scowl at me, but I made this declaration without wavering. I thought the decision to be inevitable, and for the best.

'Splendid!' Mycroft Holmes cried, suddenly at his ease. 'When your good landlady has served the excellent coffee of which I know her to be capable, but which you have neglected to summon, I will tell you everything.'

The bell was rung. Mrs Hudson came and went, then came and went again, and we sat, cups and saucers in hand, with the biscuit jar on a low table between the three of us. When he had refreshed himself and replenished his cup, Mycroft Holmes took a deep breath and began to speak.

'Dreyfus is altogether innocent, of course.'

I thought for a second that Holmes might erupt; but he maintained his control upon himself, and listened, grim-faced and silent.

'That is not to say,' Mycroft continued, 'that he is the hapless

victim of some deliberate plot. His involvement came about in-
advertently. No, Sherlock—hear me out. Suffice it to say that if it had
not been him whom Fate had cast for so tragic a role, it would have
been someone equally blameless, and for whom, I don't doubt, you
would have been engaged to act. So be it. Now, I do not need to ask
whether the name Walsin-Esterhazy means anything to you?'

'No, Mycroft, you do not. Just tell us it all, without gloating.'

'I beg your pardon. Well, the fact is that this Esterhazy is a
mountebank who has consistently lived above his means. He
entertains delusions of grandeur, yet was not above making the
almost fatal mistake of marrying for money. It appears that, like our
own former Prince Regent's, in a similar situation, his wife proved to
be both clumsy and, er, avid, and as a man of self-professed sensibility
he had to pay a fairly heavy price for the use of her funds. However, he
got through a good deal of them before he was brought up short by
her relatives, who separated her fortune from his reach. The
consequence was that he slipped ever deeper into debt. His possibilities for social prominence were curtailed, whilst, at the same time,
his military career was stagnating. He was an ambitious man in both
spheres. It occurred to his cunning mentality that he might retrieve
his situation by offering to sell secrets to a foreign power. Naturally, he
chose that which France fears most—Germany.'

'That is the most blatant treachery!' I cried involuntarily.
Holmes's silence was its own rebuke for the interruption and his
brother acknowledged me by only the briefest of glances.

'Esterhazy is a rogue,' the latter continued, 'but he possesses an
extremely nimble mind. He wields a clever pen, and has written
widely upon military topics. He would be well aware, therefore, what
could be published, or conveyed to other ears, without breach of
national security, and also what could be passed across under a
semblance of confidentiality so as to make it appear secret matter
without its actually being so. It was in this spirit that he presented
himself quite openly to the German military attaché in Paris, Colonel
von Schwartzkoppen, offering to trade "secrets" for money.

'He ran some risk, but not a great deal. There was the possibility
that the Germans, out of some ingratiatory motives of their own,
would report him to his own superiors. There was the risk of being
seen calling at their Embassy, sometimes even in his uniform. He

would need to have some excuse ready for either of these eventualities. Well, he had one. You see, Esterhazy is also intensely ambitious. He regards himself as God's gift to the French Army and had been pressing hard in recent years for promotion, decoration, advancement to the general staff, and all those other things which look well in an officer's record of service. He had his friends in high places and was gradually attaining his objectives. Yet, he was not getting there quickly enough. He was not much admired or trusted by those whose decisions counted. Therefore, he conceived this audacious means by which to demonstrate his initiative. He would offer his services to the Germans, provide them with some plausible but harmless information, with the promise of more interesting things to follow; but, instead of concealing his activities from his own side, he would let them know what he was doing. In short, he would go to his superiors and say, "I have infiltrated the German Embassy. I have gained the confidence of their Intelligence service. All that remains is for me to be provided regularly with information which we should like the Germans to believe to be true, and I will ensure that they receive it." Thus, at one stroke he would gain his superiors' esteem, and perhaps further promotion, whilst accomplishing a financial bargain with the Germans which would help to get him out of his private difficulties. This is precisely what occurred.'

During the little break in Mycroft Holmes's narrative during which he helped himself to more coffee I sat appalled that any so-called officer and gentlemen could use his position thus. Had it been a purely disinterested act of initiative, I might have appreciated it, although I could not have condoned any course of this kind which did not carry authorisation. The risks attendant upon it seemed enormous.

'And he got away with it,' Mycroft Holmes went on, breaking into my very thoughts. 'But, being the sort of man he was, it was not to his country's Intelligence service that he reported what he had achieved. He went to the place where he might hope to gain the highest recognition for himself: to where the military and political hierarchies intertwine. I refer, of course, to the War Ministry.

'Now, whatever opinions either of you might entertain about the administration of the British Army (and we in Whitehall have our reservations about certain policies and not a few individuals, upon which and whom we are keeping an eye) our top echelons are in immaculate shape as compared with those of France. The French Army at all levels is a seething mass of jealousies, intrigues and even hatreds. *Esprit de Corps* may be a French term, but it is a quality sadly lacking in their army today. Our men are true comrades in arms. Our officers are a band of brothers, whose devotion to one another comes second only to their care for the welfare of their men, and third to their pride in their respective regiments and corps. Believe me, this is not the case in France. The French people are accustomed to look upon their army as their country's most stabilising force. Well, it may be so, as compared with their other institutions; but if they knew the extent of the laxity and rivalry which permeate their army, and in particular its general staff, they might well shake in their shoes at the prospect of depending upon it to sustain them through another war. Insularity and self-advancement are what count most; and every senior officer fears the approach of that "smyler with the knyf under the cloke", of whom good old Chaucer wrote so felicitously. Esterhazy gambled upon this, and won. He knew that the War Ministry would not report him to the Chief of Intelligence, but would keep the knowledge to itself and employ Esterhazy for its own ends, ensuring him of commensurate rewards.

'The French are a nation sadly unprepared for war; which, incidentally, is one of her Majesty's Government's chief reasons for wishing to stave off for as long as possible the European catastrophe which it is believed must eventually happen. The Germans know that France could not match them, but they do not know to what extent. The War Ministry felt it most desirable to make them believe that the disparity was not nearly so great as it actually is; so Esterhazy and his bizarre plan were welcomed. He was told that he should develop his relationship with Schwartzkoppen and hand him documents contrived to make Berlin believe that the quality and quantity of French artillery and other weapons, and the skill of her forces in using them, were of a very superior state. Thus, you see, far from betraying his country, Esterhazy actually proceeded to serve it.

'But he did so unknown to the Intelligence Department, who, unknown to the War Ministry, had their own link with the German Embassy in the form of a cleaning-woman, whose duty it had been for years to collect the contents of the wastepaper baskets and deliver them to French Intelligence, who diligently examined them for useful information. This was how the *bordereau*, in which Esterhazy had listed items of information which he proposed to obtain for Schwartzkoppen, came into the hands of Major Henry, the deputy of the ailing Chief of Intelligence, Colonel Sandherr. Henry pieced the scraps of this document together and realised that he had found sensational evidence of a French traitor. He conferred with his closest associates—though not his chief—and they convinced one another that the traitor was Dreyfus.'

'But how?' I was compelled to demand. 'Out of all the army . . . !'

'Not quite, Doctor. There were several indications as to the sort of man who must have written the list. He seemed to have access to information more likely to be possessed by a staff officer than by a regimental one. The preoccupation with artillery details suggested that he belonged to that corps. *And* someone examining the writing chanced to remark that it put him in mind of Dreyfus's. From that moment, Alfred Dreyfus was their man.

'Think of it. He fitted the requirements, as deduced from the document itself. He was a Jew and a native of Alsace, and therefore capable of suspicion of having divided loyalties. He was not much liked personally, and his aloofness and self-assuredness were resented, as was his rapid progress up the ladder of advancement. And, it has to be conceded, the writing on the document did indeed resemble his to a certain degree.'

'Are you telling me,' Holmes demanded loudly, 'that the War Ministry learnt of this suspicion of Dreyfus by the Intelligence Department, and did nothing to clear him?'

'I'm afraid I am. The essential part of the scheme was that Esterhazy should remain beyond the Germans' suspicion, to go on conveying false information. Sherlock, the look in your eye tells me that you are about to retort that there could be no moral justification for such an arrangement. I must forestall you by arguing that the deception of the Germans which Esterhazy's enterprise had made possible might well be accredited in history with having spared hundreds of thousands of lives, the over-running of France and her neighbours, and perhaps even of England herself. So, now can you see why, having found that you had come so close to, and yet remained so far from, the truth, I have had to use all my means to halt your mistaken progress? Your hypothesis, if I am not entirely mistaken, has been that treason against France was being conducted, and that the traitor's accomplices or friends were covering his tracks by means of a conspiracy of which Dreyfus was the victim. The truth is that everything Dreyfus has had to endure has been, if he had only known it, towards his country's and Europe's interest. Surely that puts a very different complexion upon the matter?'

Holmes answered slowly, 'I doubt that he envisaged any such thing when he so proudly enlisted. It certainly alters my case, however. I confess, Mycroft, I had not for one moment suspected such a situation as you describe. The magnitude of it frankly overwhelms me. It makes me wish almost to fall down upon my knees and start praying for the salvation of the souls of all concerned in it—not least your own.'

His brother raised the palms of both hands, fingers spread in a gesture of helplessness. I ventured to intervene in the discussion.

'Surely, Mr Holmes, we are not to be given to understand that the court martial proceedings were contrived to have Dreyfus committed?'

'Regrettably, yes. Oh, the members of the court were innocent enough of any irregular behaviour. The Intelligence Department, convinced that it had nailed its man, adduced all the evidence it could to that end. As you know, much of it was circumstantial and even prejudiced, and the case was going badly for the Prosecution. It was saved for them, not by their own efforts, but by the quiet intervention of the War Office. Seeing that Dreyfus might be acquitted, which could have led to some enquirer seeking an alternative traitor, and discovering Esterhazy, it manufactured the evidence which, reputedly too secret to be produced in open court, convinced the judges of Dreyfus's guilt. In other words, the Intelligence Department prosecuted him, but it was the War Ministry which got him convicted; yet there was no collusion whatever between them.'

'Ye Gods!' cried Holmes. 'And all upon the strength of this *bordereau*, which itself was a false document originated by the War Ministry to mislead Germany about France's preparedness for war! A case of treachery without a traitor.'

'But with a host of guilty men,' I suggested.

'Not really,' Mycroft Holmes told me. 'Henry, Lauth, du Paty de Clam and others believed they had caught a traitor. Having amassed evidence against him, and with their suspicions of him deepened by his poor showing under interrogation, they convinced themselves and everyone else that they were right. There was no going back from that. If they had been proved wrong by some over-zealous journalist, or by the Dreyfus family abetted by my brother here, they would have lost face irreparably. Once committed to their stance, they had to maintain it, even if it meant producing extra pieces of "evidence" to support themselves. We have no doubt at all, by the way, that the most recent documents to have appeared are forgeries.

'As for the War Ministry people, they have behaved equally sincerely, according to their lights. Esterhazy presented them with an excellent chance to mislead the Germans. When the piecing together of some scraps of paper seemed likely to spoil it all, they were only too glad to seize upon the coincidence of Dreyfus's trial to save their agent from discovery and enable him to go on operating. They believed they were acting for the greater good of France. So, who are we to blame any of them?'

I realised at this moment how grey and tight had become the skin of my friend's face, which had grown almost skull-like in aspect. In a voice which might have echoed from some tomb, he asked, 'Tell me this, Mycroft: how much longer is Dreyfus expected to go on with his martyrdom to this patriotic cause, of which he knows nothing?'

Mycroft Holmes looked more uncomfortable than I had ever seen him.

'Don't ask me, Sherlock,' he almost pleaded. 'I am not responsible for what the French do—merely for watching them do it. It is in our country's interest to know the ramifications of relations between France and Germany, in order to assess our own situation vis-à-vis them both. If it will enable you to see me in any better light, I will say that I personally pray his durance will end sooner, rather than later. Either Esterhazy's usefulness will come to its end; or there will be some sort of public eruption which will produce a crisis which the French authorities simply cannot pass off; or . . .' He spread his palms again. 'Who can say?'

'But I may do nothing?'

'You *must* do nothing, Sherlock. It would help no one—least of all Dreyfus.'

A bleak silence hung in the room. I felt a numbness in my mind. It was as if I had been informed that I was suffering from some dread disease for which there could be no cure, and which I should have to learn to endure until death, or a miracle, brought final relief. I fancied that Holmes must be feeling much the same.

'In all my career,' he said at last, 'I have never resigned from a case in which I believed. I have been pleaded with, begged, cajoled, warned, blackmailed, threatened ... Yet I have insisted that if a result awaited my discovery, I would carry on until I reached it. I flatter myself that I have not often failed to achieve that objective. On a very few occasions I have regretted what I found at the end of my quest. Mostly, I have completed my work with the feeling that I have contributed a little towards the overall sum of justice or the betterment of some poor wretch's condition.

'For once, however, I find myself stalemated. I could carry on. I have promised not to do so with the aid of what I have just heard, but I could persist in other directions, hoping to come upon a line of enquiry which would lead me by some other set of moves to a position of advantage from which to influence events. I have to accept, though, that it would be in no one's interest were I to do so. In fact, my only useful course appears to be to concede and leave the field. So be it. My part in this wretched business is at an end.'

He placed his pipe upon the mantelpiece with a little clatter of the briar bowl upon the marble and strode to the door to his own room. At it, he paused and turned to me.

'Watson,' he commanded, in his coldest tone, 'pray never mention this affair again within my hearing. Gather up what documents there are and stow them away in your own archives if you wish, but never more bring them to my sight. There is in my mouth just now the sourest taste I have ever known.'

Without a word of farewell to his brother he strode out, and the door closed firmly behind him. Mycroft Holmes rose slowly to his feet, exhaling a long sigh.

'What else could I say?' he appealed to me. 'Heaven knows, the taste on my own tongue is bitter enough, and I have had to live longer with the unappetising truth than Sherlock has.'

I felt no contempt for him. My bitterest instincts were all concentrated towards those men who had manipulated the life of an innocent man in order that a spy might prosper in a course of action undertaken for no higher motive than to assist his own pocket and help sustain his vanity. To an extent, I supposed, patriotism had motivated them, and I had throughout my life regarded patriotism as one of the most noble instincts any man could possess. Yet the aura of professed patriotism surrounding the case of Alfred Dreyfus seemed to be composed far less of nobility than of pusillanimity and malice, and it occurred to me that these were prices too high to pay.

Mycroft Holmes was moving towards the outer door. One further thought struck me.

'Mr. Holmes . . .'

'Yes, Doctor Watson?'

'Would it be impolitic of me to ask, in confidence of course, how you come to know all these details, which no one in France is aware of in their entirety?'

'Oh, we have our own access to certain wastepaper baskets, you know. And a certain, rather charming lady was persuaded to give us some information with which she had feared to trust anyone before— even yourself, I regret to say.'

'Well, well, well! A final detail then—possibly irrelevant, but I have puzzled over it rather. The murder of Adolphe Meyer. You said it had no direct bearing, yet your brother remarked that you evidently knew the truth of it. Might I ask what it is?'

He had stopped, standing with one hand upon the doorknob, the coat which he had gathered up draped over his other arm and his hat and stick in his hand. The dark, melancholy eyes regarded me for some moments. Then he sighed again.

'Perhaps you will write about all this some day, though we must all hope that it will be many years hence, and that history by then will have provided you with a happy ending. Adolphe Meyer was killed by Albert Gonselin, some hours after you met Gonselin at the Diogenes Club.'

'Gonselin! But . . .!'

'A left-handed man, coarse-grained enough to swig his drink from the decanter. According to Inspector Lestrade, that was what my brother suggested to him. It was my duty to instruct Lestrade, however, that the matter was not to be pursued.'

'You ... knew it was Gonselin?'

'You know that he was sentenced to the Islands for mutilating a woman in Marseilles? It was his defence that she had helped her protector betray him to the police on a false charge of theft. The court disregarded such specious nonsense, of course; but throughout his years of imprisonment Gonselin never forgot it, because it was the truth. When I recruited him into our service he mentioned it to me and said that his days were numbered from physical decline, yet his remaining ambition was to revenge himself upon this man who had ruined his life. If he could have that reward, he would ask none other. He named the man—Adolphe Meyer.

'Not for a moment did my mind connect the name with that of the spy in London. It was only when Meyer began to be active in the Anarchist movement, and we enquired into every detail of his former life, that I found he had spent his younger days in Marseilles, where he had acquired a police record for offences whilst living with a dancer also known to the police. She, Doctor Watson, was the girl whom Albert Gonselin mutilated with a penknife.'

'Great heavens! And you ... you told Gonselin that Meyer could be found in London?'

'More than that, I am afraid. We had discovered all we needed to know about the movements of Meyer and his Anarchist associates. He could be nothing more than a potential danger to the state in future. In short, we wished to be rid of him—and Albert Gonselin, through his part in my brother's adventure to Devil's Island, had earned his reward.'

I stood dumbfounded. Mycroft Holmes nodded sadly.

'I remarked earlier in our discussion today that you might think none the more highly of me for what you might hear. There you are, then. But consider this, Doctor Watson, when eventually you sit down to compose your narrative of this business: Meyer was becoming a menace to our country; and Albert Gonselin had saved Sherlock's life. His innocent soul cried out for only one reward upon this earth, and a brief visit to London could obtain him it. Perhaps, Doctor, there is a trifle more justice meted out from behind the dispassionate façades of Whitehall than you may credit.'

I could bring myself to say nothing in retort. Mycroft's mien softened suddenly, his eyes glowed wistfully.

'A most adroit young lady, eh Doctor? Most . . . interesting.'

'Mademoiselle Claudine?'

He retrieved his great coat and hat from the stand and whispered: 'Good afternoon to you.'

EPILOGUE

TRUE to his resolution, Sherlock Holmes never discussed the Dreyfus Affair again. When, from time to time, there came a resurgence of it into the London newspapers I would observe that he was reading intently that portion of his copy corresponding to the one open before me, and knew that what held his attention was the account of the latest development. When I saw that he had finished it, I would sometimes look across, hoping to catch his eye and provoke him into comment. I never succeeded, and I knew better than to broach the subject myself.

The reader who has remained with me throughout my narrative will no doubt be curious to know how events transpired—unless, that is, he is already acquainted with the details of a case which is universally known by the name of its central figure, but is only vaguely familiar to most people as a matter of treason and miscarriage of justice. I therefore append the following brief summary of subsequent events.

Colonel Picquart, more convinced than ever that his life was in danger, lodged a full account of all he knew with his attorney. The latter, without the authorisation of Picquart, communicated it to the Vice-President of the Senate, whose mind was already deeply disturbed by the notion that Dreyfus was innocent and another guilty. The Vice-President's attempts to persuade the general staff to re-investigate the case were brushed aside in a manner which convinced him that the truth was being deliberately suppressed, and he felt it his moral duty to acquaint the Dreyfus family with what he had learned.

This was enough for the ardent Mathieu, who proceeded at once to write an open letter to the War Minister, accusing Esterhazy, and to demand a new hearing. This put the cat amongst the pigeons with a vengeance, and sent them fluttering in every direction. A campaign to discredit Picquart's integrity was set going. Esterhazy was "investigated" and tried by a court-martial which was so obviously a staged sham that its acquittal of him caused the novelist, Emile Zola, to publish his sensational denunciation *J'Accuse*, proclaiming the guilt of the War Ministry, the staff, and the individual officers who had procured Dreyfus's conviction and Esterhazy's acquittal.

All France was in an uproar, and at a time when a General Election was imminent. Picquart was dismissed from the army for having passed information upon military matters to a civilian, his lawyer. Zola was tried for libel and convicted, but managed to fly to exile in England. To the Dreyfuses' dismay, the change of administration caused by the Election brought about the appointment of a new War Minister, a man who could be expected to back up the military hierarchy to the full. He proceeded to do so, producing in the Chamber of Deputies new documents which seemed to prove Dreyfus's guilt conclusively. When Picquart challenged their authenticity the Minister ordered his arrest, but found himself compelled to investigate the source of the documents. They were traced to Picquart's former deputy, Henry, now a colonel and head of Intelligence.

Henry was arrested and committed suicide. The War Minister had no alternative but to resign.

These events provided the cue for Madame Dreyfus to re-submit her appeal for her husband's case to be heard again. Several months of investigation and legal submissions followed, before, early in June 1899, Dreyfus left Devil's Island to be transported to France for re-trial. So it came about that, almost five years after his arrest, Alfred Dreyfus again endured the painful uncertainty attendant upon a trial which he must have sensed was intended less to ascertain his innocence than to confirm his guilt. By verdict of the majority of the court he was declared guilty with 'extenuating circumstances', and sentenced to ten years' imprisonment.

On this occasion, however, the press of the entire Western world had watched the proceedings. A unified howl of disgust and anger arose, and outside French embassies and consulates in scores of cities violent demonstrations raged. I shall never forget the spectacle of tens of thousands of men and women massed in Hyde Park to listen to speech after speech condemning this mockery of justice, and vilification of the character of a nation which could tolerate it. With one accord they fell into ranks to march upon the French Embassy, where many of the sentiments were repeated in tones ringing enough for its occupants to hear; and amongst that band of marchers was myself, the only one of them all who knew the even more shameful truth about Dreyfus. As I stepped along amongst them I wondered with what amazed horror they would hear of our own country's part in it, were I to mount a stand and tell them that which I could have done.

Inevitably, the politicians accorded Dreyfus a pardon. It was not enough for him; he was determined not to rest from the fight to prove his complete innocence and be rehabilitated without a stain upon his name. Reunited with his family, he lived quietly in Geneva, recuperating from his years of mental ordeal and the deprivations of his life upon Devil's Island. In 1901 his book "Five Years of my Life" appeared in many languages and evoked universal sympathy. Yet, a further five years of his allotted span were to pass before the convoluted legal and political proceedings attendant upon his case culminated in yet another court hearing, and, at last, a unanimous proclamation of his innocence.

He was restored to the army with the rank of major; Picquart, too, was reinstated, with promotion to brigadier-general. A week later, the drums and drilled tramp of feet sounded again, to an accompaniment of crowd noises, in a courtyard behind the Military College in Paris. Again, Alfred Dreyfus, silver-haired and frail now, was at the centre of the proceedings. This time, however, his badges of rank were restored to him and the insignia of the Legion of Honour pinned upon his breast by the general commanding the First Cavalry Division, who then embraced him and assured him emotionally of the pride which his old formation had retained in him.

With trumpets blaring and drums thundering the troops marched past the two men, each sectional officer raising his sabre in salute as he passed. 'Long live Dreyfus!' cried the crowd. With his heart no doubt beating fit to burst, and his head swimming with the emotional memories of that day when he had stood pitifully in the courtyard adjoining, his head bared, his uniform in shreds, and his own sabre reduced to metal fragments, Alfred Dreyfus replied in his customary flat tone: 'No, my friends. Long live the Republic! Long live Truth!'

Patriot that I myself profess to be, I doubt very much that, in his place, I should have responded in altogether such dignified terms.

For Sherlock Holmes and myself there came a dramatic sequel of our own.

One listless evening in the year following these last events Mrs Hudson showed in a stranger whose card introduced him as a journalist named Fitzgerald. He was an angular figure of a man, middle-aged, clean-shaven, black-browed and hook-nosed. He explained that he was of Irish-French parentage, and that after many years' residence in France he was now permanently domiciled in England, where he was serving as correspondent to several French newspapers.

'I have been invited,' he explained, in an odd accent which owed far more to French than to Irish, 'to contribute a series of studies of persons behind the scenes, as it were, of English affairs. I jotted down certain possibilities, and the personality and methods of the most eminent of unofficial criminal investigators came very near the top.'

'I am duly flattered,' replied Holmes, who seldom showed irritation at being disturbed, welcoming any distraction from the restlessness which invariably beset him when he had no deep matter on hand. 'However, my own chronicler sits beside you. I make it a rule never to give interviews.'

Our visitor sighed, but smiled. 'So I had been led to believe; which is why I risked intruding upon you personally, rather than receive the almost certain rebuff which a letter would have invited. Pray forgive me.'

'Not at all. I admire enterprise. All the same, I regret I must still decline your invitation.'

Instead of rising to leave, Fitzgerald remained silent for some moments, his eyes searching Holmes's. Then he asked hesitatingly, 'There is another request which I beg leave to put to you.'

'There is no harm in your doing so.'

'Thank you. It is this. If I may not write about yourself and your celebrated methods, would it be asking too much that you provide me with an opinion, with or without permission to quote your name in its connection, upon an important public matter to which I find no reference anywhere in your distinguished chronicler's writings?'

'It would depend upon the matter.'

'It is one which I am certain must have engaged your formidable intellect, if only through sheer curiosity. I refer to *l'Affaire Dreyfus*.'

My friend's reaction was no more than the drawing of his pipe from his mouth to examine its contents. To our visitor it could have had no significance, although he was watching Holmes closely. To me it spoke of sudden wariness on the latter's part. He responded casually, 'Of course, I followed that business in the newspapers. I would not claim to have reached any deductions of my own about it.'

'You surprise me. When all the world and his wife were up in arms about it, the least one might have expected of you would have been an opinion.'

'As to what precisely?'

'Why, as to whether the truth has ever emerged.'

'I was under the impression that it had all been cleared up. Captain Dreyfus was finally exonerated and honourably reinstated.'

'Oh yes,' Fitzgerald answered. 'He is widely regarded as a martyr.'

'You are not expecting, surely, that I might question his innocence?'

The black eyes of the interviewer suddenly seemed to resemble coals before the instant of combustion. He leaned forward and, in an entirely new tone, demanded, 'I am asking you to tell me the unrevealed circumstances behind the case.'

Holmes's eyes flashed in return, but he restrained himself from any sharp retort. 'I do not understand. Do you suppose that I possess information unknown to others? If so, I must assure you that ...'

'I know you do,' Fitzgerald interrupted. 'I know that you were engaged in this matter on Dreyfus's behalf. You, and your friend here.'

'That is an outrageous remark to make!' I protested.

'You deny it, then? On your honour, Doctor Watson?'

The invocation of my honour was enough to cause me to hesitate fractionally. Fitzgerald saw it and waved aside any reply by me. He smiled unpleasantly.

'I believe I have my answer without pressing for it.'

'You have nothing of the sort, sir. You have come here uninvited and taken advantage of Mr Holmes's good nature. You have flung at him a provocative assertion which you hope will persuade him into giving a response capable of being twisted into copy for whatever gutter rag you serve.'

'Not at all,' came a smooth rejoinder. 'As a responsible journalist I have my duty to discover and pursue matters of public interest. I can assure you that the readers of the Parisian press will be only too interested to be told that a case of the greatest importance to their national security had involved representatives of the country whose late queen was closely related to the emperor of that other state from whom France has most to fear. The implications are limitless.'

I protested vehemently against this slur upon her late Majesty. My instinct was to take this fellow by his collar and bundle him from the room. Holmes evidently noticed some movement on my part which presaged this, and gave me a glance of restraint.

He said to Fitzgerald, 'I will not enquire the source of your alleged information that I was concerned in the Dreyfus affair, because I know you will not reveal it. Nor will I continue this discussion.'

Fitzgerald sat still, smiling even more arrogantly.

'Your friend is itching to eject me by main force; I can sense it. I dare say that you would be capable of it between you, but I must warn you that it would provide me with a splendid opening to the account which I propose to pen. However, if you will not answer my questions, so be it. To many people's minds such a refusal is tantamount to an admission. So, I must draw my own conclusions and publish my own speculations. After King Edward has gone to so much trouble to establish this *Entente Cordiale* with France, I fear his good work will have to be undone.'

He paused for a moment. I could imagine Holmes's brain racing in pursuit of some solution to the dilemma. I myself could see none, but Fitzgerald had one ready to offer.

'Of course,' he continued, 'there is an alternative. I shall be very well paid by some editor for my story, but after that the knowledge will be public property and I personally may expect little further reward. You, on the other hand, will face endless inconvenience and no doubt personal and professional embarrassment. Let us say, then, that out of consideration for yourself and the good relations of France and Great Britain, I will refrain from publishing in return for the payment of a sum of money which we will mutually agree.'

'Blackmail!' I cried. 'Holmes . . .'

'No, Watson!' he ordered, as I jumped to my feet.

I wished he had told me to break the other's neck. All I could do was stand and glower. Fitzgerald had risen quickly, to be free to defend himself. Holmes got up more slowly and came to stand close to the two of us.

'This little charade has been played out,' he said. 'It has had its points of interest, and it would be untidy to end it violently.'

Fitzgerald returned him a surprised look. 'You . . . agree to my proposition, then?'

'Not unconditionally.'

'What does that mean?'

'Simply that if you publish details of what you believe to have been my involvement in the Dreyfus case, I shall cause to be published, both in France and here, the full particulars of what I *know* to have been yours—Major Esterhazy.'

Of all the unexpected revelations I had ever heard from my friend this brought me the greatest surprise. Clearly, it had the same effect upon our visitor. His face paled and he stammered, 'My . . . name is Fitzgerald.'

'Your pen-name, don't you mean? The name under which you have been writing scurrilous articles about this country, whose hospitality you have enjoyed since your conduct made it no longer possible for you to live in your own. Your Irish pose is as counterfeit as everything else about you.'

'That is nonsense! You are raving!'

'Really? Am I deluded, then, in confirming that this series of studies which you claim to be preparing is quite genuine?' Holmes turned to me. 'Its general title, Watson, is *"l'Angleterre Inconnue"*— "Unknown England"—and it has been commissioned by that rag in which we have sometimes been interested in the past, *l'Eclair*. Really, Major Esterhazy, you cannot expect men who, to use your own phrase, move behind the scenes of public affairs, not to gain access to certain privileged information in the course of it. I know a good deal more about you. I know that the reason you cannot return to France is because a conviction for false pretences hangs over you there, as a result of your embezzlement of considerable funds which belonged to one of your own cousins. I know that you made another cousin your mistress, used her money and then betrayed her. I know that until quite recently in this country you have been living off another woman who keeps a house of ill-repute, which seems to me a most appropriate *milieu* for you. Do you wish me to continue to graver particulars?'

The mien of our visitor had changed utterly during this relentless recital, which Holmes had delivered in his bitterest tone. The black eyes no longer burned. All the rigidity of defiance had left the man's frame. Looking at his sagging features, I pictured the big black moustache which had been one of their salient points, and wondered why I had not recognised him earlier, although I had had no cause to do so.

'If I am brought low,' he muttered, his eyes cast down, 'it is by the ingratitude of my country. Dreyfus is honoured. I am cast aside. My occupation is gone. I am virtually penniless; an exile from my beloved motherland. Such has been my reward for serving her.'

I could have pitied him momentarily, but Holmes dispelled any such temptation.

'The service of which you speak arose from your own treachery. Your original motive was to sell yourself to a foreign power. As to your description of your motherland as "beloved", did you not once write a letter in which you expressed your ideal of happiness as being a captain of Uhlans sabring down your despised countrymen and women as a prelude to the pillage of Paris by a hundred thousand drunken soldiers? No, Esterhazy, your protestations are as false as your heart. You are beneath all contempt. But I am glad you came here tonight. I am glad to have met the creature who precipitated the events which led to what may come to be recorded as the greatest perversion of justice in history, because it has enabled me to express my loathing of you. Now, get out! You will never write any article about me, so I have no fear of the consequences of pitching you headlong down our stairs.'

Esterhazy lingered no longer. He left almost at a run and the slam of our street door shook the building. Holmes strode to the sideboard, poured himself a glass of whisky, and drank it at one swallow.

'How did you know?' I asked, following his example.

But my friend's passion was aroused. 'Once, Watson, I had occasion to remark that this case had left in my mouth a bitter taste. Neither time nor the strongest spirit will ever dispel it. I beg of you, let us never discuss the odious affair again.'

He refilled his glass excessively, took it back to his fireside chair, and stretched himself out. I was charging my own glass again when I heard him say, 'Bring the decanter over here. I fancy we are going to need it to hand.'